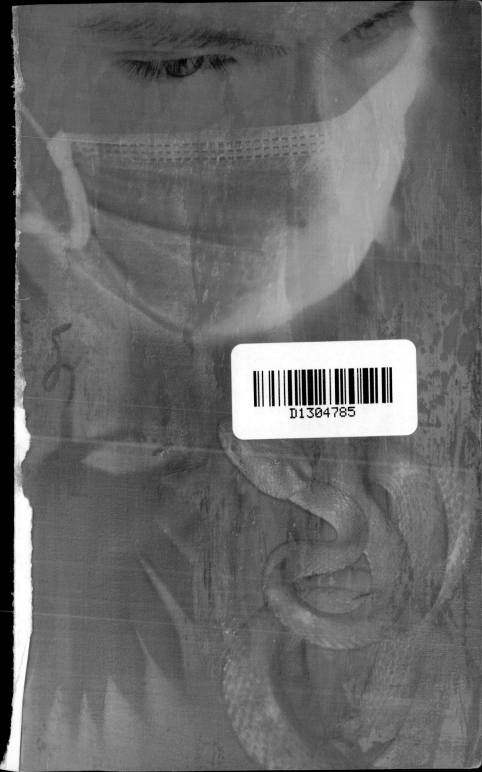

Praise for the novels of Arthur Rosenfeld . . .

A Cure for Gravity

"A Cure for Gravity *roars along at the pace of an open throttled motorcycle."*
—*Miami Florida Herald*

"A Cure for Gravity *is a constantly flowing mix of jarring, earthbound reality and soaring flights of fancy."*
—*The Boca Raton News*

"*It will be the rare reader who turns the last page without a lump in the throat and a smile on the lips."*
—*The Sun Sentinel*

"*[A] charming tale. . . . There's a bravura innocence at the heart of this offbeat novel."*
—*Publishers Weekly*

"*A zesty, comic, high-speed American gothic."*
—*Kirkus Reviews*

"*A touching ghost story that eludes easy comparison to any other book.... An amazing voyage that is as rewarding for the reader as it is for the protagonists."*
—*Booklist*

"*Rosenfeld uses the tangle of lives he has created to tell a story that has its mystical moments—but is every bit about the needs of the living. This makes it a love story, of course, and a sweet, telling one at that."*
—*The New York Daily News*

"A Cure for Gravity *may be seen as mainstream fiction, that just happens to be fast, funny, outrageous, and full of heart."*
—*The San Jose Mercury News*

"A Cure for Gravity *roars along at the pace of an open-throttled motorcycle."*
—*The Tribune, South Bend, IN*

"A Cure for Gravity, *by Arthur Rosenfeld, is a charming tale of one teen-age boy's lucky bank robbery that takes us not only cross-country, but also across a few spiritual dimensions such as the one separating life and death.*"

—The Daily Courier, Prescott, AZ

"A Cure for Gravity *is a constantly flowing mix of jarring, earthbound reality and soaring flights of fancy.... It's the way life could, or should be.*"

—The Boca Raton News

"A novel of surprising imagination and stylistic daring . . . . A Cure for Gravity *rises to near greatness as a piece of home-grown Magical Realism. Touching, scary, hilarious.*"

—Knight Ridder News Service

"This wonderful novel doesn't just cure gravity, it cures all matters of heart, mind, and soul. I felt better after reading the title alone, imagine how I felt after reading the whole book."

—Neil Simon, Pulitzer Prize - winning
playwright of The Odd Couple, Lost in
Yonkers, and Brighton Beach Memoirs.

"Rosenfeld has woven a very unusual yarn that intrigues and grips the reader. A colorful collection of unique but believable characters, thrown together in a series of bizarre event help to create an imaginative and suspenseful tale that doesn't let up until the last page.'

—Barbara Taylor Bradford, New York Times
bestselling author of Where You Belong

"This book is like reading a story and listening to music at the same time. A page-turner with rhythm, and a most unusual narrative voice. I loved the characters, the views of an America I haven't seen, the unexpected twists and turns. A wonderful book."

—Jack Paar, former host of The Tonight Show

"Mr. Rosenfeld's work inspires the deepest emotion one writer can feel about another: envy. These days I manage to get through barely two books a year. Having just finished A Cure for Gravity (its title being

only the first of the many treats in the pages which follow), I am now ready for my second—which will be a rereading of this amazing book.
—Larry Gelbart, creator of M*A*S*H, Tootsie, and A Funny Thing Happened on the Way to the Forum

"Arthur Rosenfeld's A Cure for Gravity is a noir mystery, a supernatural thriller, a crime caper novel, a love story, and an American road-trip adventure—all seamlessly woven ml one moving, magical book. If the ghosts of Jack Kerouac and Jim Thompson could collaborate with Alice Hoffman, this is the story they might write . . ..
This novel twists, spins, and rages like an Oklahoma tornado, and it'll fling you up into the cruel sky before bringing you back down to the good earth . . . safe, but shaken. Hell, it'll make you fly.'
—Bradley Denton, author of BLACK BURN and LUNATICS

Diamond Eye

"A great read in the noir tradition."
—Cluesunlimited.com

"Rosenfeld dexterously blends cinematic scenes with intricate, often humorous personality studies in what may be this year's most promising detective series introduction."
—The January Magazine

"Exploring cop-struggling-against-criminal-desire themes hauntingly reminiscent of Hammett's Red Harvest, Rosenfeld crafts a high-action suspense thriller with plenty of wry humor and cultural commentary."
—Publishers Weekly

"Rosenfeld's crisp writing, vivid characters and incisive humor that make Max Diamond a treasure to discover."
—Book Browser

"Rosenfeld writes a muscular prose that moves along at a brisk clip… smooth and fast, and it provides plenty of bang for your entertainment dollar"

—*The Sun Sentinel*

"This is, to put it bluntly, one of the freshest, most enjoyable mysteries to come along in the last couple of years."

—*Booklist, (Starred Review)*

"…quite delight of a mystery…"

—*The Washington Times*

The Cutting Season –
A Xenon Pearl Martial Arts Thriller

"Arthur Rosenfeld's The Cutting Season is a marvelously entertaining blend of many different genres: medical thriller, psychological suspense, fantasy, martial arts adventure, romance, and crime drama, all neatly packaged into three hundred engrossing pages…"

—*MostlyFiction.com*

"Highly recommended, and not just for martial artists. This is a well written story that all will enjoy."

—*Larry Ketchersid, Author of Dusk Before the Dawn*

"It takes a bold author to attempt the creation of a new category of popular fiction. That's the task crime novelist and tai chi master Arthur Rosenfeld set himself with his ninth novel, The Cutting Season."

—*Chuancey Mabe, The Sun Sentinel*

" A gripping story…. a page-turning mystery…. Rosenfeld's medical knowledge and martial-arts expertise reinforce an authority and clarity to the work…. that's storytelling!"

—*Walter Anderson, Chairman & CEO Parade Magazine*

The Crocodile and the Crane–A Novel

Also by Arthur Rosenfeld...

Novels
The Crocodile and the Crane
The Cutting Season
Diamond Eye
A Cure for Gravity
Dark Money
Dark Tracks
Harpoons
Trigger Man

Nonfiction
The Truth About Chronic Pain
Exotic Pets

QUIET
TEACHER

ARTHUR ROSENFELD

YMAA Publication Center
Wolfeboro, N.H. USA

YMAA Publication Center, Inc.
Main Office
PO Box 480
Wolfeboro, NH 03894
1-800-669-8892 • www.ymaa.com • ymaa@aol.com

© 2009 by Arthur Rosenfeld

Editor: Leslie Takao
Cover Design: Axie Breen

ISBN-13: 978-1-59439-126-2 (soft cover)
ISBN-10: 1-59439-126-2

10   9   8   7   6   5   4   3   2   1

Publisher's Cataloging in Publication
Rosenfeld, Arthur.
   Quiet teacher / Arthur Rosenfeld. -- 1st ed. -- Boston, Mass. : YMAA
Publication Center, c2009.

   p. ; cm.

   ISBN: 978-1-59439-126-2 ; 1-59439-126-2

   1. Martial artists--Fiction. 2. Neurosurgeons--Fiction. 3. Serial
murderers--Fiction. 4. Immortality--Fiction. 5. China--History--
Fiction. 6. Florida--Fiction. 7. Mystery fiction. I. Title.

PS3568.O812 Q54 2009   2009927702

813/.54--dc22   0906

Printed in Canada.

For Herbert, Julie, Ethan, and Camryn.

Kowtows to David and Leslie for the great counsel and teamwork and to Dr. Lloyd Zucker for bringing out the inner neurosurgeon in me. No Lloyd, no Xenon. Nine bows also to Dr. Rodney Cohen for his darkly inventive medical suggestions, to Detective Jim Dees for vetting certain technical details, to Dr. Ron Weisberg for his ongoing advice, to Pamela Barr for a masterful edit, to my marvel of a wife, Janelle, and last but not least to Master Yan, once more, for teaching me all I know about Chinese history, philosophy, and martial arts.

1

I am an insubordinate puppet in the pitiless hands of karma, and try as I might I cannot cut the strings. Day in and day out I struggle among the ten thousand things, pulled one way by the desire to shun the world and another by the need to save it. Back and forth I go, sometimes exercising suture and scalpel, other times heeding a dark and terrible call. I want to be a better man, but my violent compulsions stay me. I am never more at peace than when I am cutting; I am never more tortured than in cutting's red wake.

My new stepsister, police detective Wanda Berkowitz, knows nothing of my inner turmoil. Although she could see easily enough that nearing the prison sent me into a toxic swoon, she could not know that it was because a thousand lifetimes worth of judgments and sentences fill my head. As she propelled me toward the penitentiary door, I unconsciously rooted myself to the floor.

"Oh no," she said, taking my elbow. "You're going through with it, buddy boy."

"Please," I said.

"You're not out of the woods yet. There are still charges floating around and people waiting to pounce if you slip up. Any and all reminders of prison life are good for you and even better for our family."

Two control room guards watched our dance with mild interest. Wanda pressed her badge to the bulletproof window. "Detective Berkowitz," she said.

"Everything under control, detective?"

"You better believe it."

The guard opened the security drawer. Wanda dropped in her badge and reached back somewhere for her cuffs. Then she loosened the jacket of her gray suit and pulled her duty Sig-Sauer .45 from a nylon shoulder web.

"Holster those eyes, doctor," she snapped.

I didn't. "Watching a woman undress has never been quite like this," I said.

"Shut up and give over your knife. I know you've got one."

"Don't be silly."

"The metal detector will find it."

"There's nothing to find."

Holding my eye she feigned a cough and magically came up with another, smaller gun. I managed a smile.

"And where'd that come from?"

"Kahr PM40," she said. "Forty-caliber death puppy. Nothing flatter, nothing finer."

The guard pushed out a clipboard for us both to sign.

"Chaplain's office," said Wanda.

"All the way down the hall, first right, second left."

Once before Wanda had tried to scare me straight by taking me to the Broward County Main Jail. It hadn't worked, though I still remembered the terrible stench of sweat and disinfectants and toilet. Up here in South Bay on the lower edge of Lake Okeechobee, smack in the middle of what used to be magnificent Everglades and was now chemically polluted sugar country, all I got was a whiff of burning cane. The hallway was brightly lit, and the orange and yellow color scheme said school as much as maximum security.

We found the chaplain's office and Wanda introduced me to a man whose shopworn face revealed a faith still strong after much testing by rapists, murderers, child molesters, and punks.

"It's really quite astonishing to get a renowned brain surgeon to come to prison to lead a meditation," he said, seemingly unable to stop staring at my ponytail. "Do many of your colleagues do this kind of work?"

"I don't know any others who do," I said. "And I wouldn't exactly say I'm renowned."

"I'll leave you two to get acquainted," Wanda said. "There's a prisoner I have to interrogate. Zee, I'll meet you at the car in an hour."

She left and the chaplain stared at me in fascination. "Tell me about your meditation techniques," he urged. "A Zen master has been doing a monthly session here for about five years, but I'm sure he doesn't have your technical qualifications."

"Sounds like I don't have his," I said. "Meditation is just an escape for me."

"And for the men," the chaplain smiled. "The only escape, or so we hope. Shall we go see them?"

He led me down another hall to a little windowless room where barefoot men in fatigues waited cross-legged on the floor. A statue of Buddha stood on a draped bookshelf at one end and there were prayer flags, two tiny incense cauldrons, and a stack of inspirational books.

The chaplain made a few remarks about me being a celebrated surgeon and meditation master, describing an impressive man who did not sound the slightest bit like me. Then he slipped out of the room and left me alone with the inmates. I made it a point to shake everyone's hand. The group's leader was tall and gangly and ruddy and thin. His ID tag said Irwin. I figured he was there for the same reason as the other men—to break the monotony and find an incorporeal route past the barbed-wire fence and the cameras and fences and guards.

"We got a few sick brains in here, Doc," he said in a Southern drawl. "Probably all the neurosurgery in the world won't help."

I started to chuckle but saw he was serious. I motioned for the men to rise. "I have a few exercises to calm the body and make meditation easier," I said.

"*Jing to qi, qi to shen,*" said a man standing front and center.

His nametag read Neptune, and he bristled with the kind of hard, shiny muscle only endless hours at the weight rack can bring. His ears were as perfectly formed as a young girl's, and his look said he was working the angles, always monitoring how he struck others and how he could use whatever impression he made to his best advantage. His gaze was intense and challenging. He looked at me as if he knew what I was hiding. I found myself holding my breath.

"There's a saying in Mandarin Chinese," I explained, giving myself a chance to recover. "*Jing to qi, qi to shen* means transforming essence to energy, energy to spirit. *Qi* is the operative word. It means life force or energy. Meditation, together with the exercises we're about to do, uses this life force to transform your essential fluids into a deeper spirit. The exercises are called the Eight Pieces of Brocade."

"They are martial arts exercises, yes?" Neptune said. "What's a doctor doing bringing martial arts to prison? You know that's not allowed here. Why are you even practicing if you're a healer? This inmate wants to know."

"I'm a martial artist, but these are not martial exercises," I said. "The set is just for health."

They were the first movements my teacher, Wu Tie Mei, shared with me during the years she taught me *gongfu*, medicine, energetics, and philosophy. A superbly trained fighter, Tie Mei (Chinese people put their given name last, family name first) was a Chinese Jew rescued by my maternal grandfather's rabbinical congregation in a 1970s international outreach. Most people don't know there are Jews in China or that they cluster in a city called Kaifeng at the end of what was once the Silk Road. Kaifeng's Jews have no connection to world Jewry, but they engage traditional practices such as eating unleavened bread on Passover and resting on Friday night to honor the Sabbath.

"Oh they're martial," Neptune went on. "You can fool them but you can't fool me."

His persistence made me uncomfortable. I wished Wanda hadn't left me alone. I wished the chaplain had stuck around. I tried to focus on the exercises.

The first movement in the Brocade sequence had the men

reaching for the sky or, more precisely, the fluorescent lights nine feet above our heads. Looking up, I saw dead moths and flying roaches trapped behind the plastic covers by their lust for the light. I wondered about their reincarnation cycles. Perhaps they had already come back as men, had tested the laws of karma, and were on their way here to serve prison terms as inmates; perhaps they were already buzzing around outside again.

The second movement was called the archer because it separated the arms in a bow-stretching action.

"Gotcha," said Neptune, lining up his imaginary arrow with my forehead.

The third movement was a big spinal twist. Mercifully, Neptune had nothing to say about it. The fourth movement was similar. The fifth was a low circle that worked the belt vessel—good for weight control because it stimulated the metabolism. Bending low, Neptune aimed his fist at my groin, striking the air just inches from me.

The next movement was a toe touch. The one after that was a tensed punching exercise. Neptune lined himself up with my face and went through the motions with grimacing and grunting and harsh breathing and a murderous look in his eye softened only by a humorous glimmer. "For your health, of course," he said, his curled thumb just inches from my nose.

He kept his counsel for the last movement, which entailed rising to a toestand and then dropping down onto the heels.

"That's it," I told the group. "Now we do our meditation. We stand rather than sit because standing does a better job of encouraging the flow of your life force through all your meridians. The Chinese believe that these meridians carry energy to all parts of our bodies. On our feet, we open the channels for circulation and energy and nourish the vital organs, appendages, and bones. Sitting closes off some of those channels."

"Appendages," snickered someone in the back.

Chuckles spread in a wave, chaos and violence lurking beneath like shark and rocks, but then the group settled down, hands folded over navels.

"Feel the energy come up from the ground," I said. "Imagine it coming into your feet and up the back of your legs and following the line of your spine to your head, rolling up over your crown and back down the front of you to collect behind the navel in what the Chinese call the *dantian*."

After ten minutes of standing, I came out of my reverie long enough to check on Neptune. He appeared to be deep in meditation, but the moment my gaze settled on his face, his lips turned up into a smile that said he knew I was watching. Irwin began to rock back and forth. Another inmate, a Filipino man with a stocky build and youthful features, sobbed quietly, his hands still in place, tears rolling down his face.

I went back to my own practice and tried to remember my past lives. I wanted to see images from the Song dynasty or the Ming. I wanted to smell the battlefield or, better yet, a long-lost lover. I wanted to see a panoply of flowers laid out for an imperial celebration, to recall a feast of dumplings, to see snow on a pristine mountaintop before there was acid rain to stain it or strip mining to gouge holes in its profile. I wanted to get to know my cohorts, those people whom Chinese metaphysics said traveled with me during the transmigration of souls, making pit stops at the way station, the bardo, for the purpose of signing new contracts in the seemingly endless cycle of living and learning and dying and living again.

I had visions not of past lives but of this one. I saw my blade, Quiet Teacher, flutter over a woman's eyebrows and I saw her tiny hairs shower down. I saw my sharp steel slice a mulberry-sized mole from a man's neck. I saw that inescapable steel sever an arm from a shoulder, and then I saw it hack a body into bits for easier disposal. My eyes jerked open to find Neptune's lips at my ear.

"You're a fake," he hissed. "The dark and the light all confused and running to gray. You're a healer, yes, but an avenger too, and you've got a bill of goods to sell us. You're a hustler of the spirit, a doctor of deception with no goddamn right to preach."

My eyes snapped open like blinds with springs run amok. Irwin clapped the gong signaling the end of the meditation. The men came out of it with slow breathing and peaceful expressions, but the scorpions in my belly nearly bent me over with their stings. I avoided Neptune's gaze as I shook hands all around and answered a few questions. The men noticed my agitation, but I was in no condition to explain. I left as soon as I could.

Outside at the car, Wanda seemed pleased by my wan expression.

"So maybe the life of crime really *isn't* for you," she grinned.

2

On the way back to Fort Lauderdale, the air inside the SUV grew chilly. I wasn't dressed for it, but Wanda was logy from the donut she stopped for just outside the prison and said the car heater would put her out. My offer to drive got me only a hard stare.

"You want to tell me about it?" she asked.

"It was fine. The men were interested. I think they got something out of it."

"If it was so fine, how came you came out looking like you were going to puke?"

"I don't know what you're talking about."

"Really?"

"There was one guy got under my skin a little."

"Tell me his name; I'll look him up for you."

"Doesn't matter," I said. "He didn't really do anything."

"Oh, he did something. Maximum security always means a rough crowd. That's where violent offenders end up."

"I mean he didn't do anything to me."

"Then why are we talking about him?"

I shrugged and we drove in silence for a few minutes. I reached casually below the seat, found the knife I had left there, slipped it into my pocket, and shivered.

"Aha," Wanda crowed. "So you did have one with you."

"Keep your eyes on the road, will you?"

"I didn't have to look. I could smell the steel."

"You're ridiculous," I said. "Have I mentioned that?"

She smiled and played piano on the steering wheel. "Been exercising your sword lately?"

I looked out the window. There was a hard line of clouds to the west.

"Zee?"

"Not much."

"A little is too much. We had a deal."

"I've been using a machete, okay? Stainless steel, twenty-three inches, made in El Salvador. Good and cheap.

"You've been cutting trees?"

"Trees, bushes, saplings. There's a park in Lighthouse Point, near the Intracoastal. The hurricane damaged it last year. I've been doing my own private cleanup. Park workers saw me and told me I should be paid."

"You know cutting is a sickness with you, right?"

"I thought you'd love this news," I said. "No people, just wood. Nothing illegal. I'm performing a service."

"How often?"

"Now and then."

"How often, Zee?"

"When I feel like it."

"And how often is that?"

"Give it up."

Friday was winding down and traffic was heavy. By the time we reached I-95 in West Palm Beach a light rain had begun to fall. It wasn't enough to require wipers, but I could tell the road was slick. Since I get around by motorcycle, I pay particular attention to a road's coefficient of friction. I know that after a long period of dry weather in South Florida this light rain was bringing oil and gas up out of the asphalt and turning the interstate into a roller rink.

Wanda seemed not to notice. "How long has it been since you've worked?" she asked as we passed southbound through Delray Beach.

"I go to the office."

"I mean operate."

"Five months."

"Does someone like you get rusty?"

"I hope not."

"When are you going back to it?"

"As soon as they'll have me."

"Broward Samaritan isn't the only hospital around," she said, referring to the fact I'd been suspended for operating on my own girlfriend—a clear violation of policy—and for other more violent transgressions against hospital regulations and rules.

"The hospital district runs as a unit," I said. "The administrators talk to one another."

"Don't they need you? I thought there was a shortage of brain surgeons."

"There *is* a shortage and they *do* need me, but I pissed them off. My office is still open for existing patients, but they aren't sending me any new ones. They're strangling me slowly."

Her look said that she thought I had gotten exactly what I deserved. "Word has it the DEA is looking at you for writing too many prescriptions for pain killers."

I was startled and tried not to show it. "How do you know about that?"

"I'm a good cop. Besides, you're family now."

"Some guy from the DEA came to my office thinking he knew more medicine than I did. He didn't like it when I told him he was wrong."

"What was he wrong about?"

"People have a strange prejudice about pain. Some think its punishment from God and they deserve it, others think it's good for them. Easy when it's someone else's pain, but when it's your own, people change their tune."

"And junkies?"

I shrugged. "Plenty of people abuse pain meds just like they abuse booze or street drugs. That doesn't change the sick person's need for medicine."

"A new cause for Zee to champion."

I laced my fingers together in response to the jibe. "A cop sees one side of this, a doctor sees another. These people are desperate. Wouldn't *you* be in order to agree to have a drug pump implanted in your spine or to have nerves cut so you can't feel anything at all?"

Wanda gave me a sidelong glance. "I got the DEA guy off your back."

"You did?"

"For now. Doesn't hurt that you're not operating anymore either. He seemed quite pleased at that."

*   *   *

On the edge of Boca Raton, a motorcycle passed us. It caught my attention because the orange color meant it was a KTM, the exotic Austrian marque all the rage with the motorcycle press. In the forced leisure of my recent life I had been reading motorcycle magazines as fast as publishers could print them.

"Look at that guy," Wanda said. "If you weren't in the car, I'd pull him over right now."

"You'd never catch him."

Wanda tightened her hand on the wheel. I touched her shoulder. "That wasn't a dare," I said. "Those bikes are crazy fast. I doubt he'll even see your lights."

Indeed, the rider seemed possessed. The professional motorcycle racer, high-mileage tourer, or experienced motor cop uses spare, subtle motions to guide his machine; this guy sped up and slowed down and whacked his handlebars from side to side, clear evidence that he was either addicted to adrenalin or just plain stoned. "Some riders just want to die," I said as we watched him disappear between trucks up ahead.

"But not you."

"Nope. I just ride for the feeling—second best I know."

Wanda screwed up her face. "Oversharing," she said.

As we left the Boca city limits, the rider split lanes between a large tractor-trailer and a VW Bug. His speed surprised the truck driver, who reacted by twisting the wheel. The trailer fishtailed dangerously. Wanda stepped up the pace to stay with the bike.

"In California it's legal to split lanes like that," I said.

"Not here," said Wanda. "Enlightenment begins in the East. You of all people should know that."

I grabbed the dashboard as she picked up the pace. "You'll never catch that guy."

"We'll see."

"You're going to bang up this nice Ford."

"It's a lease truck. We got it on a HIDTA grant."

"English?"

"High Intensity Drug Trafficking Area."

"Which means it was bought with confiscated drug money."

Wanda grinned. "You really *are* a quick study. Don't worry; policy says I can't pursue him unless he commits a violent felony. We'll just stay with him for a bit. If the road opens up, I'll pull him over."

We passed through Deerfield Beach at triple digit speed. The traffic and the rain were heavy, but the KTM did not slow down. A white Porsche suddenly jerked sideways out of the fast lane to let him by, then came up behind him with bright headlights flashing. The rider gave him the finger and scooted off in a diagonal that took him across three lanes of traffic. He could have stayed in his lane and proceeded on his way, but the Porsche driver set off in pursuit, making the same sweep. Brake lights turned the shiny blacktop red.

"You know the difference between a porcupine and a Porsche?" Wanda asked above the din of the big Ford's emergency equipment.

"Joke all you want; they're beautiful cars."

The Porsche came up on the bike hard, and the bike darted away again, slow lane to fast. The Porsche wouldn't let it go and set off in pursuit, roaring past and dousing the rider in filthy spray.

"A porcupine's prick is on the outside," Wanda said, carefully moving to the center lane.

On the beat of her last word—later I would remember that quite distinctly—the world in front of us turned into a bloodbath. The Porsche's tires lost their grip on the road and shot a rooster tail to the sky as the car went sideways then back to front. Out of its lane it moved into the path of a tractor-trailer that slammed on its brakes and jackknifed across the road.

Presented with a wall of metal, the motorcyclist went down. His bike slid under the trailer, tangled briefly with the wheels, and continued through. The Porsche driver regained control of his car and sped away in the fast lane. The truck rose on its passenger-side wheels and flipped over. A midnight blue Subaru Forester plowed into the overturned truck in front of us, hitting right in the V between the trailer and the cab. The truck folded around the car, squashing it into the shape of an arrowhead. Wanda screeched to a halt and I jumped out.

Cold air sharpened my mind and cold rain soaked my short-sleeve shirt. Cars were sideways all over the road and the breakdown lanes were full. The bitter smell of brake-pad asbestos filled my nose as I sprinted for the driver's side of the Subaru. The driver was a young woman wearing sweats. Her face showed airbag burns and her neck bore a hundred tiny cuts from the glass of her shattered windshield. The front doors were completely crushed, so I took off my jacket, wrapped it around my hand, and used it to clear away the glass.

"What's your name?" I asked.

She blinked her eyes.

"Your name," I asked again.

Her voice wavered, but it was clear. "Kimberly Jenkins."

"I'm a doctor, Kimberly, and before I move you I need to ask you a few questions."

She tried to release her seatbelt. Her hand shook, and she

couldn't do it. She turned around, trying to look behind her. "Tierra," she said.

The headlight glare of Wanda's Ford Expedition made it hard to see inside the vehicle. It took me a moment to discern the car seat and the child in it. The rear airbags had deployed, both side and front. Deflated, they formed a cocoon around the little girl. She was awake and watching me. I went around and tried the side door, but it was crushed. Unlike the windshield, the side window had come away cleanly. I leaned in and saw blood on the C pillar and on the side of the little girl's head.

"Are you all right?" I asked.

Tierra nodded, and reached out her arms toward her mother. "Mommy," she said.

"Your mommy's stuck right now," I said.

I went forward to Kimberly. "Did you hit your head?"

"I don't think so."

"It's going to take a little work to get you out."

"How's my baby?"

"She is injured, but she's conscious."

Tears came. "Oh no. I tried to stop, but everything happened too fast."

"You did fine," I said.

"I can't move my left arm."

The belt pulled down her blouse, and I could see a bruise developing on her clavicle. "Where do you hurt?" I asked her.

"My neck."

"Mommy!" Tierra cried again.

"I'll be right there, honey."

Wanda came up behind me. "Paramedics are on the way," she said.

"Go check on the guy in the truck."

"What about the biker?" she asked.

"I doubt there's anything we can do for him."

I turned back to Kimberly and asked her to lift her arm. She managed but only from the elbow.

"Good. Now can you shrug your shoulder?"

She tried without success. I brought out four inches of bead-blasted stainless blade and a textured aluminum handle. It opened with a click. Kimberly watched me with the eyes of a person whose entire world has constricted to a small space where every detail shines with importance.

Wanda cleared her throat. "It's a switchblade?"

I sliced neatly through the seatbelt. "They're called automatics now."

Shaking her head, she moved off. I put my jacket around Kimberly's neck. "I'm going to wait for the paramedics to take you out," I told her. "You could have an injury I can't see. We'll find out at the hospital."

I went back to Tierra. She looked sleepy and that worried me. I asked her to squeeze my finger and found her right hand weak. Her left pupil dilated as I watched it. I smiled at her. The smile she gave me back was lopsided.

Wanda came back. "The truck driver's trapped. He's awake but weak. Cursed the Porsche. Doesn't seem to realize the motorcycle slid under him."

"The girl's brain is bleeding into her skull," I said quietly. "We've got to get her to the OR right away. There's a clock on an epidural hematoma, and it's ticking. Where are the paramedics?"

"They'll be here," Wanda soothed. "I know it feels like forever, but it's been only a couple of minutes. Where's that legendary surgeon cool?"

"So many variables," I muttered. "It's chaos out here. I don't know where to turn first."

"Welcome to a cop's world. And by the way, you were wrong about the biker. He's alive and talking. You're not going to like the look of him, though."

As if on cue the rider appeared, walking upright like a regular guy, his leather riding suit in tatters, a piece of his skull completely gone.

"Are you guys cops?" he asked. "'Cause this wasn't my fault. That prick in the Porsche...."

"Prick," Wanda interrupted. "Exactly."

The rider noticed the open rear hatch of Wanda's SUV. "Wow," he said. "Look at all those guns. You guys preparing for war or what?"

I took his arm. "Let's sit down for a minute."

"I'll look for the missing piece," said Wanda.

"Don't worry," said the rider, thinking we were talking about his bike. "My insurance company will fix it."

The paramedics arrived in a storm of sirens and lights. I went back to Tierra.

Her eyes were closed.

3

First on the scene was a strapping young blonde with stubble on his chin. He regarded the ambulatory, half-headless biker like an entry to *Ripley's Believe It Or Not* and frowned when I identified myself and steered him toward the Subaru. I joined Wanda at the tractor-trailer, where a Florida Highway Patrol trooper used the Jaws of Life to work the door open. The driver was a big man with a big belly and a full beard going white.

"How you feeling?" I asked.

"Who wants to know?"

"The doctor standing next to you."

"Weak," he said. "But not so weak I won't strangle the life out of that guy in the Porsche if you drag him over here."

"I get that," I told him. "The troopers will have you out of here in no time."

Wanda tapped me on the arm. "The ambulance is leaving."

"You know what? I'm going to ride with the kid."

"I'll pick you up at the hospital."

"Don't worry about it. I'll get a ride. Anyway, I may be there a while. This much head trauma all at once—they may need my help."

I ran over and climbed in and the burly kid shut the door behind me. The seal was so tight I could feel the change in air pressure and the noise of the road was suddenly gone. We might as well have been in a tomb. Tierra's eyes were closed and she was as pale as a corpse. Her mother held her hand.

"She'll be fine," I said, even though I was not so sure. "We just need to relieve the pressure on her brain."

The driver maneuvered his way through what was left of the

rush-hour traffic as if he were water seeking its level, finding holes and sliding through them without any fuss.

"You're good," I said, leaning through the divider.

"Thanks."

"Don't talk to him," the burly blonde kid said. "He needs to pay attention to the road."

I ignored him and kept at the driver. "You do martial arts, right?"

The driver smiled. "You got that from the driving?"

"Something in the way you handle the wheel. What style?"

"A little aikido."

When a martial arts guy says he does something a little bit, you can be pretty sure he's a veteran, particularly when he's in his forties and has a U.S. Marines tattoo on his forearm. "Desert Storm?" I asked.

"It's that obvious?"

"I didn't figure you for Grenada. Where can I find you if I want to be in touch?"

He gave me a card from his shirt pocket. It had a school name and number. "I'm there evenings, Monday through Friday."

*   *   *

The ambulance pulled into the bay at the hospital, and I went straight to the nursing station. "I'm Dr. Pearl. Who's the neurosurgeon on call?"

There was a flicker of recognition on her face. "Pearl . . . "

An orderly pushed Kimberly past, immediately followed by little Tierra.

"I don't work here anymore, but there go two trauma cases with two more on the way. You're about to have more patients than surgeons."

"I'll have to check with Dr. Khalsa," the nurse said.

My former boss, John Khalsa, was the Chief of Neurosurgery

in the hospital district's division of surgery. The consummate politician, his influence seemed to grow by the hour. Lately, I'd heard talk he might be running for office.

"You didn't answer me about who's on call," I pressed.

"Dr. Tremper."

Scott Tremper is a competent surgeon. He was at my right elbow during the case that killed my career.

"Who else?"

"His partner, Dr. Weiss."

"I don't know Weiss."

"He's new. A young man."

"My replacement, you mean."

The nurse blushed and looked down at the phone. "They say he's very good. I'm sorry, but I really need to ring Dr. Khalsa."

"Then do it."

They brought in the truck driver and started a chart on him. It said his name was Edson Erkulwater. I stuck my head into the treatment cubicle. A physician's assistant I didn't recognize was working on him. "Dr. Xenon Pearl," I introduced myself. "How's he doing?"

"*The* Xenon Pearl? I heard you were canned for crazy."

"You're swamped. We'll see what Khalsa says. In the meantime, scan Mr. Erkulwater's neck. I'm betting you'll see something at C5, C6."

The assistant looked at me evenly. "Already ordered," he said.

I went in search of little Tierra. She was in a room with Dr. Jean Morris, an ER doc I'd dated briefly. There hadn't been chemistry, but we remained friendly and I gave her a peck on the cheek.

"Wow. Xenon. What are you doing here?"

"I came in on the ambulance. The wreck happened in front of me. There are other patients, and I knew the duty surgeon would need help."

We examined Tierra together, agreed she was crashing quickly and that we should prep her for surgery.

"Dr. Weiss is on his way," Jean said.

"I'll do it. If we wait just a bit, she loses any chance for accomplishment or achievement in the future. If we wait longer than that, she dies on the table. How's the mother?"

"I haven't seen her, but I heard she's stable. Look, I hate to ask this, but do you have hospital privileges?"

"I'm privileged enough to know how to save this little girl."

She looked pained. "This cowboy stuff is what got you fired. If you take a wrong step now, they'll sue you around the block and back."

"I didn't come in to make trouble. I was on the road, that's all. You know how fast they go when the fluid builds, Jean. I don't want this on my conscience and neither do you."

She nodded, her decision made. "All right. I'll back you up."

On the way to the locker room, I passed the motorcyclist sitting up on a gurney talking to Vicky Sanchez, my favorite OR nurse. She was trying not to stare at his naked brain.

"You think Ferraris are fast, you gotta let me take you for a ride on my bike," he said.

"Dr. Pearl!" Vicky said. "So nice to see you. Are you back with us?"

"For tonight I am. We have a trauma overload. How's Galina?"

Her face brightened at the question. "Can you believe she's talking a blue streak? All those months of silence and now I can't shut her up."

The little Russian girl had been orphaned by events of the previous year, and I had been instrumental in helping Vicky adopt her.

"Your loving home did the trick," I said.

She smiled and pointed at the biker. "Anyway, meet Charles Czarnecki."

"How do you feel, Charlie?"

"Tired," he answered.

I took Vicky by the elbow and walked a few steps. "Keep him away from reflective surfaces," I said. "I don't want him to see himself. He's in a kind of fugue state right now, sort of a heightened denial. We need to get him into surgery before infection sets in."

"We're waiting for Dr. Tremper," Vicky said. "It shouldn't be long now."

I went to the OR locker room. Weiss's name was on my old locker. I took the empty one above it and dug around for scrubs. Dressed for work, I used my cell phone to call Roan Cole, anesthesiologist extraordinaire and my best friend and former partner in crime. "I'm about to do a epidural on a little kid. Care to help me?"

"What? Where?"

"Samaritan."

"Come on."

"No joke. Car accident happened in front of me on the road, and I came in with the ambulance. Multiple casualties. Tremper's coming in and the new guy Weiss, too. They need one more."

"Get her prepped and into the OR. I'll be there in twelve minutes."

I went out to my old operating suite. I cruised the room. Almost everything was the same: my boom lamps, the scan reader in the corner, the trays and instruments, even Roan's tool chest with the familiar Arrogant Bastard Ale sticker and the black-and-yellow Batman oval, along with a temporary tattoo of the Sandman and a Wonder Woman sticker frayed around the edges. I was suddenly overwhelmed by nostalgia. It bent me over and I reached out for support. That was how John Khalsa found me—propped up on an operating table with wet eyes and a stricken expression and shaking slightly in a fashion strictly taboo for any kind of surgeon.

4

"You want to tell me what you think you're doing here, or do you want me to leap to my own, incredibly disturbing conclusion?"

Khalsa had grayed slightly at the temples in our lost five months and if I wasn't mistaken there was an extra set of lines at the edges of his mouth. The changes only made him seem more distinguished, and I couldn't help admiring the guy's spit and polish and the way everything the world had to offer folded readily under his wing.

"You think I've become an ambulance chaser," I said. "That's not the way it happened."

"I know. I spoke to the paramedics. You were with some detective."

"My stepsister," I interjected, "though I'm sure you'd rather believe I was in custody."

He stared at me for a moment, and I could see the politician in him fighting with the surgical boss. "I was hoping not to argue," he said.

I nodded. "The last time I saw you, I told you I was sorry for not being a better team player and I meant it. I haven't been brooding and I haven't been looking for an angle back in. Mostly, I've been taking care of Jordan and thinking about my life."

"And practicing your karate," he said.

"*Gongfu.*"

"Whatever. I called Jordan last week and she told me she stood unaided for the first time."

"She used her hands."

"Her progress is remarkable. And very encouraging."

"She had a good surgeon."

Khalsa actually laughed. "She sure did."

"Speaking of good surgeons, how is David Weiss working out for you?"

"He's very good, Zee. Maybe as good as you, and down from Harvard with the latest techniques."

"Easy to work with, I bet."

"A real *mensch*."

I smiled hearing America's best-assimilated Indian use a Yiddish word. "So what are we going to do here?" I asked.

As if on cue, an orderly wheeled Tierra into the OR. Prepped and pale, she might have been a corpse.

"This one is for you," Khalsa said. "Go ahead and fix her up. The truck driver's in line for Weiss, the mother seems out of the woods, and Scott Tremper will attend the remarkable Mr. Czarnecki. Since you're operating in my hospital again, I expect you to be around for postop if you pull her through. After that we'll see how everybody gets along."

"Right," I said. "Do you need me to sign anything?"

He handed me a contract renewal. "Same as the old one," he said.

I went straight to the bottom line and signed it.

"Believe it or not, I'm glad about this," he smiled. "You strengthen my team."

He went out as Roan Cole came in. Roan and I get together every couple of weeks, and it is always good to see him. He hooked Tierra up to his magic potions straight away, and only when she was stable and asleep did he lower his mask enough to give me a grin.

"I forgot how ugly you are in scrubs," he said.

"We both know I'm the best-looking surgeon in South Florida."

"Ah, that was only true until the redoubtable Dr. Weiss graced us with his presence."

"I hear he's a helluva guy."

"Believe it."

"The kind of guy who wouldn't, for example, mention the

Wonder Woman sticker on your cart."

"Screw you," said Roan. "Someone put it on there as a joke. When I find out who, I'll kill him."

"You could take it off," I said.

"Tried. Look at the edges. The prankster used superglue. If I pull, I'll leave a crater on the cart."

"You could cover it," I said.

"I'm looking into it."

"The Sandman tattoo's a good one."

"The patron of my art," said Roan. "Gotta pay my respects."

Monica Dietrich, a solid surgical nurse, came in to assist. I shaved Tierra's head and dropped her shorn locks in a plastic bag. Some folks believe that virility, longevity, and strength are stored in hair, and returning a patient's shorn locks is a custom as old as the story of Samson and Delilah. Once the shaving was done, I cleaned the skull, made a curvilinear incision, elevated the temporalis muscle, and had a look at the break.

The news wasn't good. The fracture was across the vascular groove of the middle meningeal artery. I drilled a burr hole to relieve some of the pressure, turned the flap of bone, and saw the blood clot right away. It was a gooey, gelatinous clump sitting on the dura mater, the thick layer surrounding the brain. Gently, I used an instrument to elevate the clot. As it came free of the ruptured vessel, a stream of blood hit the lamp above me and made a thin arc over Tierra's draped body. Monica stepped back involuntarily and I felt a tiny surge of panic at the force of the blood.

"Zee," said Roan. "The bleeder."

I took a deep breath. I had been away from work for six months, but my martial training—the constant seeking of a relaxed state of equilibrium, the thousands and thousands of repetitions of loosing the tension from the neck down—helped bring me back. The tension left my shoulders and chest and my hands went soft and my focus returned and I teased the bleeding artery to its origin.

Unlike the brain, the meninges—the three protective layers

around the brain, of which the *dura mater* is the outermost—have a robust collateral circulation. Loss of blood supply to an area of the brain can be dire, but the meninges take the sacrifice of a single vessel with impunity. I cauterized the artery, lavaged the area, replaced the bone flap, and closed the wound without incident.

"I'd say that evens the score," Roan said.

I knew what he was talking about and Monica did too. The last time I'd had a child on the table he hadn't made it. It hadn't been my fault, he'd been dead going in, but the way it happened and what I saw when it did—a true white soul going up toward the light like a butterfly—had savaged my career and changed my life forever.

"Thank you," I said, thinking that wherever the little boy was, I hoped he'd seen me do a better job for the little girl than I had done for him.

Monica saw my tears and gave me a squeeze that was almost a hug. Roan came over and put his hand on my shoulder. I let it rest there until it was time to bring Tierra back to the real world so she could be with her mother.

"Go home and get some rest," Roan said once Tierra was breathing on her own.

"I can't," I said.

"The surgeon's fever is in you," Roan said.

I nodded. Monica smiled.

"It's been a while since I've put something right in the world," I said. "It's a certain feeling, that's all."

*   *   *

I went down the hall to talk to Kimberly and found her pacing anxiously, her arm in a sling.

"Tierra," she said.

"She's fine. The surgery was a piece of cake. She had a skull fracture and some blood pooled up on top of the brain."

Kimberly put her hand to her mouth.

"On *top* of the brain," I said. "Not in it. We got it in time. Relieved the pressure. There shouldn't be any damage. She'll bounce back quickly. Kids do that."

"I don't know how to thank you."

"Glad to be able to help. The word I get is that you have no damage to your neck."

She nodded. Even the nod was reassuring in its normality, its smooth casualness. "They said something about a nexus under my arm. I think that's the word they used."

"Brachial plexus."

"That's it."

"Just a bunch of nerves. They got bruised. They'll be fine. You might need a little rehab; you might not. Do we need to notify Tierra's father?"

"He's not in our life. It's just my little girl and me. Look, I use a computer at work. How soon will I be able to type again?"

"A week of rest, maybe two. Tell you what. I have a little magic potion at my office. Chinese herbs. If you drop by early in the week, I'll give you some. It'll ease the bruising and speed the return to movement."

I could see she had more thanking in her, but I interrupted. "They'll be bringing Tierra into recovery about now. Go and be with her."

Still in my greens, I went back down the hall. Looking in the window of the theater next to mine I saw Scott Tremper working on Charles Czarnecki. Things had slowed down enough for me to consider how I felt about the mad motorcyclist. I decided I didn't blame him for the accident. He was reckless, yes, but it had been his own life he was endangering this time, not anyone else's. It was the Porsche driver who held credit for the tragedies of the day. He was the one who hadn't been able to hold his temper, who had gone off and reacted when he simply should have moved out of the way for the bike behind him. I hoped Wanda would find him.

I pushed the OR door open and quietly went in. Scott Tremper raised his chin in greeting.

"Heard you were skulking around," he said.

"Mr. Czarnecki here's a piece of work."

Tremper nodded. "I thought he was juiced, but his blood work said he was clean. I couldn't believe it when I pulled the ABD aside."

ABD is our word for gauze. I wanted to tell Tremper he should have seen him before the bandages, blazing gloriously along on his speedy orange bike.

"Motorcycling is its own kind of high," I said.

"You would know."

"Yes, I would."

"His piss test may be clean, but he's no virgin. We're having trouble keeping him under."

Recreational drugs follow some of the same pathways as anesthesia. A user has different requirements than a nonuser, making anesthesia difficult. I noticed that the anesthesiologist had a BIS monitor set up—an instrument that monitors the depth of anesthesia by looking at the prefrontal EEG. Brain activity tells the critical story of a patient's level of awareness. No surgeon wants to get caught in the nightmare of operating on someone who's silenced by muscle relaxants and can't scream at every slice.

I watched Tremper rotate a piece of Charlie Czarnecki's scalp up and over to cover his exposed brain. It wasn't a permanent solution—that would come later when Tremper could put in a piece of prosthetic bone to repair the skull—but it got Czarnecki out of trouble.

"Nice," I said.

"Thanks. How did it go with the kid?"

"Fine."

"Feels good to have you back on the team. If you're back, I mean."

"We'll see," I answered.

"Helluva thing," Tremper said. "Needing a third surgeon today."

"Never rains but pours."

I left the suite and went down to meet Weiss. He looked like he was still in high school, quite the feat since you can't really start working as a neurosurgeon until you're well into your thirties, by which time the stress of the job draws dark lines on most faces. There wasn't anything dark about him. Blue-eyed, towheaded, and fit, he might have been a surf champion.

"Dr. Pearl, I presume. Heard you saved the day."

"Right time and right place, that's all. How's Edson doing?"

"Subluxation at C5-6. I screwed in the pins and pulled, but traction isn't doing it."

Two of the vertebrae in the truck driver's neck had come out of alignment. Weiss had tried pulling on the spine to realign them.

"How much traction did you use?"

"Thirty pounds. Why?"

"More traction would make the surgery easier," I said. "There'd be less work to do to get the neck stabilized, less trauma to the patient, less complexity to the fusion. I've gone twice that high."

Weiss frowned. Roan drifted over. "It's true. I've seen him do it."

I put up my hands. "Your case, your call. I'm just offering help if you want it. We used to do sixty pounds in residency. I think it's just a question of what they did where you were trained."

I saw Weiss war with my suggestion. If we injured Erkulwater further it would be his responsibility, but if we succeeded the surgery would be much easier. To his credit, he nodded his assent. I lent a hand, and we stretched the driver's neck. When everything looked good, Weiss went in from the back of the neck. He made a perfect incision along the midline, bloodlessly separated the muscles, found the spinous processes of the vertebrae, exposed the laminae, and put screws in the lateral masses. With everything lining up, it was a straightforward procedure to attach the rods that fused the neck. Weiss did it quickly and smoothly.

"Beautiful work," I said.

"Thanks," he said, sounding a bit surprised at the compliment.

"Zee doesn't deserve his evil reputation," Roan confided.

"An evil reputation can come in handy," Weiss said with the utmost seriousness. "I wish I had one."

5

Sometime after midnight, Roan offered to give me a lift. He had a comfortable Saab convertible, and the rain had stopped so he lowered the top. I settled back into the leather seats and looked up at the crescent moon squatting low in the western sky, feeling the humid air on my skin. I got a whiff of Japanese honeysuckle, which flowered in winter.

"You seem calmer than you've been," said Roan.

"You're saying work agrees with me?"

Roan seemed to consider his answer carefully. "I think you've been casting about for a way to fix yourself. You seem a bit less bent on that tonight."

I shrugged. "I've got my demons," I said. "Being busy keeps me from thinking about them."

"Being with Jordan doesn't help?"

"In some ways it does."

"You want me to take you to see her?"

"It's late. Since she moved in with her mother I get the stink eye if I show up after eight."

"From Jordan or from the mother?"

"The mother, Jordan, whatever."

"I heard she stood on her own this week."

"Yeah. Her balance is still weak, but her legs took some weight."

"She'll be back," he said.

We both knew she probably wouldn't. Standing wasn't walking, and in truth she'd only leaned.

"I gather the mother still blames you for what happened."

"She's not wrong there, is she?"

Roan shook his head. "Strange comment from a guy who believes in karma and signing contracts before stepping into life and all that. You seeing things differently all of a sudden?"

"I don't know what I'm seeing," I said. "I just wish she'd get better."

We crossed the causeway to the barrier island on which I live, just south of the Hillsboro Lighthouse, which for more than a century has been keeping mariners from running aground on the rocky outcropping by the Hillsboro Inlet. My house sits on a corner lot directly across the street from the beach. Back in 1957, when it was constructed, it nudged the edge of the sea grapes and the dunes. Twenty years later, some smart real-estate angler found a hole in the city code, did a little measuring, and made space for a narrow lane and more houses along the shore. Now mansions in the sand block the ground-floor view, but I can see still see the ocean from my second story—along with a nice view of my Australian black bean tree, yellow crotons, and Mexican Firebush arbor.

I waved good-bye to Roan and went inside. There was a phone message from Wanda saying she had run the plate on the Porsche and had a name, and another from Jordan just calling to say hello. Exhausted but not ready for sleep, I went out back with Quiet Teacher, the magnificent blade Jordan had crafted for me. The yard is my refuge. An eight-foot board-on-board fence encloses a small swimming pool and hot tub, and a riot of passionflowers, orchids, jasmine, Bermuda cherry, Jamaican strawberry, and citrus scent the air around a gazebo I built for meditation.

The grass was slick from the rain and there were cricket frogs trapped in the pool. I rescued half a dozen before starting my sword exercises, rinsing them with the hose to get the chlorine off them because I know it burns their skin. Then I started my routine. At first I moved slowly and carefully. The glint of the hand-forged Damascus steel was hypnotic, the wavy lines picking up the faint moonlight and reflecting it into my eyes. I stood on one leg for a time, with the sword extended, and when my breath told me I was ready, I picked up the pace. I focused my attention on spiral movements of my core, softening and lightening my torso and arms until the blade effortlessly expressed my intentions.

Wu Tie Mei always scoffed at teachers who exhort students to become the sword. She always reminded me that a sword has no mind, and in that regard, along with many others, it is merely a tool and far inferior to a human being. "No matter what you hold in your hand, you behave the same way," she said. "Keep the same focus, the same internal harmony, the same equilibrium. You behave this way with a scalpel. You behave this way with a sword. You behave this way with a calligraphy brush or a screwdriver and the same way with a lover's hand."

I remembered my teacher's words and I remembered her lessons, but sad to say, I found it hard to see her face in my mind's eye anymore or to hear the tones of her voice. My longing for her guidance was the keenest, sorest reality of my life, fully as omnipresent and painful as my guilt and regret over the attack on Jordan. When Wu Tie Mei's shade came to me in the locker room six months before, I had been shocked, unbalanced, even worried it was a sign of schizophrenia. Now, in the deafening silence— unguided and alone—I pined for the sweet aroma of almonds that heralded her appearance and for the cool evanescence of her impossible departure. I wondered if she might be silent now because she had freed herself from the tethers of her karmic obligation. Perhaps her time as a wispy presence was over and she had moved on to life as a dolphin or an embryonic restaurateur. Perhaps she was back in Asia, patiently waiting in the womb of a Communist Party member, or perhaps, because she had once been a Chinese Jewess, she was a developing fetus in Egypt soon to become an avatar of Middle East peace.

What I knew for sure was that she had left a queen-sized hole in my world when she died. When she came back—that is to say, when her ghost appeared and talked to me—she set me back on the path I'd followed for eons but lost. Then she disappeared again.

Losing her the second time was worse than losing her the first. Without the guidance of her shade, the violent path of the vigilante left me confounded by moral doubts and I realized that she had set me on a path to enlightenment but abandoned me before I reached my goal. By taking either a wrong turn or getting bogged down in a spiritual quagmire, I had become a freak at best and a madman at worst. Incomplete as they were, her gritty martial teachings were all I had.

I dropped down and forward onto my risen foot, raised my left hand high in the air, and thrust the sword straight out. "Where are you?" I shouted.

The path in front was obscured, but even the steps she had taught me as a child lacked details any adult would want. I yearned for a connection to the history of her style, a name for that style, characters and lineage I could learn about and study. I tried my best to find these answers in books, discourses, and drawings; though I had found pieces of what Tie Mei had shared here and there, no single source brought it all together enough to help me move forward. I needed another teacher to help me make sense of so much translated, second-hand, and oft-conflicting information; the *gongfu* forest was just too dense and dark and impenetrable to navigate without one.

My front foot slid out on the wet grass, pulling my groin. I went down. The pull wasn't a bad one, but it was enough to stop me from continuing. I lay the blade across my chest to keep it dry and stared at the stars.

"I'm losing my grip, Tie Mei," I whispered to the sky. "I feel terrible things coming and I hate myself for them already. If you don't answer, I don't know how much longer I can keep myself together. At least give me a sign that you're out there and listening."

I scanned the heavens but all I saw was a bevy of high-altitude jets heading for Fort Lauderdale and Miami and a couple of low-flying prop jobs on final approach to the little Pompano Beach airfield. Desperate, frightened, and alone, I went inside.

*   *   *

"Who's dead?" my grandfather answered his phone breathlessly.

"Nobody's dead. I just called to say hello."

"At one in the morning?"

"I know you don't sleep. I can hear the music playing."

Grandpa Lou laughed his crazy, 1950s, beatnik laugh. "All right," he said. "So I'm awake."

"You used to like it when I called you."

"I still like it when you call me. It's just I know you're bored now because you're out of a job and not such a big shot."

"I'm not calling because I'm bored."

"Then you need something."

I carefully put down Quiet Teacher on the coffee table and sat back on the couch. "I want to know about Tie Mei," I said.

"We've been through this so many times, Xenon."

"I want to talk with people who knew her before she came here."

Across town in the Fort Lauderdale neighborhood of Sailboat Bend, Grandpa Lou took a long pause. "You've asked me before," he said. "I don't know what to tell you."

"There's asking and there's asking."

"So now you're really asking?"

"You always taught me that a man needed a special passion to keep him sane. Well, mine is the martial practice Tie Mei taught me. I've gone as far as I can go with it, I'm stumped, and I need someone to finish teaching me what she started. I figure it might be one of those Chinese Jews."

"So after all these years you're interested in Chinese Jews. Well, I've told you all I know. The congregation made a donation to help Jewish victims of religious oppression. Five Chinese refugees came over on the boat. I saw Tie Mei at the dock and she was beautiful and I know a little about what happens to beautiful women alone in the world so I offered her a job with your parents even before I asked them. Remember, your mother and father were working a hundred hours a week on the business back then."

"What happened to the other four?"

"I told you. They ran away."

"What does that mean? People can't just disappear in this country."

Grandpa Lou gave a bitter laugh. "No? What do you think happened to your grandmother?"

I didn't want to get into that with him. After my mother finally succumbed to her long bout with cancer, my grandmother, Grandpa Joe's bride, simply up and left. No effort to find her had drawn any water.

"You don't remember any of their names?" I said. "You don't know if any were Tie Mei's friends?"

"There was one young man who liked Tie Mei and came to your house sometimes. I don't know if there was anything there."

"I want to meet him."

"That was decades ago, Zee. I don't even remember his name."

"Think about it, okay? Mom was gone and you were gone and Dad was always working. I feel like I'm losing it again and this is the only thing that can help. I'm alone on this, Grandpa. Can you understand that?"

"Being alone is something I understand," he sighed. "I'll see what I can dig up."

6

Jordan's father, Thaddeus Jones, was a man who believed in life insurance and lots of it. If he hadn't, his widow never would have been able to afford her Boca high-rise condo. The place was in one of the older waterfront buildings down near the Deerfield Beach line. There was a doorman and marble in the lobby, but none of the pretentiousness of the most expensive buildings in a town trying to be a chichi retreat for snowbird New Yorkers.

The doorman hadn't seen me before, and he took me for biker trash. He gave my new black Triumph Thruxton the stink-eye. "What can I do you for?"

"Jones," I said.

"You know how many Jones we got in this building?"

"Jordan and Amanda."

Forty-something, he looked like he might have lost his job as a mid-level manager somewhere. He frowned at me. "Are they expecting you?"

"Give a call and find out. I'm Dr. Pearl."

He rang, got permission, and pointed to the elevator.

Upstairs, Amanda opened the door and stared at the helmet in my hand.

"When are you going to buy a car?"

"When Jordan tells me she doesn't like the bike anymore."

Amanda has Jordan's features, or, rather, Jordan has hers, but the uncanny resemblance stops at the neck. Where Jordan is tall and lanky with a swimmer's shoulders, her mother is shaped like one of Tie Mei's pork dumplings. She wore a floral dress that day, a bad choice for her figure, and deep maroon lipstick best on a 1950s *Folies Bergère* dancer. I figured the choice of dress might have been for Jordan's benefit. My lover adored flowers; her own home had been a veritable arbor and many of her favorite botanical beauties had been transplanted here.

Jordan wheeled over and met me halfway. I knelt to her, dropping the helmet, and closed my eyes as we kissed. Her mouth felt fevered.

"I have some new feelings today," she whispered. "Down there. You know."

"New sensations require a thorough neurological exam," I whispered back.

I scooped her out of the chair and held her to me. She wrapped her arms around my neck and pulled me tight.

"I've been working my abs," she said, lifting her blouse so I could see the result.

"We have to get you modeling," I said.

"Modeling," Amanda sniffed. "That'll be the day."

"Strengthening my stomach stopped the pain in my back," Jordan said. "Will you take me for a ride? I can hold myself up now. I know I can. Look."

She sat up straight in her chair, legs dangling limply. She twisted her torso to convince me. "I'm gripping with my thighs," she said. "Come feel. In combination with my arms, it's enough."

I handed her my helmet. "Let's go," I said.

Amanda stepped up, eyes blazing. "I forbid this."

"Mom," Jordan said quietly.

I didn't know much about the issues between them, but I did know that they had drifted apart after Thaddeus died and that things had been strained between them since Jordan was hurt. Jordan always said it was because it was just too painful to be together without her father, that the hole between mother and daughter was so iron-heavy that its gravity threatened to pull them down. I figured it had more to do with female issues. I sensed Jordan had taken her mother's place in her father's eye, and the proof of Amanda's resentment was the utter absence of Thaddeus memorabilia in the apartment—not one photo, not a single one of the late swordsmith's magnificent blades.

"We'll see how she manages just around the parking lot," I told Amanda. "Nice and easy."

Amanda set her jaw, but I scooped up Jordan.

"You could wheel me," she whispered.

"And miss a chance to hold you? No cigar."

Her smile was worth her weight, and we necked waiting for the elevator to come. Downstairs, the doorman followed us outside and watched me put Jordan on the bike. Designed to convey a racy, solo-rider-only image, the Thruxton has a plastic cowling over the rear seat. I asked the doorman to keep it safe then fastened the helmet under Jordan's chin while pretending not to notice her tears. I climbed aboard in front of her and placed her hands around my waist.

"Road test first," I said. "Are you ready?"

"Born ready," she answered.

Keeping my feet on the ground, I moved the bike from side to side, feigning cornering angles we never could achieve on South Florida's flat, straight highways. Jordan's grip tightened, but she didn't slip. Using the clutch and the brake, I inched the bike forward then stopped it hard, simulating unexpected traffic stops. Her helmet hit me on the back of the head.

"Sorry," she said. "I know better than that."

I tried the exercise again. She kept her head straight. I leaned the bike as far over as I could without dropping it. She stayed aboard.

"All right," I said. "Now for the shakedown cruise."

I eased out onto the beach road, heading north. There was a gentle breeze and it brought the smell of the ocean.

"Happy?" I asked.

"Deliriously."

I snuck a look back at her and found her glowing. I sped up and passed a car over the double yellow, gunned it over the bridge at Camino Real, and came down for a view of the Boca Raton

Inlet. Hundreds of boats bobbed in the protected water and the pink towers of the Boca Raton Resort and Club glowed against the deep blue sky. The caps over the open ocean to the east made me think of the fiery demise of a vintage speedboat I'd seen go down in a hurricane sea.

Just shy of Spanish River Boulevard, couples walked the beach together. I made a silent prayer that someday soon we would, too. Jordan must have thought the same thing, because she squeezed my hand. To our left was Gumbo Limbo, a nature preserve with a raised walkway. "I want to go there sometime soon," Jordan yelled into the wind. "I like those crazy banana spiders that come in springtime, the yellow ones all over the trees."

"I went to work last night," I called back.

"What?"

"There was a car accident and a few people were hurt and there weren't enough surgeons. I happened to be there. John Khalsa let me operate on a little girl."

"That's wonderful, Zee. Did it go well?"

"It wasn't like the last kid. I don't think there'll be any residual beyond a white line under her hair."

Jordan knew all about white lines. Her back was riddled with the scars of the incisions I'd made and closed over her injury. I thought I heard her say she was glad it went well, but it might have been the wind.

"I'm thinking Delray for breakfast!" I yelled. "How does that sound?"

"Too close! I want Palm Beach."

So we motored on. Cars came up behind us. I accelerated, made space, then slowed down again. It was possible to go too fast along this road, to miss wonders in the ocean, to blur the sight of the magnificent houses and their imperial gardens.

"Khalsa asked after you," I said.

"He called me," she said. "I want you to tell him how well I can ride."

I glanced back. She was straight in the saddle, and her grip on me was still strong.

"They hired a guy to replace me," I said. "I met him."

"Nobody can replace you."

"You say."

I felt her sigh as much as heard it. "Yes, I do."

We passed through Boynton Beach. At the parking lot in the inlet, I saw a boy in the surf bring up a small shark on a line. We continued north through Lake Worth and into Palm Beach, followed the zigzag of the beach road, and then turned on to Worth Avenue so Jordan could see the shops. I idled the bike in front of a store that sold rare Meissen china: delicate blue-and-white pieces. Tie Mei had loved the style, and I remembered my father had bought her a teapot.

We chose a popular eatery five minutes up the road. I carried Jordan to a table under a yellow umbrella. People stared. Jordan had Niçoise salad and ice tea. I had my hamburger medium well.

"I need the restroom," she said when we were done.

We went there together. I knocked then took her into the stall and went out until she was finished. A woman standing at the sink started to say something, but I shut her down with a look. Afterward, I held Jordan up to the sink while she washed her hands.

"Sometimes this is so hard," she said quietly when we got back to the bike.

"Hard?" I joked. "The engine's doing all the work. A year from now we'll do the same ride on bicycle."

"Sure," she said. "A bicycle."

"Everything's going to be fine," I said.

"I'd like to think so, but it's not just about me. I worry about you, Zee. I worry that you'll go back to your night work."

I didn't want to answer, so I gunned the engine and the motorcycle leapt into the fray.

7

I went in to see young Tierra on Sunday morning. The incision—while still fresh and oozing slightly—was clean and tight and the little girl was awake and talking with her mother.

"I play the cello at church," Tierra continued. "And I play at school. I did a solo at our autumn fair. My aunt and uncle came from New Jersey and my cousin played the triangle."

"You'll be playing better than ever when you get out of here," I said. "I put a little cello magic in your brain when I had the top of your head off."

"You had my head off?"

I nodded. "While you were sleeping."

"What's cello magic?"

"It works only if you're very good and listen to your mom and take care of yourself so the wound heals."

"But what *is* it?"

"It's a certain magic only for musicians. It takes good cello players and makes them into great ones."

"You're very kind," Kimberly said.

"I have a girlfriend named Jordan," I said. "Maybe I can bring her to hear you play sometime."

With that, I gave them two thumbs up and went to see Edson Erkulwater. The truck driver was awake in his bed, but his neck was immobilized and he looked pale and drawn.

"You did this to me?" he said.

"Dr. Weiss was your surgeon. I just lent a hand."

He tried a smile. "Just kidding. I guess I owe you both."

"The hospital will take care of me."

He tried a nod then winced. "I bet they will. Tell me about the people in that Subaru. What happened to that little girl?"

"Some blood built up on her brain. I relieved the pressure. She'll be fine. She and I were just talking about playing the cello."

"And the mother?"

"A bruised armpit is all. Nerves are a little tender. Her arm will be in a sling for a while."

The tension went out of Erkulwater's body, and he sank down into his bed. "I heard there was a biker," he said. "Gotta say, I didn't see any motorcycle. Remember a white Porsche is all."

"The Porsche kept going. I'm sure the police are looking for him. The bike went under your truck. The guy will live. He's very lucky. I've seen less do worse."

Erkulwater clucked. "Some of those bikers just have angels riding with them. It's like they give up on common sense and put their faith in something bigger. The Lord watches out for all of us in his own way."

"I never thought of that," I said.

He looked at me hard. "No?"

I shook my head.

Erkulwater closed his eyes, and I took it as my cue to leave. I went down the hall and looked in on Charlie Czarnecki. He was sleeping, and the nurse on duty said he was stable. I wanted to spend more time at the hospital after that, but there was no reason to. I didn't want to seem too eager, didn't want any of the staff to start talking, and didn't want to run into Khalsa and rock the boat.

So I left.

*   *   *

My father, Asher, met me for lunch at Jerry's Famous Deli in Miami Beach, close to where he lived with his new wife, Rachel. The restaurant started in the San Fernando Valley, California, and branched out all the way to Florida. My father liked it because it was convenient and the soups were good. I liked it for its encyclopedic menu; there was always something new to try.

"So you're back to work," he said.

"I've made a step in that direction."

"You keep your office?"

"I had to let some staff go."

"You still have the dwarf?"

I winced. "He prefers little person. Medically, he's a midget."

"So the dwarf still works for you."

"Travis keeps the office open," I said. "We do follow-ups on existing patients, and I see people for diagnosis when they're referred."

"So other doctors are referring to you again?"

"Nobody actually has," I said. "Maybe now that will change."

"You look pretty healthy," he said.

"You too."

And he did, which surprised me. Rachel is a terrific baker and I expected my father to gain weight after their marriage, but he was getting leaner every week. Rachel put him on the stationary bike in front of the television every night and bought him tennis lessons, which he claimed to hate but really loved. Izod shirts were his new passion—he'd raised me with the profits from his own men's store on Miracle Mile in Coral Gables—and sitting in front of me, with a deli menu in his hands, he wore a baby blue one and a terrycloth sweatband around his wrist.

"Today, I'm having mushroom and barley," he announced. "You?"

"Matzoh ball."

He leaned confidentially across the table. "I wouldn't. Lately, they've been heavy."

The waiter came. I ordered blintzes with extra sour cream.

"I still worry about the Mafiya," my father said, referring to a tousle that I'd had with Russian mobsters.

"Don't," I said. "Whatever personal vendetta there might have been is over. Done. Nobody's thinking about me anymore and they're certainly not thinking about you."

"From your lips to God's ears," he said.

Soda crackers in a basket appeared. I ignored them in favor of the steel bowl of sour tomatoes in the center of the table, using the tongs to pull out the tomatoes and the scissors provided to make bite-size slices without squirting green juice all over myself.

"Your mother loved sours," he said. "Personally, I can't stand them."

"I know."

"Tie Mei loved anything salty. All the Chinese do—soy sauce, *hoisin* sauce, oyster sauce, *ponzu* sauce."

"What she really loved was chocolate."

My father smiled, his eyes drifting into a memory. "She tried to keep that a secret. She was always so serious, always so practical."

"Listen, I want to ask you about something. When Tie Mei first arrived in Miami on the ship, she came with a group of Chinese Jews, yes?"

My father nodded.

"Who were they and what happened to them?"

"You'll have to ask your grandfather. I wasn't involved in all that. It was his congregation that put the money together."

"I did ask him. He said there were four others and that one of them came around to see her."

My father took a long time addressing my remark, so I knew I'd hit a nerve.

"There was a *schmo* who used to come around," he said at last. "Tall and thin. They had a history. I asked her about it once and she put her finger on my lips."

"A history as in a romance?"

My father shrugged. Romantic references to Tie Mei disturbed him and they disturbed me too because I resented the fact my father hadn't done the right thing and married her. I knew they'd loved each other. Tie Mei was more than a nanny and far more than my father's employee. I could only guess that some guilty allegiance to my dead mother had kept my father from offering his hand.

"The guy was persistent, I remember that much," my father said. "I didn't get involved; Tie Mei was hardly the kind of person to ask me for help fending off unwanted advances."

"Hardly," I thought, thinking of how she had died saving my father's life in a robbery.

"So what brings all this up?"

"I want to find the guy," I said.

"Still looking to the past for answers, huh? My advice is to lift your head and look forward. It's the present and the future that need your attention."

"The three of them blur together for me."

My father closed his eyes and wiped his face. "I think you need some professional help, son."

I couldn't remember a time Asher had called me son. It didn't sound like him.

"I'd just like to ask the guy some questions," I said.

"Isn't there someone you can go to quietly, one doctor to another?"

"So you don't even know where I should start?"

My father sighed and looked around. "The guy was bad news. Besides, he could be anywhere by now."

My father's soup came, along with blintzes dense enough to make matzoh balls look like clouds. I smothered them in sour cream and put some jam on the side of the plate for good measure. My father watched disapprovingly.

"Imagine," he said. "A doctor who eats like a Teamster."

"A Jewish Teamster," I said.

"A thug."

"A thug with a sword," I muttered under my breath.

He raised an eyebrow. "That's all over, yes? Whatever that was? Craziness, fantasy, a suicidal impulse, the *dybbuk* of the old country alive in your heart?"

"Whatever it was, yes it's over."

"You have Jordan to think about. Not to mention a cop in the family."

"I said it's over," I replied, diving into the blintzes. "By the way, I took Jordan on a motorcycle ride yesterday."

I watched him work the angles: his own history with motorcycles, the trials and tribulations of life in a wheelchair, the sadness, the dead end of it. I was pretty sure he was going to yell at me, but instead he nodded. "Wonderful," he said at last. "She could sit up?"

"She's been working her belly muscles, and her thighs did a job holding onto the seat."

"A beach ride?"

"That's right."

"Tie Mei's friend was a pharmacist," he said. "Or the Chinese equivalent—an educated man. I don't know how much that helps you. People start over. I remember her saying he didn't have anybody. Of course *she* had us, an instant family, a place to belong. That's what women want."

"Everyone wants a place to belong, Dad."

"Maybe they do. I remember I felt bad for the guy. He had no license to drive a car much less dispense drugs, and he barely knew a word of English."

"I thought Grandpa Lou figured out all that in advance. Bringing people here from the other side of the world."

My father put down his soup spoon. "He freed them from tyranny, don't get me wrong. Ah. That's it. Now I remember. His name was Solomon."

"Solomon?"

"That's what he wanted to be called. It was a hard name for him to pronounce, but he was here because he was Jewish and he wanted to honor that by taking an Old Testament name. He was very young then, but he'd be past his prime now. Late fifties, I'd say."

My cell phone rang. It was Wanda. "Highway Patrol is bringing in the Porsche driver."

"Why them and not you?"

"It's their jurisdiction. The accident happened on I-95."

"But you were right there."

"It doesn't matter who brings him in."

I almost argued the point but held my tongue.

8

During the height of things, I'd had quite a crew at my office, and the front door had opened and closed frequently enough for the glorious smell of the gardenia in front to waft in as far as the supply closet. That afternoon, the place smelled stale. The only one there was Travis Bailey, the man my father referred to as a dwarf.

He waved a greeting. "That bastard landlord won't water the shrubs," he said.

"There's a drought."

"Now there's a drought. Six months ago, a hurricane. Lake Okeechobee's a reservoir, for God's sake. You can't just let plants die."

"They'll come back," I said.

"The hell with that. I dragged a hose over from my place and watered them myself."

"Khalsa let me back in the hospital," I said. "I did one surgery and assisted in another."

"What? When?"

"Friday night, late."

"We gonna bill for it?"

"Sure we'll bill for it."

"Good, 'cause things are a bit thin around here."

I was grateful he didn't say anything about the loyal staff—including his girlfriend—whom I'd let go when I got fired.

"How's Marta?" I asked.

"She moved in with me."

"She did? Wonderful news."

"I think so," he said. "But she won't let me smoke my Cubans."

"That's probably because they're not real Cubans."

"Oh, they're Cubans all right. Joe Montefiore gave them to me."

"The bastard landlord Joe Montefiore who won't water the plants?"

"That's him. Said his cousin smuggled them in from Sicily."

"Marta won't let you smoke them in the apartment, or she won't let you smoke them at all?"

Travis jumped up on the desk where he did my insurance billing and pulled a box from behind a stack of mail. "She won't let me near them at all. Here, I brought the rest for you."

They were Cuban Montecristos, some of the best cigars in the world. I opened the box and let the rich smell of the cedar lining and fine tobacco reach my nose.

"I don't want to turn these down," I said, "but maybe we should talk about setting some ground rules. I mean, she's the one moving in with *you*."

He shook his head. "I knew you were going to say that, but a man has to pick his battles."

"Give in over a box of cheap Mexican sticks if you must," I said, "but these beauties are worth the fight."

He sighed. "They're still just cigars."

There was a sound at the door. He hopped off the desk and ran to the window. "Cop car!" he hissed. "Hide the box."

I pushed them behind me as Wanda walked in. She looked around and sniffed the air.

"Cuban cigars?"

Travis paled.

"Travis, this is Wanda. Her mother is my father's new wife. Wanda, Travis. He keeps my office running and smuggles contraband Cuban goods. Sometimes he also runs drugs in from Cuba and hustles rich people out of their life savings with promises of sure entry to heaven with a paper ticket."

Travis coughed a greeting and scuttled out. Laughing, Wanda asked for the hospital update.

"Everyone should recover. The biker will need a toupee and the trucker won't be driving for a while. Are you charging the Porsche guy?"

Wanda stopped smiling. "He lost control of his car on the slick road in the rain. After fighting for his life, he regained control."

"That's his story and he's sticking to it, huh?"

She nodded. "He claims not to have seen any motorcycles."

"Didn't see it but chased it all over the road."

She pursed her lips. "He says he has no idea there was an accident."

"What's the guy's name?" I asked. "What does he do for a living?"

"You don't want to know."

"But I do."

"He's an adult film mogul by the name of Jay Boniface."

"Adult films?"

"You heard me. He lives in Weston, in a mansion."

Weston is a western development of Fort Lauderdale, a swath of land made habitable by the canal system that dried the Everglades. Twenty years ago it was swamp; today it's a thriving bedroom community full of lakes and golf courses and mile after mile of subdivisions peppered with tract homes and ritzy enclaves.

"I gather he has a superstar lawyer."

"You have no idea."

"So the insurance companies eat the bills and this guy skates across the pond."

"And all this time I thought you believed in karma and the restoration of balance to a world gone mad."

If I didn't know better, I would have thought she was asking because she was hoping for some of my particular brand of justice. I felt a surge of excitement at the idea, and the surge worried me. Violence, Jordan had repeatedly told me, was not the answer. Look where it had gotten her. Look where it had gotten the world. She claimed the planet was trying to save itself from the human race by activating something in our genes to get us to kill one another.

"You have an address for this guy?"

The way Wanda looked at me, I knew I should not have asked. It had been some time since we had done our little dance—the cop and the outlaw—and I had forgotten how subtle and delicate a thing it was.

"I shouldn't have mentioned this," she said. "Not to you. It was stupid of me. I'm sorry."

"Never mind. Here, have a cigar."

She waved it away. I lit up my illegal gains, savoring the slightly bitter taste of the wrapper tobacco on my lips and the many-layered flavor of the smoke. She just watched me.

"Time to get back to work."

She was gone before I could see her out. I walked over to the folding Chinese screen that is the centerpiece of my consulting office. I looked at the peasants rendered in gold paint on the black lacquer and bent close to examine the horns of the water buffalo they rode as they forded a river fed by a waterfall tumbling down from beautifully drawn mountains. I wondered if I loved the piece because in some past life I had crossed the river myself, or if it just evoked China for me. Tie Mei and the contrails of my many lives had left me with a romantic obsession with that distant land.

I brought the cigar to my belly as if it were a sword, picked up one leg, and leapt across the room, stabbing the cigar into the air in the movement Tie Mei called "Hungry Tiger Pounces on Prey." The motion felt hollow, weak, and unstable. My feet didn't connect properly with the ground. I was an iron lollypop—top heavy, tense, and unable to sink and relax. It was an infuriating feeling, all the more because I knew better.

Travis came in. Startled, I dropped a bit of cigar ash to the floor.

"Listen," he said. "I know you were just kidding around . . ."

"Don't worry," I said. "It was just my stepsister in to say hello."

9

Grandpa Lou accompanied me to his old synagogue, but he did so under duress. His story was that he stopped being a rabbi after my grandmother left, but I knew there was more to it than that. A rabbi is a teacher, and Lou could no more stop teaching than a falcon can stop hunting—it was an everyday affair with him, arising naturally in his moment-to-moment interactions with others.

The temple was in Coral Gables, not far from where my father's store had been. It was a small terracotta building set well back from the road. The parking lot was crushed coral. Cardboard, Queen, and Alexander palms and a tough tangle of rhododendron were at war with the edge of the lot. A large rock bearing a bronze Star of David mottled with oxidation was the sole clue that it was a Jewish house of worship.

"People have a strange idea of this country," my grandfather said as he pulled his old Volvo into the parking lot. "Or at least they did. Now, who knows? These days our primary export is genetically engineered beef, calorie-free carbonated water in ten different flavors, and whatever policy suits the current administration's goals to achieve hegemony over people willing to buy cheaply built goods they don't need with money they don't have."

"I don't think it's so simple," I said. "Immigrants come here for all kinds of reasons, and not just because they love burgers and cola. There's freedom, for one thing. . . . "

"Whatever that means to them."

"Maybe it means the right to worship whatever they want, the right to walk down the street without being told what to do, the right to pursue a better standard of living. . . . "

"A big-screen TV," he growled.

"A decent education for their kids," I countered.

"Our educational system is among the worst around, unless, of course, you're talking about teaching people to worship money."

"That's painting with a pretty broad brush."

He shot me a disgusted look. "I'm just saying true freedom is on the inside, and this country has become more about the outside than ever, more about consumption and instant gratification than it's ever been."

I thought about freedom being on the inside. I wondered when I was going to be free of myself. "Most people in the world are ducking bullets and worrying about their next meal," I said. "From that point of view, this country looks pretty good. Listen, Grandpa. You seem stressed about coming back to your old stomping grounds. We're not out of the car yet. We can still turn around."

"We're not turning around. I didn't leave the temple in shame. I quit teaching the Torah, that's all. I left to pursue quiet contemplation."

"In your garden."

"That's right, in my garden."

"For thirty years."

"You're the only one counting. You can be sure nobody working here will ask or care or even remember me."

*   *   *

By the time we got to the glass doors, my motorcycle boots were covered with coral dust. Inside, I wiped them carefully on the mat. My grandfather took no such precaution but forged ahead to a door marked "staff" and went inside. "I'm looking for records," he said.

An elegant, white-haired woman looked up at him in surprise. "I know that voice."

Grandpa Lou stopped scowling. He looked at his feet.

The woman got out of her chair. She wore a gold *chai* around her neck, the Hebrew sign for life. Each and every aspect of her wardrobe matched, not just in color and style but in overall shape and feel. The effect was mesmerizing. She had beautiful blue eyes.

"Rabbi," she said.

Lou waved his hand. "I'm not a rabbi anymore."

"A rabbi is always a rabbi. Only his congregation can change. Do you remember me?"

"Yael," he said reluctantly. "You haven't aged a day."

"And you're still the charmer."

He introduced me. We shook hands. Her grip was cool and dry. "We're here about the Chinese Jews," I said.

She furrowed her brow in concentration. "You mean the five who came over on the boat about thirty years ago?"

"That's right."

"It's so long ago. Didn't one . . . "

"She came to work for my parents," I said. "She raised me after my mother died."

"There must be files," Lou broke in.

"Things have changed, Rabbi. Those old files are in boxes in the back. We use computers now. Your successor is a great believer in technology."

"Good for him," said Lou. "Maybe he can find God with a telescope. Where are the boxes?"

"I'd have to rummage around."

"So rummage," Lou said.

"He's doing this for me," I said. "Don't mind his manners."

"There's nothing wrong with my manners. She said she'd have to rummage, so I said go ahead and rummage."

"He was always like this," Yael told me, as if she were telling me something I didn't know. "The files are in the shed where we keep the garden things, the lawnmower and the like."

"If you have a moment, it would mean a lot to us to find them," I said. "My nanny passed away. We're trying to locate her relatives."

It wasn't strictly true. Wu Tie Mei had been dead for years, and as far as I could recall, we'd made no such effort. But it was simpler than explaining my complex preoccupations and more likely to yield results.

"Perhaps you'd like to meet the new rabbi while I have a look."

Lou shook his head. "I'm Buddhist now. He wouldn't like me."

Yael paled. I searched for something to say as we followed her across the swale to a metal shed. She worked the key in the lock. Inside, there were tools. I moved a bag of fertilizer out of the way to clear a path to a stack of cardboard boxes.

"Black widow spider," my grandfather said, pointing.

Yael took a step back. I scooped up the spider on a folded envelope and tossed it out the door.

"How is your wife?" Yael asked.

"We're divorced," Lou answered. "She lost all faith after our daughter died and she moved north somewhere. She never writes or calls. I really don't know a thing about her."

"I'm sorry," said Yael.

"Happened thirty years ago. I've been alone all this time. I've got sprites in my fountain, though, and confabulations in my heart."

Yael was speechless. My grandfather started ripping through boxes. I tried to help, but he brushed me away. "Save your fingers for brains," he said.

We found the files after a while. There were ghosts in them for my grandfather, remnants of his glory days in Miami when he'd been hailed as a reformist thinker, a generation-bridger, an interfaith pioneer. Seeing the way Yael looked at him, I was sure she had ghosts of her own.

"Here," my grandfather said, tossing a stack of manila envelopes at me. "These are the records, though I doubt they're much good now. Dinosaurs went extinct in less time than has passed."

"They're not extinct if you're still around," Yael said, then touched his arm as if to say she meant it in a good way.

Lou gave her a look I'd never seen on his face before.

*   *   *

On the ride back to Fort Lauderdale, I opened the file. Tie Mei's passport photo tumbled out. My grandfather snatched it and held it on top of the steering wheel while he drove, moving it a few degrees to the left and then a few degrees to the right.

"I forgot she was such a beauty," he said.

"I remember," I said.

"Not Tie Mei. Yael."

In the envelope were documents in Chinese, some on crude paper with thick ink, some looking surprisingly modern—blue with red lettering. There were copies of the letters between my grandfather and the rabbi at the Jewish synagogue in Kaifeng. Tie Mei's profession was listed as schoolteacher. I hadn't known that, but it explained the easy way she conveyed such wide-ranging information to me over the years—everything from Chinese history and sword techniques to acupuncture treatments, the preparation of healing concoctions, and the anatomy of *dim mak* death strikes.

There were details of the other three people in the group, too, but frankly I skimmed over them. It was Solomon I was looking for, and I found him by his photo. Listed as an herbalist, he was a tall, slim, elegant man. I showed the picture to my grandfather.

"I remember him as being very polite," he said.

"Here it says his name was Yu Ying."

"Ying," my grandfather repeated. "I don't know."

"Dad says he called himself Solomon."

"Ah yes, Solomon. I remember him now."

"I bet there are other things my dad could help you remember. You haven't met my new stepmother. Maybe it's time to give him a call."

"I don't hear from him, he doesn't hear from me."

"I think Yael would like to hear from you."

"Younger women," he said wistfully.

"She's not that young."

"Not to you."

"If I brought Jordan and my father and Rachel to see your garden, would you receive them?"

"Maybe you should take the bus from here," he said, pulling to the curb. "You'll make it home within the week."

10

The Triumph Thruxton is named for a British racing circuit popular in the early 1960s. It's a retro bike with retro performance rather than the rocketlike speed and ultrastable handling of a modern performance motorcycle, and as such it gives a great deal of feedback through the handlebars. I felt the crosswind push the wheels on my way to Weston that night and imagined I could even feel the slight gravitational tug of the winter moon. I felt the sting of the scorpions in my belly more strongly. My violent alter ego was in control of the bike, and I smiled and hated myself for it.

Quiet Teacher, freshly oiled and sharpened, was lashed firmly across the seat behind me as I wove my way through the thin late-night traffic. I followed I-95 South to I-595 west and thence to I-75, Alligator Alley, toward Naples. I don't care much for riding the alley even in the daylight, as it is a long, straight, boring road that provides none of the thrills for which a motorcycle is made. At night and with temperatures in the forties, it was a chore. My neck froze and my fingers were stiff, and I thought about Lou's exhortations to save those precious hands of mine for brainwork.

I had plotted my route on the Internet at home, and after taking the second Weston exit I turned south into a division called Weston Hills Country Club. I stopped shy of the guard gate and used a tiny flashlight to read the Google printout lashed to my tank bag. Once I had my bearings, I avoided the gate by gunning the Triumph up and over the curb. I traversed the berm, crossed someone's backyard, passed the edge of a golf course and the side of a lake, and unceremoniously entered the paved world of ostentatious mansions that looked like upgraded versions of Scarface's Mediterranean-style spread.

Adult-film producer Jay Boniface's house was on a corner lot. I tucked up behind a broad-based bottle palm and surveyed the scene. Spotlights numerous enough to turn night into day lit the driveway and grounds. I was sure there were cameras, too. Even in black leather, they'd pick me up in no time.

I plucked a jasmine blossom from a bush and sniffed it, enjoying the hunt. Memories flooded in: Xenon with a sword on a continent far away, sneaking up on jungle prey, crossing desert dunes to assault an oasis, navigating the way downriver in a fertile valley, treading on river rocks so as to leave no footprints. Somehow I knew I had come up the backside of more than one mountain to surprise an enemy, and I had hidden for weeks in a damp cave just to conjure the element of surprise.

Electronic surveillance technology provides new challenges, but they are not insurmountable ones. I stayed low and kept my helmet on. I heard the flutter of wings as an ibis beat a fish, the rustle of cane toads, the hoot of an owl, and the stealthy stalking of night herons in the water. When I detected a hissing sound next to the lake, I crept forward to investigate, an idea forming in my head.

The Florida state record for an alligator is fourteen feet, and ten-footers are seen from time to time in the Everglades. The specimen at the edge of the lake was nowhere near that big, perhaps five feet, and it was sluggish in the cold weather. It seemed not to notice as I wriggled closer. Adrenaline coursed through me.

Like most people, I am simultaneously fascinated and repelled by reptiles. I've seen very few up close, as my father forbid scaled pets when I was a kid, and even Tie Mei seemed to regard them as nothing more than a source of some useful medicinal tonics and powders. I touched the tip of the gator's tail and found it hard and cold. It pulled away but did not dive into the water. I reached for it again and closed my hand this time, waiting for it to turn around and attack, my heart hammering, my entire nervous system in hair-trigger mode. I gave a tentative pull. The animal was strongly rooted—the consequence of a low center of gravity and the power of four feet and claws digging into the ground. I dug in my feet and tugged harder and slowly began to draw it backward. My breath was hot in my helmet. By the glint of the nearby floodlights, I saw blood on the gator's head, perhaps from a tousle with another gator, perhaps from a potshot. I continued pulling it slowly toward the edge of the circle of light. I got it there, and swiveled it around so it was facing the driveway. Then I stood up and stepped hard on its foot.

The effect was instantaneous. The alligator shot across the driveway and, as two motion-sensor floodlights on the garage went on, froze in the wash of a thousand moons. An alarm sounded and within two minutes a private security car came up the drive. I watched the driver get out and stare at the alligator then take out a walkie-talkie and start discussing the situation. With the distraction in place I crept around to the back of the house and went to work on the French doors by the pool. In the medically idle days of the past half-year, I had spent time applying my digital dexterity to various projects and gotten pretty good at vanquishing locks using surgical instruments. The lock gave fairly easily.

Even in the near darkness, the house was a wonderland of porn-film memorabilia, posters, outfits, a framed set of matching whips, bikinis, and lingerie. The living room was a sunken affair with an open fireplace in primitive chic. Near the spiral staircase was an enormous marble penis, fully erect and a good six feet tall.

With the house alarm still sounding and the alligator still in the spotlight, I headed upstairs to find Mr. Boniface.

*   *   *

I have discovered that home invasion is like neurosurgery: everything has to be done quickly and the stakes are too high for errors or sloppy work. Because it was late and the house was mostly dark, I moved immediately upstairs. I checked five doors before finding the master bedroom. The porn king had a reading light on and was sitting on the edge of the bed, clearly fearful of what the alarm might mean. There were fluffy pillows behind him and an open book by his side. He wore pajamas and yanked a big blue gun from his bedside table at the sight of me.

"This is a .44-magnum Smith&Wesson Mountain Gun," he said, coming up off the bed.

My mouth went dry.

"You remember what Dirty Harry said about the .44, don't you?" he quaked.

"I remember," I said, my voice muffled by the helmet.

"So you're gonna put the sword down," he gestured at the floor with the barrel.

That single moment when he pointed the revolver away from me was all I needed. I brought my sword hand to my chest in a scooping motion that knocked the gun out of his grasp. We ended up wrestling for it on the floor.

Before I knew it, I was in a joint lock. He bent my sword hand back so hard my wrist screamed for relief and I was forced to set Quiet Teacher free. The blade clattered to the floor. I had a moment of pure panic. What a fool I was to do this to my life again, to embrace my karma without considering the possibility that things might not go my way.

Boniface's breathing was quieter than mine, and he smelled of vetiver soap and sour, nervous sweat. He was surprisingly strong, and I took his moves for the sort of Brazilian jujitsu I'd watched in cage-fighting matches, though without the fit, manic ferocity of paid fighters. He'd probably learned them at one of the local strip-mall schools. I spiraled around the point of contact, easing the pain in my shoulder and the stress on my elbow. Boniface grunted as I reversed the lock.

He cast about for the gun, which lay above his head, close to the bed. I tightened up until I felt his shoulder tendons vibrate. Unable to reach his weapon, he went for my helmet. His fingers clawed at the darkly tinted plastic visor, trying to lift it.

"Lemme see your face, you bastard," he grunted.

I flipped over so I was on top of him and applied my knees to his neck. I saw a flicker of resignation in his eyes as the blood flow through his carotid artery failed, and within a few seconds he went limp. I rose to my feet, retrieved my sword, tucked the revolver in my pocket, and looked out the window at the driveway. The alligator was gone, and the security car with it. I returned to the bedroom and slapped Boniface on the cheek a couple of times. He stirred.

"Your road rage almost killed four people," I said.

He opened his eyes, massaged his neck, licked his lips, and leaned against the side of his king-size bed to sit up. I saw a flicker of recognition behind his eyes.

"You're here about that? It was nothing, man—a moment of irritation, and more your fault than mine. How'd you find me, anyway? I thought you were in the hospital with half your brains hanging out."

It took me a moment to realize he thought I was Charlie Czarnecki, the motorcyclist he had pursued. "Wrong," I said.

"That's what the cops told me."

I raised my sword over him. He looked up at me, but instead of terror I saw defiance.

"So that's it? This is how it ends? You're right; I shoulda kept my cool. I got carried away. But you're gonna waste me for it? I'm about peace and love, man. I spent my life making movies about getting together, not tearing each other apart. I take more heat for sex scenes than the networks get for airing shoot-'em-up shows to children, but I never did one rough shot, one piece of real bondage, never showed so much as a spanking on film. Now I get a little hot under the collar when some maniac scares the shit out of me on his bike, and what happens next? The very same maniac breaks into my house to hack off my head. You know what? Go ahead. If that's the way the world really is, you can have it and good riddance."

I looked at Boniface as if for the first time. I noticed the bald spot on his head and the sag under his chin where a second fold of skin was beginning to form. I saw the first faint age spots on the back of his hands, and I saw in his calves, exposed by our tousle, varicose veins. I looked at the gun in my hand, at Quiet Teacher's crisp edge, and at the copy of the Dalai Lama's *The Art of Happiness* sitting open on the bed next to Boniface's glasses.

"You were ready to shoot me," I said.

"No bullets," he said.

I flipped out the revolver's cylinder, saw it was empty, and tossed it on the bed.

"I try and get clean with the world and all it does is shit in my mouth," Boniface said. "Nobody understands me. Nobody knows the man I am deep down. First I lie awake all night worrying about the press from this thing, worrying about the law suits, sure that what tiny reputation I have will be destroyed, and now you come in with your sword. I just fucking give up. If you're going to cut me, get on with it. If not, just leave."

Surprised at his vituperation, I backed away. The wind that had taken days to fill my sails to billowing suddenly died. Becalmed, overcome by the sudden knowledge that Jordan was right in everything she said about violence and madness and me, I turned and ran down the stairs like a goat fleeing a wolf. Boniface came after me, the edges of his robe dancing.

"Get the fuck out!" he screamed after me. "Get out and stay out!"

Outside, the night seemed ten degrees colder, but inside my helmet, sweat poured down my cheeks. I dashed to my bike and rode quickly down the grassy slope. On the way home, nothing I had done seemed to have relevance or consequence.

Loathing myself more than anytime in the last six months, I rode away a deflated fool.

11

I brought chicken wings with spicy barbecue sauce to Jordan for lunch.

"Her bowels don't work normally," Amanda snapped.

Jordan paled.

"It's not anything to be ashamed about," Jordan's mother went on. "The intestine has a muscular wall. It requires stimulation. To digest properly, a person has to be able to walk."

"Amanda, I'm a physician. I know how the digestive tract functions."

"You brought spicy chicken wings, so apparently you don't."

"I'm listening to music a lot since what happened," Jordan said, holding up the pink iPod I gave her. "I download a song from the Internet every day. I'm making a real study of it, something I never did before. I'm trying to understand international influences and get a sense of history in pop tunes and classical music, too. There's this great African singer Ayub Ogada. What a hypnotic voice. And Lang Lang's return to China for native music is just unbelievable. What a pianist."

"She thinks listening to world music takes the place of being able to travel," said Amanda, attacking a chicken wing with a fork.

"Why do you people talk about me like I'm not here?" Jordan asked.

"Maybe she loves music because she has fewer distractions these days," I said.

"Distractions," Amanda muttered. "Right."

"Will you two stop it?" Jordan cried.

I wheeled her out onto the balcony. I rarely went out there with her—not because the view wasn't salubrious, it was, but because I couldn't see that sparkling ocean without thinking of the time—in a fit of vindictiveness—I had thrown a human arm off a similar balcony twenty miles to the south.

"I paid a visit to the guy who drove the Porsche," I said.

"The one who caused the crash?"

"That's right."

"What kind of visit?"

I didn't answer right away.

She turned to me, eyes flashing. The energy in her eyes gave me hope that someday she would regain the use of her legs. I could not imagine how a wheelchair could contain such a blaze forever.

"You went to cut him?"

I put up my hands. "I know violence isn't the answer," I said. "But four people . . ."

"You know violence isn't the answer but you go on cutting anyway?" She raised her hand to slap me, then stared at it and put it back down by her side.

"I didn't do it," I said.

"You mean it didn't go as planned."

I looked down at the beach. A couple walked arm in arm, toes in the lapping surf. A worker raked seaweed away from the front of a building. Far off, a single squall moved across the horizon like a traveler. "I didn't go through with it," I said. "I realized what I was doing and I stopped."

Jordan moved her light brown hair away from her face. When I met her, she had kept it cut short, reinforcing the competition swimmer's look given by her broad shoulders and narrow hips. Now it fell straight, nearly reaching her shoulders. I preferred it short, the better to see her deep gray eyes, but for some reason I had not told her. I found it strange that her hair could grow so fast while the rest of her remained withered.

She nodded. "That's something, Xenon. It really is. You weren't hurt, were you?"

"I'm fine."

We had a silent time. I could see she was thinking hard. "You need to build on this," she said at last. "You need to find a way to keep not doing it."

"I've thought about that," I said.

"Not boozing the way you were starting to before I got hurt."

"Definitely not boozing," I said.

"Therapy, maybe?"

"Maybe, but I've got another idea."

"What is it?"

"The martial path leads to peace. The martial master seeks no violence because he has nothing to prove. He seeks peace because he knows what violence feels like and knows it's the lowest form of human interaction. It holds no magic for him."

"Your nanny, Tie Mei, was like that, yes?"

"She certainly was."

"You're saying you want to learn to cut better so you won't cut at all?"

"You don't understand how this works," I said. "I have to go deeper in order to find a way out. It's not something I can force to happen from the outside. It's the natural evolution of what I do. Right now I'm stuck in the middle of a process."

"This sounds like nonsense, Zee. It sounds like rationalizing. It sounds a bit weak, frankly."

"I think it's my only way."

We sat with that for a moment. "Who *was* your would-be victim anyway?"

"His name's Jay Boniface."

She actually laughed. "The porno king?"

"Should I ask how you know that?"

"Who doesn't? He's always in the news. He's a big philanthropist. Donates money to culture and the arts, sees his work as legitimate filmmaking, gives to starving children. . . . "

"You should see his house," I said. "The artwork alone. . . ."

"So you broke in."

"All right, I broke in. But I told you I stopped before I hurt him."

"Why, exactly?"

"Why did I stop? Because I saw him differently than I thought I would. He had a moment of road rage. It can happen to anyone. It's happened to me. He didn't mean anything by it."

She wheeled herself to the edge of the balcony and pointed at the squall with her finger, tracing its path like a child drawing on a board.

"I guess I wanted to hear that you stopped because you promised me you would."

"That too. It all goes together. The way you've got me thinking changed the way I responded to him."

I bent down to kiss her, but she turned away. I pursued, but she evaded. I brushed her neck with my lips. "How do you feel today?"

"Like I want to stand against the rail."

Her mother went absolutely crazy when Jordan went anywhere near the rail. I glanced over my shoulder. Amanda was watching television in the kitchen. She had her back to us.

I lifted Jordan out of the chair and brought her to the edge, my hands around her waist. She put her hands up to steady herself. "Let me go," she said.

"Jordan . . . "

"I sat on a motorcycle, I can stand on a balcony."

"Sitting isn't standing. You want to practice standing by yourself, let's go inside."

"Let me go."

"No."

She twisted to face me wearing the expression of someone whose tooth has just hit a hard pit. "You have to," she said. " I need you out of my life."

"Please don't say that," I said. "Please."

"Violence has a vibration, Zee. It's with you all the time. It poisons you."

"No poison," I said, knowing I was soaked with it. "I told you I was dealing with it. I told you I have a plan."

"You should work that plan, Zee. You really should. And I need to work my own plan. I need to work on me. I need to turn a new leaf, too."

"Let's turn leaves together," I said.

"Look at me," she said, but keeping her head turned away. "Look at what your sick heroics have done to me. Haven't you learned anything?"

"I have," I said. "I've learned so much. That's why I told you how it unfolded. I wanted you to see that."

"Half a year goes by and you go out with your sword again. I knew it would happen. I've been waiting for the day, fearing it every time I turn on the news, fearing it every time the phone rings. It's in you. I've just been kidding myself—about you and a lot of things."

"You're having another bad day is all."

"And you're having a bad *life*—crazy and destructive and ruinous. Look what it's doing to me! Look what it's *done* to me!"

"We'll get through this," I said. "Everything is changing."

She put her hands on my shoulders and pushed me away with surprising force, teetering by the edge as a result. I grabbed her and put her back in the chair.

"Nothing is changing," she said ferociously. "Not in my legs and not in your head. I mean it, Zee. I can't take it anymore."

"Just relax," I said. "I've got the healing path all mapped out."

"Your path is a self-deluding ruse, Zee. It's pathetic. We've discussed this over and over. You told me no more, and then you went out with your sword. You did it and you will do it again."

"This is because I'm the one who put you in the wheelchair," I said slowly.

"That would be a good reason, but that's not it. You're spinning it now, Zee. I've made it clear as I can. You said it yourself. You're stuck in a romance with lives you think you've lived before, with a woman long dead, with a sick urge you can't beat. I want someone in a romance with *me*."

"I *am* with you," I protested. "You're all I think about."

She made a fist and waved it. "You think about diagnoses and cures. I want to forget about this chair every time I see my man, not reminded that I'm in it by medical details and prognostications and expectations that wake me up at night."

"So it *is* about me putting you in the chair."

"You didn't put me in the chair. Horrible people did that to me. I know that. I just can't be saddled with a man who can't break free of himself, and, frankly, you don't need to be saddled with a woman who can't walk."

"I'm not saddled."

"I'm telling you how I feel. I'm not the girl you knew for a couple of weeks before this happened. You don't really know me, and despite your guilty conscience you really don't owe me anything. I can't be worrying about you all the time. I have to focus on *me*. I have to get back to being a person not a patient."

Amanda opened the sliding door behind me. "What's wrong?" she demanded. "She's sick just from *looking* at those wings, right? I knew it."

"Please go," said Jordan. "I mean it."

She turned away then. I made a move to kiss her, but she raised her hand in dismissal.

"Xenon's leaving, Mom,"

"She's just having a bad day," I said.

"Just do what I ask and leave me alone, Zee."

"Maybe you better go," Amanda said quietly.

*　　*　　*

On the ride home, wishing for a quick way out of this life and into the next, I considered steering my bike straight into a wall. When I got home I ate an entire bar of Venezuelan chocolate spiked with red pepper. The chocolate filled the pit in my stomach, if only temporarily, and I washed it down with white tea—yin and yang, the dark and the light, the solid and the liquid, the bitter and the sweet. In a numb blur, I checked my mailbox and found an envelope from Neptune, the inmate I had met at the prison. I wondered how he got my address. Inside was a letter written in a clear hand, in pencil, on a yellow legal pad:

> *Dear Dr. Pearl,*
>
> *I feel a connection to you. I have martial training too. Spending time in prison, a man grows sensitive to what he sees in others, yes? Men forge alliances with and against each other here, and recognizing what is true and false keeps an inmate alive. We are not so different, yes? I have a feeling you'll be joining me in here a lot sooner than you think, and then we'll get a chance to discuss true nature, yours and mine.*
>
> *Sincerely,*
> *Neptune Cohen*

I stared at the note a long time before picking up my machete and heading for the door, intent on cutting anything and everything I could find—grass, trees, bushes, anything. When I opened the garage door I found John Khalsa in the driveway. He wore a seersucker suit, mirrored sunglasses, Bally weaves, and an open collar.

"Gee, John. You look like a Mafia hit man," I said.

"Says the man with a machete in his hand."

I ushered him inside. He looked around. "I've heard this was a terrific house," he said. "The open beams are a nice touch. Are all the pieces from the Orient?"

"Yes."

"What's wrong? You look like a fish pulled out on the dock."

"Tough morning is all."

He took his glasses off. His eyes were shiny. I marveled at his shave. He hadn't missed a single whisker and his skin was as smooth as molded plastic. Sometimes I wondered if he might not be a department-store manikin, supernaturally operated. Since the events of the previous year, I believed in any and all manner of miracles.

"I came to talk about reinstating you," he said. "If we're going to do that—if we're going to forge a pact I won't regret—we're going to have to be more candid with each other. Can you agree to that?"

"All right."

"So tell me what's wrong. A few nights ago you were glowing with purpose. Now you look like hell. I understand the brilliant surgeon can have his moods and I'm not trying to start an argument—I just want to know if there's anything I can do."

"Jordan doesn't want to see me anymore," I said. "She told me an hour ago."

Khalsa sat down on my couch. "Probably just a lover's tiff," he said. "She needs you desperately."

"She doesn't think so. She thinks I keep her from flowering as a person."

Khalsa picked a piece of imaginary lint off the crease line of his trousers. "She told me she knew you for a only few weeks before the attack."

"She called it an attack? When I'm around, she and her mother refer to it only as 'what happened.'"

"Do you think she's right in what she says?"

"Of course not. I love her. I want to be with her."

"Even if she spends the rest of her life in that chair?"

"She won't be paraplegic forever, and even if she is she's the most fantastic woman I know."

71

"Maybe you need to get out more," said Khalsa. Then he put up his hand. "Of course, I'm not saying she isn't all that. You could be friends. You don't have to let go of her completely. Maybe holding her so close is just a constant reminder to her of a future that can't be. Maybe it's painful for her. Have you thought about that?"

"I don't think our newfound candor extends this far, John."

He shrugged. "Just trying to help. The hospital board has rescinded your dismissal. They've acknowledged you're an important asset to the hospital district. Keeping busy will help with all this, I'm sure."

"Keeping busy will keep me busy, that much is true."

He stood and put his hands on my shoulders. I could not remember him ever doing that before.

"You'll find someone else," he said.

"Every fiber of my being tells me to stay with her."

"Telling sounds different than wanting. And fibers stretch, change, and wear out. You know that from the OR."

I liked Khalsa better as an abrasive adversary than as this self-styled therapist and big brother. "I'll think about your point," I said.

He smiled. "Good. Now here's a new beeper. Congratulations. You're my man again starting now. My office will get in touch regarding the schedule. Your daily on-call retainer is back, too, which, looking at this beautiful home, I'm sure you can use. I'm sorry about Jordan, I really am. If you need to talk, you know where to find me."

I sat down to the sound of the front door closing gently and cradled myself. Trying to ease the pain in my heart and the harsh effort of each breath, I rocked back and forth, my arms folded to hold myself.

Jordan.

12

The ambulance driver's business card showed wallet wear, but it was heavy with promise in my hand. The driver's name was Kurt Vanderkamp, and he called his Fort Lauderdale school Winter Moon Studio. I found the place next to a T-shirt factory in a warehouse district west of I-95, just north of the center of town, a cardboard sign in a blacked-out window the only identifier. I put the kickstand down on the Thruxton, took off my helmet, felt a couple of drops of rain on my face, and considered what I was doing.

My childhood lessons with Tie Mei had always been conducted in secret for fear my father would find out and stop us or even fire her. With consequences so dire, I never even attended a tournament and rarely used what I knew on the schoolyard. I had never set foot inside an aikido training hall, but I knew that a famous fighter named Morihei Ueshiba created it from Japanese fighting arts. Sources I'd read said Ueshiba was a great fighter but also a pacifist and built a great deal of compassion into the system's no-nonsense moves. I'd never thought of trying the art before, but Jordan's judgment was pushing me to a place I had been avoiding. Even more, my tousle with Jay Boniface told me that despite my one-time battle with the Russians, I lacked much gritty, real-world experience. There was nothing gritty about a dojo—particularly this one, with its white walls and *shoji* screens and its large clean canvas mat and air redolent of jasmine—but it was a start. I lacked experience in the vicious finality of real life combat. I didn't expect to find it in a dojo.

A silkscreen likeness of the Buddha hung on the back wall alongside a photo of an elderly, white-bearded Ueshiba sitting with his legs crossed and one finger in the air. From across the room I could see the size of the old man's hands. Near the molding were small framed Japanese *kanji* characters. I have some knowledge of

Chinese characters from years of calligraphy study under Tie Mei, but even so I was not sure I could read them. There was a small locker room in one corner and a cubicle in the other, where I saw Vanderkamp doing paperwork at a makeshift desk.

"Can I help you?"

I recognized the thickly built man who stood in my way as the young paramedic in the rescue truck that night on the highway.

"You shaved," I said. "But I'd know you anywhere, even in a skirt."

"This is a martial art school," he said, touching his chin and trying to look flinty-eyed. "It's not the best place to run a smart mouth. This is not a skirt. It's called a *hakama*. It's a traditional garment."

"I'm Dr. Pearl," I said. "We met the other night on the road. I rode back to the hospital with the little girl and her mother."

Recollection took him. "The neurosurgeon," he said. "I thought you looked familiar. What brings you here?"

"Your teacher invited me."

Vanderkamp came out of the office and floated across the floor in seconds. Up close, his face was more pockmarked than I had seen it to be in the ambulance, and he was taller than he had seemed at the wheel.

"Dr. Pearl," he said, offering a ceremonial bow. His voice was very soft and his arms, visible under the hard cloth top, were knotted with veins.

"Thought I'd check out what you do."

"I'm very glad you came."

A few more guys walked in. One wore construction clothing, the other two were in fine suits and nice ties. Nods and a few words were exchanged, and everyone went to change clothes.

"Looks like you have a good crew," I said.

"Dues are $250 a month," answered the blonde paramedic.

Vanderkamp put his hand on the young guy's shoulder. "Preston helps me keep the doors open," he said. "He's been with me since I opened the place eight years ago. He started as a teenager."

"I became a paramedic because of him," Preston said.

"We got off on the wrong foot the other night," I told the kid. "I don't like being told what to do either."

"I know how to assess an accident victim," he said.

"No doubt you do. It's just I was already on the scene."

"So you studied the arts when you were a kid and now you're thinking about getting back into it, is that the idea?" Vanderkamp interrupted.

"That's right."

"Meeting in the ambulance was a happy coincidence then."

"Coincidences," I smiled. "I can't say I believe in them."

"Take a seat on the bench over there and watch. See what you think. We'll talk after the class."

I sat down quietly and closed my eyes to compose myself. Men came in, talking softly. A recollection of Tie Mei floated into my head. She was on the beach outside a South Miami Beach hotel, under a pink parasol. She wore a white blouse of lace flapping open over a one-piece swimsuit and loose pants covered her legs. Beach visits were rare because Chinese women eschew the sun and my father had always feared the water, but nonetheless we were there to celebrate my nanny's birthday. They had stayed in one room together, and, all of nine years old, I had stayed alone. I hadn't remembered that detail until just now, not in all the conversations I'd had with my father about his relationship with her and why they hadn't married.

"You're a Gemini," my father had said, toasting her with a bottle of champagne in the sand. "That means there are two of you. I know one. Perhaps Xenon knows the other."

The allusion to my secret training was right there, but even under the influence of alcohol no further truth was revealed. They talked. My father mentioned how happy he was that he had just paid off a long-standing debt. Her face said she suddenly realized the weekend away was as much about him as it was about her, but despite the sweltering heat she kept her cool.

My father went to the room to fetch some ice water. While he was gone two young bodybuilding Latin boys came up and addressed Tie Mei in Spanish. Imperious, she shooed them away with her umbrella. They would not go. They wanted to see her in her suit. They wanted her to swim with them. Finally, in broken English, they professed to be entranced by the opalescence of her skin.

When she demurred again, I threw sand at them. They ducked away and feigned great injury. I snapped at them with my beach towel, which made them howl with laughter. One picked me up like a grouchy doll while the other one went right for Tie Mei, declaring that he was going to introduce her to the pleasures of the tropical Atlantic.

His fingers never reached her. Darting out she intercepted them and there was a cry of pain as my captor cartwheeled a good ten feet. I heard the bones snap as he went down, crying, into the sand. A few people around us noticed and broke out in applause as she rescued me smoothly and easily.

"They care enough for entertainment," Tie Mei muttered in disgust, "but not enough to help."

"You didn't need help."

"They didn't know that."

Even after a break and a throw she was completely unruffled. I realized with a small shock that never, not even once, had I seen her sweat.

"I have a feeling I'm going to mix it up with these aikido guys," I said silently. "Please come back and share some of your cool."

She didn't answer, and another memory floated in. This time it was Jordan on the beach, and we were under the beam of the lighthouse near my home. The only company we had was the lapping of the surf on the jetty and the distant barking of a dog. It was our first night together, and we lay gazing into each other's eyes, our fingers interlaced. I drew a deep breath and tried to remember the smell of the sea and the scent of her perfume, half washed off, but all I got was a faint whiff of jasmine. I felt an overwhelming sadness and then all visions were gone.

I opened my eyes. There was a woman in the dojo. She was petite and blonde and must have arrived dressed for battle because there had been no time for her to change from street clothes. She had green eyes creased at the edges, wide feet, high cheekbones, and a dimple in her chin. Her *hakama* hung straight and ample and her thick jacket disguised her shape.

"Bow to the founder," Vanderkamp said.

All eight students bowed to the picture of Ueshiba. After that they jumped out onto the mat and began stretching into splits, bending and rotating their shoulders, kneading their feet and wrists, rolling their necks, and practicing falls. When they were finished, Vanderkamp pointed the woman in my direction.

"I'm Melissa," she said. "Sensei asked me to give you a primer. We've just finished warm-ups. Next we'll do the first set of partner drills, which are all about following the opponent's energy without the slightest kink or break."

"I never figured a martial arts school would smell like this."

Melissa smiled. "I keep a bowl with jasmine flowers behind that *shoji*. A fan blows over it. By the end of the evening the water has evaporated, but even then you'll smell more sweat than blood; aikido's founder, O Sensei, was big on compassion.

The men paired up and practiced lapel grabs and joint locks. I liked their fluid movements but noticed the circles they made were primarily around the axis of their waists—flat circles, like sending salt to someone across the table on a lazy Susan. Tie Mei had always stressed verticality in martial arts circling and three-dimensionality more than that.

"Horizontal circles throw people away," she said. "When they're away, they get up and come back for more. Vertical circles send them to the ground. When they're on the ground, especially after they fall hard, hit them with your elbows and knees. Remember to spiral not circle. Climb your opponent like a snake climbs a tree and bring him to your center like a tornado."

I did not see a lot of climbing, but I did see a lot of flying through the air. Melissa soon joined Preston in practice and the two of them moved joyously, harmoniously. The grabs and throws were like dancing; the force was augmented by momentum and the pain looked to be diffused by soft, practiced rolls. Melissa caught my eye once or twice during the routines, and I nodded in appreciation.

After grappling came defenses against kicks and punches. I knew the first instant of contact was all important, but I saw none of the complex touch I'd learned from my teacher through the endless drills in the park—exercises that became more and more challenging until, when I reached my teens, the attacks were filled with actual menace. In contrast, the *aikidoka* attempted to anticipate the direction of the attack and then begin moving with it so that initial contact was light. Punches that contained an upward component, even if it was a slight one, were directed upward. Punches with left or right English were encouraged to follow their deviation. Punches that tended slightly downward were followed to the ground in a way that had the attacker ultimately pulled there.

After an hour, Preston finally invited me onto the mat. I wore a golf shirt and my usual cotton climbing pants, which are light and comfortable with a gusseted crotch that won't let them split.

"Your shoes," he said, pointing.

Tie Mei always had me train in shoes because she claimed we didn't walk around barefoot and one should train the same way one lives. The pair she favored were thin-soled Chinese slippers, which offered little support and gave great challenge to the tendons of the foot, the plantar fascia, and the toes. I shucked them off.

"Shoot me a punch," Preston said, pointing at his nose.

Vanderkamp and Melissa were watching. I threw a strike off the rear hand but kept the speed down. He saw it coming, reached for it, and threw me.

There was a moment of exhilaration as I went past him. Truly, I felt like I was flying. I landed roughly because I had never practiced falling much, but the mat protected me.

"That was fun," I said.

"You held back," said Preston. "Don't do that."

Vanderkamp cautioned Preston to keep it light. I tossed him a faster punch. Preston waited this time, and when it got to him he threw me again. I landed harder, taking the brunt of it on my shoulder. It didn't feel too good.

"Again," said Preston.

By this time, the other students had gathered around to watch.

"Your turn to punch," I said.

"You haven't learned the technique yet."

"When you punch, I'll practice."

Preston grinned as if to show he was going to enjoy hitting me. The punch flew and I stood watching it. I saw it coming as if in slow motion even though it came in at full speed, far harder and faster than I had hit him. There was meat behind it and practiced precision. At the first touch, I became the snake. I moved the point of contact from one spot to the next, locking Preston's arm first at the elbow, then at the shoulder. He went up on his toes and then crashed downward in a heap at my feet. Holding him in that position I made three quick strikes: a knee to his throat, a fist to his temple, and a knife hand to the back of his neck. I pulled all three strikes so they just tapped him lightly, but they made my point potently.

Preston got up red-faced.

"Did I do it right?" I said.

"Fuck you," he answered, but only with his lips so Vanderkamp wouldn't hear. There was a general titter among the other men. Melissa came forward.

"Might I have a turn?" she asked.

"Sure."

"What is it you study?"

"I learned some Chinese *gongfu* when I was a kid."

Melissa was much more challenging than Preston. Her movements were softer and there was the hint of a spiral to her punches and locks. I found the exchange intimate and a bit disconcerting. I had only moved martially with a woman twice previously, once training with Tie Mei and another time in a life-or-death struggle with a Russian mobster. I tried treating Melissa gently, but executing the techniques I knew properly required a very particular body alignment and when the alignment was there and the spiraling emerged, the result depended far less on the power I put in to the defense than the energy she put into her attack. When she punched, she landed close to me, twisted and vulnerable. She got up and bowed to me; I returned the favor.

"You move well," Vanderkamp acknowledged. "Weapons part of your show?"

"Once in a while," I said.

Preston came out from behind one of the *shoji* screens with a pair of wooden swords. He handed one to Vanderkamp and another one to me.

"*Bokken*." Vanderkamp said. "Japanese practice swords."

The *bokken* felt more like a staff than a sword. "Pretty dense wood," I said. "Do you use protective gear?"

"Oooh. The pretty neurosurgeon worried about his hands?" said Preston.

Melissa turned to him. "Don't be a jerk. If he's a neurosurgeon, he *should* be worried about his hands."

Preston colored. Vanderkamp assumed an attack position, sword overhead in classic Japanese fashion. He moved in slowly and I stepped diagonally, slicing his jacket softly as I went past. We did a few more movements slowly and then picked up the pace.

I saw more holes in Vanderkamp's swordplay than I saw broken windows after last year's hurricane. At one point I parried his blow, ducked down, and let him run right into my sword. I figured this would discourage him, but he was a Marine after all so he just came in faster and harder. I slapped him on the side of the thigh, gave another stab to his abdomen, pulled back at the last minute, and tripped him up with a feint and a lock. He looked up at me from the ground and grinned.

"Let's go back to open hands."

We put the *bokken* away. I stepped in with a punch and he worked a lock. I spiraled out of it and we stalemated, kneeling.

"Preston's got some work to do," I said softly in his ear. "But Melissa is terrific."

He grinned. "Why do you think I married her?"

I was surprised at the revelation and he took advantage of me by leaping up and going at me again. I parried, neutralizing his second hand by twisting it out of the way so he could not reach me. He dropped down, swept my leg, and ended up on top of me with my wrist in two of his hands, working it so hard I had to tap out.

We kept it up for a while. He understood spiraling very well and got the better of me more often than I got the better of him, but our strong suits were different and it was close. Afterward, with Preston glowering and Melissa clapping and the rest of the guys watching me with genuine curiosity, we retired to his little office.

"You know things about the sword I don't fully understand," he said. "Your sensitivity is terrific, your body is solid, your movements are integrated, and yet for all that you're a rube."

I nodded, rubbing my sore wrist. "I don't get out much."

"I mean there were opportunities. If I hadn't been playing by the rules. . . ."

"I know."

"You could come here, but I don't think we have what you're after. "

"Where can I get it?"

He rubbed his jaw. "We martial artists are clubbish and lawsuits have killed school feuds. Truth is, I don't know who's around these days. I guess I'd advise you to keep doing what you're doing but just step it up a bit."

I nodded. I didn't feel like telling him my teacher had been my nanny and that she was long gone. "I owe you one," I said, giving him my card. "Call me sometime and let's get a beer."

On the way out, Preston wouldn't look at me but Melissa gave me a smile big enough for the two of them.

13

I should have gone to the hospital the next morning to check on my patients, but I retreated to my hot tub instead. Nursing my sore wrist and my banged shoulders and knees, I stared at the sky and tried to get one decent breath through without it catching against my ribs. It took me a few minutes to realize that the pain I was feeling was not from the hard hands of Kurt Vanderkamp but from the separation from Jordan. My Jordan. The Jordan I had avenged, the Jordan I had pieced back together. The Jordan whose life my love had destroyed.

The breakup hit me like a sledgehammer. I should have expected it. All these years my emotions have sported a built-in delay switch. Tie Mei used to tell me it was a good thing for a martial artist—a natural advantage. It stopped me from reacting in anger, she explained, and stopped me from making premature decisions based on fear. While she thought time would diminish my feelings, I knew better. My delay circuits only gave my feelings time to marinate and simmer. Guilt and loss doubled me over.

I have felt the pain of drowning firsthand and it was Jordan who pulled me from a briny grave. Now she was the one holding my head underwater. All I could see, over and over, was the anger in her eyes and the way she raised her finger and pointed at the door. It wasn't the ending I was looking for—not the storybook recovery and not the happily ever after. Jordan was right about violence and she was right that I was stuck and her being right made everything hurt even more. My thoughts and feelings about her were a clouded mélange of guilt and yearning, attachment to a fantasy romance that never had a chance to bloom normally. Certainly my parents had not offered a model. My mother died before I was old enough to get a sense of my parents' marriage, and my father's relationship with Tie Mei had always been shrouded by guilt. There were no clues there for me regarding the truth about love.

None was to be found in my personal history either, replete as it was with affairs and attachments. My modern life as a first-generation American son of a Russian Jew was clouded by fears of another Holocaust, and my memories of past lives in China did not include romantic wisdom or specifics. No matter what I conjured during meditation, I could find little guidance in matters of love. Did I love my father? Yes. Did I love the memory of my mother? Yes. Did I love my grandfather? Did I love the ghost of Tie Mei, with her rustling silk and her almond smell? Yes and yes. But Jordan? As a scientist, I understood the complex of variables that had to coalesce in order to bring forth real passion—the neurotransmitters, the tentacles of history, the guidelines of culture and experience and reason. I thought those might be there, though she was right to say we'd had little time—a matter of only weeks—before tragedy struck. Certainly we had shared lust and the first exciting titillation of romance, but those paled before the guilt and obligation I felt toward this complex and damaged woman.

I put my head under the surface and pressed my forehead to the jet. I let the pressure massage my temples so hard it rattled my brain. Under there, in the warm water, I imagined I was floating in my mother's womb again, that I had wound back the clock and was about to emerge and start the whole thing again. Why did we have so many lives, anyway? Why couldn't we just be done with it and ascend to the realms of pure joy the masters talked about, unfettered and unconcerned, our suffering finally at an end? I wondered what Jordan might have done to be forced to the place she was right now, wheelchair bound, needing help just to get to the toilet. I ached to hold her, to stroke her hair, to hear her moan and giggle when I rubbed her feet. I shot out of the tub in an agony of wanting and landed roughly on the stone around the pool. Impulses raced through me, mostly about cutting and more cutting, but this time I knew they would not ease my pain. Wrapped in a towel, I set to straightening the house. I emptied the dishwasher, took my laundry to the washer, watered the indoor plants, made my futon bed up tightly, and brought in the mail.

A second letter from Neptune Cohen was at the bottom of the stack.

> Dear Dr. Pearl,
>
> I get dark violent images of you in my meditation. You keep circling back to violence and then hating yourself for it. You think that violence is the last resort of the weak, but you're wrong; it is merely the inevitable consequence of who we are and how we work and the way nature guides us. You're right about one thing, yes? You weaken yourself with doubt, and doubting you lose your way. Your meditation should help you discover this truth, but not as long as you hide from yourself.
>
> Humbly,
> Neptune Cohen

I sat with the letter for a while. This guy was onto me. I was a ticking bomb spiraling into something too painful to consider. After a time my belly rumbled. I thawed some vegetarian pot stickers in the microwave, then put them in the oven to bake them brown. When they were ready, I doused them in soy sauce, shredded some fresh ginger over them, and sprinkled a bit of rice vinegar as a flourish. I sat down and ate, then picked up the phone and called Jordan.

"She doesn't want to speak to you," Amanda informed me. "You know this isn't right."

"I know no such thing. I know she was well and whole and happy, then you came along and she lost everything."

"She'll walk again, Amanda. This is just temporary."

"That's the problem with you. You're irresponsible and childish.

You toy with her and give her hope where there is none just to keep an impossible dream alive. If she didn't boot you out, I'd have had to do it myself. Now don't call here again. Think of her for once instead of yourself."

The rejection and pronouncements only steeled my resolve—another defect in my character or at least Tie Mei always thought it was. Unlike the emotional delay, which she saw as a martial asset, she saw my stubbornness as a liability. A great fighter never gets stuck, she said. Great swordsmen have had minds that cannot be trapped. Like a butterfly, the master's thinking moves up and down and sideways and slantways. Unpredictable, alighting nowhere for more than an instant, it can never be anticipated or outguessed.

Amanda was an obstacle. Jordan's current view was an obstacle. Obstacles could be removed. I had removed them before. Gritting my teeth, I went back to the computer and pulled up my Internet browser. I did a search for Yu and watched the results scroll in. There were hundreds. I tried another search, this time for "Yu Solomon." Again the list was long, but there were several entries I dismissed right away: a Texas cockroach exterminator, a California accounting firm specializing in bankruptcies, a Chinese listing that I could read only slightly but which seemed to refer to a purveyor of fine silk.

On the third page, I found a listing for a Dr. S. Yu, a professor of pharmacology at the University of Miami. I picked up the phone.

"Dr. Yu is in class," his assistant told me.

"I'd like to leave a message for him."

"All right."

"Before I do, could you tell me his age?"

"I beg your pardon?"

"I knew him a long time ago."

"Where?"

"I beg your pardon?"

"Where did you know him?"

"In Miami," I said.

"Dr. Yu has been in the country only two years. He came here from Shanghai. Could you perhaps have the wrong man?"

"I'm sorry to trouble you," I said and hung up.

I continued down the search results and found another Florida entry. This one was for an acupuncturist on Commercial Boulevard in Fort Lauderdale. The name was Ye. Not exactly the same, but close. Mr. Ye answered the phone.

"Beachside Acupuncture," he said.

His voice was heavily accented. I tried as hard as I could to dig it out of my memory, but like the voice of Helen, my mother, there was no trace of it in my head.

"I'm looking for Mr. Yu," I said.

There was a long pause. "This Mr. Ye."

He said it with a short e, and I was unsure of how he might spell it. I tapped my fingernail on the surface of my desk. "I'm sure I don't have the name wrong. Might I ask if you've changed it?"

"Change name?"

There was something in the way he said it that sounded like it was leading to an explosion, something like outrage and vituperation at the merest suggestion that someone from a culture that holds names and heritage so dear would ever, ever change his name.

"Chinese people sometimes take American names," I said. "Do you use the name Solomon?"

"Name is name," he said. "Not new. Not American. Taiwanese. From Republic of China. Who is calling?"

"Sorry," I said. "Wrong number."

I put the phone down and stared at the screen again. I went back to the search window and typed "Solomon Yu Florida."

The sole listing appeared instantly: "Solomon Yu. Exotic animal imports."

I tried to get my mind around the idea that a man trained as a pharmacist or a doctor could have come from China thirty years ago and wound up importing exotic creatures to what was the zoological melting pot of the United States. I did a separate search for his business, Slither & Crawl, and found a simple website featuring data on an outfit in Davie, southwest of Fort Lauderdale. The photos showed myriad reptiles and miles of aisles of metal tubs and plastic containers in a warehouse teeming with people. There was no photo of Solomon Yu.

I picked up the phone then put it down again. I hadn't had much luck with the telephone lately.

It was Triumph time.

14

I strive to achieve the blissful place I know I have touched in previous lives, if only for a few minutes at a time. In that glorious zone I don't chastise myself for my itchy sword fingers and don't hate my dark side so much. I don't worry that I should be meditating on a mountaintop instead of getting blood on latex-clad fingers. I don't worry about love and I don't examine every move I make and find myself coming up short. The taste of enlightenment is faint, tantalizing and hopelessly distant, and yet I know that the key to grasping it is to be found in the relinquishment of judgment.

Despite my lofty ambitions, Slither & Crawl left me cold. How could a man with sufficient taste to admire Wu Tie Mei create such a place? Everything about my late teacher was so clean and clear and high and fine, so elevated and principled—both to my child's eye and to the neurosurgeon confronted by her shade—that I found any link to this bizarre world farfetched. The place was a vast artificial jungle of camouflaged creatures waiting to explode out of sand or bark chips if a visitor got too close.

A young woman approached me, one of a number of athletic-looking employees. Her lower lip was pierced and there was a spider tattoo on her neck. Her tattered blue jeans hung off her, and she wore Birkenstock sandals and a tight tube top. Studs in her ears offered purchase to a large chameleon clinging to her shoulder, stabilizing itself by grabbing on with claws that looked like tiny gloved hands. Her nametag said Darlene. I asked her how long she'd been at the shop.

"I've worked here since '99," she said. "I was still in school then."

"Did you always like snakes?"

"They're not my favorite now, but they grow on you. I prefer lizards. This is a panther chameleon. His name's Ezra. Hey, what kind of bike do you ride?"

"Triumph."

"British, yes? I like Hondas better."

"There's a little more soul in the bikes from Europe," I said.

"Animals have souls. Bikes don't. So what can I do for you? You're a tree python guy, right?"

"I'm just here to see Solomon."

"He's working with the hot snakes. We're not allowed to bother him. If he gets distracted he might get bitten."

"Did he play with reptiles back in China?"

"Oh yes. Solomon lives, eats and dreams herps—that's what reptile people call them. He says it's a lifelong love affair."

"Good guy to work for?"

Darlene frowned. "He's a sweetheart, of course. Why do you want to know?"

"Just making conversation."

She opened a tub and a giant lizard lunged at her. She tapped it on the snout to distract it and pulled out its dirty water bowl. "This is a water monitor," she said. "My girlfriend and I went to Thailand last year. We took a river cruise in Bangkok and one of these came right up to the boat. Must have been seven feet. Had a bad eye, which I figure was from a fight with a croc. Not much else could hurt one of these when they get big."

"People want something like this as a pet?"

She filled the dish with a hose and carefully put it back in the tub. "It's best to raise these by hand from babies. This one was caught in the wild, so he sees everything as either food or threat."

"Solomon married?"

"Are you sure you're not a cop or something?"

"What would a cop want with Solomon?"

"There's Solomon. Why don't you ask *him*?"

*   *   *

Standing at his office door, I heard Solomon Yu's voice before I saw his face, and the high tones of it brought back a memory from my fifth year of life. Just as Tie Mei bent over the teakettle, our doorbell rang. She turned and the steam caught her ear. As her hand flew to the scalded flesh, a strand of her thick black hair fell to the stove and caught on fire. Tamping out the smoke, she glided to see who was calling, the acrid smell of burning hair following her. It was Solomon. She would not let him in but he peered around her shoulder, his eyes devouring the details of our Miami home, the heavy European furniture my father favored—before Tie Mei redecorated our house in Asian style—the vaulted ceiling, the Tiffany lamps, and the generous kitchen.

Now, more than a quarter century later, Solomon looked at me with the same curiosity and spoke to me in the same voice, though now his English was flawless.

"Can I help you?"

"I believe so."

"Wholesale or retail?"

"I'm Xenon Pearl. Wu Tie Mei was my nanny."

He recoiled like one of his reptilian charges.

"You came over on the boat with her. It was my grandfather who brought you here. Tie Mei worked for my family. You came to our home in Miami."

We looked each other over carefully. He was a handsome, vital man—tall and lean and long-limbed for a Chinese. His skin was clean and clear, his eyes bright, his posture straight and true. His nose was aquiline rather than rounded. With the right clothes and the right haircut he might have passed for Native American, though perhaps he was too narrow of bone.

"That was a long time ago," he said.

"But you remember her."

"Certainly. And I remember you—as a little boy, of course."

"May we speak somewhere more private?"

He led me to the front office and sat down behind a desk. I took a chair. He moved his computer monitor out of the way so he could see me.

"Tie Mei is gone," I said. "She died ten years ago in a robbery. She saved my father's life."

"I read about it in the newspaper. What brings you here?"

"I looked you up because I wanted to talk to you about her, to learn about her life before she came to America. There's so much I don't know about her."

"All of that is long ago and far away," he said. "I'm sure I can't help you."

"You were a doctor in China, is that right?"

"I was a pharmacist," he said. "What you would call a scientific researcher. All that is ancient history; I am a businessman now."

"Were you and Tie Mei in love?"

He colored. The phone rang. He took the call. Listening to the exchange, I learned it was a pet shop in Kansas City. They wanted to know what was holding up their order of Mandarin rat snakes.

"Is that the kind of snake you played with as a little boy?" I asked.

"They are from southern China and I am from the north. I suspect you know about Kaifeng and my Jewish blood."

"Yes."

"Could I see one of those snakes?"

He hesitated then shrugged. "All right."

Solomon led me to a quiet corner of the floor. The snakes were gray with bright yellow bands.

"Very colorful," I said.

"The most beautiful of the rat snakes," he said.

"Tie Mei was beautiful too, yes?"

He avoided my eyes. "I try not to sell them to beginners. They die quickly in captivity unless you have a special touch."

"And you do?"

He opened his hands. "I treat an animal like a treasure and respect its feelings. I do not open a cage and yank out an animal whenever I please. I wait for the right time and I breathe quietly when I'm around living creatures. I walk softly."

"Tie Mei tried to teach me that skill. I'm not sure how well I learned it."

"She was strong willed. She wanted things her way."

"All her movements were soft. That's what made her so fast. She taught me *gongfu*, but when I asked her about lineage, history, the names of moves and teachers, she just put me off and said she'd tell me some day. She never got the chance. I was hoping you could fill in the blanks."

Solomon busied himself with putting the items on his desk into straight lines. "If I remember the story right, her *gongfu* got her killed."

"She fought burglars."

"If she had not known what she knew, she would have stayed still. If she stayed still, she would not have died. It is better not to know such things. Now, if you will excuse me, I have to get back to work."

"Can I come back? Can we talk some more? You're my only link to her."

He shook his head. "I cannot bring your nanny back and I don't know any *gongfu*. Now, I'm sorry but I have work to do."

The dismissal was clear, but instead I reached over, picked up a letter opener from the desk, and ran at him with the blade extended. I saw him relax his body in an instance through a series of key acupuncture points—*jian jing* in his shoulder wells, *qi men* under his nipples, *zhang men* beneath his floating ribs, *qi chong* at his inguinal crease—and assume a wedgelike defensive stance, effortlessly deflecting the letter opener and pulling me down to the floor, hard.

I stood up and brushed myself off. The fierce pain in my wrist was worth the gambit. He knew he'd been found out.

"This is my place of business," he said, obviously annoyed. "Please take your childish tricks somewhere else."

He pointed at the door and I went out, but I knew he knew I would be back.

15

My long history of sleep disorders includes lucid dreaming and fugue states. Neurologically speaking, such disorders may be linked to visions, which is why I have never been quite sure whether Tie Mei's ghostly visitations are in any sense real. What I can say with certainty is that a certain combination of meditation and trauma has opened the doors of my past lives to me.

The night after I met Solomon Yu I lay on my couch and journeyed to the deck of a giant warship of the Northern Song Dynasty rebel Admiral Chu Ling-Pin, ten decks up from the Yangtze River. The dream was tangible, complete with smoke and fire. Previously, I had felt the past descend like a surreal curtain, but this time I slid down into my previous incarnation the way a cork goes back into a wine bottle. I watched Chu pace the prow as we came about to face the enemy ships of Emperor Taizu. The imperial ships were smaller and faster and more maneuverable, and they harried us like wasps. The emperor's skilled archers rained arrows down upon us and a man beside me fell with one in his ear. I went to pull it out but saw in the light of the flames that his eyes were staring open and it was too late. I pulled the arrow anyway and went to the edge to vomit.

The admiral screamed an order. Men came up from the lower decks bringing barrels of petrol. I was no weapons wielder but a sailor for the lines and so manipulated the sails as the second mate instructed. This was a task of no small significance because our giant warship flew huge sheets that needed to be worked with the rudder to turn the ship. The admiral kept yelling, but he wasn't the only one and it was harder and harder to hear because of the dying all around me. At one point the hail of the arrows grew so dense it darkened the sky. I put a tin bucket on my head just as an arrow grazed my arm. Another soldier, bigger and stronger and with no loyalty to the cause, tore the bucket from me and used it for himself.

I wasn't Xenon Pearl and yet I was, and the immediacy of mortal danger and the rush of battle were terrifying but exhilarating, too, because the window on my past—the grit, passion, glory, suffering, fear, and ultimate triumph of my own immortality—had been closed to me since the night I learned of Jordan's maiming. I turned my attention back to the battle. Hell is merely imagined by civilians but actually lived by soldiers, and here I was a soldier and it was time for the enemy to burn. The weapon was a gunwale-mounted nozzle fed by a large square tank mounted on the bow by the admiral. The pitch-filled buckets were dumped into the tank and the piston bellows were set to work by a pump handle. When the flammable liquid issued from the nozzle, some brave soldier lit it—there was always the risk that at the moment of ignition an arm might be consumed or at least a hand or fingers—and death sprayed on the imperial ships.

I thought the first ship immolated might be the command ship but couldn't be sure because I knew imperial naval commanders were crafty. In the lead or no, the men burned quickly without regard to rank. Some jumped into the water like comets of capitulation while others burned where they stood, leaving a column of ash. We took another ship quickly thereafter and then another, working a smooth symphony of rudder, leeboard, sails, wind, ropes, and that deadly muzzle. I heard Admiral Chu Ling-Pin laughing and the sound chilled me. While victory was sweet, we had many of our own casualties and no right-minded human being celebrates burning men to death.

The fourth small ship fell back, and in our zeal we chased it. We were almost within firing range when there was a sudden shift of wind and our forward motion faded and with it our power to maneuver. The wounded among us seemed to sense the sudden stillness and quieted down. That was when the smell came over us. It floated in, rancid and stinking sharply of combusting life and singed hair and charred skin. I retched again right alongside the barbarian who had taken my bucket and heard my fluid hit the river in the ominous quiet.

Black smoke blew in on the shoulders of a sudden north wind and a moment later we were in the thick of it. I looked to our other vessels but could not see them. Some of our men cried for help from their brothers and because sound carries so well on water we answered, though it was hard to get a bearing on them.

Our ships were bigger and we had the flamethrowers, but for all the formidable advantage that terrible weapon bestowed, the wind turned the tide of battle. The imperial vessels had slaves to row and we did not, and all of a sudden what remained of the emperor's force was betwixt and between us, darting here and there and giving us only random glimpses of a prow, a stern, a mast, or an oar. The admiral, lost in madness, screamed at us as we fought blindly and breathed in particles of burning flesh. Desperate, the cannoneers on all our ships sprayed fire at will, but the wind took the flames and turned them back on us. Incoming arrows took the blaze, and when they landed they set fire to our timbers.

I understood the magnitude of the defeat at the same time I understood that I would not survive it. Alone and frozen in my beach house, I tried to scream as the fire drew close to me. As a student of neurology, I knew the medical dimensions of the pain I would soon suffer and the agony of others, too. This time—perhaps because I was neither skipping from life to life as I had done nor hearing of my own exploits from the lips of a ghost—I felt dread so keenly it drove me aft right through the officer's line and to the very feet of Admiral Chu.

Able to see him up close, to see the blood on his legs, I knew him at once for the man who in a later life would be my teacher's lover. The face was different, but his soul was Solomon Yu's. Tens of thousands of men might have lived if he had simply abandoned the attack and fled, and I implored him to stop the fire. More prideful than wise, he looked at me as if considering taking my head for my insolence then kicked me down the stairway.

I tumbled past the chain of men bringing the petroleum from the bowels of the ship. They seemed a string of forest ants bearing booty, staggering upward then dashing below again after dumping their barrels into the tank. They paid me no heed as I struggled back to the deck, the side of my face throbbing from Chu's kick. I did not dare get close, but even in the smoke I could see his expression, hear the orders he gave, and watch the nervous play of his features. I saw him clap his hands at each refill of the flamethrower.

I don't think the admiral realized he was setting his own ships ablaze until some lieutenant had the temerity to tell him. Huddled behind a stanchion on the forecastle, I overheard the exchange, and the smoke parted just in time for me to see him recoil at the news just the way he would recoil a thousand years later in his reptile shop at the sound of my name. Suddenly, a cinder on the wind caught the upper flare of our forward square mast. A dozen men scrambled aloft to quench the blaze, but they were assailed by a host of flaming arrows as the emperor's sailors took the cue.

Without oars and bereft of sails, our giant warship became one more coffin to add to the stack that the smoke and flames were making of our rebel force. The admiral hiked to the bow over the cries of his officers. I followed him. A gust of wind gave a clear window on the carnage. Our fleet was in shambles. The floating debris of imperial ships was visible, but more ships were sailing in and their bows parted the bodies of our own burned men riding the waves. Somehow, I knew that even though I had seen ramparts besieged and would see villages overrun and brigades slaughtered in the sands of the Taklamikan and Gobi, I would never bear witness to a massacre such as this one. The officers started wailing and the wailing caught on. The imperial soldiers had no mercy in their hearts and the piteous sound did not even slow their arrows. The wailing soon turned to weeping and then to pleading as sailors jumped into the river, trying for clear spots between the flames. Two of our burning vessels collided with a terrible crash and the rampageous roar of splintered wood.

When things seemed as bad as they could get, the wind increased. The stream of fire Chu insisted on maintaining arced through the air and came back to our own ship, lighting the admiral's cabin and the bridge and the wheel along with all the charts, instruments, and maps. The pilot ran from the wheelhouse with his armor ablaze and sailed toward the water, catching an arrow in his chest in midair.

Without a hand on the rudder, our burning ship began to gyrate and the first sail disintegrated in favor of the second. By this time there was pure chaos at play and I walked to where Chu stood and he looked at me and I saw he was crying. He started to say something but his voice would not work. Even if it had, the disaster was beyond words; we had been a force of 150,000, and not a soul would be going home. The rout was complete, and since we were the flower of the rebellion all was lost in the worst possible way.

Chu scanned the surface as if looking for a diamond, and when he found what he was after—a patch of particularly brightly burning water—he jumped off the boat and straight into it. The jump itself was a gesture not of shame and not of defiance but of despair so deep it craved utter and complete annihilation. As he sank, the flames found me and I looked down at my burning feet and gave a cry of my own and came back to my body and my house by the beach. Frozen, I waited to hear men howling and smell flesh burning, but there was only the whistling of a winter wind outside and the faint odor of night jasmine coming in around the doorjambs and the window seals. I sat quiet and desperately afraid, as I had been for a while, that the dream, and with it my vivid and certain awareness of past lives, meant I was truly, deeply crazy.

*   *   *

After a time, I went to find my wallet. In an interior pocket behind some movie ticket stubs and a plumber's number jotted on the edge of a paper placemat, I found a business card I hadn't used in some time. I dialed the number on it, and Dr. Diomedes Ramirez, the county's best psychiatrist, answered the phone.

"Sorry to call your home at this hour," I said.

"For you, no hour is too late. How is Jordan?"

"Better every day," I said.

"She is in my prayers. What can I do for you?"

"My patient has had another episode."

"I see. Am I right in thinking things have been quiet for a while?"

"Very quiet."

"And she has been sleeping?"

"Soundly."

"And she is taking the medication I prescribed?"

We maintained this fiction, Diomedes and I, that I was consulting him about an imaginary female patient.

"No."

"I see. And how long has your patient been off the medication?"

"Quite some months now. The medication produced untenable side effects."

"I remember suggesting long-term therapy might be an idea."

"I thought about that. Passed the suggestion on. She hasn't called you?"

"No she hasn't," Diomedes said dryly. "Has the ghost returned?"

"No ghost," I said. "But there are other hallucinations, very distinct, very real. There was an episode just half an hour ago—a sequence of great vividness, right down to odors."

"Were any other senses involved?"

I rose from the couch and paced with the phone. I touched the side of the room, feeling the paint and the drywall behind it. The coolness of it was reassuring, and the minor imperfections of the surface grounded me.

"Yes," I conceded. "There was a fire and she felt great heat."

"Was there sex?"

"What?"

"Was it a sexual experience?"

"No sex," I said. "It was a military campaign."

"So there was violence?"

"Beyond imagination," I said.

"And you were a soldier?"

"A sailor. She was a sailor. And she could feel what it was like to be in a smaller body."

"A smaller body? A child?"

"A Chinese," I said.

"A Chinese," Diomedes repeated. "I see."

"So what do you think?"

"The episode has passed?" he asked.

"It has."

"Any residual effects? Nausea? Weakness? Blurred vision? Dry mouth?"

"None that I'm aware of. The patient has gone back to work."

"Remind me. She works as a reporter, is that right?"

"A librarian," I said.

"My goodness, how lucky for the books," he said.

"I am a bit concerned that she may return to her violent behavior."

Diomedes was silent for a long moment. "Have there been new episodes of violence?"

"Abortive ones, I think."

"What does that mean?"

"I think she went out with the intent of committing violence but then balked at doing so."

"Balked?"

"It didn't pan out," I said.

Diomedes made a sound with his lips, and I realized he was working his pipe. I heard the click of a lighter and the flare of flame.

"Self-inhibition is a step in the right direction," he said.

"But a return to violence is not."

"No."

"I'm afraid there may be more episodes," I said.

"I repeat my recommendation for talk therapy."

"I'll pass that along."

"Be good to see the patient back on medication, too," he said.

"A month ago that might have been possible, but now that the patient is working again the medication poses certain problems."

Diomedes sucked on his pipe. I could see the smoke in my mind's eye, and it brought back the river battle. I imagined rich smells.

"Would you agree that the risk of not taking medication outweighs the side effects?"

"I suppose it does, yes."

"Well then. Will the patient consider the medication?"

"I'll ask her."

"Please do. And report her answer, would you?"

"All right," I said.

"In the meantime, I suggest the patient get as much sleep as possible, eat well, exercise strongly, mind her diet, and leave alcohol and all recreational drugs completely aside. Do you think she can do that?"

"I think she can," I said.

"Good night, Xenon."

"Good night, Diomedes."

I hung up, feeling all the better my friend was out there but still afraid I might depart again. I sat back down on the couch and waited there until I was sure I was me and would stay me—not the etheric, transcendent me, but just plain Xenon Pearl.

It was a full hour before I could take myself upstairs to bed. I lay with a bottle of antipsychotic pills on my chest, but I did not remove the cap. During the night, I kicked the bottle onto the floor.

16

That afternoon, Kimberly Jenkins came to see me at the office. She was dressed to the nines in a print skirt with a wide belt and an elegant silk blouse. I was exhausted from the previous night's ordeal but had enough presence of mind to compliment her on the outfit.

"My grandfather was from Argentina," she said. "That's my only connection to Latin flair."

"I think you've got plenty."

"You're nice to say so."

We were in my consulting room. She pointed at the folding screen with the water buffalo on it. "Is that very old?"

"Yes."

"From Thailand?"

"China."

"It's in amazing condition."

"The gold paint is flaking off in a couple of places, but imperfection is part of its beauty."

"You like Asian things. Is the potion you have for me Chinese also?"

"Potion?"

"You told me to come pick it up, remember? You said it would help my shoulder heal faster."

I suddenly became aware of Kimberly's perfume. It was spicy, with an undertone of clove or cinnamon. "Stabbing pain or aching pain?" I asked.

She moved close to me. The aroma of her perfume grew stronger. "It's sharp," she said. "But I don't know whether to call it stabbing. I've never been stabbed."

"Good to hear. Let's try an herbal poultice. It might speed things along."

During downtime at the office I'd picked up an antique Chinese apothecary cabinet and placed my herbal remedies in it. Kimberly watched as I transferred a few ounces of my bruising liniment—known in Chinese as *dit da jow*—to a small glass bottle for her. The recipe was Tie Mei's, and I had jars of the stuff that were fifteen years old. The twenty-six herbs, suspended in alcohol, were pungent and strong.

"You were great with Tierra," she said. "You have her believing you've changed her brain and now you're all she can talk about."

"She's a great kid. Now come with me and let's see what we can do about your pain."

I led her into the examination room and gestured for her to get comfortable on the table. Gingerly, I removed her sling and palpated her shoulder. The brachial plexus—the bundle of nerves and blood vessels that runs from spinal nerves C5, 6, 7, 8, and T1 under the collarbone and down into the armpit—was swollen along its course and I could feel the tenderness in her scalene muscles.

"I'd like to try some acupuncture on you," I said.

Her toes went rigid. "Needles? Isn't the poultice enough?"

"The solution will help, but acupuncture can work miracles. There are bonesetters in China who put a needle in a broken arm, stop the pain, feel the bones through their fingers, and set them back in place with just gentle pressure. They don't use pins and they don't use screws; they just ease the edges back in gently and wrap the arm in cloth soaked in herbs. Compared to those guys, our trauma surgeons are like typists wearing oven mitts."

"So neurosurgeons don't usually do this?"

"Not usually, no. One of my teachers was Chinese, so I had the benefit of both Western and Eastern training."

"Will it hurt?"

"You don't have to worry about the needles, Kimberly. They're very tiny. You'll barely feel them go in. They'll help the inflammation and bring healing to the area."

I put my fingers on her wrists in the technique of Traditional Chinese Medicine and felt her pulse to be vacuous and wiry. The pulse in TCM reveals far more than the pulse in allopathic medicine, which primarily gauges heart rate. The other traditional place to look is at the tongue, and Kimberly's was skewed to one side.

"Have you had any dizziness?" I asked.

She shook her head.

"But the shoulder pain is still there."

"Yes."

I began her treatment using a needle shallowly inserted into the Heart Channel 1 point in the center of her armpit. On the opposite side of her chest, just under the depression of the collarbone, I put a needle into the Lung Channel 1 point and another into a point on her Gall Bladder Channel 21 point at the top of her shoulder.

She kept her eyes closed during the treatment, but her feet stayed rigid and her hands made fists.

"Try to relax," I said.

"You're funny," she said.

"Tell me about Tierra's music then."

"She has real talent, perfect pitch, and the temperament to practice. That she gets from me—the temperament I mean."

"Her father's a hothead?"

"That's a nice way of putting it. He's a hard, rough man, but underneath his bullying he's weak. Anyway, like I told you, he's hardly around. Tierra wanted me to bring you white roses and I thought it was a great idea so I did, but then I left them outside."

"You did?"

"By the door," she said, wincing as I adjusted one of the needles. "I got cold feet I guess. I didn't want to give you the wrong idea. I feel stupid about it now."

I put another needle into her leg, this one at Stomach Channel 38 point, on the same side as her sore shoulder. She cried out at that one, all the more when I rowed the needle in place. I patted her hand and put some meditation music on.

"You hold tension in your stomach," I said.

"It's kirring me right now."

"I beg your pardon?"

"My stomach. It's killing me."

For just a moment, I thought she slurred her speech. I had a few more points to hit, but instinct told me to stop. "How do you feel?"

"A little dizzy."

"Light-headedness is a common side-effect of acupuncture. When did you last eat?"

"A few hours ago."

"I'm going to bring in the roses." I said. "Exactly where did you leave them?"

"Just to the right of the door, behind the bush."

"I'll get them. Just try to relax for a few minutes."

When I reached the front of the office, the flowers were gone. My office is in Lauderdale-By-The-Sea, in an old strip mall between the ocean and the Intracoastal Waterway. It's a beach community of old apartment duplexes and a few motels, and there are transients in the area. I figured someone must have picked them up.

*   *   *

Back in my consulting room, I rummaged about in the apothecary cabinet for the trauma pill I favored. I'd done a careful job of organizing everything, but there were sixty drawers and I wasn't yet good at finding things in it. It was a Chinese patent formula, a standard medication following a widely available prescription. In the terms of traditional Chinese medicine, the formula breaks blood stasis, tonifies blood, stops bleeding, strengthens sinew and bone, dredges and opens acupuncture channels, and relieves pain. I used the pills often for training injuries and had relied on them heavily the previous year after my war with the Russian mobsters. Finally, I located it and put a few tablets in a bottle for Kimberly.

Back in the treatment room, she appeared to be asleep. I pulled the needles out and asked her how she was feeling. She moaned but did not open her eyes.

"Wake up. Treatment's over. You're just dreaming," I said, rubbing a bit of the liniment into her shoulder.

She sat up. "Whir emmm I?" she slurred.

My stomach clenched up. "Kimberly," I said.

"Dogder Burl."

I helped her lie back down and rushed out to Travis. "Run outside and flag a cab," I ordered. "I have an emergency."

"Shouldn't I call an ambulance?"

"She'll be dead by the time it gets here. Get the cab."

As I ran back to the treatment room, all I could think was that I should have trusted the pulse and tongue exams that told me Kimberly was in danger of a stroke. I told myself I was rusty from not having done a TCM exam in a while, but in truth I had ignored the signs and trusted logic over intuition—exactly the tendency Wu Tie Mei had so often warned me against.

I removed the needles and carried her out to the front. One of her shoes fell off. Travis removed the other for safekeeping. The cab arrived. I slid into the back. A coconut air freshener hung from the mirror. The Haitian driver had wooden beads draped over his seat to keep him cool. The line of his hair on the back of his neck sloped off to one side. Kimberly's eyelids fluttered as I told the driver where to go.

"Drive fast," I said. "If we get a ticket, I'll pay it."

We pulled up to the ambulance entrance a few minutes later. I paid, leapt out, and carried Kimberly into the ER.

"I need a CT scan of the neck right now," I told the admitting nurse.

As Kimberly had only just been discharged, they had all her information handy. A moment later she was whisked off on a gurney. I sat down and waited for the scan results, torturing myself over the diagnosis. There is more to keep in mind with TCM than there is with a Western medical exam, which follows a logical diagnostic tree but has room for neither energetic considerations nor any of TCM's complex relationships between the human body and food, mood, stress, seasons, nature, activity, and the world at large. I wished I had ordered more extensive scans when she was first admitted and paid closer attention to what I saw at the start of the TCM exam.

"Idiot," I muttered to myself.

A crash cart rolled past me, moving in the direction of the CT lab. I had a bad feeling seeing it and followed to quiz the orderly pushing it.

"What's going on?"

"Some young woman stroked in the middle of the scan," he said.

I ran into the lab. Kimberly Jenkins lay on the table, eyes wide open and sightless, looking into the bardo. The scan technician stood beside her, in obvious shock.

"One moment she was awake, the next minute she was flopping around. I tried to restrain her, but before I could do anything she . . . "

I grabbed the paddles off the cart and shocked Kimberly. Her back arched, but her expression did not change.

"Temporal hemorrhage," the technician muttered.

I shocked her again, watching the flat line of the EEG and thinking about Tierra, whose father was out of the picture and whose mother was now out of the world. I tried a third time. Nothing. The fourth shock lifted her off the table, and a barrette fell from her hair, exposing a patch of forehead covered with makeup and heavily bruised. The technician touched it with his finger, the makeup came off, and the bruise showed big and deep, right up at the hairline.

I tried one more shock, but it was no use. I sat down on the floor, exhausted. The technician sat down beside me. He looked like he was going to cry.

"First time?" I asked.

"She's so pretty," the technician answered. "I remember her from the other day. That bruise wasn't there when she came in off the road. We looked her over. We would have seen something like that."

"You're sure?"

"How could I forget that crazy night? No, she had to have hit her head again. Or somebody hit it for her."

I felt a hum in the air and looked quickly around the room. I smelled almonds.

"Tie Mei?"

"I beg your pardon?"

I peeked under the cart, jumped up, and checked every nook and cranny of the lab, but there was no sign of my dead teacher. The technician stared at me. "She was twenty-eight years old," he said, trying to cover my strange behavior. "What a shame."

"Scan her head," I said.

The technician blanched. "But she's gone."

"Just do it. If we wait for the autopsy, it'll be days before a result."

He readied the machine and ran the scan. It showed a massive brain insult. We both stared at it.

"Now we know," he said.

I took Kimberly's stiffening hand in mine and spoke to her silently. I told her I was sorry I'd failed her. I told her I would look after Tierra.

I told her I'd find out what had happened.

17

I met Wanda at an ice cream parlor in Wilton Manors, a community slightly south and inland from my house. A teenage girl named Bimini had introduced me to the place, and I'd become a regular ever since. I had a waffle cone with two scoops of pineapple basil sorbet. At my suggestion, Wanda tried a scoop of coconut ice cream and another of macadamia nut with chocolate bits.

"Oh, no," she said. "Not again. I will *not* look into the whereabouts of the girl's father."

"What if he beat the wife? She said he was a bully."

"You're remembering the woman with the cigarette burns, aren't you?"

"Gloria Brownfield."

"That's right. And you carved the husband like a Halloween pumpkin."

"I don't know what you're talking about," I said.

"Of course not. How's Jordan?"

"Listening to a lot of music. This morning I downloaded Ray Charles's *I Got A Woman* from iTunes and emailed it to her."

"Kimberly Jenkins might have fallen down, Zee. Not every husband beats his wife."

"This one did."

"You don't know that. It's total conjecture."

"My gut says he did it."

"And my gut says you're trouble," Wanda frowned.

"That gut of yours should be bigger with all that ice cream you eat."

"Macadamia nut chocolate owns an automatic exemption from all rules, and, no, I don't eat it every day and, yes, I work out like a madwoman and, yes, I know you're trying to change the subject."

"Well you do look pretty trim these days," I said.

"That's the second time in a week I've told you to keep your eyes to yourself. And how you can eat pineapple with basil in it I'll never know."

"It takes a sophisticated palate."

"How about I pop a couple caps in that palate of yours?"

"Why Detective! You would never do such a thing. You love me."

"Like I said, you're trouble."

A couple with three kids walked into the place. I thought about Tierra. I wondered who would take her for ice cream. "If you think I'm trouble, why did you give me Jay Boniface?"

"I was frustrated by his high-brow lawyer. It was a moment of stupidity, and I regretted it a second later. Thankfully, you knew better than to act on the news."

"Thankfully."

"That chapter in your career is over. Let's keep it that way."

"Of course. But the little girl is going to need someone. She's completely alone."

"I'm sure the hospital has social workers for cases like this. I bet they're already on it, talking to the insurance company and all that. It's up to them to find the father."

"The mother had been discharged for only a day," I said.

"And she fell and hit her head."

"Hard enough to cause massive head trauma, but she didn't mention it in her office visit. Why do you suppose that might be?"

She finished her ice cream, rose, and tossed the cup. "You can think what you want but stay out of it. Order an autopsy if you think it will lead to something important. If there's criminal evidence, we'll investigate. But confine your cutting to the scalpel. Clear?"

"Clear. By the way, Neptune has already written me twice from the prison.

He seems to feel some sort of kinship with me. It's not a good thing."

"Kinship, huh?"

"The way I read it, he thinks I'll be his bunkmate soon."

"Let's hope he's wrong."

"What should I do about the letters?"

"Don't want any more letters, don't write back. Don't want to be his cellmate, keep your sword in the closet. Easy enough, right?"

"Sure."

"Anything else, Zee?"

I almost asked her to do a background check on Solomon Yu, but something stopped me. Wanda's favors were budgeted by time and her schedule. The more I asked for, the less I was likely to get.

"Nope," I smiled. "I've said my piece."

*   *   *

I know that Tie Mei had stood against injustice in many past lives, and the smell of almonds around Kimberly Jenkins in the scan room told me my old teacher had been close by and watching. Ironically, the details of her life with me this time round were a blank slate. No matter how hard Solomon Yu tried to rebuff me, I was going to fill it in.

I called Slither & Crawl and invited Darlene to meet me for lunch.

"I'm not sure that's a good idea. I pick up on some weirdness with you and the boss and I don't want any part of that."

"No weirdness at all. He'll like me soon. You'll see."

"Well, maybe the weirdness is about you."

"Let me set your mind at ease."

I named a diner I'd spotted by the shop. She was waiting beside a lime green VW Beetle when I pulled into the parking lot.

"Let's talk out here," she said. "I'm not hungry."

"Are you sure I can't buy you a cinnamon roll or something?"

"Just tell me specifically what you want to know. If it's about business, I'm not going to answer. You say you're a doctor, but I think you're ICE."

"What?"

"U.S. Customs," she sniffed. "Like you don't know."

I handed her my hospital ID and she inspected it.

"Could be fake," she said.

"That could be fake snake shit too, but I don't think it is."

She followed my glance to the chalky stain on her jeans.

"Not snake. Lizard. Skink, to be exact."

I gave her my driver's license. I gave her my hospital key card, which opened certain security doors. I handed over a business card. She examined each one closely.

"They look okay, but they still could be fake. I'm no expert."

"Pretty unlikely though, right? I mean, why would I go to all that trouble just to talk to you about Solomon?"

"His research. Duh."

"What research?"

She rose from her cross-legged position with surprising ease and grace. "I'm outta here. This was a bad idea."

"How long has Solomon had the business?"

"Ask him."

"I'm asking you. You work there."

"A while. Years. Maybe ten or fifteen."

"Does he have a family?"

"No."

"Never married."

"No."

"Any pictures of women in his house?"

She started to answer and then stopped. "I don't think I like you."

"I'll take that for a yes. And ten to one, at least one of the pictures you saw was of my nanny. She raised me like a mother.

She's dead now. She and Solomon came over together from China. I miss her and I'm trying to find out more about her past, more about her life. I thought Solomon might be able to help."

She twirled a blade of grass around her finger. "This is about your nanny?"

"That's right."

"That's so weak it has to be true. Why don't you just ask him about her?"

"I tried. Listen. Does he have a soft spot?"

"What the hell does that mean?"

"Chocolate, old watches, cigars—I don't know."

"Goodbye *Doctor* Pearl."

"I'm just trying to change his mind about me," I called after her. "If I knew about snakes I'd make a present of the rarest snake in the world just to get him to talk to me, just to get him to feel he owed me a conversation."

She looked at me over her shoulder. "You want to buy him a present?"

"There must be something super rare or expensive, something a competitor has that he'd love to get his hands on. I'm just trying to honor him, to get him to see I'm sincere."

Darlene chewed her lip. "Now you don't sound like a cop, 'cause for sure this is entrapment."

"I told you I'm a doctor."

"And you say you loved this nanny?"

"My mother died when I was four. Tie Mei was all I had."

"Tie Mei," she repeated.

"Will you think about what I asked? About a gift of some snake?"

"I'll think about it."

And I might have left it there. I was raised to be patient, to wait for all things to unfold. I might have let her go and gone home and waited, hoping that she would come up with a gift idea for Solomon or influence him in my favor. Instead, I started my bike and zoomed after her and pulled into the warehouse parking lot just as she was getting out of her car. I walked right past her and strode into Solomon Yu's office. He wasn't there. I went out onto the floor of the place. He wasn't there either. I looked in a room labeled for spiders and another one for frogs. No sign of him. I went to a room with a sign on the door that said "NO," tried the handle, found it locked, and knocked loudly.

Darlene came rushing up. "What's wrong with you. That's the hot room. Venomous animals. You can't go in!"

A few customers stared. I knocked again, louder this time.

"Don't knock," Darlene yelled. "He could get bitten if you startle him."

A second later, Solomon Yu opened the door. His mouth was open as if he were about to yell. When he saw me, he stopped short. I reached into my pocket and drew out a black silk mask with cutouts for only the eyes.

"I found this in her dresser drawer," I said, thrusting it into his hands. "I thought you'd want it. It still smells like her."

Staring at me, he brought the mask slowly to his nose. He closed his eyes. His inhale was deep and full. He stayed there a long time, with everyone watching. Finally, he opened his eyes.

"I really want to talk to you," I said.

Just before he closed the door, I caught a glimpse of something incongruous sitting on a shelf. It was a plastic water jug with flowers jutting out.

White roses.

18

I needed to stop and see Tierra that evening, but I was reluctant to do so until I had something to offer her—a plan, an idea, some news. That's what I told myself, anyway. I ducked into a mixed martial arts school located near a local plant nursery I frequented. I'd long been impressed by the grim mien and muscularity of the fellows streaming through the door and knew that mixed martial arts drew from a variety of disciplines to train guys in rough and tumble cage fighting for fame and prizes. If I'd find real fighters anywhere, I'd find them here.

There was no aroma of jasmine when I went through the door—in fact, the place smelled strongly of sweat and something much worse. A young man taking off his shoes by the door saw me wrinkle my nose and smiled. "It's blood," he said. "There's a sausage factory next door."

What I knew of sausages was that pretty much anything warm-blooded was a fair ingredient. The stench shot up my nostrils and seemed to ooze from every surface in the school. "You get used to it," the young man said. "After the first few classes, I thought it had made me sick, but then I realized I was nauseous from the workouts. I lose five or six pounds of water during the class. If you're going to bow in, you better have water with you."

"Just here to watch," I said.

"He doesn't let you."

"What?"

"The coach. He doesn't let people watch."

"Which one is he?"

"He's in the back. He'll be out in a minute. You'll know him by his dirty belt."

There was a different feeling in the school than there had been in Vanderkamp's aikido dojo. This was no temple to self-cultivation; it was a fighting gym and the smile I'd received in explanation of the school's aroma was the first and last of the evening. Warm-ups—hurdler stretches, frog stretches, Chinese splits—were conducted individually and in total silence.

To a one these were big men without an ounce of fat on them. I expected the same from the coach, but when he emerged from the changing room he was five foot two at most, neat and trim and sleek as a missile, his hair slicked back, his feet perfectly parallel with every step. He put out a hand inviting everyone to a line, and they formed one while I took a folding chair to watch.

He stared at me and grunted, "You are here . . . "

"To watch," I said. "I'm interested in training."

"No watching allowed. Didn't anyone tell you that?"

"They did and I thought perhaps you might make an exception."

"Why would I do that? Are you exceptional?"

"My nanny thought so."

Nobody laughed. The teacher came off the mat and stood so close to me that we would have been nose to nose if he'd been taller. "Do you have an attitude problem?"

"No, I have a genuine desire to learn what you do here and I cannot do that without watching it performed."

"There are no performances here. We train fighters."

"I'd like to know more. What would you suggest?"

"I would suggest you obey the rules and make an appointment for an interview."

"I can interview you by watching. I don't need extra time."

The smart-ass comment got the attention of a few of the guys on the mat who made their way over to stand by their teacher. It was that teaming-up move that cleared the picture for me, for in that moment I noticed what I had not noticed before: the rubber-soled shoes and the hair-trigger looks and, off to the back, just outside the changing room, the clothing hung carefully on hooks so as to drape over the shoulder holsters.

"I'm sorry," I said, extending my hand. "We've gotten off on the wrong foot. I'm Xenon Pearl. I got a sister on the job. Broward Sheriff's Office Detective Wanda Berkowitz."

The letters BSO had the mollifying effect I was looking for, but as soon as I spoke them I realized I should have kept Wanda out of it. My visit might get back to her and there was no point in letting Wanda know what I was doing.

"Wanda Berkowitz," I heard someone mutter. "Never heard of her."

"I have. She's SID."

"Is that right, Mr. Pearl?" the teacher inquired, ignoring my hand. "Is your sister part of the Strategic Investigations Division?"

"She is."

"Wanda's not married," said the student. "How come you don't have the same name?"

Somebody in the back row suggested maybe it was because I had taken my wife's name, but they said it very softly and the comment generated no chuckles.

"She's my stepsister," I said. "But don't tell her you saw me here or she'll kick my butt."

Again, my attempt at humor fell flat.

"Sign a waiver," the coach said abruptly, and as if by magic, the young man who had spoken to me at the outset put one in my hand.

"Is everyone here a cop?" I muttered under my breath as I signed my life away.

"I'm not," the kid said brightly. "But I'd like to go to the academy some day."

I confess I got a little tingle out of being in a room full of trained police fighters. Adding to the danger was the little matter of being a wanted vigilante. I had a sense that if I attempted to convince the officers that violence was a good solution for violence they might respond by beating me within an inch of my life.

The paper signed, I was allowed to watch while the class went through a series of group exercises: rolling and kicking and punching and rolling again, followed by calisthenics designed to ensure the heart had no rest. When those exercises were over the teacher gestured for me to join a human fireplug named Axe on the floor.

"Axe?" I asked. "Is that really your name?"

"Avery."

"You BSO too?"

"Miami."

"You come all the way up here to train?"

"I'd drive to Jersey to train with these guys. Now tell me, what kind of background you got?"

"Chinese *gongfu*," I said.

"Like in the movies?" He said it derisively and I didn't like it.

"Weapons training mostly," I answered. "Spears and swords."

"Yeah? I like my weapons practical. Give me a shotgun and a Glock .45 and I'm ready to rumble. Now, coach wants me to start you with a few basic throws and locks. Before I do that, I need to show you how to fall."

"I know how to fall," I said, even though it was surely the weakest of my skills.

"You signed the waiver?"

"I signed it."

Axe sighed, reached over, grabbed the collar of my shirt, and threw me over his shoulder. I landed a bit hard and more or less on my head.

"I thought you said you knew how to fall."

"I fell, didn't I?'

"Like a rock. Here. Let's do a few. We'll start kneeling and . . . "

"I don't have to start kneeling."

"Okay, we'll start standing up and you'll crack your shoulder."

"We'll start kneeling," I said.

We played it that way for a while. Tie Mei had always maintained that I didn't need to learn to fall because if I learned what she taught me, I would not go to the ground. I was eager to work my stuff on Axe but figured my time was better spent learning new skills.

When he was satisfied with my falling skill we moved on to trying a throw. I was eager to feel the thick of him, the density Tie Mei always said came with internal practice, which I realized described the style she was teaching me. Tie Mei eschewed gymnastics and muscle building—though she was astonishingly lithe and flexible and strong—in favor of standing meditation and *qigong* routines. She scorned the conversation endemic to all martial arts but hers, the tit for tat that required your actions to be a response to your opponents'.

"Watch yourself, not your enemy," she said. "Feel what happens to you. Anticipate the way in which you will be deprived of your equilibrium and protect it. Move to stay in perfect harmony at all times. Move to protect the unimpeded flow of *qi*. That's your one and only mission. Do what you must to accomplish it. If your enemy breaks his arm as a result, that's not your problem; if you happen to break his neck, that's not your problem either."

I seemed unlikely to break either Axe's elephantine arm or neck, but as always it was a challenge to avoid the give and take that seemed so compelling, immediate, and natural. As he advanced on me, the teacher looked our way and when he did, Axe threw me with a bit more gusto.

Tie Mei had always told me to use as little force as possible, to cultivate my external strength with the exercises she gave me but not to use that strength directly against my opponent. "No force against force," she said. "Feel the direction he's going and take him even further that way; go down to go up, go right to go left."

She meant that the initial movement, that all-important first instant of contact, had to be artful, light, spiraling, and subtle. I held back on all of this with Axe. The teacher noticed and came over, his jaw muscles quivering.

"You're playing," he said. "We don't play here. Either show what you know or get out of my school."

"I came to learn."

"You're not learning anything that way."

I was, actually. I was learning that other than a bit more verticality in Axe's attacks, the same intricate three-dimensionality that had been missing from most of the players at Vanderkamp's school was missing here too. Compassion did not rule and the cops were faster and stronger, but in principle I really did notice the same problem.

I shrugged. The teacher moved Axe out of the way and took over his job. He did not invite me to attack him for a throw but came at me with a real barrage. I was caught off-guard by his sudden intensity, and he hit me hard with a right hook on the cheek and then came in with a sweep. Once I was down, he knelt, gave me a kick to the belly, and tangled me in a painful leg lock. I tapped out, but he took his sweet time letting go.

Tie Mei always presented our martial arts lessons within the context of spiritual development. They were to cultivate the self, she said. "In an age when everyone has a gun, what do you think I teach you all this for? It's to make you a better man. It's a place for you to discover yourself, to find the rough edges and smooth them, to detect the weakness and strengthen it, and to tone down your excesses."

This cop coach didn't seem to be about smoothing any edges. He was pure ego and it grated on me. Rising ruefully from the mat, sore in the right hip and knee from his unnecessary cruelty, I figured I'd had just about enough frustration for one week: I'd lost a girlfriend, I'd lost a patient, I'd landed no better than a draw at an aikido school, and getting Solomon Yu to even talk to me was like a tooth extraction. All in all, I was in no mood to be tossed around by a sharp-talker with a bad attitude.

So I mentioned weapons again.

"This is not a weapons school," the coach said. "You want to play with swords, go to a Renaissance fair."

"Even a stick is a practical equalizer," I said.

"You pull a stick out there on the street, the other guy pulls a knife. You pull a knife, he pulls a gun."

"Historically, we learn a lot from weapons," I said.

"Lay off the sermon."

"I'm just saying they reveal our most basic tendencies, our underlying proclivities, our excesses, too, and our fears. My teacher always told me to study them first then work backward to empty hands."

The room was silent. The coach stared at me. "Get a load of this guy, will you? Historically? Proclivity? You some kind of college professor?"

"I'm a brain surgeon," I said. "And I'm just trying to make the point that it's always better to fight with a weapon if one's around. Weapons level the playing field.

"Bang, bang, you're dead," said Axe.

The coach smiled. I couldn't help marveling at how much subtle information the human face provides. He condescended to people, this man whose name I did not even know. He held others in hostile regard. The world was his bunker when it might have been his oyster. He was burdened with karma so rancid that his school smelled like sausages.

"Okay, Doc," said the trainer. "Let's cut the shit and get to work, shall we?"

He raised his hands, but that was only a feint. He swept my leg and as he did I rolled my leg behind his. Trapped, his leg went forward and he winced, dropping into a forced split. I stepped around behind him and drilled him twice in the head—once with a round kick and once with a vertical punch to the side of his jaw. I felt the bones grate and knew I'd cost him some teeth.

As I stepped off him, Axe was there and kicked me in the face. I felt the blood vessels in my left eye burst, watched the world narrow into red as the lid swelled instantly. I drew back to engage him while the teacher moaned on the floor, but the young kid I'd talked to and a couple of the other students pulled us apart.

"You'd better get out of here," the boy whispered in my ear. "They'll kill you if you stay, even if you really *are* a brain surgeon and your sister is a cop."

I grabbed my motorcycle boots and made for the door. On the way home, my eye swelled shut. It made for an interesting ride, as the road was half as wide as it should have been and twice as dangerous.

19

I slept on an icepack, and the shiner I woke to would have been much nastier if I hadn't dabbed another of Tie Mei's *dit da jow* formulas carefully around the eye before bed. I went outside, lifted a *Dendrobium* orchid from its hanger on one of my bird-of-paradise trees, and sat down to smell it. Tie Mei taught me that this class of fragrant plant relieves stress, as do jasmine flowers and gardenias, which is why I have so many around the house. I thought about Solomon and about the white roses and I thought about the beating I'd given and the one I'd received.

I also thought about the latest letter that had arrived from Neptune Cohen.

Dear Dr. Pearl,

I commended you to more meditation, but now thoughts of you take over my own sessions. It's happening more and more, yes? I go to this place that is not physically real, which of course I like to do because physical reality here is something to escape. And so in that strange place that is not this world and not exactly another I find you with a sword in your hand, a sharp one, and you have the devil in you and your face is steaming and your victims are bleeding and all that is good—no, it is great—but you fight this pleasure and it makes you careless. You take too many risks, yes? I know what I'm talking about. I took them too, and look at what happened to me.

You see the hand of God sticking his fingers into the glove of your life and moving you like you might not wish to move. True, those fingers have sharp nails and you are his manifestation. You are doing what you are supposed to do. Don't listen to the doubters. Don't listen to the weak. Don't listen to those who have never felt God the way you do, felt the fingers in the glove of life.

Celebrate your darkness.

Respectfully,
Neptune Cohen

I found myself utterly disinterested in Neptune's relentless campaign to land me in jail by exhorting me to do more and worse. I did have a problem with violence and I was sure I was on the right track to solving it, even if Axe and the other friendly folks at the mixed martial arts school had not been a big help.

I had yet to drink my morning tea, the side of my face was pulpy, and there was a yawning hole in my heart where Jordan should have been. I felt I was reliving her tragedy all over again: watching the beating on a video disc, vomiting eggs and toast all over my own floor, finding the telltale tattoo on her back in the middle of the life-saving surgery I believed I was performing on a stranger.

I walked back inside for a shower and all I could think of was that I'd been so busy attending to Jordan every moment of every day since the surgery that I hadn't allowed my feelings to flower, hadn't acknowledged the full weight of the guilt or what I stood to lose if she really would not have me.

I am a guy for whom second dates are more rare than first ones, which in turn are more rare than red moons; a guy who finds flaws and obstacles and problems in relationships faster than he finds succor. I was sure there was no other Jordan out there waiting for me, no other female master swordsmith whose strength of spirit had sustained me from one life to the next. I knew very few people who could suspend judgment enough to believe in both vengeance and ghosts; Jordan is truly one of a kind.

So I emailed her another song. I looked for a reply to the first one but found none. I wasn't surprised. If there was one thing she had shown me in the six months I'd watched her in rehab, it was an iron will. Once she made her mind up to do something, she went after it without surcease. I chose The Beatles' *I Want to Hold Your Hand*. I knew it was corny, but if Jordan was making the study of music she said she was, she knew all about the British Invasion, and said incursion never would have happened without that particular song.

It was also true that I wanted to hold her hand.

*   *   *

The doorbell rang. I peeked around the blinds and saw the long thin side of Roan Cole's head. I was in no mood for company and considered playing possum, but Roan would have none of it

"Open up," he banged on the door. "I know you're in there. Your bike's in the driveway."

I opened the door to let him in and saw he wasn't alone.

"You want breakfast?" I asked.

"Actually, we came to take you out. Hey, you got a shiner there."

"Nothing much. I bumped into a wall. And I'm not hungry, thanks, but how about introducing me to your friend."

"Zee, meet Lysandra. Lysandra, this disheveled prankster is the famous Dr. Xenon Pearl."

Lysandra was young and slim and blonde and very pretty. Roan gave me the wink. "You really look like hell," he said. "I thought you'd be fat and happy now that you can start chiseling on brains again."

"Jordan wants out," I said.

"What do you mean?"

"She doesn't want to see me anymore."

"You have a lovely home," said Lysandra. "Are you Chinese?"

"Does he look Chinese, bubblehead?" Roan chided her.

The girl whacked him hard enough on his arm to make him wince. "I am not a bubblehead. Your friend has dark eyes. He could be part Asian. Look at the furniture. Look at the paintings on the wall. What I said is a conversation opener. You could learn the art of conversation from me if you pay attention. Charming openers are not your long suit."

Roan's mouth went slack.

"I don't know the first thing about you," I told Lysandra. "But already I can see you're a treasure."

"Jordan's just in a mood, right?" Roan asked. "She's got a lot on her plate, after all."

Lysandra broke in. "Excuse me. Are you giving relationship advice?"

"Come in and sit down," I said. "Can I get you anything?"

She blew by me and went straight to my library. "Books!" she said. "Nobody reads books anymore. Look at all these. Chinese philosophy. See? I knew he was part Chinese."

"She's like that," Roan muttered, as we followed. "A friggin' thunderstorm. Just blows this way and that, wherever she wants."

"You've known her how long?"

"A month."

"And you tell me now?"

"Lot of false starts," he said. "You know how it is. I didn't want to jinx this one. I'm really sorry about Jordan, Zee. I'm not exactly sure what to say. There are so many angles."

From behind, I admired Lysandra's straight back and long legs and the ash tinges in her blonde bob. The more I looked, the lovelier she got. She might have been a runway model.

"We met at thirty thousand feet, since I'm sure he hasn't told you," she said.

"Lysandra's a flight attendant," Roan explained.

She pulled out a copy of the *I-Ching*, a book of divination and the most famous of all Chinese tomes. "This is the book that has you sort yarrow stalks or flip coins to see the future or get guidance, isn't it? Do you have questions about your life? Are you searching for answers?"

"I hear you met at thirty thousand feet and I've got a question all right."

Lysandra smiled. "He's funny, Roan. Maybe not original, but funny."

"Oh, he's original all right," said Roan, gently putting the book back on the shelf.

"I had a Chinese nanny," I said. "She told me about a lot of these books, even translated some for me, but I've only actually started to study them formally during the last half year."

Lysandra pulled out a Tibetan volume about karma and reincarnation. "Roan's always being called away at night. I guess when you're a big-shot surgeon, you have time to read."

"I had time because I was fired," I said. "Now I'm working again."

She seemed not to hear me, or if she did she had the good grace not to ask for details. "Karma's interesting," she said, thumbing through the volume. "I think it's more useful as a study in causation, as a reminder that what we do creates what we have. I'm not sure I believe in the principle across lifetimes, though."

I opened my mouth to spill the beans. I wanted to tell this complete stranger that I had visions of my past lives and knew my cohorts from the bardo. I wanted to tell her that Roan had been with me before, as had Khalsa, Solomon, Tie Mei, and my father. I wanted to tell her that Jordan had variously been my mother, my nephew, my doctor, my priest; I even considered mentioning that I may have known Lysandra herself in a previous go-round.

"You have to admit the possibility is intriguing," I said instead.

"Human relationships are complex enough without worrying about what happens after we die."

"Go ahead and turn metaphysical on me," Roan told his girl. "I'll just stand here and smile at the furniture."

Lysandra gave him a withering look. "Roan tells me you do Chinese medicine. That's Buddhist, right?"

"Daoist," I answered. "The medical ideas started thousands of years before Bodhidharma brought the Buddha's word to China. The principles of following nature, of observing all the small cues we Western docs aren't taught—smells, facial features, the tongue, various pulses, the affect and the flow of energy, the temperature of the flesh—these are the insights of great Daoist teachers. We tend to laugh at things like 'ancient sages believed the world was flat' and forget that those same wise men also invented the very yin/yang theory that underpins the digital revolution. In the East, thinkers gain understanding by putting the world together. In the West, we understand things by taking them apart."

"Synthesis verses reduction," Lysandra murmured.

"Wow," I said to Roan. "Where did you find her?"

Lysandra gave me a peck on the cheek.

"Maybe I should leave you two alone," Roan grumbled.

"Oh stop it. You're the man for me and you know it, you sleep doctor you."

"I think that's a compliment," Roan looked at me. "I mean it is one, right?"

Lysandra took his face in her hands. "I'm the biggest compliment I have to give," she said, squishing his cheeks together.

*   *   *

I had bittersweet feelings about the visit. Roan had found a good woman and that only made me think of Jordan. I knew she liked to take the air every morning at 11:00, so I went upstairs, dressed in a dark pinstripe suit, white shirt, and red tie, and rode up to Boca in hopes of catching a glimpse of her. On the way I had the strange feeling I was being followed. I checked the mirror but nothing caught my attention. Chalking it up to my general disquietude, I turned my attention to the view of the sea. A stiff breeze drew current lines in the green, green sea, and the white sand below turned the water postcard turquoise. I saw dark shapes offshore, but I couldn't take my eyes off the road long enough to determine if they were rays, sharks, or large shoals of small fish. A year ago I had seen an American crocodile just a bit farther north. They stray up from the Keys sometimes. My suit jacket flapped so hard I worried it might tear my buttons and my trousers wrapped around my ankles.

Traffic was light and I arrived ten minutes early. I waited in the sun on the south side of the building with a view of Jordan's usual route. I went through the eight-posture *qigong* routine Tie Mei had taught me and after that meditated quietly, standing, my eyes in slits. Within two minutes I was twitching and shaking as if suffering a seizure. That happens to me sometimes. Tie Mei likened the phenomenon to a carton of milk shaken and then set down on the counter. The liquid sloshing around inside makes the carton bounce in the same way unsettled *qi* moves the body. I never intend to move when I meditate; I never force energy to flow according to my intention.

The rods and cones of my eyes—photosensitive cells—responded to the bright winter sun by turning Amanda's condo building into a tapestry of tiny dots. The dots remind me that my body is nothing more than a collection of billions of cells, some cooperating with one another, some on missions of their own. Consciously or not, we all hold ourselves together by sheer force of will, resisting the temptations of entropy— the first law of thermodynamics—which has all of us disintegrating into our component parts in the same way that galaxies fled the site of the Big Bang.

When I opened my eyes, I saw Jordan riding a hand-crank bicycle down the sidewalk. Her limp legs were stretched out in front of her, strapped in tight to the sides of the wheel, while her hands did the work. I was stunned. I knew she had fantasized about riding a bicycle again and the two of us had looked wistfully at some sporty models, but she had turned the fantasy into reality. Her biceps bulging, she moved the bike so well I had to jog to keep up.

We covered a few blocks before she noticed me in the rearview mirror she wore clipped to her cycling helmet. She slowed and stopped, breathing hard.

"This is pretty great," I said. "Wow."

She licked the sweat off her lips and looked up at me through her sunglasses.

"Gets my heart rate up," she said.

"Did you get the songs I sent you?"

"I got them. You look like an idiot, running in that suit."

"Well *you* look beautiful."

She shook her head. "No, I don't. I look like a paraplegic. But I'm getting exercise. I haven't had my heart beating so hard since the attack."

She called it an attack. That was new, too.

"I can think of a time or two I got it beating."

She nodded. "Of course you can. But this isn't about you."

"You're in the anger phase now," I said. "That's probably healthy, but you don't have to go it alone."

"You graduated high school in two years, isn't that what you said?"

"Jordan."

"And college? That was just two years also. You started medical school at eighteen. You zoomed through your internship and residency. You're the youngest neurosurgeon in history."

"Not in history," I said. "Please stop this. It's not about me."

"Oh, yes, it is. This time it's all about you. Because you became a doctor too soon."

"What's that supposed to mean?"

Her gaze bored into me. "You should have let me die."

"Please don't say that."

"It wasn't up to you to save me."

"Yes," I said. "It was. And I'm glad I did."

"I'm not."

My tears came up so fast they surprised me. I turned away so she wouldn't see them, and when I did she turned her hand-crank bike around and began wheeling furiously back toward the condo. I started to follow, but she must have seen me in her mirror, for she took one hand off the crank and raised it in the air, fingers spread wide in a gesture that would have stopped a stampeding elephant.

No, it said. I don't want you. Leave me alone.

20

At 3:00 A.M. the next morning, while I was lying in bed mentally replaying every detail of the scene with Jordan, I heard someone in the backyard. I went quietly down the stairs, chose a spear from the weapons rack, opened the French doors, and slipped out into the darkness.

My backyard is made private by a tall board-on-board fence and screening foliage: an African Daisy, a hedge of Bougainvillea I favor for its thorns, an Australian flame tree whose flowers create their own light at dusk, and a row of Tasmanian tree ferns that provides moist, cool shade for fence lizards and tiny cricket frogs. My privacy is important not only for solace but also because this is the battlefield for my practice, the territory in which I negotiate with imaginary and remembered opponents.

The interloper was no phantasm from the bardo but Solomon Yu's girl friday, Darlene. I found her with my spear when I detected movement behind the passion-fruit vine. She pivoted around then ducked and rolled away, headed for the fence, and used the tiny imperfections in the wood to grab on and climb like a gecko.

She was dressed in a dark blue sweat suit. The fit was generous but not so loose that I couldn't see the muscles in her back and thighs. I felt her power as I yanked her down and knew instantly that she had trained hard for them. She went to the ground but jumped up, hands at the ready.

"Stop," I said, putting the sharp spear point to her throat.

Her eyes considered batting at the spear and ducking out of the way.

"Don't try it," I said. "This tip is Damascus steel from Indonesia. Very old but very sharp."

Her eyes went left and right, looking for a way out.

"You must have heard the old adage 'Don't fear the ten thousand kicks I've practiced one time, fear the one kick I've practiced ten thousand times.' Well, I've practiced the spear thrust a lot more than that. Been doing it since I was nine. Done the fly on the rice paper thing. Killed the fly but left the rice paper intact. And I've been practicing lately, just like you."

"I don't know what you're talking about."

"Sure you do. It's obvious."

"You're whacked."

"Fine. I'll just call the police."

"I'll say I'm your girlfriend and tell them you assaulted me."

The word girlfriend ratcheted it up a notch for me. "Like I'd date you."

That one hit home. Her eyes flashed. She grabbed the spear shaft and pulled, yanking me off balance, then launched a kick at my head. I blocked it, tried to grab her foot, and failed. She put a jab within a quarter inch of my chin.

"You think you're better than me," she panted.

"Solomon taught you to fight?"

"Not your business."

"You made it my business when you skulked into my yard."

She glared at me.

"This is stupid," I said. "We both know Solomon sent you. If he wants to talk to me, why doesn't he just call?"

She chewed her lip. "Who said he wants to talk to you?"

"All right then. I'll call my sister, the BSO detective, and tell her you broke in and we'll see who she believes."

She took a deep breath. "You asked me what sort of snake you could get him so he would talk to you. I've come with an answer."

"You snuck in to tell me about a snake?"

"It's a delicate subject."

"He doesn't trust me so he sent you to check me out."

She picked up the spear and threw it behind her. "*I'm* the one who doesn't trust you."

"Back at you. Tell me about the snake."

"You got something to drink?"

"This isn't a restaurant."

"You're curious and I'm dry. Make a good decision."

I liked her assertiveness right then, liked the way she played her hand even when it was empty, so I led her to the gazebo and went in for a glass of water. I half expected her to be gone when I came back, but she was still there.

"Solomon does venom research," she said, sipping daintily. "There's a snake he'd like to study, but he can't get it because it comes from Australia and Australian animals are illegal to import and he's got a little history with contraband."

"But you know a smuggler."

She took a sip of water. "Florida Fish and Game is on us 24/7."

"24/7 includes 3:00 in the morning?"

"Relax. Nobody followed me here. Now show me your house."

"I'm not sure I should invite you in."

"The indignant doctor thing doesn't suit you," she said. "I wonder why that is? Look. Doctors have money. I figured if you really were one, if you really had some dough, I could tap you for this project. You'd get your audience, he'd get his snakes, and I'd get some bonus points."

"Tell me about the white roses," I said.

She looked confused.

"White roses?"

"The white roses I saw at Solomon's shop."

"I don't know what you're talking about."

"Of course you don't. Never mind. You can come inside."

*   *   *

Darlene complimented the Asian furniture and the high ceiling, then stopped in front of an old black-and-white portrait I'd put up in the corner of the living room near the hallway to my home office. Slightly blurry, it showed Tie Mei holding a pair of binoculars and wearing her mysterious smile under a broad, white-brimmed hat. My father took the shot at the Pompano Park Race Track.

"This is her, right?"

"She loved horses."

"So where's your bag?"

"I beg your pardon?"

"Your kicking bag. Where is it?"

"I don't use one."

She frowned then popped up the stairs like a goat. She poked her head through a few doors, found my bedroom, and went straight for my closet. "Little shoe fetish going, huh?"

"I just like them shiny is all. You can't look neat if your shoes look beat."

"They're shiny all right. All four hundred of them."

"Get out of my closet."

She touched my safe with her foot but had no comment about it. Downstairs, she was just as nosy with the contents of the garage.

"No car?"

"I prefer two wheels."

"That Triumph's an old fart's bike."

"I wouldn't say that."

"Of course you wouldn't."

She knelt by the Thruxton and touched the polished engine casings—one of the best style points on the bike—then wiped off the smudge with her sleeve. "It's just so old-fashioned."

"It's simple. I like that about it."

She sniffed. "My high school boyfriend had a crotch rocket. A bunch of rich guys would get together and each put five or ten thousand on a race. He'd smoke 'em and take the pot every time."

"You ride on the back with him?"

"Just once."

"If I were on the track, I'd want a racer. On the street they just hurt your wrist, neck, and back. The high pegs cramp your legs, too, and shorten your hamstrings. No good for kicking."

"The practical, medical view of the donorcycle."

"Exactly."

We went back inside and she asked if I had anything sweet. I opened the chocolate cabinet. Strategically chosen to be far from the heat of cooking, it preserves my favorite indulgences: Richart box sets, Vosges truffles, Lake Champlain, MarieBelle, Chocolaterre, Chuau of Venezuela, Valrhona, and others.

"That's some stash," she said admiringly.

"Actually, I'm a bit low. I've been diving in more than I should."

"So pick one for me."

I did and as she took a bite a line of perspiration appeared above her lip. She spit into her hand.

"Nice. I show up in good faith and you try to poison me."

"It's very high end."

"Give me a Mars bar anytime."

"It's a Vosges Black Pearl truffle," I said. "Ginger, wasabi, sesame seeds, and dark chocolate."

"Wasabi like sushi mustard?"

I smiled.

"You're a cock."

I smiled again.

"No," she said. "I'm not kidding."

I popped what remained of the truffle into my mouth. "I love the contrast. Here, try this."

She narrowed her eyes.

"It's a trust game," I said.

"You lost when you gave me a hot mustard candy."

"This one's not like that."

She tried it. "All right," she conceded. "Not bad."

"Coconut and curry but mild."

She licked her fingers. "Like I said, you're weird and so is your taste in chocolates. And I don't like the way you're looking at me."

I didn't like it either. "Tell me about the special snake," I said.

"The Latin name is *Oxyuranus microlepidotus.* Some people call it the Inland Taipan. It's the most venomous thing that crawls and a mean son-of-a-bitch, too, from what I hear. Solomon says it'll chase you down just for looking at it."

"How can I go about getting it for Solomon?"

"You can give me five thousand dollars."

"I don't have that much here."

"I bet you do," she said. "I saw that big safe in your closet. You're telling me you don't keep enough hurricane emergency cash to get you out of town if you need to get out, enough to buy what you need when everyone else needs the same thing?"

"Wait here," I said. "Don't move."

When I came back down with the money, she was at the chocolate cupboard putting a few more truffles in her pocket.

"They'll get smashed if you carry them that way," I said. "Just take the box."

She put out her hand for the money. "I'll bring the animal to you when it comes in," she said. "Then we can deliver it to him directly."

"I don't want it anywhere near me."

"Of course you do," she said. "You want to impress him with your cool. That's what a *gongfu* warrior needs, isn't it?

"Now we're getting somewhere. So you admit he's your teacher."

She bit into a truffle and looked at me over fingers oozing chocolate. "You're pretty seat-of-the-pants with this aren't you? You assume he knows something because your nanny did. . . ."

"I didn't assume anything," I interrupted. "It was a calculated guess. They were close, they came over together, her commitment to the art was so total that if he didn't know something they wouldn't have had much to talk about."

"That presumes all kinds of things."

"All right, I'm flying by the seat of my pants, but I know he's a master. Admit it."

She grinned. "Beyond belief. He understands the music behind the moves."

"Thank you," I said. "Now it's time for you to go and for me to go back to bed."

She put the money down her blouse. "I'm your meal ticket," she said. "Cheap at twice the price."

With that she waved her fingers and walked out the front door without looking back. In the distance, I heard a door slam and a car start. When the sound trailed off, I went back inside and emailed Jordan another song: *Be My Baby* by the Ronettes. Recorded in 1963 and produced by Phil Spector, it pretty much said it all.

21

I wanted Khalsa to know I was firmly back in the saddle, so I rode to the hospital in the predawn darkness and made rounds. I stopped by to see Charlie Czarnecki first.

"Word is you're gonna build me a new skull," he said.

Normal color had returned to his face, and the bandages did a good job of hiding the fact that the top of his face had been pulled tight in the skull resection. He wasn't going to win any beauty contests, but he was presentable and seemed in a good humor.

"Not me—Dr. Tremper."

"I kinda think of you as my doc, seeing as how you were out there on the road, you know, the night it happened. One of the nurses told me you ride."

"Triumph Thruxton."

He frowned. "Slow."

"I've just been through all this," I sighed.

He brightened as I looked at his chart. "At least you're stylin' when you're ridin'."

"How are you feeling?"

"A little fuzzy," he said. "Sometimes I forget people's names, or I get up from the bed and find myself in the hall and don't remember why I went there or what I'm supposed to be doing. Not ready to get back on the bike, but that day will come."

"Maybe time to give it up."

He took hold of my elbow and dragged me close. His lips were dry from the medication and there was spittle on his chin when he talked. "Come on, Doc. Next best feeling to sex, right? Sometimes *better*, so long as a truck doesn't jackknife in front of you."

I had to laugh at that one.

He shook my arm fervently. "A brain doctor that rides—you gotta be a guy who understands."

"Your parents were dead set against you riding, right?" I asked.

"My father told me he'd never sleep through another night in his life when he found out I bought a bike."

"But that didn't stop you."

He shook his head. "Hell, my mother said the same thing—their problem, not mine."

"We don't live in a vacuum," I said. "This accident must have taught you that, if nothing else."

"Taught me to stay wide of semis," he said. "Taught me not to weave past white Porsches. Did they arrest that guy?"

"The accident happened behind him," I said. "I don't think the police can charge him."

"Some kind of justice system. You know a lawyer?"

"I do, but I don't think he does that kind of work."

Czarnecki finally loosened his grip on me. "Doesn't matter. I'll find one. I'm gonna sue that Porsche-driving prick down to a Hyundai."

I went to see Erkulwater next. He was sitting quietly in his bed, eyes closed, listening with a pair of fancy headphones. I touched his arm gently and he took them off.

"Dr. Pearl," he said. "I heard you helped out putting me back together."

"I gave a Dr. Weiss a hand, that's all. How are you feeling?"

"Well, you know."

"Neck's a bit stiff, huh?"

"I'm going to have to get used to checking my mirrors by turning my waist," he smiled, tapping his ample belly. "The good news is my middle could use the exercise. Tell me, will the fusion hold?"

"Steel plate screwed into your bones. Once your incisions are tight you can twist away. No reason to worry. What are you listening to?"

"Puccini's *Turandot*," he smiled. "I'm an opera buff. Can't say I like the sound of these headphones, though. Don't like transistors and I do not like CDs. I've got enough good old vinyl to never run out, and I listen through electrostatic speakers and vacuum-tube amplifiers. The confabulation of the sound is almost human. Voices, doctor, that's what does it for me. Voices of angels on earth."

"You listen in your truck?"

"Too noisy. But I think after this, I'm gonna retire. I figure the settlement with that Porsche driver should give me a nice nest egg. Tell you the truth, I've put a good bit away already. Got a piece of land in Hawaii ready and waiting."

"Have you talked to the police?" I said.

"Sure. They were here. Took my statement. Insurance company, too."

"And they say Boniface will pay?"

"That's his name?"

"He's an adult-film producer."

He laughed. "Perfect. Ah, what the hell. So long as he's loaded, I don't care if he's a ballerina."

"I don't think you're going to get any money out of him," I said. "The cops can't charge him. The accident happened behind him, and he had no contact with anyone."

"You shoot somebody, you don't touch them either," said Erkulwater. "I got a good lawyer working on it. The guy will pay or his insurance company will. Then I'll just take my wife and we'll move out there to volcano land and I'll crank up Caruso and Joan Sutherland and Milnes. You ever hear Sherrill Milnes?"

"Who is she?"

Erkulwater winced. "Not she. He's an American baritone. Famous for his Verdi."

David Weiss stepped in before I could learn more, and I left the good doctor to his postsurgical exam.

*   *   *

I found Tierra's father sitting by the little girl's side as she slept. He was a tall large-boned Cuban dressed in a fine summer-weight wool blazer and a simple white shirt open at the collar with French cuffs. A white part marked his thick shock of black hair and his beard was heavy with the night. His eyes went to my ponytail as he offered his hand.

"Oswardo Lopez-Famosa," he said.

"Dr. Pearl."

"You're the doctor who saved her. I owe you everything."

I thought about Kimberly. I looked at his hands. They were big and thick, but the fingernails were polished with a clear coat.

"I'm sorry about your wife," I said.

"Kimberly was not my wife."

"I'm sorry for your loss anyway."

Lopez-Famosa stroked Tierra's hair gently. "Be sorry for the child. It's terrible to lose a parent, but she will have everything, I promise you, Doctor. She will have love and she will have all she could want or need."

A nurse came in to check Tierra's vitals. "Don't wake her," I said.

The nurse shrugged, looked at the monitor, made a few notes in her chart, and left.

"It's a pet peeve I have," I told Lopez-Famosa. "Nobody gets any rest in the hospital, even when rest is what they need most."

"It is good to hear a doctor say such a thing."

I went to the window and pointed out past the parking lot to the Interstate. "I can see the spot where the accident happened," I said.

Lopez-Famosa stood up. He was half a foot taller than I am. "I was shocked at Kimberly's death," he said. "She told me her injuries were minor."

"They were. Something happened to her after the crash. A blow to her head burst a blood vessel in her brain."

"I don't understand."

"It's not complicated. Someone, or something, hit her head—hard."

I thought he paled, but it might have been the fluorescent light. "Kimberly was a well-intended woman," he said. "But she made poor choices."

"Was leaving you one of them?"

He clenched his fist and looked about to answer, but then Tierra stirred and he went to her and stroked her cheek. I flipped through her chart. She was recovering nicely.

"She shouldn't have had my daughter in a small car," Lopez-Famosa said. "I offered her a Suburban. Do you think this would have happened to Tierra in a Suburban? No, it would not."

I went a bit closer and tried to sniff him. Sometimes I did that. Tie Mei had taught me that an opponent's scent was a rich source of information. I got a whiff of cologne and something metallic. He had a strong physical presence. Wu Tie Mei would say he vibrated with *qi*.

"When did you last see Kimberly?" I asked.

"Are you married, Doctor? I see no ring on your hand."

"No."

"Then perhaps these questions are outside your area of expertise."

"They're not marriage questions, Mr. Famosa. Tell me, what's your business?"

He handed me a business card. "I manufacture men's clothing."

"My father had a haberdashery in the Gables," I said. "Right on Miracle Mile."

Glancing at my gusseted crotch chinos and my short-sleeve silk shirt decorated with little palm trees bending in a wind of stitches and thread he said, "Since you prefer the casual look, I can find you a nice 120 series suit that you can wear with an open collar. I would consider it a pleasure to help you upgrade your wardrobe. I promise my people will fit you as never before—all on me, of course."

I nodded. "Very nice of you. Have you told Tierra about her mother?"

"Yes," he said. "She took it remarkably well."

"She hasn't yet realized how alone she is. It'll take a while for that feeling to set in."

"She's not alone," he answered. "She has me."

22

All men know the tingle of underlying threat perceived, but for martial artists the tingle has taste. I licked it off my gums and tried hard to remember, from the confines of my karmic cage, in what life I had met Lopez-Famosa and to what cue I owed the intuition that he had killed Kimberly Jenkins. The big Cuban made me crazy. I wanted to punish him. Neptune came to mind, his voice taunting me with the warning that, as he predicted, I would soon join him behind bars.

The battle inside me was exhausting. My world grew dark and all my trappings hateful. Where once I had found satisfaction, I suddenly felt distress; where before I had seen beauty, I now saw limitation. Looking down at the Thruxton's narrow tank, it seemed insubstantial, unimaginative, and wrong. It was slow and underpowered, a relic of the past just like I am. Darlene was right and Charlie Czarnecki was, too. It was an old man's bike.

Maybe I could not change *me*, but I could certainly change my bike. With a tug on the handlebars I was heading south from the hospital instead of north, heading toward downtown Fort Lauderdale and a motorcycle dealership that carried exotic Italian machines.

A baby-faced salesman met me at the door. I doubted he was twenty years old. "Ready for something with a little more oomph?" he smiled.

I nodded. "But still comfortable."

He took me first to a Moto Guzzi police bike. "Shaft drive instead of the chain your Triumph has," he said. "Less maintenance but still that Old World charm. More comfortable, too, and with room for a passenger."

"I want sexy and speedy. Some young girl told me the Triumph was for geezers."

"Right this way," he said, leading me to a row of Ducatis.

I always notice when a Ducati rolls by. They sound marvelous and they look even better. The lineup did not disappoint. The kid picked out the sleekest model first. Bright red, it screamed speed.

"The Desmosedici," he said proudly. "It's their top of the line, based on their race bike, and represents the future of the marque. Ultra high-tech and will hit nearly two hundred miles per hour."

"How much?" I asked.

"If you have to ask, it's too much."

"And this?" I asked, moving down the line.

"Pure sporting heaven. Watch the Japanese bike riders drool as you sing by."

I put my hands on the bars and leaned forward. This much weight on my forearms would kill my elbows and wrists—not to mention my neurosurgeon's fingers—and the spasms were already starting in my neck from the way I had to lift my head to see in front of me.

"Not for long miles," I said.

"Not for around town either. That's the Sunday morning rider, pure and simple."

I chose a more upright model next and tried to envision Jordan on the back. Darlene's image popped up instead, and with it the feeling of her pressing against me. I shook it off.

"The Hypermotard 1100," the kid said. "Urban street fighter if ever there was one. Lean and mean for performance and handling. You read the bike magazines?"

"Sometimes."

"The journalists say this thing has the perfect engine."

The bars felt a bit wide to me, and when I leaned the machine slightly from left to right it was very, very light.

I noticed another group of bikes in the corner. The kid followed my gaze.

"1970s retro Café racer," he said.

"I love the look, but retro I've already got. I need a reliable everyday machine that has modern guts and speed and power."

The flicker in the kid's eye said nothing on the floor was right for me. I thanked him and left. Mentally I ticked Italian bikes off the list. I didn't want another Triumph and found Harley Davidsons too bulky. KTM made an excellent machine, but the brand brought Charlie Czarnecki's wild ride to mind, along with the image of his brain hanging down along his face. That left only the BMW. I knew the local shop because I'd been there hunting up parts for the vintage bike I'd restored and given my dad. A short bald salesman named Ernie greeted me and inspected the Triumph.

"Beautiful," he said.

"I like it, too."

"Triumph makes a nice bike. Since they went out of business and came back, the quality's much better. They finish parts on the inside, where you never even see them. You going to keep that beauty or trade it in?"

The guy was so smooth, I was already buying a bike from him; we were merely haggling over the details. "Trade it in," I said.

Ernie touched the fine finish work of the instrument panel and ran his hand lightly over the gas tank. "Want a little relief for your neck, too, huh? Any long trips in the cards?"

"No."

"High-speed rides across Alligator Alley in the wee hours before the Highway Patrol wakes up?"

"I'm too likely to hit a sleeping bird."

"Of course. What about dirt riding?"

"Not my thing."

We went inside. I could feel his eyes appraising me in a professional way.

"Lawyer?" Ernie inquired.

"Doctor."

"Had to be one or the other. You don't have an accountant's

fingers. Surgeon?"

"Bingo."

"Wait until you see the bike I've got for you."

He led me past touring rigs, sport machines, dirt models, and cruisers and finally stopped in front of a blue and white bike that was long and tall and fully as outlandish as a rolling Titanic.

"Meet the Megamoto H2," Ernie said, waving his hand like a vaudeville performer. "King of the street fighters—BMW's ultra-high performance city bike. Power, torque, handling; nothing can touch it. It's exclusive, mostly hand-built, all but impossible to find, and perfect for you."

"Expensive?"

"Obscenely."

"It's fantastic," I said. "But I can't buy it."

Ernie smiled. He'd heard the line before. "Sure you can," he said. "You deserve it, and if you blink it'll be gone."

"I ride with a lady on the back. It's only got one seat."

"I never trifle with matters of love," Ernie said. "Buy it and keep the Triumph for two-up rides."

I stroked the bike, noticing a hundred little touches only a hard-core biker would: the liberal use of exotic metal, the after-market-spec Akrapovich muffler, the sensuous curves of the painted blue frame, the exotic Ohlins shock absorber. Most of all I noticed the latest incarnation of the flat twin-engine design that had been conceived in 1923 and spoken reliability and class ever since.

"I'll throw in a handheld GPS," Ernie said. "On this machine, you might find yourself in places you've never been before."

I put a leg over. I felt like Superman.

"Sold," I said.

23

Big Steve Lovrich rebuilt The Grace Note from the ground up as a testimonial to the people who had died when the original owner burned the place down for the insurance money. As I pulled up for the opening celebration, I saw the bronze plaque by the door bearing the names of the dead. I hoped the victims were at rest, particularly the little girl who had died when she came in to tell her hard-drinking father it was time to come home.

Steve is a big, thick man—a bald-headed biker who carries his tiny fawn-and-white Chihuahua, Luna, around like a purse. He stood at the curb, surrounded by a small crowd that included a writer and a photographer from the local paper. Emma the Dilemma was beside him, looking as rebuilt as the bar. The acne scars I remembered were barely in evidence, telling me she'd had some work done. The club's star singer cropped her sunset hair like a Marine but had such innocent gray eyes and such a long creamy body that not even a bullet could take her for a soldier. I saw her fingers brush Steve's and was glad for the union.

"You look beautiful," I told her. "And the place does, too."

She kissed me softly. "Thanks for coming."

Steve pointed at my new ride. "That's some bike," he said. "Looks like a freakin' spaceship."

"I just bought it. Rode right over from the dealer."

"Dump the Triumph?"

"I'm holding on to it. The BMW folks are dropping it off tomorrow."

"How's Jordan?"

"Recovering," I said. "She bought herself a bicycle she pedals with her hands."

Inside, the place was modern and fresh, with Art Deco flourishes that included angular crystal shot glasses, brandy snifters, champagne flutes, and highball tumblers. The lampshades, exposed ceiling beams, and air-conditioning ducts were all painted in a subtle coordination of magenta and gray. Even the drink napkins were colored to match, with the monogram TGN.

Steve had built Emma a real stage—a raised platform big enough for a grand piano and a bud vase and a microphone, with room to swoon and sway left over. She shone as she posed for photos, and her happiness made me realize that not everyone is doomed to repeat his mistakes the way I am. Despite the hard knocks I knew she had taken—police record and all—Emma had the talent to pull off a new life and had obviously done the work required. I hoped that what I saw between her and Steve would strengthen and last. I thought of Jordan and felt a squeeze in my stomach.

Roan Cole came up behind me, Lysandra in tow.

"What're are you doing here?" I whispered to him. "I thought you hate Big Steve."

He waved his hand. "I came for Emma. Think she'll sing?"

"One song, maybe two. It's not a daytime joint."

"That monster ride parked outside your new toy?"

"Makes me feel like a new man," I said.

"Hear from Jordan?"

"I've been emailing her songs. Cuts for her iPod."

Lysandra squeezed my arm. "Music and flowers," she said. "And don't forget chocolate. Roan tells me you're good with chocolate."

Emma picked up the microphone and cleared her throat. With a small blues band behind her, she covered *King Bee* as if she wanted to leave her stinger in each and every one of us.

"Like a young Koko Taylor," Lysandra breathed when she was done and the applause went quiet. "Looking at her, you'd never imagine. I always thought a big voice needed a big chest."

"Lysandra," Roan sighed.

"I don't mean that. I mean, you know, that women who sing like that are usually fat. Emma's skinny as a rail."

We squeezed together at a high two-top, bar stools crowding. Roan ordered a beer and Lysandra had a Cosmopolitan. I opted for a booze-free O'Douls.

"Tierra's father came in to see the kid," said Roan.

"I met him."

"He wasn't married to the mother."

"No."

"How terrible that poor woman died," said Lysandra. "Roan told me all about the accident. What happened to the others?"

"The rider's going to need a lot of reconstruction," said Roan.

"He'll be all right," I said.

"How do you think we missed Kimberly's frontal contusion?"

"We didn't. It happened after she was discharged."

Roan stared at me. "What?"

"Someone knocked her down, or maybe she fell. She'll never tell us."

"You know this?"

"I reviewed the films with the scan tech. There was nothing there when she was admitted."

"Had to be the Cuban."

"The two of you are so clichéd," Lysandra sniffed. "Women have lives, you know. We keep men, even though no man wants to hear it. Maybe she was with five guys and one of them did it— nothing to do with the kid's father. Maybe the lady tripped and hit her head and didn't think it was important enough to mention."

"You keep men?" Roan repeated.

Lysandra lifted a lovely hand and stroked my friend's cheek. "Yes, darling. The female predator is alive and well."

"This could be the scariest day of your life," I told Roan.

Lysandra stroked him. "Don't worry baby, I'm not two-timing you. I'm just saying things are not always what they seem."

Roan grunted. "My money's still on the dad. Occam's razor.

The simplest answer is usually right. Personally, I'd bash the guy's teeth in."

"I'd like to see you use a sword sometime, Zee," Lysandra said. "Or maybe a spear. Roan says it's like watching ballet."

"I've got to go home," I said. "It's almost rush hour."

24

Dear Jordan,

I hope you won't be annoyed at me for saying I'm proud of the way you've taken to the hand bike. Your arms look great already. I've attached another MP3 file to this message for your iPod. This one's Bob Dylan's 1963 A Hard Rain's a-Gonna Fall. *I chose it because of the front coming in and because I'm a little blue right now and it's a forbidding song nearly as beautiful as you are. Even without the haunting melody—which also makes me think of you because you haunt my every waking minute and my sleeping minutes, too—the words are sheer poetry. Dylan may be last generation's poet laureate, but he has a subtle influence on everything we listen to as well.*

I've scanned a copy of a magazine article about a new steel forging technique. After seeing the state of your biceps, I'm certain you'll be back to your shop soon and figured you might want to look into this new technology. From what the article says, there's a way to put steel on steroids. While I can't imagine anything sharper and finer than what you forged for Quiet Teacher, I know you like to expand your horizons, and this addition of boron to the forging process seems quite clever to me. The makers put a specially designed tool into the blade and turn it to create frictional heat, and that creates micro-structural shearing that breaks down the granules of steel. I confess that despite all you've explained to me, I didn't realize steel was granular. Anyway, the smaller grains make the steel denser and better able to take an edge and hold it almost indefinitely. As the charts in the article show, the edge never needs to be sharpened, and it's incredibly resistant to staining as well.

*Both those properties mean it's perfect for a practice sword
I can use to hack up small trees, dowels, and other practice
targets.*

*I saw Roan earlier this afternoon, and he sends his love.
He's got a new girlfriend, and she's just what the doctor
ordered. John Khalsa wishes you his best, too. There are
some other things going on, but they're better told than
written so I'm going to call it an evening.*

Enjoy the music. Let me know if you'd like a visit.

With all my love,
Zee

After I hit the send button, I wandered slowly about the house,
not quite able to sit down. I sensed an emotional Humboldt
Current at work—powerful enough to rattle the continents within
me but so deep it barely showed at the surface. I closed my eyes and
walked with it, letting martial patterns emerge, curling my hands
into fists and uncurling them again, stepping high in what could
be a series of low front kicks, meandering ever closer to the false
picture frame in my bedroom behind which Quiet Teacher slept in
the secret compartment I built for it after Wanda made an official
police request it be retired.

I might have been a boozer dancing around his bottle or a
junkie romancing his stash. I opened the compartment and the
beautiful sword came into my hands so fast it seemed to fly on the
bat wings of its guard. I talked soothingly to it, caressing the ebony
handle and wiping the black diamond pommel with my thumbs. I
angled the etched black blade so the light picked up the wavy lines
of the folded Damascus steel. I let my addiction overtake me, and
I swooned with it.

"It's cutting season," I said out loud.

Then I dialed Oswardo Lopez-Famosa's office.

"Tech support here," I told his secretary. "We have Mr. Lopez-
Famosa's personal laptop upgrade ready."

"He didn't tell me anything about that."

"Bosses. How late can we show up?"

"He leaves at 5:30," she said.

"Can't make it by then. I'll email him an auto-install file."

"You sure he can do it himself?"

"Of course. It runs itself. Don't worry."

"Great," she said.

*   *   *

The clothing factory was a brick-red three-story building in the Miami Design District, a quick twenty minutes down I-95. On the Triumph I would have been buffeted by the backwash of eighteen-wheelers, moved from lane to lane by the crosswinds brought by a cold front coming through, and jarred by the rough road surface, but the pavement-devouring omnipotence of the high-tech BMW made the ride quick and smooth. Several times I had the feeling I was being followed, but there was no way to make anything of it in the sea of headlights behind me. When I got off the Interstate I stopped and started a couple of times, even did a U-turn without warning, but traffic went by without incident so I chalked up the feeling to combat jitters and pressed on to my goal.

Out front the company offered glass doors to the trade. In the back alley I found a heavy security door with a burgundy Bentley Continental GT Coupe parked beside it. At 5:20 I stashed the bike out of sight behind a dumpster and hunkered down to wait. My fingers felt glued to Quiet Teacher's ebony handle. I rejoicing in the dense, smooth surface and relished the grip of the grain. I checked my reflection in the blade, distorted and nearly invisible against the black lines. The bright angles of the blade narrowed my face, turning me into a wolf. I raised my snout and sniffed. The chic Design District sits on the southern edge of Little Haiti and picks up the pungent urban odor of burning trash overlain by the exotic aroma of bananas and spiced tomatoes. I found it delicious.

Trying to relax, I watched my breath. It was high and fast, and I let it drop and slowed it down and thought about how the desire to please Jordan had helped me smother my dark urges in the months since my battle with the Mafiya. She was my ballast, my heavily weighted keel. I'd climbed partway out of the pit by choosing medicine and healing to atone and grow, but alone again and with no word from Tie Mei I was the vigilance man once more.

I thought of Kimberly Jenkins. She had been young, talented, attractive, and kind. She had her whole life ahead of her and a child who depended upon her. Moral outrage readied my muscles and increased my awareness. I reminded myself of my victim's size. I cautioned myself against the power of his temper. Take it easy, I told myself as my heart began to pound. Stay calm and centered.

I was still talking to myself when Lopez-Famosa came out the back door. He wore a taupe seersucker suit and carried a Mark Cross briefcase. He hustled toward the Bentley, holding a remote ignition key. The car started, obedient as a vassal. I sprang forward, my face obscured by my helmet, Quiet Teacher in my hand. Lopez-Famosa froze. I closed in. He threw the briefcase at me. I twisted sideways and it flew past. He turned to run and I darted forward and sliced his Achilles tendon with my blade. He screamed and collapsed.

"Hesitation does it every time," I said. "Just that one little moment. That's the thing to beat."

"My God, what have you done? What is this? Who are you?" He was panting, cradling his ankle. Blood soaked between his fingers.

"You know," I said.

I tried to keep my voice low, but he recognized me despite the helmet.

"The doctor," he said, wheels turning, angles of intellection creeping in past the pain. "The brain surgeon."

"And you know why I'm here."

The pain in his ankle worked its way through his brain, and a slow dawn took his face, replete with heavy clouds. "A sword," he said. "Are you completely crazy?"

"Yes."

He licked his lips. "People are coming out of the building," he said. "They're coming through the door."

I put Quiet Teacher to his chin. "Get up."

He glared at me, put a hand on his car, and lifted himself up.

"Move," I said.

He grimaced, took one step, and collapsed with a cry.

"I said get up."

"Somebody will see us," he groaned.

"It's dark. Nobody's going to see anything. Now walk."

Again, he tried to put weight on his severed ankle. He screamed louder this time.

"Hop like a bunny," I said.

"I can't."

I touched his neck with my cold steel, right below the ear. He hopped.

"You could lose a few pounds," I said. "Your suits would fit better, too. Tell me, did you hit her or push her?"

"She fell," he said. "I swear, she tripped and fell."

I put the sword to his throat. "This blade is so quiet and sharp I can take your head off with less than a whisper. So sharp I scarcely know the damage I'm doing—not good when I'm so close to all those blood vessels feeding your brain."

"We were arguing about Tierra," he moaned. "I told her I was going for full custody and she went crazy."

"You threaten to take her kid because she has a car accident and you don't think she has a reason to be mad?"

"What do you want? For God's sake, tell me what you want. Can't be money, a man like you."

"I want to hear it all."

Lopez-Famosa leaned against the trunk of his car. He was panting now. The pain in his leg increasing by the second as the initial shock of the clean cut began to wear off.

"Call an ambulance," he said.

"I said I want to hear it all."

"You're sick. There's something wrong with you."

I nodded. "Oh, yes. Most definitely there is. That's why I want to hear all of it. Do it like sportscast. Tell it like you're on TV."

His good leg couldn't hold him any longer and he slid down the wall. There was glass on the floor of the alley and he sat in it not five feet from his expensive car. The glass cut through his suit and into his buttock. His cut foot flopped to the side. The Bentley's taillight showed the blood soaking through his trousers. He looked at it incredulously.

"You have to help me."

I touched Quiet Teacher to the inside of his thigh. "This is the line of the femoral artery," I said. "No ambulance can help you if I cut you there. You'll bleed to death before you even hear the siren."

"If you kill me, Tierra will have nobody. You have to help me."

"The sportscast."

His eyes seemed glued to my blade. I was not surprised. The double-edge sword is just a long dagger with a short handle, and Jordan's grind line down the middle—perfectly bisecting twenty-eight inches of Damascus steel—is a glorious demonstration of fevered intent.

"She called to tell me about the accident. I went to her place to see Tierra."

"Play by play," I said. "That's the way I want the scene."

"Why?" he whispered.

"So you can relive it."

He looked up at me with something new in his eyes. "Don't you think I relive it every minute of every day?"

"Relive it again. Every excruciating detail."

He shook his head. I drew a tiny line in the flesh of his legs. He touched his blood with his fingers then started to talk.

"He goes into the kitchen. She is standing by the stove. 'You're an unfit mother,' he says. 'It wasn't my fault,' she answers. 'You were driving in the rain in that shitty car,' he says. 'It's not a shitty car and the accident wasn't my fault. The judge won't see it that way. Spend your time praying not hating,' she says. 'Pray for our little girl.'"

"She said that?" I interrupted. "She told you to pray not hate?"

Lopez-Famosa nodded. His chin sank to his chest. There seemed no energy for anything beyond resignation.

"Go on."

He started to, but just then a police car paused in traffic at the end of the alley. Lopez-Famosa made a vain, pathetic attempt to wave and shout, to reach out and grab the car with his hand like a child trying to leave his thumbprint on the moon. The traffic light changed and the cop drove off and Lopez-Famosa collapsed to the pavement, weeping with guilt and rage and impotence. "I didn't hit her that hard," he whispered. "I didn't mean for anything to happen. I still don't understand it."

"She hemorrhaged," I said. "A vessel burst in her brain. Sometimes it doesn't happen immediately after injury. Get back to the sportscast."

"He grabs her shoulders. She breaks away. He yells, 'You almost killed my little girl.' She yells at him that he's distorting the facts and that it won't work and that he'll never get control of her or Tierra again. She screams at him to stay away from Tierra and to get out of her house. She keeps yelling at him to get out of her house."

He stopped.

"The rest," I said. "The end of it."

He pulled his foot up and looked at it dangling. "He punches at her face," he said. "She ducks. He hits her in the forehead."

"The mother of your child," I said.

Far away, there was the sound of a helicopter. Lopez-Famosa

glanced up at the sky, for a moment thinking it might be deliverance from aloft, but the sound faded and the light in his eyes did, too, and he just stared at me.

"Kill me," he said. "I deserve to die."

"No," I said. "Better you should live with what you're feeling right now and know it will never go away."

"Cut my other ankle," he said. "Cripple me forever."

"You've done that to yourself."

"You're evil," he said. "A cruel doctor."

"Yes," I said.

He threw his neck back and screamed. The sound struck the windows of his factory and reverberated down the alley. For the first time, I worried someone might find us.

"Cut me again!" he yelled.

And then he had my leg. Taken off-guard by his fit of remorse, I hadn't seen it coming. He yanked me off-balance and I went down. He moved his mouth to my gastrocnemius, the big muscle of my calf, and I felt the heat of his breath and as he began to bite down. The Kevlar fabric woven through my riding jeans protected me some, but the feel of his teeth was painful. I hit him on the top of the head with Quiet Teacher and felt the hard face of the black diamond on the pommel sink into his fontanel, the spot on the skull that is soft in newborn babies.

He exhaled, loosening his mouth a tad, and I pulled away. My first thought was AIDS, but even without it human bites are among the dirtiest in the animal kingdom. I raised my blade, ready to finish him, but let it down easy as he gurgled and looked up at me, dazed.

"Tierra mentioned an aunt and uncle and a cousin attending a recital," I said.

"They live in New Jersey."

"Tell the court you can't care for her. Say you're too busy with work. Send her up north."

Lopez-Famosa put his head in his hands. "You're sending me

to hell."

"I hope so."

"Why would you do this?"

"It's my nature. And know this: an autopsy can match your fist to Kimberly's head even now. If you go to them about me, I'll make sure I order one. I'll tell Tierra about you, too. I'll tell her you killed her mother. So see a private physician for your wound. Someone you can trust. No official report of the injury. Do you understand?"

I sheathed my blade when he nodded slowly, looking at the ground.

I walked to my bike and powered away to the sound of those two big German cylinders pummeling each other like boxers.

25

Back home, I sniffed around for the lingering aroma of almonds, for it has been true that Tie Mei knows when I draw blood and she comes to me. The house was stuffy, but I found no telltale fragrance. I threw the windows open wide and let the sea breeze blow through while I cleaned my sword. I opened the bottle of antipsychotic pills Diomedes had prescribed and took one. I knew I'd get a dry and fuzzy mouth for my trouble, and I knew my hands might give a tremor, but I wanted—needed—another view of my world.

Thus fortified, I checked the wound Lopez-Famosa had given me. His bite had not broken my skin, but the area was tender and I knew it would bruise. I used another of Tie Mie's liniments, this one an antiseptic, and felt my flesh tingle as the herbs soaked in. I used downward strokes along the meridian lines to massage the area, hoping to lessen damage to the underlying muscle.

I was so keen on the work that I did not hear Darlene pull up, and I gave a start when I saw her staring at me through the window.

"You're jumpy for a kung fu jock," she said.

I didn't want to tell her I was half expecting Wanda to come and cart me off. "Are you familiar with the concept of a doorbell?" I asked.

"Wow, you're uptight. Tension's bad for your blood pressure. You should know that. Is that a new bike?"

I opened the front door for her and saw she had a box under her arm.

"Just bought it."

"It's cool," she said. "I didn't know BMW made bikes."

"For more than eighty years," I said. "They were among the first."

"I dig the color scheme. Is it fast?"

"Yes. What's in the box?"

She started to answer, but the phone rang. It was John Khalsa.

"I heard you stopped by to check the patients," he said.

"Done it a couple of times."

"You ready for regular office hours? I have some referrals."

"Born ready."

"Good, because the board has cleared you all the way."

"Thank you."

"Perhaps we can have a meal sometime soon."

"That would be great, John."

When I put the phone down, I saw that Darlene had taken a snake from the box and was dangling it precariously from a telescoping hook. It was brown and narrow and nervous.

"See how alert it is?" she said. "It's not just the most venomous snake in the world, it's smart and quick and mean, too."

"Great news. How about you put it away."

"I just wanted you to see what your money bought," Darlene said.

"I am consumed by pride over what is obviously a killer deal."

"Sarcasm is an unattractive trait," she said. "Perhaps that's why it suits you."

"You're very nice. Would you put the snake away now?"

She flashed that familiar smile. "Two drops of his venom can kill a quarter million mice."

"Sounds like overkill. Please put it back in the box."

"The desert it comes from is so hot and dry and dangerous that the prey has to drop dead quickly if the snake is going to be able to find it and eat it—thus the crazy venom. Death occurs almost instantly."

"The best way to go. If you don't put it away, I'm going to have to leave my own house."

"The alertness and the venom and the aggressiveness all work together. Seeing it in person, I can understand why Solomon wanted one so badly. He loves this species."

Right then, the snake came off the hook and glided across the floor and under the couch. I took a step backward. Darlene hopped up on the coffee table.

"I begged you," I said.

"Oh, be a man, will you?"

"Get it back right now."

"I'm trying, okay?"

"Trying? You're standing on the table."

I went to the couch and bent to lift it.

"Watch your fingers under the edge," she warned. "It'll go for them for sure."

My heart pounded. The human bite on my leg ached. I didn't want a worse one on my hand. "You ever notice how the universe works in twos and threes?" I asked.

"What?"

"For instance, you hear the name Xenon for the first time in your life and then all you hear is Xenon the noble gas, Xenon the Greek philosopher, the Theban general."

"Theban?"

"Never mind. What happens if we get bitten? There's an antivenin, right? A serum?"

"There's a venom center in Miami. I don't know if they have anything for this snake. I've never heard of anyone keeping one around here, so they probably don't. Regular taipan serum might work, or help anyway, but that's not my area."

"Not your area? You brought the damn thing into my house. Now get it back in the box."

Darlene gingerly stepped down from the table and pushed the couch with her foot. No sign of the snake. She pushed it a little more. Still nothing. She slid it to the middle of the room, but no snake was visible.

"It's gotten into the upholstery," she said.

Together we turned the couch over. The cushions fell off and the taipan moved quickly toward the hall.

"If it makes it to my study, it'll hide behind my bookshelves and we'll never get it out," I yelled.

"Get me the styrofoam box," she ordered.

I came back with it just as snake reached the study door. It struck with an open mouth and she fended, hooked it, and dropped it into the box and covered it in one smooth motion.

"Let's go see Solomon," she said.

26

I sat with the Styrofoam box between my legs.

"How does it feel having the girl drive for a change?" Darlene asked.

"I'm more concerned with this snake between my legs."

"You best mean the taipan."

"I'm too scared to mean anything else, but you know you love me. You follow me everywhere."

She shifted in her seat. Her short dress crept up showing muscular thighs and the edge of frilled panties. "I don't need to follow you to know you like to drive," she said.

"Where does Solomon live?"

"Victoria Park. A couple of blocks off Las Olas."

Victoria Park is yuppie central. Close to the beach and east of Federal Highway, it is an extremely desirable neighborhood popular with gay couples, ad execs, writers, and artists. Even after last year's storm the vegetation was still tropical and lush.

"I expected he'd live somewhere out west by the shop."

"He's smart and he's Chinese. He knows Victoria Park is prime real estate."

So Solomon had become a man of substance. He had arrived on American shores with nothing but had utterly changed his circumstances. Tie Mei used to tell me that change was the basic ingredient of life. Watch how you react to it, she said. Only by relaxing into the flow of life's changes can you set yourself free. Solomon had found business success and Emma had found love. Maybe there was hope for me. Maybe I could escape my repeating pattern, too. Like an alcoholic swearing off booze, I told myself I would not go out with my blade again. Lopez-Famosa was the last one. It was a hollow bit of self-deception and it made me vaguely ill.

"I bet you're glad you found him," I said.

"I bet you are, too."

* * *

It took us twenty minutes to get to Solomon's bend in the road. His house was old and surrounded by the kind of old trees and mature plantings I remembered from my father's Miami neighborhood.

"He's done a ton of work on the property," Darlene said, ringing the bell.

I looked around while we waited. The house had a stately feel, with shutters and columns and a birdbath in the front yard. In it's water I could see the partial moon, distorted by the ripples the wind made. Dust devils danced and the air took newspapers aloft. One clung to my leg like a spoiled child.

It took Solomon a long time to come to the door, and when he did I could see why. He was in yellow silk pajamas and his eyes were crusted by sleep. I glanced at my watch. It was just 9:00 P.M.

"I'm sorry to wake you," Darlene said deferentially.

"Well, what is it?"

"We have a present for you," she said. "A gift."

His eyes rested on me without expression then shifted back to her.

"We?"

Darlene nodded. "May we come in?"

He moved aside. I noticed that his silk slippers matched his outfit and that the tops of his feet, like his hands, were white and fine and unlined and delicate.

The foyer had textured yellow wallpaper, a chandelier, and a high ceiling. Behind it I could see traditional Chinese furniture, tapestries, and porcelain pieces on pedestals. A lifesize bronze statue of Guan Gong, patron saint of the martial arts, glared at me from an alcove.

"The statue is beautiful," I said. "And I smell incense. Cedar mixed with mugwort?"

"I retire early," Solomon replied. "The morning is my time."

"The incense is for the snakes, right? It calms them?"

Solomon's eyes narrowed. "What do you know of snakes?"

"We brought you something," Darlene said.

She handed him her hook and pushed the trashcan forward with her toe. "The doctor's gift to you. Please open it with care."

Solomon extended the hook with a practiced motion, taking the lid off the box and holding it as a shield just the way she had.

The snake came up like a jack-in-the-box and, once airborne, twisted in flight so as to aim right at its new owner. My heart went to my throat and Darlene sprang away, but Solomon just laughed, threw down the hook, and snatched the animal out of the air. I had never seen anyone move like that, not even Tie Mei. His fingers laced about the snake, playing the scales like notes. Through it all, the snake slithered and coiled but seemed utterly disinclined to bite.

"*Oxyuranus microlepidotus*," Solomon cried, his mood utterly transformed. "How is this possible? How did you get him?"

"I have another in a box in my car," said Darlene.

I jumped at the news. She grinned. "It was in the trunk."

"Bring it in at once," Solomon said.

She was back a moment later with the cooler. "Dr. Pearl funded the expedition," she explained. "He is very keen to spend time with you and I thought this would make you happy."

Solomon Yu unsealed the cooler and hooked the second deadly serpent, gracefully depositing it into his waiting palm. "Female," he said.

For a moment he had both snakes in his hands. They moved quickly, climbing his arms, circling his neck, their tongues flicking into his ear canals.

"You said these were the missing keys to your research," Darlene said.

"Yes, yes. Exactly so. Now please bring me water. They are terribly thirsty."

He ushered us into the house and sat with me on a richly upholstered couch. Darlene brought a dish and Solomon put it down on a lacquered temple table and lowered the snakes one by one until their tongues were wet. Side by side they immersed themselves in the liquid, their powerful jaw muscles pulsing as they drank. When they had their fill, Solomon lifted them up carefully and put them gently back into the box.

"You may go," he said to Darlene.

I could see she was hurt by the dismissal, but she bowed and backed away.

Solomon offered me a slight but formal bow. "I am grateful to you. The taipans are magnificent."

"They were Darlene's idea. I'm glad they please you. I hope you liked Tie Mei's mask as well. Her fragrance . . . "

"She used medicinal oils," he said. "If they are sealed, they last a long time."

"I know. She taught me herbal medicine. I recorded many of her formulas and use them in my medical practice."

"Good. It would be a shame to lose them."

"Being an herbalist yourself, you must have many more."

He crossed his legs and waved his hands and pushed back into the couch pillows. "Tell me, Doctor. What is it that you want from me?"

It was the opening I'd been waiting for, and the floodwaters rushed through. "I want to hear about her," I said. "Everything and anything you can tell me."

"She might as well have been your mother. How can you not know her far better than I did?"

"She shared nothing of her past."

"Ah," he said.

"When did you last see her?"

"I came to your home one day when you were a small child,

and she told me not to come back."

"You never saw her after I grew up?"

He looked at me evenly. "She was with your father."

Right then I felt his pain over her, and I wanted to tell him that she was all right, that she was in a safe place and watching us all, that she had come to me as a ghost and smelled of almonds no less intoxicating than her medicinal potions. I wanted to tell him that she been with me through the hardest time this life had yet offered but that recently she had been very, very quiet.

"She taught me more than herbs," I said. "She taught me weapons and forms. She taught me her *gongfu*."

"So you said. You have yet another treasure from her. What does that have to do with me?"

I sighed. "Her *gongfu* must have had a tradition behind it," I said.

"Suppose it did?"

"That tradition was part of her and now it's part of me. Trouble is, I don't know the first thing about it."

"You're an American physician," he said. "That makes you the high priest of your society. What could you possibly want with Chinese *gongfu*?"

His look, his feigned casualness, the way he folded his hands— it all said everything was riding on my answer.

"The American culture you mention lacks coherence," I said. "The founding principles have been washed away by a sea of consumption. The martial philosophy Tie Mei shared with me gave me an anchor. It helped me understand the way the world works and gave me roots and a center. And that's just the mental part. Physically, most Americans tear their bodies down with exercise. Hers made me feel younger and stronger every day. I'd like to learn more."

Solomon stood. "That was a pretty speech, even for a doctor, but it had no substance and neither do you. Thank you for the gift. It was a very nice gesture. Please leave now."

"Wait a minute," I said.

He had been walking toward the door, no doubt to open it for me. He stopped.

"Yes?"

"You're right. It was bullshit. The truth is, I use the art badly. I hurt people with it. The bloodlust takes me and I lose all reason and I can't stop."

"Now this is more interesting," he said. "What do you mean you cannot stop?"

"I get these urges to use what I know and I find circumstances that justify my urges. People have suggested therapy and medication, but I've tried that and it doesn't work. I'm hoping you will train them out of me."

"You think you are sick, see a doctor."

"I *am* a doctor. I'm going to lose everything, including the woman I love, because I can't stop myself."

"You think the martial path has the answer."

"I need to kill the thrill," I said, growing more agitated with each passing moment. "A martial-arts master has tranquility and peace and self-restraint and a disinterest in violence because he knows it's low and he has nothing to prove. Tie Mei stopped my training when I went off to school and then she died and I couldn't continue."

"Kill the thrill," he repeated.

"I'm addicted to violence," I said. "I'm stuck halfway up the mountain."

Looking at me hard he said, "Every teacher knows better than to teach a student with low character. If you want to stay that hand of yours, become a monk."

"It's too late to become a monk. Believe me, I've considered it. It would be the easy way out but it's not the answer. I need to make amends for so much."

"You have a discipline problem."

"All right! But I'm a worm and I need to be a butterfly. I need to shed who I am and grow. I need to transform!"

He sat down on the couch again. He put his head in his hands and rocked back and forth like men I'd seen at an orthodox synagogue. Then the rocking stopped. It was as if something had suddenly occurred to him. He sprang from the couch, tucked the snake boxes under his arms, and motioned for me to follow. He led me through a disorienting warren of corridors and stairs. Both wallpaper and floors varied drastically from room to room. It was a house to make a rushing man seasick.

"The place was built in stages," Solomon explained. "It started out as a bungalow and then a series of additions made it the home it is today. We are heading for the basement now. Not the usual thing to have a level below ground here in Florida, but there is a slight rise in this part of Victoria Park—the remnant, I am told, of an ancient coral reef."

"Tie Mei had my father buy a number of pieces of furniture like the ones you have," I said.

"I remember them," he said. "An armoire was one, yes? And a long, low table?"

I nodded. "I still have them."

"Good pieces are built to last."

We stepped into what was obviously a training hall. A heavy bag anchored by chains leading to steel plates was bolted to the floor and a small, suspended speed bag hung from the ceiling. There was a latex torso atop a water-filled base that was covered by colored dots at his vital acupuncture points. Around a large, clear, central area, presumably for forms practice, were racks containing spears, swords, poles, axes, and myriad other martial weapons. A mural of a mountain scene covered one wall.

"We are behind the garage," Solomon said. "I had a contractor tunnel into the rise a little bit. It's stable because of the limestone, though it required some shoring."

"Did you paint the mural?"

"I did."

I used my finger to lightly trace the outline.

"It's an energy pathway," I said, showing how the water curled and the land rose and the flow of the stream above had a certain, spinal shape. "The governing and conceptions vessels from Chinese medicine. It's the human body interpreted."

"Very good."

"Tie Mei shared some theory with me. Do you teach big classes in here?"

"Big? Certainly not."

"But you teach private students like Darlene."

"She told you that?"

"She wouldn't say anything, actually."

"The taipans were expensive, yes?"

"Yes."

"Participating in their importation involved legal risks. Did Darlene tell you that?"

I couldn't help thinking how advanced and free of accent Solomon's clear and formal English was compared to Tie Mei's simple, heavily foreign way of speaking.

"She let me know she was having them smuggled in. I gather I could go to jail for being a part of it."

"Yet you agreed."

"So will you teach me? I have a thousand questions."

"Yes, but it is late now. I was asleep when you arrived."

"I'm sorry. I'll let you get back to bed. But before I go, can you show me something to inspire me? Tie Mei inspired me every day."

"I remind you I am not Tie Mei."

"Just a small demonstration," I said. "Please."

In response, Solomon took my hand in his. His touch was smooth but very, very heavy. His hand felt like a piece of cool marble, polished to a high, white shine. He placed my palm against his breastbone, which felt dense and superficially soft, but hard one level deeper.

"You know how to use a stethoscope, yes?"

"Of course," I said.

"Your hand is your stethoscope. Tell me what you feel."

It was an intense moment. I hadn't been able to get this man to even speak to me, and now, thanks to the purchase of a pair of dangerous snakes, I was standing alone with him in his private training room with my hand on his silk pajamas. He was not smiling anymore. In fact, his gaze was hard and dark and it nauseated me slightly. Some of the old Chinese texts Tie Mei translated said the eyes could emit *qi*, but I had never felt such a thing before. I wanted to ask him about it, but I did not dare.

"You are thinking, not feeling," he said. "Pay attention. Banish your thoughts. Quiet your mind. Focus on your sensations."

I closed my eyes to avoid his gaze and did as he bade me. I like to think my fingertips are more sensitive than the average Joe's, but what I felt didn't make sense. Solomon seemed to be disappearing beneath my hand. I stared at the patch of fabric on his chest, confirming visually that I was in contact with him.

"You're sinking," I said.

"Dropping my *qi*. How do you feel?"

"Unsettled."

"That is because I am underneath you. I could overwhelm you at will. Fighting me would be like trying to stand atop a beach ball. I am under your feet, so nothing you can do to me has any effect. Push like you mean it and you will see that you are the one that moves, not me."

I pushed and the result was as he predicted. I tried again, shoving downward this time, figuring to get under him the way he claimed to have gotten under me. The result was the same. I tipped forward. I tried left and I tried right, but no matter the angle I just popped off in the direction I was pushing while he seemed as rooted as an oak. I gave a sudden upward shove seeking to disconnect him from the ground and found myself flying downward. I landed in a twisted heap at his feet.

"Thank you, again, for the snakes," he said. "Now it is time for me to rest."

I had found a teacher.

27

Try as I might, I could not sleep that night. My palms were sweating and I had a twitch in my eye. I wondered if it was the medication or some pernicious consequence of Solomon's demonstration. I rose from my bed, parted the curtains, watched the broad, white-lipped tongues of seawater lick the sand, and imagined the tiny crabs scuttling back and forth across the littoral. Nature was clicking along, everything was in its place, but as so often before, Morpheus would give me no peace.

I ached for Jordan's smile and her touch and the sound of her breathing. I yearned just to talk to her, to tell her about my day, about my new master and his snakes and his underground studio and how strange and powerful he was and my hopes and dreams of what I might learn from him. I knew she really wanted to hear all of it and that she cared about me the way I cared about her, that we were meant to be together despite her admonition to stay away. I knew her ban ran against the true current of her heart. Her limitations were nothing to me; I knew she would get better, would walk and skip and boogie and run. I just wanted to be with her when she did.

I returned to bed and screamed her name into the pillow, wrestling the duvet across my face to keep my private agony from the ears of possums and geckos and roaches and rats. Her absence was a knife turning inside me, cutting, its target always unpredictable and always near. Nothing could be right without her. None of what was happening for me—neither the blossoming of my surgical career nor the appearance of a new teacher—felt right without her there to share it.

I rose and went to the phone and called her. Amanda answered, sounding fogged.

"Hello?"

"It's Zee for Jordan."

There was a pause and the sound of shuffling furniture.

"Xenon. It's after midnight. Jordan and I are asleep. When are you going to get it through your head that she doesn't want to talk to you?"

"Please," I said. "I just want to know how she's doing."

"Better without you," she said, breathing heavily.

"I understand you're angry," I said. "But we've been through this. It's not about me. . . . "

"Of course it's about you!" Amanda hissed. "You went up against the mob and they punished you by crippling my daughter. You want redemption. Stop calling here. This is harassment. I mean it. We don't want to hear from you."

She hung up abruptly. I was torn between anger and sorrow, between understanding what she was feeling and wondering if she wasn't poisoning Jordan against me every waking minute and perhaps sleeping minutes, too. I had this momentary vision of her bending over my slumbering love, whispering, "It's all Xenon's fault" into those beautiful, delicate ears.

Powerless, I went to the computer and composed an email. I started to pour out my feelings but appended a song file instead, a Joni Mitchell classic from 1974, the selection colored by my inability to touch Jordan's heart. I sent off *Help Me*, went back to bed, and managed to fall asleep.

*   *   *

My pager rang early and I was glad it did. I dressed quickly and went downstairs, where I discovered a delivery truck pulling into my driveway with the Thruxton. I signed a receipt, put it away in the garage, and rushed off on the BMW without eating breakfast, popping an unintentional wheelie at the stop sign at the end of my street.

Vicky Sanchez met me at the elevator. "They told me to wait for you," she said. "Khalsa got into trouble with a patient, called Weiss to help, and they're both in over their heads. Hope you're up for it; you look like hell. What's that, a black eye?"

"Late night," I mumbled. "Is there a muffin or a bagel around? I haven't eaten."

Rolling her eyes, Vicky went off and came back with a coconut-dusted doughnut.

"What's the latest news of Galina?" I asked, wolfing it down.

"She's onto some Japanese video-game toy—a little baby that needs constant feeding."

I nodded. It made sense to me that a child whose family had been violently ripped from her would try to reconstruct one of her own, even if in miniature and in plastic.

I headed for the locker room. To my surprise my name was up on the door next to Weiss's. It felt good to see it there. I changed quickly, scrubbed, and went into the OR.

Even without the radar of a brain surgeon and the sensitivity of a warrior reborn three hundred times I could sense the sharp edge of catastrophe unfolding. Khalsa, ever the picture-perfect fashion plate, looked like he'd been through a carwash. His surgical cap was soaked with sweat—his thick, dark hair showing through the blue paper. He and Weiss were crowding the space above the skull of a middle-aged woman whose legs were kicking spasmodically on the table. A technician stood nearby, manning a cart laden with electronic devices, and another doctor in scrubs stood next to the patient holding her hand.

Khalsa looked at me with visible relief. "Thanks for coming," he said.

Weiss glanced up at me, took a deep breath, and stepped back from the patient. "It's a DBS," he said.

Deep brain stimulation is a treatment on the frontier of technology and is most often used to treat advanced Parkinson's disease but also sometimes depression, a disorder of involuntary tics and vocalizations called Tourette's syndrome, and even severe obsessive compulsive disorder. The idea is to position an electrode deep within the patient's brain and use it to send electrical signals to control the symptoms.

Khalsa's patient had a frame attached to her head. The frame looked like the lower half of a Greek battle helmet stabilized around the chin and built up on top of the head. Its purpose was to steady the insertion of electrodes, which are pushed through a burr hole drilled in the skull and precisely placed according to a stereotactic map created by an earlier MRI of the patient's brain. An amplifier connected the probes to speakers on the electronics cart. Software analyzes the electrical signals from the probe. When the signals match the kind of chatter an afflicted area generates, the speakers bark with static. The sound is the surgeon's sign he's on the right track.

Khalsa took me aside. "Dave's having a bit of trouble getting all the way in," he said.

"I'm not having trouble getting it in," Weiss hissed, mindful that the patient could hear him. "I'm having trouble finding the right structure for the patient's tremors. There's not a peep out of the speakers.

"He's made two passes and he's not sure where to make the third," Khalsa said.

I gave Weiss a look that tried to communicate that I understood how humiliating Khalsa could be. "It's a tough one," I said. "Finding the exact spot is a crapshoot anyway. I've been through this plenty of times."

"We thought maybe you could do it," Khalsa said.

"*He* thought that," said Weiss.

This was no opportunity; this was a minefield. If I succeeded, I'd humiliate Weiss. If I failed, the patient wouldn't be helped. I didn't like the odds and I didn't like the options. I tried to think of another way.

"A real expert in this trained me a couple of years ago," I said.

"Maybe you've heard of Alem Benabid."

Weiss's eyes went wide. "The Ben gun guy?"

"I went to Europe to do an intensive with him," I said.

"Nobody told me you knew Benabid," muttered Weiss.

I started to sift through my tray. It was in the corner of the room. I was pretty sure I had what I needed there, but it had been a while. The neurologist came over to me. She was pretty and willowy and tall. I'd met her before but couldn't think of her name.

"I'm Karen MacDougal," she said. "I take care of Jordan now."

I blinked. "You take care of Jordan?"

"She came to me about two weeks ago. I thought you knew."

Two weeks told me that Jordan had known well ahead of time that she was going to cut me loose. I felt like I'd been kicked in the solar plexus and struggled for breath behind my mask and gown.

"There are some promising nerve growth factor trials going on," MacDougal continued. "I'm sure you know about them."

I nodded, not looking at her. "And this patient?"

"Her name's Penny. She's a CPA with two boys in the Marines. She's been wrestling with the Parkinson's for years. This procedure is a last resort—she's dystonic, has pain, can't hold things, bends over and falls while walking, can't feel her arms half the time. We've got her quieted down, but the way her legs are kicking she might as well be running track."

Dystonia meant Penny's spasms were uncontrolled, making her life a living hell.

"I'm sure the DBS will help."

"If we can find the right structure, maybe."

I continued to pick through my tray. At last I found what I was looking for and took the equipment over to the field. The Ben gun looks like a plus sign. It's a guide that allows more than one electrode to be manipulated at the same time. I fitted the electrodes into the gun. Before I did anything, I introduced myself to Penny. Her head was locked in position, but she followed me with her eyes.

"We'll get this figured out," I told her. "We're the kind of guys who don't quit until we do. You're going to feel a lot better. This technique really helps."

She smiled a gentle, long-suffering smile. "They drilled five holes in my head," she said.

"Six, actually. Five for the head brace to hold everything perfectly still in case you move and one last one to get into your brain. But don't worry, they'll all heal just fine."

"My boys need me," she said. "They're fighting in the desert over there."

"They'll have you."

"Not just alive but stable. One got wounded yesterday. Shot in the belly, out near Mosul. I found out right before I came in. They said he wasn't in pain, but I know they lie. I need to be able to take care of him."

I figured her calm was the work of the light anesthesia, but MacDougal, not similarly dulled, paled at the news.

"I didn't know," she mouthed to me.

"You'll be able to do everything," I told Penny. "And your boy will be fine."

She patted my hand. "Of course he won't. He'll have to wear one of those terrible bags to catch his shit."

Weiss moved out of the way and I stepped in. The technician fiddled with the dials, scanning frequencies and adjusting electrical sensitivity. I was going directly through the folds of the cerebrum right into the primitive brainstem, the reptilian part of the brain. I thought about Solomon's taipans as I guided the electrodes through the material manifestation of millions of years of evolution, the layer after layer that differentiates us from fish and frogs and snakes, the folds of complexity—the nature, some say, of consciousness.

The electrodes were quiet. I felt myself beginning to sweat. I knew now what Weiss was worried about. I'd never gone in this far without the reassuring chatter of static indicating I was closing in on the correct bit of tissue.

"Nearing the subthalamic nucleus," I said.

Weiss looked a bit triumphant that I seemed to be making no better progress than he had.

"This really is a stupendous technology," Khalsa said to Penny. "It would have been pure science fiction just a few years ago."

I wondered why he was so vocally keen on a procedure that did not seem to be working.

"I wonder if the leads are bad," said Weiss.

"The lines are fine," said the technician.

"The electrodes, then," said Weiss.

The technician shook his head. "One bad electrode, maybe. Five? No way."

I continued navigating my way carefully through the piece of tissue that made Penny who she was. The muscles in my back grew tighter by the moment, and I tried to relax and sink and release my tension. The deeper I went, the more satisfied Weiss's expression became. I felt a tremor coming on, courtesy of Diomedes' medicine. It took all my will to suppress it, and I noticed that Khalsa was watching me.

All of a sudden the lateral electrode lit up and the technician gave a yelp.

"Ha!" cried Khalsa, as a steady stream of static came out of the speakers.

MacDougal whispered something in Penny's ear. I moved the gun back and forth a tiny bit, nursing it over the same path again, just in the opposite direction, my hands gentle, my fingers coaxing.

"There," said the technician.

The static was loud.

"I hear an ocean," Penny cried. "It's so beautiful."

Khalsa smiled. The electrodes stimulating the brain often produced auditory or visual hallucinations. It was a good sign and MacDougal smiled at it, too. I looked at Weiss.

"Stimulator?"

He nodded. The technician mapped the point precisely so that we could return to it with ease, and I gently pulled the gun out.

"Your turn," I said to Weiss.

I had done the hard part and he knew it, but the triumph of the day was still to be his. He took the stimulating electrode and began the insertion. Once it was in place, we would calibrate it with a specialized instrument then implant a small pacemaker-like device under Penny's collarbone to power it.

"That's it," said the technician, when Weiss reached his destination.

I went to Penny's side. She couldn't turn her head because of the brace so I took her arm and leaned over her and lifted it up.

"Can you feel me holding up your arm?"

"No," she said.

"Are you sure?"

"I can see that you're holding it and I can feel a bit of the pressure of your fingers, but that's about it."

Weiss nodded to the technician, who turned on the current, stimulating the affected part of Penny's brain. I watched Penny's face carefully. Despite the coverage of the brace, I could see her eyes widen.

"Oh, my goodness," she said, wiggling her fingers "Oh, my Lord, I can feel my arm in space."

"That's what we like to hear," I said.

"Now I'll be able to hold my boy," she said, and began to weep.

Khalsa shot me a glance that said he'd like to use the line in a fund-raising campaign for the hospital.

"Let's try a leg," I said.

Penny's legs had been twitching since the moment I walked into the room.

"Would you lift your right leg off the table, please?" I asked her.

Her leg came up. When it did the tremors quieted with her intention. The scan showed activity in an area slightly dorsal of where we had the stimulating electrode. Weiss moved his probe there, glancing at the electrode brace with concern even though he knew the frame was bolted in so tightly she'd have to kick the ceiling before her head would move.

"Current," I said.

The technician applied juice. For a moment, Penny's tremors got worse.

"More juice," said Weiss.

The technician increased the power. Penny's eyes fixed on a spot on the ceiling as the tremors began to subside. A few seconds later, the leg hung in the air as perfectly still as an Olympic gymnast's. "No," said Penny, licking her lips. "It can't be true. No, no no."

"Yes," said Weiss, flashing me a grin.

"Now that's neurosurgery," said Khalsa.

I bowed out then, wanting to leave Weiss to bask in the sunshine. On my way to breaking scrub, I sniffed eagerly for the smell of almonds. Surely, this was enough of a moment for Tie Mei to show me she was watching.

But the air bore only the bright smell of iodine tinged with nervous sweat.

28

I was showered and dressed by the time I heard Edson Erkulwater was dead. The news came to me in a trickle, not a shout—a hushed admission by the floor nurse when I stopped by to check on him and found his chart missing from the door.

"He died? When?"

"Just a short while ago," she answered, looking at me as if she thought I was blaming her.

"What happened?"

"He was off the monitor," she said. "We were getting ready to send him home. When we found him, it was already too late."

"The body?"

"Still in there. The morgue guys are coming to take him down to the cold."

I pushed through the door of the truck driver's room and went to him, the nurse right behind me. He was hanging off the bed, one thick arm over his head so that his fingers brushed the floor, the other—IV still attached—gripping the bedclothes. His eyes were open and staring.

"What do you think?" the nurse said quietly.

"I concur with your diagnosis," I answered.

She blanched and I regretted the sarcasm at once. She was young, with freckles and red hair. I could tell she hadn't seen death as many times as I had. I suddenly had the urge to tell her that Edson was on his way to a cosmic waiting room, a place where he would decide what to do next about life—whether to come back as an alpine marmot or a white flamingo, say, or maybe a telephone repairman or a priest. "Sorry," I said instead, closing Edson's eyelids. "It gets easier. Not easy, but easier."

She dabbed at her eye with a cotton ball. "It looks like he thrashed around," she said. "It's terrible. I can't understand why nobody heard him."

"It was probably a stroke," I said. "Or maybe a heart attack. He was overweight and had been sedentary for a while."

"Maybe a pulmonary embolism."

"Clots do travel," I said.

"Wasn't he in a car accident or something?"

"That's right."

The nurse sat down on the bed next to the body. "It's weird. He almost looks asleep. I mean nobody sleeps like that I guess, half off the bed, but kids do, I mean some people might, if they were really tired or they had a bad dream. It's just that life and not-life are so close."

"How do you know he's not sleeping?" I said.

"What?"

"Can you describe what's missing that tells you he's no longer alive?"

She shook her head. I thought about the Russian boy's soul leaving his body and flitting upward to the light above my operating table. It seemed like a dream now, though not even a year had passed. The memory wasn't quite as sharp as it had been. Like Tie Mei's haunting presence, it was quietly fading away.

"I can't either," I said. "I just know the spark is not there."

"You must feel bad. I heard you worked on him with Dr. Weiss."

I licked my lips and found them crusty from Diomedes' antipsychotic medication, which I'd finally started taking. My tongue felt big in my mouth. "All that effort and expense and all it buys is a few more days," I said. "Some days the job just sucks."

After she left, I looked around Erkulwater's room. There was a bird-of-paradise plant on the windowsill and it made me think of the truck driver's plans to move to Hawaii with his wife, courtesy of whatever proceeds he thought he might receive from the accident.

I wondered if the hospital had called the wife yet. Technically, the driver was Dave Weiss', patient, but with Weiss, still fine-tuning Penny's implant, sharing the bad news might fall to someone else. I figured I should volunteer, but I didn't have it in me right then. I peeked into the closet. There were clothes hanging there in anticipation of the driver's discharge—fresh and clean and pressed and ready. I held his shirt to my face.

"What's up?"

I jumped. Roan Cole was standing behind me in the doorway.

"I know I'm not. I can't believe Edson's gone."

"I heard you were in surgery, then they said you left. I figured you might have come to check on this guy."

"He's dead."

"I see that. So you like the smell of laundry detergent in the morning?"

"Show some respect, will you?"

"You're the one sniffing his clothes. What's that about?"

"The smell of death. You know. I find the aroma of soap clean and domestic and life-affirming."

"I think you're just depressed about Jordan."

I looked over at Erkulwater's corpse. "It's not just about her, but yeah, I've been calling her and she won't speak to me. Look, I feel raw about this guy. Weiss and I really tried with that traction technique."

"You made a good effort," said Roan.

"Sometimes it just seems that all that work doesn't matter. We brought four people in off the road that night and two are dead."

There wasn't much for Roan to say about that so he just helped me lift the corpse back up onto the bed and cover it with a sheet.

"Emma's playing tonight," he said, checking his watch. "Not too late to catch her."

I waved it off. "Not in the mood. Music just widens the chink in the armor."

"Get some new armor, then, or else take it off altogether and just stand in the wind."

"How's Lysandra?"

"Wow," he answered.

"I agree."

"Wow on so many levels sometimes I'm not sure which way is up."

"Sounds like love," I said.

"It's something," he answered, looking down at the floor, a grin coming and going and coming again.

*   *   *

Out in the parking lot I broke down and tried Jordan's number. I got a recording informing me that the number had been changed to an unlisted one. The pit in my stomach that opened when Karen MacDougal told me she was Jordan's doctor widened to abyssal proportions. I sat on my bike for a while just breathing then rode to Slither & Crawl.

I marched right past Darlene and into Solomon Yu's office. He was sitting behind his desk with a thick volume on toxicology open before him and three lines blinking on the phone. There was a tank in the corner with a cooling fan blowing on it and dry ice rising from a packet set inside.

"Doctor," he said. "Probably we should set formal appointments."

"Forgive me," I said. "I lost a patient today and I'm feeling empty. Would you give me something to work on? A new breathing exercise, anything at all?"

"You feel the urge to do violence?"

"I don't feel the urge to be peaceful," I answered.

He pushed his chair back from the table. I noticed that his fingers were curled tight and made note of it. Tie Mei always told me to look at a man's fingers for a measure of the tension in his body. Solomon gestured at the cool tank behind him.

"This is a tuatara," he said. "Have you ever heard of it?"

I took a few steps closer and looked through the glass. The creature inside was thick bodied, with ridges on its back. "It looks like a lizard that doesn't like the heat."

"You are correct about the heat. It prefers cool weather. It is a living fossil, a unique creature from the islands off New Zealand. Not a lizard, but something else—a member of a group of Mesozoic era reptiles."

"Venomous?"

He shook his head. "There are only two species of venomous lizards, and they are of no significance to my work. This is a special order for a customer. Very endangered. Not easy to get."

"Another smuggling project?"

Solomon gave me a pained look. "It has a parietal eye," he said.

"A third eye? Where? On top of the head?"

"Correct. And no, it is not smuggled. The paperwork is right here. It is going to the University of Miami for a physiology study."

"But you sell most of these creatures as pets."

Solomon stood up from his desk. He was wearing a leather vest over a mauve long-sleeved shirt and neatly pressed pants. He looked dapper.

"Correct."

"And reptiles can be companions?"

"They have consciousness," he said. "They are alive. They vibrate. They have *qi*. Often people surround themselves with the energy they require, the vibration their body craves."

"You're saying people come to your store and buy these creatures because on some level their vibration supports health or happiness?"

"Correct again."

"In neurology we call the reptilian hindbrain the primitive portion."

Solomon opened the cage and removed the tuatara. It was

mottled gray and green and had a long row of dorsal humps. Its golden eyes fixed on me.

"Strictly speaking, the word *primitive* is not pejorative but refers to an earlier time," Solomon said, stroking the animal's back. "As far as life on earth goes, reptiles came before we did by some hundreds of millions of years. That does not mean we are better than they are. There are affectionate reptiles and hateful reptiles, intelligent ones and reptiles that give little hint of any higher function. When people choose a pet they go for what suits them."

"Which ones suit you?"

Darlene stuck her head in the door. "Would you please take this call, Solomon? It's a pet shop driving me crazy with questions about bearded dragons."

"So how about giving me something to work on?" I asked one more time. "That sinking you did, maybe? Can you show me how to practice that?"

"I want you to study your circadian systems," Solomon answered. "You do not know them, do you?"

"What organ systems are active at what times of day? Certainly I do. I use the information when I do acupuncture."

"Practice what you preach then," said Solomon. "You are not living what you know. I can see it in your eyes."

"The phone?" Darlene prompted.

"What about something physical to work on," I said. "A new technique, perhaps for the straight sword?"

"Forget about it," Solomon said. "There is much to fix in your alignment before you touch *dan jian*."

"The phone, Solomon. Please. I swear this guy is going to send back a hundred dragons."

"When may I come to start training?" I pressed.

"Tomorrow night."

"What time?"

"At the hour of the pericardium," he said, and picked up the phone. Outside the office, I asked Darlene if he made her work on her circadian rhythms.

"Very basic," she said. "Beginner stuff."

I followed her out onto the floor. She had a dustpan and broom and began tidying up the floor around the bins.

"I owe you," I said.

"You certainly do."

"I mean, for getting him to take me on."

"It was your money."

"But without you I wouldn't have known how to spend it."

She put down the broom. "Well, now everyone's happy."

"But not you."

"I was born happy," she said. "You're the one who has to work at it."

"I touched his chest," I said. "He sank away like a ghost. I've never seen that kind of body control."

"Not even in the nanny?"

"I don't know," I said. "I'm not sure I got far enough for her to show me."

"Get some rest before your session with him," Darlene said. "Trust me, you're going to need it."

29

I wanted to go see Tierra but was afraid I might run into Lopez-Famosa so I went for a walk on the beach instead. There was a little light left, though with low clouds and a sneaky wind the sun looked uncertain about its plans. Shadows on the sand flitted like the footprints of giants. A thicket of kelp washed up, snagged around some pieces of concrete brought up by dredging barges, and then retreated in streaks. Dredging is the local answer to beach erosion; without it, the beach at my home by the Hillsboro Inlet would return to the sea. As it was, any time there was even a minor storm the beach was reshaped into peaks and valleys, and all I had to be thankful for was that my local shoreline no longer tortured me by looking like the strip of shore on which I had lain with Jordan, fingers intertwined, afraid to breathe too deeply because the future looked so rich.

When I got back I found another letter from Neptune.

Dear Dr. Pearl,

You are scarier than I thought when we met, yes? It seemed you were hell-bent on getting in here with me and the other guys, and now I think it's because you're some kind of dimension-shifting demon. I had a dream about you. I wasn't asleep so maybe it wasn't a dream. Anyway, you came into my mind somehow and suddenly the two of us were riding horseback in the moonlight together. It was cold and wolves were howling and there were many men on our tail. The snow crunched and the horses huffed so hard I thought their hearts would stop, but we kept going and you kept screaming and laughing and waving your sword in the air. It's a picture I can't shake. I just want you to know that I know who you really are, what you really do, oh yes.

I support the dark in you.

Neptune Cohen

I put it in the trash just as Wanda knocked on the front door.

"I was just about to make some tea," I said.

"Oswardo Lopez-Famosa was treated for a cut to his ankle."

"Tierra's father?"

"Don't play with me, Xenon. You know damn well who he is."

"A tender and wholesome individual," I said.

"He got into a fender-bender on his way home from work. Seems he was driving with his left foot because his right one didn't work properly. He was losing so much blood he stopped into a rapid-care place in Fort Lauderdale. They called Fort Lauderdale PD and reported it as a knife wound, even though he swore it was an industrial accident. Said the edge of a conveyor belt cut him."

"Those pesky conveyor belts," I said, unlocking the door. "Herbal tea or the real stuff?"

"We're a long way past glib, Zee. I know you like the guy for doing the wife."

"He killed his wife with his fist."

"Are we back to cutting people on the basis of theories?" Wanda asked, leaning against my kitchen counter. "I mean, are we back to cutting people at all?"

"Did Oswardo say I cut him?"

"I just told you he blamed a conveyor belt."

"Then why are you here?"

The muscles in Wanda's jaw tightened and released, making ripples along the bottom edge of her face. "I think we need to go back up to South Bay."

"That inmate I told you about keeps writing me."

"I don't want to talk about him, I want to talk about you. Maybe it was the accident we saw on the road, maybe it's losing Jordan. Either way, I'm getting that whacko buzz off you again."

"I haven't lost Jordan," I said.

"Mom told me she doesn't want to see you anymore."

"What does your mother know about this?"

"You're not the only one who speaks to Jordan. We care about her, too."

"She's having a difficult time right now."

"And I'd say you are as well."

"The other surgeons and I saved four people," I said. "We saved them clean and clear, but for reasons I don't understand two of them are dead now."

Wanda frowned. "Two?"

"The truck driver, Edson Erkulwater, died this morning. Looks like he had a heart attack or stroke all alone in his hospital room. He was planning to retire and move to Hawaii. Last time I saw him, the repairs we made were looking pretty good."

"Sorry to hear it."

"It bothers me, that's all. Two out of four."

"Medical odds can be cruel, I'm sure. But that doesn't change the cut on Lopez-Famosa's leg. The guy's never going to walk right again."

"He'll walk," I said. "A little cut on the ankle isn't a crippler."

"I need to know if you cut him, Zee."

"Don't be silly."

"You never lied to me before. You always just changed the subject. If you start lying, we have a world of trouble."

"I do believe we are talking about a guy who killed his wife because he was angry at her for taking his daughter away."

Wanda ran her finger along the edge of my counter and followed it until she was very close to me. She cupped my cheeks with her hand. It was a strong hand, one that I'd seen hold a large-caliber pistol rock steady.

"The things you do wake me up at night, and the things you make *me* do keep me from going back to sleep," she said, giving my face a squeeze.

"I don't sleep either," I said. "Short term, I could write you a script for a pill."

"Even a cop can't do what you do—shouldn't, anyway."

"I guess that is rather the point."

"May I see Quiet Teacher, brother?"

I reached up and pried her fingers from my face. "I'll have finger marks on my cheeks," I said. "I'll have to let my beard come in for a few days."

"The sword."

I went and got it. She looked it over, unsheathed it, sniffed it, put it back.

"There wouldn't be any trace of Mr. Famosa here, would there, if I took this to the lab and washed it with reagents and gave it a microscopic look?"

"I keep my practice tools clean and oiled so they don't rust, Wanda. By the way, Lopez-Famosa is how I believe he likes to be addressed. I met him in Tierra's room. He told me a lot about his life with Kimberly while Tierra was sleeping. He was grateful to me for saving his little girl."

Wanda handed the sword back to me and walked around the room. She stopped in front of a bronze statue on a shelf by the front door.

"You buy more Asian stuff?"

"Just brought a few pieces out of the closet. I rotate them. They're all from Tie Mei—Chinese, mostly old, some valuable. They remind me about what's important, and, of course, they remind me of her."

"The Buddha statues I recognize, but who is that supposed to be?"

"Lao Tzu riding a water buffalo."

"Who was he?"

"China's greatest sage."

"And that one?"

"General Guan—patron saint of the martial arts. He's a real character from history—a war hero."

"That was hers also?"

"I believe so. It's been in the closet forever."

"What made you bring it out?"

"I've had time to decorate," I said. "Being off work and all."

"Nobody talks about that nanny, and the silence is deafening."

"She was my mother," I said. "That's the bottom line."

She nodded. "You worship Buddha?"

"Buddha was a man, not a god."

"You think he would approve of your actions?"

"I'm a doctor. Buddha was all about compassion."

"Not your doctoring—your other actions."

"Buddha saw violence as a last resort."

"And Lao Tzu?"

"He said violence is a sign all rational action has failed, a sign your sensitivity to the flow of nature is insufficient."

She nodded. "Show me another sword."

I looked at her.

"Your father says you have a bank of them: spears, swords, clubs, maces."

"He told you I have maces?"

Wanda shrugged, unconsciously touched her gun, and looked at me expectantly. I went away and came back with some things.

"Maybe you used this one to cut Lopez?" she asked, picking up a carbon steel Chinese broadsword I'd bought on a side trip to Toledo, Spain, the year I took the DBS training.

"You're interested in weapons, aren't you?"

She picked up a spear. "I'm interested in *your* weapons."

"Recently I read that anthropologists found the remains of a spear inside a fossilized mastodon and dated the petrified wood to be four hundred thousand years old."

"I didn't even know there were human beings that long ago."

"Early ancestors, but they hunted cooperatively and used spear to damage prey from a distance, thereby minimizing the risk to their own life and limb. Forgive the pun, but the spear is bloody ancient."

"It's a straight sword with a long handle."

"Very good," I smiled. "And the straight sword is a spear with a long blade and a short handle."

"You're right about what I've seen on the street, Xenon. I doubt you'd even believe how bad it gets out there: Frisbees with razors on the edge, screwdrivers with the handles taped for a better grip in a bloody fight, cranked up thugs swinging firefighter mauls around like toothpicks, smashing cars, crushing bones."

"Mauls," I said. "That's a new one."

She picked up my wolf-tooth mace. "Like this, but three times as heavy and minus the spikes. Firemen use them to crash through drywall and make holes in burning buildings when the doors are blocked."

"Sounds like a nice workout for the arms."

She looked out my French doors toward the pool. "The palms out back have gotten bigger."

"The tropical almond is the real champion."

Wanda stood up. "If you need help, you know I'll be there for you."

"Don't worry," I said. "I'm getting all the help I need."

She kissed me on the cheek then patted where her lips had been. "I hope so."

30

Just after sunrise, I rode to Jordan's building through the tourist season bustle. The BMW's upright riding position gave me a commanding view of the road, and I enjoyed the experience even though the high-tech bike's super bright headlight failed to stop two octogenarians from turning left right in front of me. There was no sight of my love on the first pass, but I made a U-turn just before the Boca Inlet and drove by again just in time to see Amanda exiting the underground parking lot in her minivan. I waited until she was out of sight, pulled up to the building, and went into the lobby. I did not recognize the doorman, but he seemed to know me.

"You can't go up, Doc."

"At least ring her," I said. "Give her a chance to say yes."

"They warned me about you. They knew you'd come."

"Well, here I am."

He was a grizzled fellow, a New Yorker by the sound of it, with bad skin and yellow teeth and a tall, hulking frame. "You're a real doctor, right? An M.D.?"

"Through and through," I said.

"So you got money. Maybe you could use a haircut, but you're not a bad-looking guy. Even I can see you got a lot to choose from in Florida. The girls take care of themselves down here, though I grant you there's high maintenance in the air. They spend all year in bikinis, so they gotta look good. Even the older ladies, they get surgery, you know—the tits, the eyes."

I started to interrupt, but he put up his hand.

"Just let me finish, okay? I know you think it's not my place to say, but I wasn't always a doorman and even if I was, maybe you shouldn't judge a guy by his job. I get paid a decent wage, I have nice hours and benefits, I help people all day long. There's nothing wrong with what I do. So I'm just trying to say maybe you shouldn't push your case with a girl who don't want you, especially when she's, you know, not all there."

"She's plenty the way she is," I said. "She and I are connected. We have history I can't begin to explain."

He shrugged. "History can be rewritten. It happens all the time. And connections, well, they can be broken."

"Ring her for me," I said. "You can tell them I was making a scene. If she won't see me I'll leave; no muss no fuss."

He looked at me a long minute. "You're sure?"

"I'm sure."

"You won't cause any trouble?"

"Just make the call."

So he punched it in and I heard the ring and then the tiny, sweet timber of Jordan's voice through the receiver. I felt something in my belly and the doorman saw it on my face.

"No," I heard her say.

I grabbed the phone from the guy's hand. I did it hard and fast and smooth. I knew he was talking sense and talking from his heart and I didn't mean to hurt him, but my thumbnail gouged a chink in his chin and his fingers went to it and his eyes grew dark.

"Just for a minute," I told her. "I've got something to tell you. We can do it through the door if you want. You don't even have to open it. You left me no choice. Your number's unlisted."

The doorman was on his way around the desk when I handed the phone back to him. I stopped his progress with a push of the receiver.

"I'm sorry about your face," I said. "I'll figure a way to make it up to you."

"I was Golden Gloves," he said.

"I figured."

"I'd like to deck you. I don't like the feel of my own blood on my face."

"I don't like it either," I said. "And I'm used to it. Mine and other people's."

"You work emergency?"

"Neurosurgeon."

He paused. "A brain surgeon?"

"That's right."

He touched a fingertip to his chin, looked at the spot of blood, and shook his head.

"You oughta have more sense," he said.

*   *   *

In the elevator, I felt my breath coming in gasps. I'd fought the Russian mob with better wind. I'd kayaked through a hurricane and not struggled so hard for air. The door opened and I walked down the hallway. Things looked different and it took a moment for me to realize that the familiar mustard-colored carpet had been replaced with a 1970s cheap hotel blue, hardly fitting for such an up-market building. I rang the bell and pressed my ear to the door to listen for the tiny squeak of Jordan's wheelchair.

"Get your ear off the door, Xenon," Jordan said from inside. "I'm already here."

"They put in new carpet," I said. "I thought I was on the wrong floor."

"Things change."

"You're seeing Karen MacDougal," I said.

"That's right."

"I did a case with her yesterday. I don't know her, but she seems nice."

"She's very thorough."

"Can I at least see you?"

"I don't think it's a good idea. You said you had something to tell me. Why don't you go ahead and do that?"

"Did you know about the phone?"

"It wasn't my idea. My mother did it without telling me."

There was a long silence. Jordan's voice came through lower the next time. Softer.

"Your false hopes and promises and forced brightness are no good for me, Zee. You say stuff I can't believe, stuff I'm not even sure *you* believe. Ghosts. Life after life. That a man can go out into the street with a sword and cut people he thinks need cutting. That I'm going to walk again."

I felt the tears come. I didn't want them to, but they did. I slid down to the floor, sat on my knees, and leaned into the door with my forehead. "Those are all true things," I said. "They're all true and they're all important."

"You're wrestling with your own reality, Zee, and I'm wrestling with mine."

"Wrestling by yourself is pointless. If you win, you lose. If you lose, you win. It's twisted. Better we should wrestle together."

There was another long silence. I pressed my ear to the door again and this time I heard her crying.

"I'm out of the wrestling business, Zee. I'm just trying to survive. And I can't make a career of rehabilitation. I told you that."

"You don't have to make a career of anything. Would you open the door, please?"

"No."

"Just for a second? Leave the chain on if you don't trust me."

"There is no chain. And I trust you plenty. It's me I don't trust."

The world brightened at those words. I blinked back my tears and the cream walls seemed creamier, the blue carpet bluer.

"Do you like the music I'm sending?"

"Yes," her voice was tiny now.

"Can I keep sending it?"

"Probably you should stop."

"It's not guilt," I said. "That's what I came to say. I'm not here out of guilt. And what you think about the short time we were together before the attack, that's not how I see it. There's no before and after, or, if there is, it's before I met Jordan and after I met Jordan. It's all one. Everything we've been through together has made us who we are. I don't mean to push you too hard. I'll stop, okay? I won't talk about you walking if you don't want me to. I'll keep my mouth shut. I'll do anything."

She opened the door, then, just a crack. "It's early," she said. "I just got up."

She wore sweat pants, a tank top, and no makeup. She looked as if she wasn't getting enough sun. Her hair needed washing and I could see by her ankles that she hadn't shaved her legs.

"Say it," she said.

"You're beautiful. More beautiful every day."

"Not that. Don't lie."

"I'm not lying."

"Say it."

"I love you. I adore you. I don't care that you can't walk. You said you needed to focus on yourself. That's fine. I understand. You don't have time to be with me right now, that's fine. But please don't shut me out."

She reached out and touched my neck. I felt a thousand volts in my ears.

"Zee, right now seeing you hurts too much. This is just making everything harder. Please go."

*   *   *

Hope moved through me like lymph, saturating my tissues by dint of gravity and the squeezing effect of my muscles. She had talked to me, she liked the songs I sent, she had touched me, and she'd given me a chance to tell her I loved her. I pushed the big BMW harder than a brand new engine deserved, blurring the scenery, tempting traffic cops, and covering the ground between Boca Raton and Sailboat Bend in record time.

It was still early morning and my grandfather's house was quiet and still. I figured I'd find him out back in the garden and, indeed, he was there when I went through the gate, standing by the fountain, twisting in a fashion I immediately recognized as part of the *qigong* set I'd shared with him, the same set I'd taught at the prison.

"Greetings, brain boy," he said.

"Brain boy?"

"What, you don't like that?"

"You're in a spunky mood this morning. I've never seen you doing the *qigong* I taught you. Do you find it helps?"

He nodded. "My back is better. Gives me energy, too. You got special movements to stimulate my juice?"

"Your juice?"

"My sperm. My spunk. My mojo."

"Try this," I said, moving my hand up my centerline and then around under my armpit and down my back. "Then do the other side."

"Looks like a dance your father used to do. I think he called it the Frug," said Grandpa Lou, copying the movement pretty well.

"Keep your hands in contact with your body. Don't take them off."

"Hard to do," he said. "I'm not flexible like you are."

"Use your hips," I said. "Make your kidneys move up and down, one after the other, as if they were on a seesaw. That stimulates your adrenal glands and helps build *jing*—that's the Chinese medical term for spunk."

"*Jing*," he grinned. "I like that."

I was about to ask him about his sudden interest in the subject when the back door opened and a woman stepped out. She looked sleepy and new to the day, and she was wearing one of my grandfather's oxford shirts and nothing else. The skin under her throat was white and smooth.

"Oh," she said, clutching the shirt to her.

"You remember Yael?" my grandfather prompted, giving me a significant look that said—What, you don't think old people have sex? "You met her at the temple, when we went searching for those records."

"Sure," I said, putting out my hand. "I remember."

"Hi," she said. Her handshake was tentative and soft.

"I was going to buy Lou breakfast," I said. "Perhaps I can take you both? There's a place he likes on Las Olas."

"There's food in the refrigerator," said Yael. "I'm happy to make breakfast."

"He's a health-food freak," I said. "Maybe you didn't know."

Yael rolled her eyes behind Lou's back and gave me a conspiratorial grin. "I know that about him and some other things you don't."

So we went inside and sat down at my grandfather's rough-hewn wood table and drank vegetable juice he made in the juicer while Yael cooked a traditional Jewish breakfast of *matzoh brei*. She brought it with applesauce and sour cream.

"Sour cream is health food?" I said.

"I don't know where she found it," said Lou.

"I never go anywhere without a pint," said Yael.

We ate on big heavy plates with leaf designs on them. They were my grandmother's handiwork. She'd been a potter. It always amazed me how long my grandfather had kept that set of plates intact, but I read somewhere that pottery is one of the most enduring material things on the planet.

"Lou tells me you like chocolate," said Yael.

"I'm a fan," I said. "But only of the pure stuff: high in cacao, no sugar, very dark."

"I was going to put chocolate chips in the *matzoh brei*. I'm glad I didn't."

Lou waved his hand at me. "Don't even try to please him. He thinks he's a connoisseur."

"Runs in the family," Yael said.

After breakfast we had some fine Russian caravan tea. I mentioned I had found Solomon Yu.

"What's he doing?"

"He's in the reptile business," I said. "He says he was an herbalist but he changed careers."

Grandpa Lou nodded. "I knew it would be difficult for all of them."

"The problem is the size of the Asian community in South Florida," I said. "If this were New York or LA or Vancouver or Toronto he might have found a living with that skill. I can tell you as someone who integrates acupuncture into his allopathic practice, it's a tough row to hoe here."

"Is he helping you with whatever it is you wanted from him?"

"It took a while to convince him, but yes."

"He harbored feelings for the woman," Lou said. "I always knew he did."

"He doesn't say much about that."

Yael poured me more tea. "Sometimes men don't talk about their feelings," she said. "Not that I know anyone like that. What's he like, this Chinese fellow?"

"He's like a black-and-white photograph," I said. "Colors are missing but the important details are conveyed."

31

Tierra Jenkins was listening to a fancy new MP3 player through a pair of expensive-looking studio headphones. She took them off when I walked into the room and gave me a sad smile.

"Nice equipment," I said, pointing at the electronics.

"My mom would never let me have one. My dad bought it so I could use it on the plane. He loaded it with Mozart and Sibelius and also some new girl singers I like."

"Where are you flying?" I asked.

"To visit my cousin in New Jersey. She lives on a farm. They have a cherry tree."

"Sounds great," I said. "How long are you going to stay?"

"For a while, I guess. I'm going to go to school up there. My dad said he'd like me to live with him but he's too busy with his job and he's hardly ever home."

"I bet you miss your mom," I said.

She looked away and nodded.

A nurse walked in. She took Tierra's temperature while I perused her chart. I had worried that Kimberly's death would depress the little girl's immune system, but she was recovering swiftly.

"We have split-pea soup today," the nurse said. "I tried it and it's delicious. I'll bring it in a few minutes."

"I'm vegetarian," Tierra explained when the nurse left. "Everybody's really nice about helping me find food I can eat."

"Vegetarians live longer than anybody," I said. "Keep up the good work."

"Do you think my mommy is in heaven?"

"Why do you ask me that?"

"You're a brain doctor," she said. "You know stuff."

"I'm sure she is," I said.

"Do you think she can hear me when I pray?"

"I do," I said. "So keep talking to her."

"Will she talk back?"

"Only when you really, really need her to," I said.

"I won't go to heaven," she said, suddenly looking sad.

"Now, why would you say that?"

'Because I think bad thoughts."

"Tell me what they are," I said.

She shifted in the bed, avoiding my eyes.

"It's all right," I said. "I have bad thoughts myself."

"I think I might hate the motorcycle man who made Mommy crash," she whispered.

"The motorcycle man didn't do it."

She sat up and glared at me, crossing her arms.

"Who did it then?"

"A man driving a car. He lost his temper and chased the motorcycle."

"What's the driver's name?"

"It doesn't matter. What happened was an accident, Tierra. Accidents are one of the bad things in life, but there are good things, too."

Her lower lip trembled. "Like what?"

"Love," I said. "Friends. Puppies."

"I like puppies," she brightened a little.

"Maybe you can have one in New Jersey."

She nodded.

"Ice cream, too," I said. "You could have some after your pea soup if you want."

"You're sure?"

"Oh, yes," I said. "Doctors have the power to make ice cream happen."

I left her with that thought while I went out to tell the nurse to bring her some. The last thing I saw was Tierra looking dreamily upward as if she could see clear through the ceiling to where her mother floated in celestial bliss.

It was good to see.

*   *   *

On his only visit back to South Florida after moving to Idaho to live with his mother my one-time and only martial arts student, Orson Cartwright, took me to a horror festival held in a hotel in Delray Beach. The event was a celebration of scary films, books, and television shows. The enthusiastic attendees tried to outdo one another in the direction of the grotesque, painting faux blood on their faces, gluing plastic axes to protrude from their hearts, wearing Crypt Keeper masks, and toting Texas chainsaws.

As I inspected the flap job Scott had performed to cover Charlie Czarnecki's brain, I couldn't help thinking that nothing any of those folks could cook up came close to being as penetratingly monstrous as what Scott Tremper had been forced to do to the enthusiastic rider. Oh, he saved his life all right, and Tremper's a competent knife, but Czarnecki had a long road back; prosthetics were involved, and from an aesthetic standpoint the man would just never be right.

"Doc Tremper said I'm getting a new head tomorrow," Czarnecki chattered as I lightly palpated the work.

"A new skull, anyway."

"Plastic, right?"

"PMMA. That stands for polymethylmethacrylate. You ever been to a hockey game?"

"Go Panthers."

"You know that clear window around the ice that keeps people from getting creamed by the puck? That's the same stuff. It should be tough enough even for you."

"Ha ha. You're funny. Hey, I hear the other drivers and their insurance companies are trying to blame everything on the Porsche guy. He's some kind of porno king. Did you know that? I've got a lawyer and we've started suing already. Could be this little spill was the best thing that ever happened to me."

I wanted to tell him that the only thing spilling was his brain, which his skull could no longer contain. "The guy's got money," I said. "I'm sure he'll fight you. I'm no lawyer, but I'd say let it go. After all, you were the one who started it."

"Let it go? Have you seen my head? Have you seen my face? I'll be lucky to ever get a taste of the female of the species again, if you receive my meaning. Somebody's got to pay for that. You say the porn king's rich—I say good news. He made that truck jackknife across the road, Doc. It wasn't my speeding that did that. By the way, the new head bones are going to fit, right?"

"They'll fit," I said. "Dr. Tremper had them made according to a computer model of your head."

"My head ain't always the same size, though," Czarnecki said, turning to face me on his bed and forcing me to confront his distorted features. He was right about one thing: even with the prosthesis, I doubted the ladies would line up for his attentions, if, in fact, they ever had.

"Sure it is," I said.

"Meaning no disrespect, Doc, but I don't think so. I've been researching this on my laptop. I read about this thing called craniosacral therapy. It's based on the pulses of the cerebrospinal fluid. The folks who work that magic say the bones of the skull move all the time. I wonder if this acrylic job will do that. I bet not, huh? And then, of course, there's my swell head. Ha ha!"

"You have a laptop?" I said.

"Sure. Right here."

He reached under his bed and pulled out a slim, state-of-the-art model.

"What do you do for a living, Charlie?"

"I'm a video-game tester," he said. "Didn't I tell you that? How else do you think I could afford such a nice bike? The insurance company bought me a new one, by the way. It's just waiting for me to get out of here."

"How does one become a video-game tester?"

"Lightning fast reflexes, of course," he grinned.

"They didn't help you avoid that semi."

"Sure they did!' Why do you think I walked away? My life is charmed, baby. C.H.A.R.M.E.D."

32

Solomon's training studio smelled of Asian pine incense and filled my nose with winter visions of far-off peaks and crisp mornings with hoar frost clinging to leafless branches under an exotic, watchful moon.

"It's pericardium time," I said, referring to the organ system cycle Solomon had bade me review. "What do you have in mind for our class?"

"Basics," he said. "Tie Mei is long gone. I am sure her lessons have faded."

My new teacher was dressed in a frog-button jacket and drawstring pants—silk again, but raw olive-green fabric rather than the fine smooth material of his night wardrobe. As a guy who thinks infrequently about clothes and tends to wear surgical scrubs too much, I admired Solomon's wardrobe and the seamless elegance he exuded no matter the outfit, the setting, or the hour.

"I think I've got the basics down pretty well," I said.

"I will be the judge of that. Basics are the foundation. The foundation supports what you are building. What precisely *are* you building, Doctor?"

There was something in the way he said Doctor that gave me pause. Not sarcasm exactly but not respect either. I wasn't sure I liked it but figured I would let it play out.

"The goal of martial training is self-cultivation," I said. "I want to be a better fighter and I want to be a superior man. I want that peace we talked about. That stability, the strength to choose instead of to succumb."

"Let me see your tongue," he said.

I hesitated, knowing why he was asking.

"Put it out," he commanded.

I did and he peered at it.

"You must stop the pharmaceuticals," he said.

"I can't."

"You can and you must. You are not in balance."

"Maybe after you teach me some new things."

"You cannot achieve the control and balance you want if you take drugs. And you cannot study with me unless you trust me."

"All right," I nodded. "I'll stop the meds."

He walked past his array of weapons, trailing his finger over sword hilts with his fingers. "You are a Jew," he said. "Your grandfather is a rabbi."

"He was."

"Jews are warriors," he said. "We have been so for thousands of years."

"Only to survive," I said.

"What other reason is there to fight?"

"People fight for all kinds of reasons," I said. "They want things. They want to protect the people they cherish. They can't tolerate injustice."

"You talk about these high principles, but you do not attend synagogue, do you?"

"Tie Mei taught me that *qi* motivates the human body the way the fingers of God move a glove. I get to know God through my actions."

Solomon blinked. "Tie Mei spoke of God?"

"She did."

"And what about when the glove wears out?"

"God inserts us into a new one," I said. "There are various interpretations of reincarnation in Judaism. You and I have shared lives before. I believe we know some of the same people."

"Like Jordan Jones?"

I tapped the punching bag lightly to hide my surprise. "How do you know her name?"

"A man brings the past to my door, I look to see if he is who he says he is."

"Looking means following, I gather. By the way, the white roses Darlene brought you were a gift to me from a grateful patient."

"Kimberly, who died. Yes, I know. Do you think she travels from life to life with you, too?"

I felt the adrenaline immediately. "How in the world do you know about my patient?"

"You have knowledge of me and you seek more. You come to me and suddenly I, too, need information. Now show me a crane stance."

Tingling with a sense of violation, I raised one arm and dropped my weight onto the opposite leg. He grabbed my arm and pushed me hard. I went down. He jerked me effortlessly to my feet. "Try again," he said.

I did and he pushed me over again.

"You do not know how to handle force," he said.

"I thought I did."

"Sink and relax and turn like a corkscrew. Imagine that your legs are the sharp point and your arms and shoulders are the handle."

He pushed me again, and this time I transferred his energy to the ground and stayed on my feet.

"The other night you wanted to know how I melted away from your hand," Solomon said. "The answer is in that corkscrew spiral—the overarching form of nature."

"Tie Me told me."

"Then you know that the spiral is the shape of galaxies and whirlpools and snails and storms. It is the shape physical forces naturally follow when unmolested and responding to both strong and subtle cues. It is the most important shape in the world. This is pericardium time. We are here to train at a time when the protective energy of the heart is affected. The spiral shape is what gives the fibrils of cardiac muscle so much endurance and contractile force."

"You talk like a poet."

"I am an immigrant. I applied myself to the language. Let me feel your punch."

He pointed at his midsection and I set myself into a bow-and-arrow stance—left foot forward, right foot back. When I was ready, I launched a whopper off my right hand, twisting it so that when it reached his silk jacket it wrapped up a bunch of the material. The punch was fueled by confusion and indignation and a tinge of fear, but it made little impression on Solomon's body, which felt, upon impact, like a thick, overfilled rubber ball.

"Pah," Solomon scolded. "That was not much. The spiral is in the entire body not merely the fist. If you relax and keep your spine straight and grab the ground with your toes, it will come spontaneously from the bottom of your feet and manifest in the hand."

"The Greater Heavenly Circle," I said, referring to the body's major energy pathway, which runs up the back and down the front to connect all the primary meridians and systems. Completing the circle opens the spirit and ensures good health.

"It is one thing to know the name and another to demonstrate the effect in your body," Solomon said. "Try again. Your mind is in the way. The fist is not a club; it is the tip of the whip. The *dantian* is the handle. Start your strike there. Draw up from the ground and express it in the hand."

The *dantian* includes the hips and the area around them. I closed my eyes, concentrated, exhaled, and tried not to think about Solomon at the hospital or near my office or, worst of all, following Jordan. I felt my belly drop and my neck and shoulders soften, but there were places in me that would not let go. I punched anyway. This time I felt the upward energy in Solomon's deflection lift me slightly off the ground, but I also felt him rock ever so slightly backward.

"Better," he said. "Do it again."

I did. He absorbed the blow like he was an oak tree and I was a sparrow landing on his branch.

"Again," he said.

I concentrated on dropping my center of gravity by relaxing into my quadriceps. All eight heads of the muscles burned. It was a familiar feeling, and I knew it would make a better punch.

I let it loose and felt Solomon take a step back from the impact.

"All right," he said. "Now on to the one-inch punch."

Reference to a punch without extension convinced me that Solomon and Tie Mei were cut from the same martial cloth. "What's the name of your style?" I asked.

"It is a mixture."

"But mostly what?"

He thought for a minute. "There are a number of influences. It is a rich blend."

I found myself vaguely disappointed. I was hoping to dive into the traditions and history of a single art. "No single one forms the backbone?"

"There is much of *taijiquan*," Solomon said. "But, of course, not the version the New Age movement promotes for exercise."

"Tai chi?"

"Yes, but an original form never seen in the West, a battlefield system taught to imperial bodyguards. My teachers tested the principles in war; they did not practice to go down a dress size. They fought with the art and died if it was no good."

"So you and Tie Mei studied together?"

"Get back to the punch, please. Move closer to the bag. Good. Now, I want you to put your fist right up to it. Barely brush it. Yes, like that. Now coil down into your legs, pull your hips back, turn your waist, and then let the punch go. Remember, punching gets power through extension as well as rotation, so you will have to find that extension inside your body rather than by pulling the hand back. Master this and you'll be able to deliver explosive power from very close range."

—— I was more relaxed now and was able to do as he asked. I let the punch fly from right up close to the bag and it popped away and into the air.

"Not good but not bad," he said.

"What about forms?"

"We'll get to them."

"You have really been at the hospital to learn about my patients?"

"You have been to my place of business and you have been to my home."

"But . . ."

He raised his hand and his look told me to shut up. I felt like a boy again. He seemed to have all the powers of my nanny, but he was a man and he was older and therefore wiser and there was a grand tradition of not questioning the teacher, of doing as you were bidden on the assumption that he or she had your best interests in mind. I felt transported and powerless, yet I also felt great joy in joining a flow that had utterly escaped me for so long now.

"Would you tell me more about your own teachers and your own training?" I asked meekly. "Lineage is something I really miss. Did you and Tie Mei learn together in the north?"

"It's time to go," Solomon said. "I have to feed the animals and get back to my research."

"I looked into venom research," I said. "Are you working on pain control?"

Solomon turned off the light. We were plunged into darkness relieved only by a glow from under the door.

"Come back in three days," he said.

33

When I arrived at the office the next morning I found Travis wiping down the Venetian blinds.

"You don't have to do that," I said.

"Just letting in the morning light. It's been dark in here so long I didn't realize the place was so filthy."

After half a year lying fallow my office was getting busy again and the atmosphere was palpably upbeat. There was a heart-warming stream of business from docs at the hospital who apparently were glad about my reinstatement.

"We'll have to get Joe Montefiore to trim those ficus back," I said, referring to the landlord.

"Just a bit," said Travis. "The tropical feel is nice."

The first patient of the day was Eugenia Wentworth, a woman in her late thirties, sent over by Karen MacDougal, Jordan's new doctor. Eugenia was a VIP, and Karen wanted me to confirm a diagnosis made by the hospital's chief of neuroradiology. I looked through the chart, read MacDougal's notes, reviewed the films, and then had Travis bring her in.

She was a lean, well-muscled woman with wide hips and a sculptured face. She was lean and well muscled. I complimented her on taking good care of herself.

"Dr. MacDougal didn't seem to notice," she sniffed. "Or maybe she was afraid to make any personal comments."

"Afraid?" I repeated.

"My husband is the chairman of the board of the hospital," she said. "I do hot yoga. Bikram. Very rigorous. You should try it."

"I do like to sweat."

"It's not just about sweating. The heat is just to help your muscles stretch. The workout is the posture. Men come sometimes and they stand in the back of the room and ogle us women, but they don't have the balance to stand on one leg and they don't have the strength to hold themselves in the postures or the patience to stay with it and let their body adjust."

"And they call women the weaker sex."

"You're not a yes-man, are you, Dr. Pearl? I don't want a yes-man."

"How can I help you, Mrs. Wentworth?"

"I have strange pains and troubles in my lower body."

"Troubles?"

"I'm Greek, Dr. Pearl. I was born in Athens. My husband met me there when he was on a cruise. Greek women can be very direct. May I be direct with you?"

"Of course. I can't help you if you don't tell me what's going on."

"I lose control of my bladder. And I get numb and my legs give way and I fall down. My internist couldn't figure it out. He thought I might be a mental case. I can assure you I'm not mentally infirm in any way, Doctor. My husband is a very important man."

"Do you have children together?"

"No."

"Have you ever had children?"

"If I haven't had them with my husband, how would I have had them?"

I smiled and gestured for her to follow me into my examination room. I gave her a gown, waited for her to change, and went in. I performed a series of basic neurological evaluations and then I ran my hand over her back at the level of T9–T10, in her mid thoracic spine. This was the level of the congenital problem her MRI revealed, and if I paid close attention I thought I could feel the bone spike the scan showed.

"What has Dr. MacDougal shared with you about her diagnosis?" I asked.

"She said she thought I might have a rare problem and she sent me to you."

"I believe you have something called diastomatomyelia," I said. "You've had it all your life; in fact, the problem started before you were born. It's a developmental abnormality."

"Honestly, I think doctors make up these words just to lord it over the rest of us. If it's been with me so long, how come I just started noticing it now? The peeing, I mean, and the little pains."

I took her left heel in my hand and lifted it. Eugenia looked at me as if she expected me to comment on the fact that it was long and pale and shapely. I lifted the other leg and compared them. I was expecting some atrophy on the left based on what I'd seen on the films, and, sure enough, the left calf was smaller, the muscle less developed.

"Diastomatomyelia is a long word because it describes something a bit complex," I said. "When you were developing inside your mother's womb, the bones of your spine made a mistake."

"What kind of a mistake?" Eugenia scowled. "My back feels fine."

"The bones split," I said. "Or, more precisely, a segment of your spinal column doubled—started to make a twin, you might say—and the spinal cord and bones split. One branch ran through one of the twins and another branch ran through the other. The rest of the bones in your spine were normal, so the cord came back together again around the spike."

"Like a detour on the highway," Eugenia said.

I nodded. "The trouble is, there are holes in the bony parts of the spine and there are branches growing off the spinal cord that should go through their assigned holes. Because of this detour, the spine is pulled up and the holes and the nerves don't line up correctly."

She pulled the paper dressing gown tightly around her and crossed her arms and legs. "Why is it beginning to hurt now when it didn't hurt before?"

"Ligaments and tendons grow less flexible with age," I said. "That changes the position of things in your spine. Also, your spinal cord has been rubbing on that bony spike for years. Over time there's been damage."

Eugenia straightened up as if all the talk about her spine made her self-conscious about her posture. She looked past me, perhaps so I wouldn't notice the moisture in her eyes.

"So am I going to be paralyzed?"

I hesitated. "You say you like straight talk so I'll give it to you. If you were to hurt your back, bad things could happen in a hurry, but you're not in any immediate danger. You might be fine for a while except for the odd tingling and weakness and pain."

"So why all the fuss?"

"Because you are married to the chairman of the board."

She laughed out loud. "You *are* a straight talker."

"But you do need to be more careful of your backbones than you have been, and your yoga teacher needs to know about your injury so he or she can help you avoid putting pressure on your mid back."

"But my symptoms will get worse."

I nodded. "The only real reason to consider surgery at this time is the inconvenience of incontinence."

"What kind of surgery?"

"If you decide you want it, and if Dr. MacDougal agrees, then a surgeon might open the sac around your spinal cord, remove the spike, and put the detour back together with the road."

"Is it dangerous surgery?"

"Knives and nerves don't naturally mix. This kind of work has to be done very carefully, and, yes, it carries some risk. All surgery does."

She got off the table. "I'll think about it," she said. "May I get dressed now?"

I went back to my consulting room and waited for her to come out. When she did, she looked hard across the desk at me.

"If I go ahead with the procedure, are you the best person to do it?"

"I wouldn't say I'm the best," I said. "There are many talented surgeons in Miami and other major cities. Some of them have more experience with this kind of repair than I do."

"You're being modest," she said.

"It's the ponytail," I said.

"I'm surprised the hospital lets you keep a haircut like that. You really *must* be good."

"I'm just telling it like it is. If you do decide to have the surgery, you should have absolute confidence in whatever surgeon you choose. It makes a difference in the outcome and in the speed of recovery."

She gave me the second smile of the visit. "I'll make sure I do," she said.

*   *   *

Eugenia was not gone ten minutes when I got a call from John Khalsa.

"Your office must be busy," he said. "I've been on hold for five minutes."

"Sorry," I said. "I'll let my folks know to put you through faster next time."

"Karen MacDougal told me she sent Eugenia Wentworth in."

"That's right."

"Diastomatomyelia."

"Looks like it, yes."

"You mean you think it's not?"

I looked over at the Chinese screen next to my desk and stared at the water buffalo carrying farmers across the river. Lao Tzu, the great Daoist sage, had reputedly left the kingdom on a water buffalo bound for a desert death alone. I wondered which of his principles I would learn from Solomon that I had not learned from

Tie Mei. The ancient master was supposed to have been a patient man. I wondered how patient he would have been if he'd had to deal with John Khalsa.

"No," I said carefully. "I mean I think it is."

"What an opportunity," Khalsa said. "I hope you're grateful."

"I beg your pardon?"

"The wife of the chairman of the board of our hospital has an illness we can treat and I'm confident you'll do a bang-up job with the surgery. It'll gain us political capital, my friend. We'll have the whole board of trustees eating out of our hand."

I could hear Khalsa pacing. I knew how nervous energy moved him when he smelled a successful gambit and was impatient to get others on his team. A breeze came through the phone as if he were standing in the wind.

"Where are you, John?"

"I'm at the yacht club."

"Checking on your boat?"

"That's right."

"I have to tell you, I don't see Eugenia as an opportunity; I see her as a patient who needs a complex piece of surgery."

"Get off your high horse, will you? I'm not wishing her ill, I'm just laying out the facts."

"I'm trying to say that I'm not sure the surgery is warranted. It's risky and she's not in that much pain."

"But she's going to need it eventually, yes? And the younger she is when she gets it the better she'll come through."

"All things being equal, younger patients do better," I said, noticing for the first time that Travis had put a vase of white roses in a corner of the room—a mute testimonial to Kimberly Jenkins, I supposed, and a nice welcome-back-to-business touch.

"Wouldn't you agree that the longer she waits, the greater the potential damage to the cord?"

"It's her decision not ours," I said.

"She'll do what her husband tells her to do. Have you met Gus

Wentworth?"

"Never," I said.

Khalsa's voice softened. "Just keep an open mind about this, all right? It really is an opportunity. By the way, have you heard Edson Erkulwater's autopsy turned up methamphetamines in the bloodstream?"

I felt a pit grow in my belly. "What?"

"The hydrochloride salt. Junkies inject it. Not uncommon with truckers, I'm told. We found a bottle under the bed—the heavy street version, dirty and powerful. You can see how these people need stuff like that to keep going and going all night on the road."

These people, I thought. I remembered Erkulwater as a solid guy looking forward to retiring with his wife. "I don't remember anything on his admission screen."

"So he was clean that night," said Khalsa.

"But then he overdosed in his hospital bed with no embolus or stroke?"

"It was purely cardiac. A classic OD."

I took a deep breath and pushed my chair back.

I felt unaccountably sad.

34

I was hopeful there might be an email from Jordan when I got home that night, but I was disappointed. In defiance of her silence, I sent her a copy of a 1965 Rolling Stones hit that pretty much summed up my mood. Once *(I Can't Get No) Satisfaction* was zooming to her through cyberspace, I went out to bring in the mail. Just outside the front door I found a carton bearing Jordan's handwriting. I opened it with a rush of excitement.

Inside, I found a ragtag assemblage of my personal effects, including a motorcycle helmet liner I used on very hot days, a Ziploc bag filled with a bar of my favorite sandalwood soap, my toothbrush, and a stick of deodorant. There was also a black turtleneck I'd been missing, a single deerskin summer riding glove, a small pocket dagger, and last but not least the rear seat cowling for the Thruxton, which I'd completely forgotten about.

It was not a valuable assortment—even the knife was nothing fancy—but it was quintessentially mine, a material grouping that couldn't really belong to anyone else. It was the personal quality that gave the slap such weight. Despite what I thought had been an encouraging exchange, Jordan was trying to rid herself of every last trace of me.

I watched myself build all kinds of dikes around my pain: rationalizations about her physical limitations, the notion that I'd tried so damn hard to discharge my obligation that any further guilt would just be silly, the fact that even if we were done in this life we'd meet again in the next and the one after that. Despite my best spiritual gymnastics, I couldn't stop the blues, so I called Roan Cole.

"You on call?"

"Nope," he said. "What's with you? Got a cold?"

"Allergies," I said.

"Since when do you have allergies?"

"Will you let it go?"

"Ah, I see. Right. You want to go out?"

"I'd like to meet some women," I said. "Beautiful women interested in my company."

"He wants to meet a beautiful woman interested in his company," Roan said, covering the phone to muffle his voice.

"I said women."

"I heard you. Lysandra has somebody in mind. I'll call you back in five."

*   *   *

Lysandra favored Sangria, a downtown Fort Lauderdale pickup joint that doubled as a Cuban fusion restaurant. There were a few tables outside, but the action was within, where a loud L-shaped dining room graced by gauzy curtains and redolent of coconut, rum, roasted meats, and perfume embraced an active bar. The inimitable word *coño*, perhaps the island nation's most expressive term, was written in giant letters across the back wall.

The restaurant's specialty was several variations of the eponymous fruity wine, but I chose a *mojito*—a simple blend of rum and mint served with a sugar-cane stirring rod. Roan had insisted on driving so that I could feel free to imbibe without violating my no-alcohol-on-the-motorcycle rule. I took up the offer with gusto.

"Don't get sloppy," Lysandra warned. "We have quite a treat for you."

Five minutes later, a leggy Castilian brunette materialized beside Lysandra. She had a long dark look, right down to her fingers, wore just the right amount of lipstick and mascara.

"I'm Xenon," I said, taking her hand. "Speak it with a Z, spell it with an X."

"Catherina," she said. "Spell it with a C, speak it with a K."

She was charming and pretty and thirsty and before too long we were in our own little world at the bar.

"I like your perfume," I said, taking a long slurp of my third *mojito*.

"It's blue lotus."

I sidled closer and took a long sniff at the pale skin under her ear. She didn't draw away, but she didn't press closer either. It had been a long day and I hadn't eaten much and the drinks were hitting me hard. Roan cast me a worried glance and made vigorous gestures to the hostess about our dire need for a table.

"Whoa, Doctor," Catherina said as I pressed closer.

"Is he always like this?" I heard Lysandra say.

I couldn't see Roan shake his head, but I could imagine it. Catherina put her hands on my chest. "Back off," she said.

There was a part of me that heard her words and respected her wishes and another part of me that couldn't stop. It was a gentle kiss to the neck, not a foray with a sword, but it was still too much. I felt a tap on the shoulder and turned around to face a couple of wiry men wearing shirts open to their waist.

"She told you to back off," said the one with the hairy chest.

"I'm sure they've got us a table for us by now," Lysandra said, putting an arm around Catherina's waist and moving her away.

"I'll handle it from here," Roan told the angry guys.

I have to hand it to my best pal—he always steps up to the plate. Thinking back I wish I had had the wisdom to follow his lead. Instead I raised my chin to the hairy man. It was just a little bit of "Oh yeah, you want a piece of me?" but it was enough to light the macho fire. He shoved me and I saw the shove coming and would have answered more delicately had I not been tight. As it was, at the touch of his hand I sank my breastbone to my navel, collapsing my chest. His wrist bent uncomfortably, and when he sank down to take the pressure off I kicked him in the face.

Roan tried to keep his head from cracking on the edge of the bar, but he wasn't fast enough. A couple of teeth went into the wood edging and one of them stuck there right along with its root, like a shrimp dripping cocktail sauce. His friend, shorter and stockier, took a swing at me while Roan was letting the other guy down easy. I moved right into the fist. I felt my lip swell and I tasted blood but took three breaths and shook my head before I felt any pain. It didn't stop there because the guy was after my teeth, and even though I ducked and covered and nailed him once in the balls with my elbow from a crouch, he took me down and Roan had to tackle him to get him off me. By that time the toothless wonder was back in the game, snorting like a camel and wailing on my back with his fancy Italian boots.

I suppose I should be grateful there were no steel toes involved because the guy knew enough to work my kidneys. Through my slow-motion, drunken fog I heard Lysandra exhorting Catherina to stop them. There was a certain logic to the suggested intercession of the not-so-injured party, but Roan was more of a help than the brunette, who seemed understandably horrified by the rapid devolution of her night out with an eligible neurosurgeon.

The waiters piled on after that. I guess the new dental décor was bad for business. I heard someone yelling about the cops so I attacked a pressure point on the attacker's standing leg and he toppled away. My own pain came then, and I imagined blood in my urine. The ladies withered me with looks. Roan dragged me outside.

"Stay here," he said, pushing me down by the bushes near the valet station.

"Where are you going?"

"I'm going to stash the girls in that steak joint across the street so the cops don't bother them. Just keep your head down."

I huddled under the ficus. The valets stared at the bloody drool rolling off my lip, but the pain in my back and mouth was nothing compared to the pain in my heart. I saw Roan cross the street with the girls and I heard a lot of shouting behind him. He pretended to go down the street, but when the shouting faded he doubled back, brought the girls to the front door of the chophouse, snuck them in, and came back out alone, the collar of his sport jacket turned up against the night's eyes.

"Let's go," he said, taking my elbow.

We got in his Saab just as a Fort Lauderdale PD cruiser pulled up.

"Keep your head down," Roan said.

I did but it lolled to the side. The leather felt cool on my cheek.

"Goddamnit, Zee, don't you puke on my car."

"I'm not even close to puking," I said.

"Well, you're close to retarded, I can say that much. Keep your lips closed, will you? Aw, man. You got blood on the carpet. What's wrong with you anyway? If that wasn't the stupidest set of blunders I ever saw you make, it was damn close."

"Catherina's nice," I said. "I'm sorry."

"Your damn right she's nice. Not just nice but fine. Do you know what the worst part of all this is?"

"I didn't get lucky," I said, nudging the window control with my nose.

"Wrong. The worst is that *I'm* not going to get lucky because I'll be listening to it from Lysandra all night. Leave the window alone, will you? And keep your head down. We'll be lucky if we don't get pulled over before I get you home."

"I don't want to go home," I said. "I want to go to Victoria Park."

"We're in Victoria Park, bozo. Jesus, I feel like I'm back in college."

"I want you to leave me just around the corner. Make a left, will you?"

"Leave you?"

"I got a friend I wanna to see. Just go back to the girls. If the cops come, pretend you don't know me. Hey, turn here."

A moment later we were in front of Solomon Yu's house.

"So who's this friend?" he wanted to know. "Shit, Zee, if you've got a woman down here why didn't you come straight away and save me all this trouble?"

"Not a woman," I said. "My new teacher. Chinese guy. Friend of Tie Mei."

He doused the lights and turned off the car and I listened to the tick of the cooling engine as he digested the information. He didn't have long because Solomon's front light came on.

"You want a friend of Tie Mei to see you like this?"

"Like what? I'm fine."

I got out, tripped on the curb, and fell into the grass along the sidewalk. One of my shoes came off.

"You're fine. Yeah, I can see that. Not exactly the kind of impression you want to make on a teacher, is it? Get back in the car, man. I'll take you home. The girls can wait a little bit. Worst that happens is a couple of rich meat-eaters pick them up. Guys like that will probably look a lot better than we do right now anyway."

"Ring the doorbell, please."

"It's a bad idea, Zee."

"It's fine. I'm fine. Just do it, okay? If he doesn't want me here, he'll call me a cab."

Reluctantly, Roan complied, watching doubtfully as I drooled blood and struggled with my shoe.

"Go on," I waved. "He's here now."

As he drove slowly away, I heard the lock in the door turning and prepared to meet my mage.

*   *   *

Inscrutable was one of the first big words I learned because everyone was always using it in reference to Tie Mei. Looking at Solomon standing with his arms crossed, I thought his picture should be next to the definition in the dictionary.

"Again you arrive at night," he said.

"It's not so late," I answered, sitting in the grass and wrestling with my shoe.

"And you are drunk."

"I had to see you."

"Come into the house," he said. "A physician should not roll around on the street."

"I'm not on the street. I'm on the grass."

He retrieved my shoe and lifted me by the elbow. I noticed, as I had before, how dense he was to the touch. He escorted me inside and put me down on the couch.

"Rest here," he said.

I lay on his couch and covered my eyes with my forearm. The world spun. I thought of dancing with Jordan, of how lovely it would be to pirouette with her in my arms. I disappeared into a fantasy waltz in a big hall with chandeliers and a high ceiling—another life perhaps in some long disbanded western court. Violins played and other dancers circled us in wigs and long gowns. A harpsichord tinkled and glasses clinked. Jordan's hair was up and she wore a ruby necklace against the fair expanse of her skin. I could see the tiny mole by her clavicle and the wondrous hollow at the base of her throat and it was all I could do not to kiss it, as I had tried to do with Catherina, but only really because I wanted Jordan. I placed my fingers on the tattoo of the scales of justice that she bore near the acupuncture point known as *ming men*, or heaven's gate, and felt her back smooth and intact.

"Sit up," said Solomon, bringing me out of my reverie.

"Johann Strauss," I said, blinking.

"What?"

"The waltz king. That was the music. *Tausend und eine Nacht.*"

"Thousand and One Nights," said Solomon, putting a bunch of tiny dark pills into my hand from a plastic bottle. "An early effort, with Arabian influences and a strong clarinet to start."

"What pills are these?"

"You do not know? Smell them."

I lifted the pills to my nose and sniffed. My nose was all mint from the *mojitos* and I felt a rush of embarrassment for what I'd done, but I recognized the pills as *Huo Xiang Zheng Qi Wan,* a Chinese patent formula for food poisoning and hangovers.

"I was just waltzing with Jordan."

"Take the pills or suffer in the morning," Solomon ordered.

"Sometimes people poison themselves because they're all alone," I said. "And because their mother left them and their lover left them and they have no compass and things seem to be getting better on the surface but underneath everything is crumbling and the poison dulls the pain."

"You talk too much," said Solomon. "Take the pills."

He put my hand to my mouth and turned my wrist and the pills went in. He gave me a glass of water and I swallowed. Then he dabbed my lip with an antiseptic that smelled like camphor.

"What?"

"Tea tree oil," he said.

With that, he plumped the pillow, pointed for me to lie down, and handed me an ice pack.

"I'll see you in the morning," he said. "If you have to vomit, do not do it on the floor. The bathroom is down the hall, second door on the left."

Then he turned out the lights and padded off. I closed my eyes and went back to the ball.

Jordan was nowhere to be seen.

35

The streaming sun conspired with my bladder to wake me. The ice pack lay warm and flat on the floor at my side. My shirt was bloody and my lip was swollen. I listened hard but heard nothing. My memory of the previous night was clear and painful. I nearly keeled over when I stood up. My mouth was dry.

I made my way to the bathroom and cleaned up. There was a note in the kitchen next to a thermos of green tea and an apple. The note instructed me to eat and drink. I did then checked my pager and found no message. I called Roan but got his answering machine. I went in search of Solomon.

The house was laid out the way Tie Mei always told me ancient Chinese temples are, with passages that lead nowhere and doors that appeared grand but hid only a small closet. I went downstairs to Solomon's studio but didn't find him. I checked the library next and amused myself looking at the books, which were herpetological titles covering the reptiles and amphibians of Indonesia, Central and South America, Africa, and Australasia.

I poked my head into the garage and found his silver Aston Martin coupe in place. I called his name over and over, feeling like an interloper but figuring that since his note hadn't mentioned he'd be out, he had to be around. I went back upstairs and opened doors until I found the master bedroom. The bed was small and low and hard—I tested it—and the room was dominated by a big old Chinese armoire of the style in which Tie Mei had decorated my father's house. I knocked on the door next to it, called his name, got no response, went through and down a winding staircase to another door and through that into some kind of laboratory.

The room was clean and white and smelled like Slither &

Crawl. An air purifier hummed. Row after row of glass cages sat on a stainless-steel restaurant rack. Solomon Yu stood at a matching table. He wore thin latex gloves and a lab coat and thick magnifying spectacles and was busy pushing the fangs of a big snake through the plastic cover of a glass vial. He addressed me without looking up.

"Never come in here again," he said.

"I'm sorry. I was just looking . . ."

"I don't care for excuses. Do not come in here again, ever."

I held up my hands. "All right."

"How do you feel?"

"Terrible."

"You'd feel a lot worse if you had not taken those pills."

"I know. Thank you."

"This is a king cobra, the largest venomous snake in the world. It has venom enough to kill fifty men, and it can move nearly as fast as you can run. Can you imagine what would happen if you startled me while I was milking it?"

I took a step backward. "I didn't know," I said.

Pearls of venom dribbled down the sides of the vial as Solomon massaged the snake's head with his fingers. When the dribbling stopped, he used a long metal hook to put the snake back in a cage.

"The venom is neurotoxic," he said. "I sell it to institutions that use it in research and to make antivenin."

I followed him to a row of rodent cages. "I worked in a rat lab as an undergraduate," I said.

He nodded, picked up a good size rat by the tail, and put it down on the steel-topped table. The rat tried to gain purchase with its front legs. Solomon took a pen out of his breast pocket, put it at the back of the rat's head, and pushed down. Then he yanked the tail. The rat died instantly. "Painlessly separates the spinal cord," he said.

I found my heart pounding and took a deep breath. It wasn't

the fact of rat death that moved me so much as the dispassionate ease of it. He reached in and took out another. It squealed and gyrated wildly in his fingers.

"They spin to break free," he said. "He'll break his tail in half if I don't let go. It's an instinct. Remember the spiral? This is another example."

He put the rat down on the table and repeated the spinal separation.

Two.

He reached in and brought up another rat. This one had black markings on the side. It didn't squeal and it didn't spin, but its eyes were wild with panic. He put it down on the table next to its dead friends.

Three.

Four.

Five.

Six.

He tossed one rat apiece into cages along the wall. As he fed the snakes, he told me what each one was.

"Black mamba," he said. "Bushmaster. Krait. Death adder. Cascabel—that is the South American rattlesnake—and your inland taipan."

"Death adder," I said. "Nice name for a rat killer."

"We must never lose regret at taking life. I kill the rats because I choose to keep the reptiles and that is what they eat."

"You can't let the snakes do their own killing? This way doesn't seem fair."

"They use venom to kill. That venom is worth more than money to me. There is no fairness in it anyway; the rodent has no more chance against the snake than it has with me."

"So the killing disturbs you?"

"How could the taking of life not be regrettable?"

I leaned against the table, checking my environment. My head was pounding and I thought I might vomit. Probably it was the hangover, but the rats, the venom, the talk of death—none of it helped. Solomon saw me grow pale and slipped off my shoes and pushed down hard on the *tai chong*, or Great Rushing—the liver point on the top of my foot between the big and the second toes. I felt my head slowly clear. Last, he pushed on *yin ling quan yin*, or Mound Spring—the spleen point on the inside of my leg below the knee. I cried out at the sensation, but he just went harder.

"Enough," I said, pulling away.

Paying no attention, he yanked my leg back and pushed again, even harder this time. I grew light-headed. He smiled a little bit. I tried to pull away. He dug deeper with his thumb. The pain shot up my leg all the way to my hip.

"Hey," I said.

He gave a final push and my head cleared. Just like that. I was soaked in sweat from the way the hurt had come on me so fast.

"People think that because snakes live lives of concealment and surprise they have little intelligence and no self-awareness. That is not the case. They speak to me, and believe me they are sentient and they have a genetic species memory. They were on this planet when it looked different than it does now, when it was all green and brown and sweet and wet. We are ruining everything, you know. The process used to be inexorable and slow; now it is inexorable and fast."

"You mean global warming?"

"Pollution, habitat destruction, all of it. Our species is a virus on the face of the planet. When we have killed it we will move to another planet and do the same there."

"And the snakes told you this?"

"You mock me."

"Not at all. You're the one who said they talk to you."

"Mammals have had our run. The age of reptiles is nigh once again. You can bet on that, Dr. Pearl. You can take it to the bank."

*　　*　　*

237

Solomon insisted that we train even though I was still hung over and an apple was scarcely sustenance enough to sustain internal martial arts practice. We started with the spear. I fancied my spear work was pretty good—I'd controlled Darlene easily enough—but he derided everything I did.

"You treat the weapon like a staff," he said, picking up his own spear and putting it up against mine. "You push left and you push right in great sweeping maneuvers. This is a thrusting weapon, Doctor! Use it to find a straight path to the heart or the throat if the heart is covered."

To underscore the message, he rotated his *dantian* in the fashion of Tie Mei's training, causing the tip of the spear to circle. He did it so quickly and was so relaxed that the spiral of his hips connected to the tip and I felt an enormous force push my spear down and out of the way. There was a sound, *braaap*, and his spear point was at my heart.

"I never move off the straight line," he said. "The point of my spear is always aimed at my target. Move aside and you give the opponent a chance to get in. When I stick to your spear and push you out of the way in spiral fashion, the fatal thrust is just a half second away. You are killed before you can get your weapon back into play. Try it. Block my thrust."

He came in again. I tried to block, but he was too fast and his spear point went right to my throat. I coughed and stepped back.

"A little feint is all it takes," he said. "If you do not hear the sound my block made, you are not doing it right. Wind your way up my spear: be a snake climbing a tree. Go around and go up at the same time. But remember, keep your spear point aimed at me every second. Never waver. Not even an inch."

I tried what he showed me, blocking and striking with one movement, using the six-foot run of Chinese waxwood to circle around his weapon like one of his scaly charges might. I saw the value of thrusting straight while blocking his advance at the same time, but the coordination required to transmit the power from my hips to the spear was a challenge.

"Twist your hands," he said, showing me how his wrists bent. "The back hand goes this way; the forward hand goes this way. This connection is an essential skill. It is not just for the spear but for open-hand fighting, too. If you can master this, if you can express your core rotation into your hands, then you have the skill to handle any attack. It is consummately practical. Do it again."

I practiced over and over. My hands burned from the rub of the waxwood. It is a smooth wood with circumferential knots like bamboo, and it was the knots, one on the other, that generated the characteristic sound of success. I found myself wondering if he had to go to work. I said something about it in between bouts and he reminded me it was Saturday.

I strove to control the spear and make that glorious, staccato sound he did, to move his weapon so effortlessly yet violently out of the way that his defense was open a little bit—his body vulnerable to my attack the way mine had been to his.

It took me a couple of hours of relentless practice but I got it at last, and when I did he had me change the spear to the other side of his and do the same maneuver in the opposite direction, diverting his attack again but this time from a different position.

"You must not be a one-trick pony," he said. "You have much to learn."

I practiced on the other side, curling my wrists the other way, bringing my spear shaft up and over the top of his to deflect his attack down and out of the way as I had learned to do from the other position. I managed that technique, too, and it actually took less time.

I was soaked in sweat that smelled like mint from the *mojitos* I had consumed and also had a certain musk I linked to my antipsychotic medication. Solomon smelled it, too, and stopped the lesson.

"You have not done as I asked."

I knew he meant the medicine.

"I have," I said. "The stuff stays in the system for a while."

He considered my answer for a moment then nodded in apparent satisfaction.

"Now we will practice some sensitivity drills," he said.

I figured I'd do well with those since perceptive hands were a must for a surgeon of any stripe. He led me to the far end of the studio and tied a piece of black cloth around my eyes. I didn't care for the feeling of being blind, and it didn't help that I was hungry and hungover and tired from the spear work. He raised my arm and put the back of his hand against the back of mine.

"There is a little patch of skin between us," he said. "Where I move, you move. Concentrate on the skin. Focus on it. Make it your world."

"There's more than skin between us," I said. "There's Tie Mei."

I felt him disconnect. I reached up to take my blindfold off, but he gripped me in the vice of his hands.

"Leave it on," he said.

"Why won't you talk about her? She's the eight-hundred-pound gorilla in the room."

"Gorilla," he repeated.

"You're so good with colloquialisms that I figured you'd know the phrase. It means something big we're ignoring. I'd like to grieve with you for her. You loved her. I can tell. You radiate the feeling, all the more because you deny it, suppress it, avoid it."

He hit me. I felt the blow coming before it struck, perhaps because of the wind it made or maybe the sound of his exhalation. It was just a slap, but it was a hard slap and my face stung badly and my broken lip split again.

"I loved her, too," I said, reaching for the blindfold, my voice coming out a mumble.

Again he stopped me from freeing my eyes. He grabbed my hand, put the back of my wrist to his, and repeated his command to stick with him. He began to move. I tried to ignore my buzzing face and stayed with him. He went low; I went low. He rose up,

I followed. I went from a crouch to my tiptoes, following him around the room as he seemed to circumnavigate the obstacles that were the training equipment.

I caught myself getting tense from the effort and used what I knew of point-by-point relaxation to sink and soften and take the stiffness out.

"That is correct," he said, after a long time. "Be like water."

So I flowed with him, abandoning all ego, moving through the darkness without a thought in my head other than to remain connected to the little patch of skin he presented. I tried not to think about his secret actions, I tried not to think about what I'd done the night before or about the slap. I tried to trust him.

His circles were smaller than mine and were growing smaller still. He made a wagon wheel out of the two of us, with him as the axle and me out on the rim. I knew the game, understood that whoever was in the center of the circle had less distance to cover and therefore got to his destination quicker. It was a principle Tie Mei had taught me as a child, in Matteson Hammock Park in Coral Gables, with wooden swords in our hands when all the other kids were out on the ball field holding bats. Back then she made me stick to her sword the same way Solomon bade me stay with his hand, though she had not covered my eyes.

The skill was still with me. I felt Solomon's surprise right through his skin and I felt some satisfaction swell up and with it a slight loss of balance. Success is just as great a threat to a man's equilibrium as is failure, and I didn't want to falter.

Hungover and uncertain and waffling in my trust, I still managed to move like water.

36

The Miami police pulled into my driveway early Monday morning. They were so quiet that I didn't hear their tires on the pavement or the slamming of the car doors. I don't know how long they had been looking around the house before they knocked, but when I responded a slight man with a mustache waved a warrant in my face and read every word of it aloud.

"Do you understand that we are here to make a search of your premises?"

I nodded. I was in an Asian leisure gown. Dawn had barely broken and I had not yet made tea. A second car pulled into my driveway and two more officers got out. The first guy through the door was tall, with a hunched back. The other looked like a human fireplug.

"Axe," I said.

His face went sharp. "Detective Avery Billings."

"You don't remember me from the mixed-martial-arts school?"

"I doubt anyone there that night will forget you."

"What brings you all the way up here?"

"It's not every day we get a warrant to search for a Japanese samurai sword. I thought I'd tag along."

"Samurai sword," I repeated. "Could I see that?"

"Did you cut some guy in Miami?" he asked, thrusting the warrant at me.

I scanned it. Samurai sword is what it said. "I don't know what you're talking about."

He nodded. "That's a nice kimono."

"Thanks," I said.

He sat me down on the couch while the other two men started searching my house. He plumped up the pillows and slid his hands under them.

"No weapons hiding here, right Doc?"

I shook my head. Things were happening fast. I wondered if it would help to call Wanda then decided it would just make things worse.

"Nice furniture," Avery said. "All from Japan?"

"China," I said. "I don't have anything from Japan."

"China," he said. "That's right."

"I don't own a *katana*."

"A Cuban gentleman with a limp says you do."

I shrugged. "The other cops call you Axe?"

He shook his head. "Different life."

"Got swords," the small detective called from the other room.

"I own several," I said. "Long ones, short ones, red ones, blue ones."

"Go ahead and be a comedian," Avery said. "But tell me, you know this guy Lopez-Famosa?"

"He's the father of a patient of mine."

"Right, the little girl. So you know him. But did you ambush him in the alley behind his office and cut his Achilles tendon with a sword?"

"Don't be silly. I'm a neurosurgeon."

Avery regarded me steadily. "About a year ago there was a guy went out at night with a sword," he said. "A weirdo vigilante who cut some woman's eyebrows and maybe tangled with the Russian mob. It was Broward County, out of my jurisdiction, so I didn't hear about it back then, but the sword angle flagged on the computer and now we got a special prosecutor involved."

"I heard Lopez-Famosa had a conveyor-belt accident," I said. "My sister told me."

"The BSO detective."

"That's right."

"Why would she mention it?"

"Father of my patient, as you said."

"First report said a conveyor. Then he changed his mind."

I adjusted my robe. "It's a shame there's so much violent crime."

"He says he bit you," Avery said.

"Kinky."

"On the leg. You mind if I take a look?"

"At my legs? You're making me tingle all over."

"Go ahead and pull up your robe, will you Doc?"

I lifted the hem a little, showing him my calf. He knelt down in front of me, gave me a look that said don't try anything stupid, and turned my foot. He paused when he saw the tiny area of discoloration left from where the *dit da jow* had done its work.

"This a bite?" he said.

"You see teeth marks?"

He looked closely. "I see a bruise."

"I bought a new motorcycle. There's a spot on the side of the engine case I'm not used to yet. I keep whacking myself there."

"You got an answer for everything, don't you?"

"No, I just happened to bump my leg."

The mustached detective came out of the back room carrying my *guan dao* and my spear. The hunchback brought both my broadswords and Quiet Teacher.

"That was quick," said Avery.

"I've got nothing to hide."

"Of course you don't."

The broadswords had no scabbards. "Be careful," I said. "They're sharp. I sliced a finger putting them up on the wall."

"You practice," said Avery. "We already know that. *I* already know that, so no bullshit."

"I cut my knee with one of them, too," I said. "Nicked my ear once."

The mustache pulled Quiet Teacher from its scabbard.

"Hooeee," he said, looking at the mosaic pattern of the Damascus steel. "Looks expensive."

"Leave it alone."

"I'm taking it for evidence."

I put my finger on his chest. Not too heavily but not too softly either. "This is between you and me," I said. "That sword is precious to me. No losing it in the evidence locker, no playing Zorro with it after hours."

The cop's face colored. He took my finger in his hand and tried to twist it. I didn't let him. The hunchback watched.

"I mean it," I said. "I want that back."

Avery stepped between us before things got hotter. "You'll get your sword back, Doc," he said. "Unless you're the man I think you are."

Staring daggers at me, the mustached cop sniffed my blade. "Bleach," he said.

"Oil," I answered.

"Sure smells like bleach. Did you use it to wash off some blood?"

"No bleach," I said. "Camellia oil. Comes from the tea bush. Keeps the rust off, living close to the beach like I do."

"You smell bleach, maybe we want to pull the drains," said the hunchbacked officer. "I'd love it if we could find some blood."

"Been almost a week," said Avery.

"At least we could lift the covers," said the hunchback, pulling some plastic gloves from a back pocket.

I sat there while they went through my kitchen and then through each of the bathrooms. Avery guarded me in case I suddenly decided to start chopping cops.

"There's an arrogance to vigilantes," he said, watching my face.

I shrugged. "I wouldn't know."

He pressed. "The average vigilante thinks the system doesn't work. Thinks all cops are dumb. You want to tell me what you know about the Achilles tendon?"

"I'm sure you know plenty without a lecture from me."

Avery nodded. "The way I hear it, these kind of slicing wounds are tough to fix. If the tendon had ruptured—say, from playing ball—you can go in and stitch the ends back together. But a clean cut kills a lot more muscle cells. There's lots of bleeding because the little cell bits required for clotting are produced by blunt trauma but not by a knife. Little threads don't form or something like that."

"Fibrinogen. Vitamin K. Platelets," I said. "You should have been a doctor."

He looked at me. "You know what's funny?"

"No, but I could use a laugh."

"You haven't asked me why this guy would say you cut him. The motive. See what I mean? If they're innocent, most people get irate. They get indignant. The first thing they say is, 'What, me? Why would I do that thing you say I did?'"

"Okay. What's my motive?"

"He says you had the hots for his wife. He says you went crazy with jealousy after she died. You know, that he had her and you never did."

"That's nice," I said. "But it's bullshit. I'm in love with someone else."

"Love makes the world go round," he said.

"Ha," I said. "I wouldn't have expected that from you."

He smiled but it wasn't a nice smile. "Like what? That it's money? Hate? Fear? Envy? Just different flavors of love, Doc. Hey, you got any celery? I like to chew on celery while I think. Good for blood pressure. Makes the body alkaline. Keeps those stomach acids at bay."

"In the refrigerator," I said, getting up from the couch. "Second drawer from the bottom."

He trundled off, opened the door, pulled out a stick of celery, and took it to the sink for a rinse. "Important to wash your vegetables," he said. "Fifty years from now they'll find out that all these pesticides kill us as sure as they kill bugs. Speaking of being a doctor, I figure a guy who chose a cut like that had to know some medicine. Coroner said even with surgery, Lopez's gonna walk half flatfooted the rest of his life."

"Maybe a football coach cut him," I said. "Those guys know anatomy, don't they?"

"We got blood," came a voice from the other room.

The mustached detective came into the living room holding a plastic evidence bag. "Drain ring from the sink in the master bath," he said.

I reached up and turned my lip inside out for Avery. "Had a little excitement at a bar the other night," I said, omitting the fact that without Solomon's slap, the wound wouldn't have bled when I brushed my teeth fifteen minutes earlier.

"We'll find out," the hunchback put in. "We're gonna run DNA."

"Aren't you going to tell me not to leave town?" I asked him.

"Don't leave town," said Avery.

"We're gonna have to take this sheath apart," the mustached cop said, raising Quiet Teacher.

"It's called a scabbard," I said. "Sheath for a knife, scabbard for a sword."

The cop smiled. "Call it what you like, but it won't look like much when we're done ripping it apart. I think we're going to find blood, Doc, because I don't see you carrying bleach around when you go slicing and dicing. I think you wipe the sword when you're done and then you put it back in the *sheath*. Like they do in the movies, right Avery? And then, when you get home, you clean the blade with bleach and then you oil it up, but you don't think about the little traces that we're gonna find inside that sheath."

"Scabbard," I said.

"Today, I think it's gonna rain," Avery said, taking a bite of celery and looking out the window.

37

The antipsychotic medication Diomedes gave me erased visions of my past lives and eased my ache for the sound of Tie Mei's ethereal voice and the aroma of almonds that heralded visitations by her shade. Withdrawing from it, I had a bad episode of tremors and dry mouth and even a rash on my thigh that faded in a day. Alone with my native neurochemistry, I came to see the broader context of my identity across many lives and to sense far deeper forces at work in the world than I had previously understood. I was beginning to wonder whether it was about me at all; I began to see myself as an agent of karma.

That delusion didn't keep me from feeling incredibly stupid for underestimating the size of Oswardo Lopez-Famosa's ego and for overestimating his love for his daughter. In previous vigilante actions, I had always figured in a deterrent, an angle that kept my victim from going to the cops. I hadn't done that very well this time, and I worried that being thrown in jail would force Jordan away for good.

I wanted to email her an explanation of my attack on Lopez-Famosa but knew email could be used as evidence in court, so instead I went to see Big Steve at The Grace Note. We sat at a two-top near the bar while he reviewed the search warrant and the affidavit the police had left with me. He looked the restaurateur more than he looked to be an attorney, but he looked the biker most of all, with the leather vest and the chains and the big belly and the thick belt. He sipped a beer. I ordered a club soda.

"Anything you want to tell me about this?" he asked, after carefully reading the entire file.

"Like what?"

"Like, what the hell are we doing having a conversation about you cutting some guy's ankle with a sword?"

"I'd like to get my sword back," I said. "And I'd like not to go to jail."

"I didn't ask you what you wanted. I asked you if you had anything to tell me."

I sipped my drink. I thought about my options. "Not really," I said.

"Look," Steve said. "We've been friends since we met. You were there for Emma when she needed you and that means a lot to me."

"Friends," I said. "As you say."

"Friends tell white lies," he said. "They look out for each other's feelings; they twist things around to paint the world rosy."

"Sure," I said. "That's what friends do."

He took a long pull on his beer and looked at me over the rim of the glass. He was big but his eyes were small and they glinted like little black stones.

"If you hack up people—even if you really think they deserve it—I have to know. It's the only way I can help. So spill it."

"There was a guy who killed his wife," I said. It was a welcome release to be able to tell someone. "They had a kid together, but she left him because he was an asshole. He hit her in the head, a blood vessel popped, she died."

Luna the Chihuahua came trotting up just then and looked at me from down on the floor with the same stony eyes as her owner. The sight made me shiver.

"She was my patient," I said. "Her little girl, too."

"You're certain this is how it went down?"

"I'm certain."

"He admitted it?"

"That's right."

"Scalpel by day, sword by night," Steve said quietly. "Might be the strangest thing I've ever heard."

"Never said I was your average Joe."

Big Steve stroked his little dog. "The healing and the hurting don't go together."

"I could tell you it's another form of surgery—that I cut what needs cutting. The truth is I can't help myself."

Steve took a look around his bar, seemed satisfied at what he saw, and drew a deep breath.

"If it wasn't so disturbing it would be comical. This isn't some Chinese fantasyland—it's South Florida and every granny has a revolver in her glove compartment. You sally forth with a sword and you're gonna end up like that sword swinger Harrison Ford shoots dead in *Raiders of the Lost Ark*."

"That's a movie," I said. "And I don't cut grannies."

He shook his head and made a steeple of his hands. "Are they going to find Lopez-Famosa's DNA on your sword?"

"No," I said. "But they might find something inside the scabbard."

He let out his breath. "Don't be flip. This could be the end of life as you know it. Even if we plead temporary insanity—which, by the way, isn't going to be easy since you took your sword to Miami and that shows intent—your reputation will be ruined, your license to practice will probably by yanked, and you'll be fired from the hospital."

"How about a job tending bar? I like the singer and the guy that owns this place."

Steve winced. "It's so bizarre it may draw jail time despite being a first offense. The courts love to make an example of people like you. How the mighty have fallen and all that."

"Maybe not a first offense," I said.

He looked at me again with those glinting eyes. "What?"

"Less than a year ago some guy with a sword tangled with the Russian Mafiya. The Miami cop who was at my house said something about a special prosecutor being involved."

Steve stood up. "Some guy with a sword?"

I shrugged.

"This may be out of my league, Xenon. I'll know more when I talk to the cops, but I won't be shy about saying you need more firepower than I've got."

"You've got plenty," I said.

He sat down again and closed his eyes and leaned back in his chair, tipping it on two legs. "I liked it better when you were just my motorcycle buddy."

"You want me to get another lawyer?"

"I want you to give me something, anything, that might help. You've read this document. Is any of it inaccurate? Did you check the date? Your address? I've got to find a procedural foul-up to slow this down—a mistake they made that'll cost them."

"There is one thing," I said slowly.

"Lay it on me."

"It's not a Japanese sword."

"What does that mean?"

"The warrant says they're looking for a Japanese *katana*. I don't have one of those."

A tiny smile started on Steve's lips. "The warrant was for the wrong thing?"

"That's right."

"How do you know?"

"I saw it."

"You said there might be blood in the scabbard."

"The sword goes in and out of it," I said. "It's smooth inside. I use oil on the sword and I clean it with bleach, which, I'm sure you know, denatures DNA."

"Is it possible some bleach got into the scabbard?"

"I don't know. I don't want the sword to rust so I wipe it pretty well."

"The oil you use, would that affect blood, too?"

"It's an organic oil from a tree. It might."

He nodded slowly. "We'll have to wait and see on the blood, but the wrong sword—that's something I can work with."

*   *   *

Edson Erkulwater's memorial service was ten minutes from my house at the chapel at Saint Coleman's Catholic Church. The distinctive spire was a stepped affair, with biblical images emblazoned on the east side and bells hanging in cubicles to the west. A long train of tractor-trailer cabs pulled into the church parking lot ahead of me. They lined up bucking and jumping into formation with a fanfare of diesel belches and the commanding hiss of air brakes. The maneuvering had balletic precision and was as gut wrenching as a twenty-one-gun salute. I watched the drivers climb out of their vehicles, many with their families, and walk into the main worship hall.

The place was packed. Dave Weiss was in the front pew to the right of the altar, and Roan and Lysandra were with him. Roan squeezed my shoulder and Weiss stood to chat with me, but Lysandra wouldn't even look my way. I knelt down in front of her and took her hand in conciliatory fashion. She pulled away.

"You're a jerk," she said.

"I'm really sorry."

"You're a drunk, too."

"Not a drunk. If I were a drunk, I'd hold my booze better."

"Catherina was horrified," she said. "You're Roan's best friend and I vouched for you. How could you?"

"I'm going through a tough time," I said. "It's no excuse, but it's a reason. I'll make it up to her. Will you give me her address?"

"Are you kidding? She doesn't want to see you ever again."

"Just to send flowers. I promise."

"I'll think about it," she said. "Would you please get up?"

I rose and went to Weiss.

"A bummer and a half about Edson," he said. "I really liked the guy. Hard to figure he'd have such a habit. I was in and out of his room a lot to check on the job we did, but I never once saw him loopy. A big guy like that can twist too far or turn too fast and spinal nerve branches can cause problems, but we did a tight job for him."

"Too bad he didn't live long enough to enjoy it," said Roan.

"He wanted to be with his wife in Hawaii," I said. "That's what he told me the last time I saw him."

Roan pointed at a heavy, brassy, strawberry blonde with a lost look in her eyes. "Speaking of the wife, here she comes. She was looking for you and Dave a few minutes ago."

"You're Pearl?" she said, when she reached our pew.

I nodded.

"And you're Weiss?"

He did the same.

"I'm Grace Erkulwater."

"Our hearts go out to you," I said, "We did our best to help Edson, and he was doing very well. He told me he was lucky he was to have a wife like you. He had plans to live with you in Hawaii. He was going to use the insurance money from the crash."

Grace was not looking for consolation. "My husband did not do drugs," she said. "I came over to tell you that."

"Amphetamines are a way of life for long-haul men," Roan put in gently. "The deadlines, the traffic, the weather and the routes. There's no way someone can meet the schedule and stay awake without them. I have a cousin who drives Abilene to Detroit. I've been in the cab with him. I know how it is."

"You didn't know Edson," Grace said fiercely. "He was an advocate for easier deadlines. He was always arguing with the dispatcher about schedules, saying he'd have to pop pills to do it. He didn't want anything to do with the stuff. Maybe he drank enough coffee to make him use the pee can more often than most drivers, but that was only because he wanted to stay awake and come home to me without running over some little Mazda or slamming into a bridge. But pills? Forget it."

Weiss took her hand. "We found the pill bottle," he said softly.

"He was using in the hospital."

Grace shook her head. "No."

Weiss kept going. "He was on medications for his heart—chemicals we used to change his blood after the operation, to keep him safe from clotting. . . ."

"You'd have to change his blood to make him take a pill," Grace said, more loudly. "That's the only way it would work at all. You'd have to change my Edson into someone else. You killed him, that's what you did. You killed him and now you're covering it up. He's dead and if you want me to keep quiet about it you're going to have to kill me, too."

The priest came down from the pulpit and a crowd of drivers swelled around Grace. For a moment it looked like they would jump us, but finally they just led her away.

"You have a truck driver cousin?" I asked Roan when we were alone again.

"Of course not."

"You made up all that about Abilene to Detroit?"

Roan shrugged.

"Jesus," said Weiss. "You scare me. Both of you do. And those drivers. Guy offs himself with pills and you'd think somebody killed him."

38

Dear Dr. Pearl,

So I've been seeing the prison shrink. I bet you see a shrink too, yes? And he gives you pills and you tell him they're for your dog or your friend or your patient, yes? I got put in solitary for looking at the prison shrink's legs too hard. She has some legs. I like it in solitary. It's quiet there—my favorite place. I love the quiet. It's where I can be me and I don't have to explain myself to anyone, and I bet you feel the same way, that explaining yourself, all that endless justifying, is just so exhausting, all the more because you know damn well they're never going to understand that the world needs you.

Before they put me away I was talking to the shrink about these visions I've been having. I wasn't talking about you, so don't worry, and even if I were I wouldn't give up your name or anything. I told her about the cutting and the blood. She thinks I might be schizophrenic. I know I'm not—we're not. The visions are real. The cutting is real. The blood is real.

I'll be seeing you soon.
Neptune Cohen

Sitting at my desk at home, I shook Neptune out of my head. Thoughts of Jordan quickly filled the space. I brought up my email program and penned a note:

Jordan,

The items you returned to me really shook me. Most of the things are just that—things. Things I probably would never miss or think about. But now each item is etched in my mind. All this time I've been fighting your desire to separate and I've been hanging on to the slimmest of threads of hope. I fight it no longer. What we had is in the past, and it is important for you to break with that past and to carve your own future. I hope the same for me.

This doesn't mean I want a life without you. On the contrary, every day I come more clearly to the realization that my love for you transcends my guilt about my role in your injury. I don't want to go back to what we had, either before the attack or after it. I want to move on to a future in which we both spread our wings and fly, holding hands and touching toes. Here's a song to help you feel what I mean.

I signed off with love and then went back and took the closing out. I attached the file for The Everly Brother's *Let It Be Me* and pushed the send button. Then I went to the phone by the kitchen and called Wanda.

"I wondered how long it would take for you to call," she said.

"It's playing out around the DNA," I answered. "There's nothing you can do."

"You need to go see your father. It might be your last chance for a long time."

"I'll do it tomorrow. Will you tell them? I'll go for breakfast."

"Call them yourself," Wanda said. "You've abandoned the family completely since Jordan broke up with you."

I didn't like that she said that. It didn't seem her place. The family she was referring to had existed as such for not even a year.

"You've told them I'm in trouble, haven't you?"

She started to answer but didn't get even one word out.

"Tell me what you know," I interrupted.

There was a pause. I could hear her wheels turning. They were good wheels, like the alloy pair on my new bike. They ran true and they had tiny gears on them that meshed with the world in great detail, picking up everything and turning and turning. I tried to calm myself down. None of this was her fault. She hadn't done anything at all.

"I found out about it only because there's a special prosecutor involved," she said at last.

"I've got a lawyer. He's looking for a way out—thinks maybe he has a loophole."

"We talked about this, damnit. I warned you off the father, the husband. There was no evidence . . . "

"There was."

"Then you should have told me. You should have made a report. This isn't your job. Don't you get that? It. . . .is. . . .not. . . .your. . . job."

"It's karma."

"What a bunch of bullshit. Your karma will blow you up like a bazooka if that prosecutor sees your lawyer use a loophole. I know the guy. You have no idea how he's going to react—believe me, you don't."

"What, he's going to aim one of those spy satellites at my house?" I said. "He's going to give me round the clock surveillance? When I use the bathroom, they're going to divert the sewage and check my shit for sharp edges?"

"If you think this is funny you're a genuine idiot."

"I don't and I'm not."

"Hope and pray your loophole is big enough to jump through. I don't know what God you believe in, but you'd better hope she comes out swinging for you."

She hung up before I was ready to, and I sat in the stillness for a while, watching through my blinds as the beam from the lighthouse ticked across my front law. It had been a quiet day at the office. I'd come home early without going to the hospital, figuring

I'd be better off staying away from Tierra for another couple of days anyway. After a bit, I got on my bike and rode over to Solomon's.

He met me at the door wearing a t-shirt and his baggy, lightweight silk pants. He had a tiny flush of beard on his chin and I saw bags under his eyes for the first time. I wondered what was bothering him.

"Darlene said something to me about the music of training," I began.

"Darlene talks too much."

"Did you study music in China?"

"Nobody studied music in China when I was young. Not unless the Communist Party put them in a school for gifted children and turned them into instruments of propaganda."

"Things are probably different now," I said.

"Too late for me. I wanted to work in the pharmaceutical industry. I studied English morning, noon, and night. Then I made an application to Brown University and went there to study biochemistry. I wanted to know my cures in Western terms. I asked Tie Mei to accompany me but she would not."

"You got a master's degree?"

"A Ph.D.," he said.

"So why did you come back?"

"Nicer weather."

"And Tie Mei?"

"It is better for the snakes down here," he said.

"But teaching? Research?"

"I have my projects," he said brusquely. "There was not so much interest in them. I fund my own research now."

"And you get to teach a different subject," I said, voicing what I'd picked up the first day I saw his crew moving lithely across platforms heavy with pythons and iguanas and giant tortoises and boas, sweeping and cleaning with focused intensity. "The young people who work for you all study *gongfu*, yes? You hire them for that aptitude?"

"You are observant."

"It's an unusual thing in this country to blur the line between business and school. I gather they pay for their lessons with their work?"

"They do what they do. You do what you do."

"I haven't paid you," I said. "You haven't mentioned a fee."

"I'll have my price when the time is right," he said.

"Sure. All right. So, about the music . . . "

He made a movement with his mouth. "It's not much," he said. "Each form has its own sounds, each weapon its own vibration. You can think of it as music or you can merely regard each sharp or heavy thing we hold as a tool used to change the body in a certain way according to a master plan."

"The master plan doesn't only train me to move differently but to think differently, yes?"

"You already know that from Tie Mei."

"And you both got the plan from your own teacher?"

"There was more than one," Solomon said.

"One for each of the contributing styles?"

"That is correct," he said.

"And this was in the north of China?"

He waved his hand. "In the north," he said. "In the mountains. Other places. Over time."

"What mountains?" I asked.

"Wudan, of course."

"I've heard of that one. Which others?"

"Song Mountain and O Mei Shan, in the south, at the end."

I felt a surge of excitement at the sound of the names. "Was Tie Mei with you at all those places?"

"Look at you, grinning like a child. You are not Chinese. You cannot understand *ku,* the bitterness that has been Chinese life for thousands of years."

"So tell me," I said.

"The Communists killed the country. The mountain temples,

the traditions, the old ways—they are all gone. The Shaolin Temple is a tourist trap. There is a cable car on Wudan for Olympic tourists to ride. China today is what your Wild West used to be; everyone is scrambling and competing and trying to get ahead. All the young monks want to be movie stars and have a blonde girlfriend and a BMW and a town house."

"But the traditions . . . "

"The traditions are dead!" he snapped. "You know only the material madness America has exported to the world—your nice house, your fancy motorcycles, your fancy hospital with high-technology tools—so you would not understand them anyway. Forget your questions about the old days. Forget these ideas you have. If you want to learn martial arts, stop asking me about the past. Focus on the here and now. Focus on what works. Focus on the body mechanics."

"Well then," I said, sore at the scolding. "What about music?"

He sighed and some of the anger seemed to leave him. "Each weapon is an instrument in like an orchestra. Together, the different weapons create a complex melody."

"What part does the spear play?"

"The spear is a violin solo—it is capable of the most exquisite melody and challenges the best players."

"And the broadsword?"

"You might think of it as the chorus or refrain."

"What's the bass, then?"

He went to the rack, chose a halberd, and tossed it to me with two hands. I caught it, nearly falling backward from the effort. It was seven feet long and weighed about thirty pounds. The pointed end was in the shape of a leaf and there was a little brass vine winding down from the tip to the handle. The giant blade was scooped and hammered in a manner that suggested great age. The edge was chipped in places but still sharp.

"The Spring and Autumn broadsword," he said.

"*Guan dao.*"

He grunted. "Correct. I call this one "Thousand Year Echo." Did Tie Mei teach you to use it?"

"A bit, yes."

"Did she tell you the logic of it?"

"She said it was used on horseback. She said the blades were used to cut a swath through infantry."

He waved his hand as if what I'd said was unimportant. "The key is the grip on the horse with the knees," he said. "The position forces you to rotate the femurs inward along their long axis. That turns the greater trochanter of the femur outward in the hip socket."

"*Huan Tiao*," I said. "The gallbladder point on the outside of the hip."

He nodded. "The point is that you need the power of three-dimensional *dantian* rotation to swing a heavy sword, especially while the other hand grips the reins. Keeping the sword to the side so it does not cut the horse means moving your hips in a figure eight around the *dantian*."

I remembered something I hadn't in a long time. When I was seven years old, Tie Mei bought me a toy gyroscope. It featured a heavy wheel inside a red metal cage. The wheel spun on an axle that had a hole through which I threaded a string, wound it tight, then pulled it quickly to set the wheel spinning. In action it resisted being turned or moved in my hand. My nanny taught me that my hips—and the area around them—were like that gyroscope, the source of all balance and power.

"The *dantian* is a gyroscope," I said.

"Yes, but a gyroscope spins in just one plane. An ocean liner or big yacht has a variety of gyros, each oriented in a different plane to accommodate the mood of seas. The way our hips are constructed lets us move freely in different directions and at angles. The basic movement is the figure eight. This skill pervades everything we do in our martial art—always relaxing the limbs, always focusing on the core of the body to make power. Because of the constraints of one hand wielding it on horseback, the logic of all our movements starts with the *guan dao*. Do you understand?"

I nodded. I hadn't ever thought of it this way, but everything Tie Mei had shown me fit the description he gave.

"Show me what you know," he ordered.

I started by facing Solomon in formal fashion, the weapon vertical and blade up in my right hand and the spear point touching the ground. I stomped, hit the spear point with my foot, kicked it into motion, and let inertia take over. I turned left, resting the shaft on my back then bringing the blade forward with my right arm, hand curling inward to my sternum. It was the movement called "General Guan Carries the Sword to Ba Bridge."

There are hundreds of techniques for a straight sword, scores for a broadsword, fewer for a spear, and fewest of all for a *guan dao*. Rather than making the form easier, this makes it harder, because there is a great deal of repetition of many movements that look the same but differ in subtle ways. I warmed into the movements and encouraged my *qi* to flow. I remembered performing for Tie Mei, using the giant blade to swipe at the first raindrops of a tropical storm behind my father's Coral Gables house.

I whirled and spun and jumped and chopped, all the while keenly aware that if the *katana* loophole was too tight and the special prosecutor had a sweet tooth for me, Big Steve would not be able to keep me out of prison and this would be my last dance with this steel partner for a very long time. A sweet exultation flowed through me—the delicious energy of a warrior reborn. The weight of the blade was nothing in my hands because I gave the blade to gravity with each downward stroke and tapped its momentum coming up. Showing Solomon what I could do, I had a taste of transcendence, for indeed I had never before looked at the weapon this way, never felt the sensation in my body and hands that I was feeling now. Twisting and leaping and thrusting and cutting, I finished the sequence without a single error of continuity and felt elated when it was over.

"Tie Mei did not teach you that," Solomon said, his face grim.

"She did."

He shook his head. "She did not. The style is not hers."

"I beg your pardon?"

"The spirals are hers but the technique is different," he said. "You did not learn this from her! You are lying to me!"

"I'm not."

"If you want another moment with me, you will tell me the truth."

"That is the truth. I never learned from anyone else. But I've told you I remember past lives, I remember the experience of battlefields and even of dying in combat. Maybe some of that crept in."

"You *cannot* remember past lives! That is pure fantasy."

"No," I said. "I remember standing on the ramparts. I remember a life in a barn, surrounded by chicken shit and pig shit, practicing my sword by chopping hay. I remember tying horsehair around the shaft of my spear so the blood of my enemy wouldn't soak my hands."

He snatched the *guan dao* from my hands and pointed at the door. "If you will not recant that craziness, how can you expect to get control of your temper? If you persist in living a fantasy, you will always be able to rationalize senseless, violent acts."

"Listen," I said. "There are all different kinds of crazy. I'm not crazy for having high ideals about the martial path. Utopian, maybe, but not crazy. I commit acts that are not in my own best interest, acts that are dangerous to me and sometimes fatal to others—that makes me sick and out of control but not crazy and not delusional either. I have clarity about who I am and what I do; I just can't stop. It was Tie Mei who told me about my previous lives, and I trust her more than anyone."

Solomon's face twisted in disgust. "You speak of her as if she were an angel and you look at me as if I am a saint. How do you think we learned the things we learned? Why would we need such skills? Do you think we were scholars? Do you think we were nursemaids? Do you think the Chinese government would have let us go because a few hundred years ago some Jews came across the Silk Road and got our ancestors pregnant and some rabbi in Miami asked that we rejoin the tribe?"

I leaned the weapon against the wall. "What are you trying to say?"

"We were doing what everyone did thirty years ago in China. We were trying to survive. We were children with no special advantages. Tie Mei might have been drowned in a bucket as an infant just the way her sisters were. She survived by luck, and she received the training she did because she was a superb athlete, a fantastic woman."

"And you?"

"I was no good at anything else."

"Don't be silly."

"I spent my boyhood gathering herbs and looking at wildlife. I loved the old medicine when everything old was erased. I loved snakes when people looked at them with hunger or fear. I was ridiculed because everyone thought my passions useless. I responded to ridicule with my fists. They were hard fists, and so I was sent off just like Tie Mei."

"Sent to monks?"

"Monks!" he snorted. "Religion was banned. Monks starved right along with everyone else. We were sent to gangsters."

A cold curtain crossed my crown. "Gangsters."

"The Triads. Criminal bosses."

"I . . . "

Solomon Yu grinned, and it was terrible to see. "You stand apart and judge," he said. "You have a picture in your mind and you paint it with right and wrong. I told you our circumstances were beyond your comprehension or experience. We were all pushed to the life by the realities of being poor and Chinese. Some of the men were just born cruel. Others did what they did to avoid the deprivations of the time."

"But they were martial masters," I protested. "The path is supposed to elevate a person, not bring them to that. If they, with their weaknesses and wants, went that way, they were no better than I am."

"I have warned you over and over about your naive romantic fantasies," he sneered at me. "You say you are not delusional, but you are. Martial artists are not saints. The martial path does not lead to enlightenment; it leads to power. My teachers were ruthless and skillful. Like us, they had been taken as children when no one else would have them or when there was not enough food at home. They paid for us and promised our parents we would have food to eat, a warm, dry place to sleep. We left our families as children and never went back."

"Your parents *sold* you?"

"I did not blame them then, and I do not blame them now."

I shut my eyes as if it would help, but all I could see was a vision of Tie Mei as she must have been as a little girl—wide-eyed, innocent, not understanding why she was being taken away by strangers. Suddenly I understood why becoming part of the Pearl family had been important enough to turn her away from her former lover.

"What about when you were children no longer," I said. "Couldn't you leave?"

"Tie Mei tried," Solomon said. "At first they would not let her go, for she was the most gifted and pitiless killer of us all. Finally she got herself caught. She was willing to be executed rather than go on, but the bosses had an investment in her. They saw to it that she was deported instead. They had business in America. They figured she would be useful here, and they sent me to keep an eye on her."

"But you fell in love," I said, rising shakily to my feet and reaching for the wall to steady me.

"Go ahead," Solomon said. "Grab onto love for balance."

"What you're telling me can't be true," I said.

Solomon laughed. "Ha! The bosses thought it was so funny that America would take a violent killer like her, that a rabbi and a congregation were so eager to help. You should have heard them slap the table and laugh at American gullibility. The government saved face by claiming she was their agent sent to rot the round eyes from within."

I felt rotted. It must have shown on my face.

"How is your fantasy now, Doctor? Is it dead yet?"

39

My father wanted a constitutional so we took a midday walk around Coconut Grove, the trendy, yuppie part of Miami that Wanda had once told me is separated from the rough currents of some of South Florida's roughest immigrant clusters by an invisible blue line of undercover policeman who wear Bermuda shorts and running shoes and carry their pistols in fanny packs.

"This used to be an interesting place," Asher grumbled. "There was a sense of community. All these chain stores were little independent businesses. Every shop looked different and smelled different, too. Have you noticed how shops all smell the same now? It's not only shops. *People* all smell the same—slick perfumes made with *faux* this and *faux* that. We're turning into doppelgängers, not human beings. And this bizarre need for air conditioning! Who wants fifty degrees blowing on them from the ceiling when it's only seventy outside? Crazy! So, are you going to jail?

"I hope not."

He stopped in front of a boutique window and looked at a dressed manikin. Clothing still fascinated my father, even though he no longer purveyed it. "No point in putting burgundy plaid pants in the window down here," he said. "No market for it. In Boston, with a beige cashmere sweater and a pair of oxblood tassel loafers and just the right umbrella—not too much metal at the tip, no loose strap flopping—you might get away with it. Down here, it'll turn to moth dust before anyone buys it."

"I'm sure."

"At least you'll finally get a haircut. They won't let you wear a ponytail in the clink."

"That's what you have to say? That I'll finally get a haircut?"

He turned to face me, and I noticed how lean his face had gotten on Rachel's healthy cooking and all that tennis; he looked desperately sad.

"What do you want me to say? That this is a terrible waste of a medical education? That you're throwing your life away just when you've built it up to a place you could attract a good woman? That my son the brain surgeon is going to get ass-fucked, lose his job, and end up living under a bridge because he has a mental disease that makes him think he's a Chinese warrior all on account of not being able to get his nanny, long dead, out of his mind? Is that what you want to hear?"

I took a deep breath. "You're not wearing tennis clothes today. Where's the headband?"

"I'm not in a tennis mood. How could you do this to yourself, Xenon? Do you hate yourself that much? Do you hate *me* that much? Have I failed you as a father? Is it the guilt? Is that what it is? About the girl who was cut up?"

"Jordan," I said. "You know her name perfectly well."

"Jordan," he said. "You think you're doing Jordan some good going to jail? She suffered so you want to suffer? She's in a wheelchair so you crave a beating of your own? Maybe some hoods will come in at night and cripple you, too. Will you be happy then?"

"I'm not so happy now, Dad. In case you haven't noticed."

"Then you're a fool."

We walked a little more. At one point I chased a bright green VW thinking it was Darlene, but when I caught up to it at a stoplight the driver was someone else. I went back to my father.

"Friend of yours?"

"I thought so," I said, not wanting to tell him that the new teacher in my life was making me more paranoid by the day.

He chose a French café for lunch. He reached out to steady himself on a metal chair by a wrought-iron table. I didn't like the change in his color, so I sat down and he did, too, and a waiter came by and my father asked for baguettes and coffee.

"How often do you talk to Wanda?" I asked.

"Often enough. She told me to tell you to stay away from Lopez, whatever that means."

"And you can tell *her* that I need to know his little girl is going off to live with her aunt."

"You tell her."

"Anyway, I found Solomon Yu."

"The old boyfriend."

"That's right. He's been teaching me some *gongfu*."

"Wonderful news. You can use it to kill people in prison."

"Aren't you at all curious about him?"

"What's to be curious? He loved Tie Mei. Tie Mei didn't love him. Or maybe she did, I can't really remember. But she loved you more."

"You mean she loved *you* more."

My father shrugged. "Maybe one shouldn't tease us apart. Tie Mei had no family and then your mother died and suddenly she had one. I remember something about Solomon going away to school to pursue his education. He wanted her to go with him; she wanted to stay."

"You would have saved me a lot of wondering if you had told me this before."

"I didn't remember. There's been a lot going on, Xenon, like you cutting people outside the operating room. Anyway, I've been thinking about Solomon since the day you asked about him."

"He went to Brown University," I said.

My father blinked. "Ivy League, isn't it?"

"In Rhode Island. He became a biologist."

"He should have become a doctor. That way he could have racked up hundreds of thousands of dollars in debt and then thrown his life away on some cracked Chinese derangement."

The waiter brought our bread. It was crispy and fresh and rained crumbs and released steam when we cracked it open.

"He's a reptile wholesaler," I said.

"A what?"

"He brings animals into the country from the tropics and sells them to pet shops. Turtles. Lizards. Snakes."

"Oy."

"He also does research on venom. I don't know what it's about. Probably pain relief. I think he's looking to come up with a pain med and sell it to the pharmaceutical industry."

"This whole thing, I don't understand," said my father.

I spread butter on my baguette and some blackberry jam, too. The butter was cold and hard but it melted deliciously on the bread.

"If God is a rodent, Solomon is in a lot of trouble," I said.

"You're the one in trouble, not him."

We munched our bread. My father called the waiter and ordered a sandwich.

"My troubles don't seem to be affecting your appetite," I said.

"I eat when I'm worried. You should know that by now. You know what gets me about you and the sword?"

"That it reminds you that violence is everywhere?" I interrupted. "Reminds you of how you left Russia for a cleaner life but were dumb enough to take a loan from the mob? How you wouldn't pay protection so they killed the woman who was more a mother to me than my own?"

His face grew pale. "You can be very cruel, Xenon."

"It's worse than you think," I said. "You judge me for avenging wrongs with my sword, but you let a thug raise me."

"What?"

"Solomon told me that Tie Me was a criminal, a killer, an assassin. Apparently she was very good at it. I think you knew. I don't think Grandpa Lou did, but I think you definitely knew. Pillow talk, if you didn't figure it out for yourself. That's why you didn't want me to find Solomon."

My father put his hands around his belly and hugged himself. "I don't want to hear this," he said, rocking back and forth.

"Whatever it is, it's the past. I'm interested in the present and the future. I want to see my son stay out of jail. I want to be happy in my life with Rachel, playing tennis, walking around town, eating wonderful food. I don't want any of this old stuff in my life."

"She was raised by triad bosses. She wanted to stop killing so she let herself get caught by the Chinese police. Grandpa Lou thought it was his doing, but the government exiled her and her masters were glad to have someone over here for dirty work."

"I said, I don't want to hear it!" my father thundered. "Don't you listen? People do what they have to do to survive. This world isn't so easy as it seems to you, sitting happily in the lucky life you are so eager to mangle."

"Funny," I said. "I heard the same thing from Solomon."

40

Until the breakup, Jordan and I shopped together twice a week at a grocery store near Amanda's condo. I went there that night and lay in wait by the organic produce, knowing that since her maiming she had become more serious about nutrition. I examined pomegranates, romaine, endive, and celery until I saw her turn the corner of the aisle. When I looked up, her wheelchair was beside me. She wore a yellow halter-top and her arms looked toned. I could tell she had lost weight by the way her cheekbones protruded. Her light brown hair was dyed red—a professional job by the looks of it.

"I knew this would happen sooner or later," she said.

"I like the hair color. It suits you."

"No it doesn't; I look like a Halloween chicken. But I had to do something to mark things."

"You mean to mark being Jordan without Zee."

She looked down at her lap. There was a basket with some cans of tuna and some spices. "I heard curry reduces inflammation," she said, holding up a bottle. "I thought it might ease the pain in my back."

"Is that something new?"

"From the bicycle," she said. "My shoulders have become my hips, if you see what I mean, and they're not quite up to the task. They get tight and my back hurts between my shoulder blades."

"You should be getting regular massages now that I'm not around. The curry might help. It's the turmeric that does it, the spice that makes curry yellow. If you don't like curry you can just take the turmeric with some honey. A tablespoon a day should do if it doesn't bother your stomach."

"I like curry," she said. "Indian food is a favorite."

I blinked. "It is?"

"I never told you because I know you don't like it and I didn't want you to feel you had to go."

"May I carry that basket for you?"

She handed it over.

"What do you need?" I said, surveying the produce bins. "Plums?"

"Please."

I put some in her basket.

"Do you really like the hair?" she asked.

"I do."

"You're a terrible liar. It's one of my favorite things about you."

"Well, all right," I said. "Maybe the red could be a bit more subdued."

"Like Emma the Dilemma's?"

"Like that. Of course, she has to work a lot harder than you do to be beautiful."

"Emma's got working legs," Jordan sighed, pointing at some avocados. "She can sing and she can dance."

"You can sing," I said.

"You're thinking about lifting me right out of the cart and twirling me around right now, aren't you, Zee? But no matter how strong you are, I still can't dance by myself."

"People rely on each other. Nobody's an island. And you've got the bicycle."

"The bicycle gets my heart pumping. It's a survival tool. It oxygenates my brain so I can think more clearly and gets the endorphins circulating so I don't need the pain pills as much."

"All right," I said. "Good."

"Deep down, you don't want a cripple, Xenon. You want a woman who can dance with you and that's not me. I'm not physical like that anymore. I don't really *want* to ride around on your motorcycle or be dragged through the aisle of a grocery store trailing my limp, useless legs. You radiate physicality. You even chose one of the most physical fields in medicine, the specialty where you act rather than diagnose or prescribe."

"I diagnose," I said. "I prescribe."

"You know what I mean. Those tiny motions you make with a scalpel require as much physical discipline and precision as the martial arts you hold so secret and so dear. I've had enough surgery. I know. And you ride a motorcycle instead of sit in a car. You have to move to feel. How can I possibly be the right partner for you? You said it yourself. You even sent it in a song. You don't get any satisfaction."

I put the avocados in the basket. "What else?" I said.

"Your impatience, for starters."

"I mean, what other fruit? What other vegetables?"

"I like those pomegranates," she said. "Pick me a few that aren't too soft. I can't eat them all at once; they have to last."

I picked three.

"One more," she said.

I picked another.

"A month ago you would have told me that a few is three and four is four," she said.

"That was then; this is now. What else do you need?"

"Organic tomatoes. I don't care if they're green."

I found some and began loading them up. When I was finished, she put a hand on my arm and turned me to face her. "Something happened that you need to know about," she said.

"Go on," I said.

"Tie Mei came to me," she said. "Last night, when I was in bed. And no, I wasn't asleep. I came to the store because I figured you'd be here. I had to tell you."

I dropped the basket. The tomatoes flew. I tried to snatch them out of the air, but I wasn't fast enough. I got one. The others hit the ground with a splat.

"Don't fool with this," I said.

"I'm not fooling," she said.

"What did she look like?"

"I know what she looks like, Zee. I've seen her picture a hundred times."

"What was she wearing?"

"Green," she said. "A green silk outfit with Chinese buttons. A faint pattern, but I couldn't really say what it was. Something Asian. Squares, I think. And her hair was up. She has a beautiful neck. Everything about her is beautiful. I can see why you adored her so."

"You had a dream," I said, cleaning up the mess.

"Not a dream. She spoke to me."

"Wu Tie Mei is dead," I said.

"She came to you, she came to me. How can I convince you? She had a message for you."

"What message? Why would she send a message to me through you? You don't even talk to me anymore."

"She said to tell you that just because she's quiet doesn't mean she isn't still your teacher. She said you have a big battle coming and that your opponent is formidable."

"Formidable? That's the word she used? That doesn't sound like her."

Jordan nodded. "She said you expect things to be what they seem, but you're going to be challenged by things that are not."

That one bent me over. I felt my breath coming hard like I'd been hit. Tie Mei talking to me was bad enough—a hallucination, a sign of mental illness, an indicator of another world. But talking to me through Jordan? Telling riddles? Could this be true?

"Did you notice a scent?" I asked.

"What?"

"My nanny had a fragrance," I said. "Her ghost has it, too. If you really had a visit, you would know what I mean."

Jordan furrowed her brow. "A fragrance. Like a perfume?"

I waited by the organic greens. I didn't say a word. I tried to remember if I had ever mentioned it to Jordan before.

"Nuts," she said at last. "Cashews, maybe, or walnuts. No— almonds. Like marzipan paste."

I felt an infinite quiet and I held on to it. My gaze flickered unconsciously around, just in case Tie Mei was poised for revelation. Nothing happened. Jordan looked at me expectantly.

"What else did she say?" I asked at last. "Did she talk about us?"

Jordan began to cry. I thought at first there would just be some tears, but her breathing grew more and more labored. I knelt down and held her and felt her diaphragm fluttering and her lungs working hard against her ribcage. I straightened her up so her chest could move more easily, and her breathing eased but her sobbing did not. It started quietly, but with her arms around my neck it became louder and louder. The sobs became wails, and they rose to the store ceiling, full of anguish for the life lost, for the terrible, terrible pain, and for the hope reborn and the challenge to belief a ghost sighting brings. My face was buried in her orange hair, but through the strands I saw an old woman standing by the melons staring at us, a boy in surf shorts and flip flops lift a bag of oranges pretending not to look, a little girl holding her mommy's hand and pointing, and a shelf clerk scanning us with his stocking gun.

"Shh," I said. "Hush."

She shook her head violently against my own.

"What did she say?"

"She told me I would walk again."

*   *   *

I sat on the cot in the back of the ambulance, holding on to the straps as Kurt Vanderkamp maneuvered smoothly and skillfully through the Miami streets. I remembered being impressed by his driving when he brought Kimberly and Tierra in from the scene of the interstate tragedy and I was impressed again. The *aikido* touch went straight to the wheel.

"You handle this thing like a go-cart," I said. "It's amazing."

Vanderkamp waved the compliment away, but Preston glanced over from the front seat. "That's why he's the master," he said.

"You guys are great to do this," I said. "Beyond great."

"It's not done yet," Preston said.

"Especially you," I said. "I didn't figure you'd come on board."

"I always wanted to be a doctor," he answered. "I didn't have the grades for it. That's my baggage, not yours, and I put it on you right from the start. Melissa and I talked about it after you left the studio that night."

I had not noticed how young he was because the anger in his eyes had kept it from me. I saw it and felt a fool for having been pulled into his war with himself.

"I should have let it go," I said. "My fault more than yours."

"I was the bad guy. Just tell me we're cool."

"We're cool. And you're not the bad guy. We're on our way to see the bad guy right now. But listen, both of you. It's not too late to turn around. You could go to jail for this. Are you sure you think it's worth it?"

"We're not going to jail," Vanderkamp said. "Targets like this have too much tucked under the dirty side of their life to squeal. He'll keep quiet."

"And if he doesn't?"

"Life's about principles," the *aikidoka* said. "There's more to it than driving a bus. A man kills his wife and gets away with it scot free, that's bad enough. A man kills a woman I saved from the road, it's personal."

"And you?" I said, looking at Preston and thinking how young he was. "You've got a lot to lose if the plan goes south."

"I go where he goes," he said, pointing his chin at his teacher. "It'll work fine. It's all blue sky."

It was a beautiful, intimate, shared moment, and it heightened my awareness of the responsibility that was completely and entirely on my head. I felt as if my disease were leaking. I felt as if my compulsion to do what I did had escaped the confines of my soul and gotten out to infect two good men.

"We could still just tell the cops," I insisted. "I could give everything to my sister."

"If the cops were going to do something, they would have done it already."

"They don't have autopsy results yet," I said. "If the fist matches the wound, the game changes."

"And he'll call it a crime of passion," Preston put in. "Temporary insanity. An accident. The guy's rich, from what you say. A good lawyer will get him out of it."

"Then the guy will knock up some other lady and there'll be another little kid who has to watch out her dad doesn't hit her," Vanderkamp finished.

So we drove to Lopez-Famosa's place. He lived in the part of South Miami Beach that is visible from the causeway. The waterfront houses are colorful in the Mediterranean style. As soon as we had crossed the bridge, we turned south, entering the neighborhood, and Kurt hit the emergency equipment. Lights and sirens going, we pulled up in front of the house. As I watched clandestinely from the back of the ambulance, the two men took the stretcher out and wheeled it to the front door.

"Last chance to bail," I said.

Preston acted as if he didn't hear me. Vanderkamp pressed the doorbell with his elbow. A moment later, Lopez-Famosa answered the door. He was on crutches and his assaulted ankle was bandaged. He wore fine khaki slacks and a yellow silk Tommy Bahama shirt with a palm tree print and seemed annoyed at being disturbed.

"Yes?" he said, seeing the ambulance and the paramedic uniforms.

Kurt's hand went high, wrapped around Lopez-Famosa's neck, and effortlessly brought him down onto the stretcher. Preston had the straps tucked around him as quickly as he had thrown me that night in the *aikido* school, and within seconds all Lopez-Famosa could do was twist his neck back and forth and yell. Kurt took care of the yelling by strapping an oxygen mask over his face. The screams dropped to a dull roar, and shortly after that Lopez-Famosa and I were alone in the back of the ambulance.

"So," I said as we drove off. "How are you enjoying our little chess game?"

"Let me go," he said, the mask muting his voice almost to a whisper.

"You called the cops, I called my friends. So, here we are."

"Do what you want to me, but you can't get to Tierra," he said.

"Why, because there's an officer outside her door? I put an anonymous note in her lunch. Told her you killed her mother. It went something like this: Tierra, remember all the times you saw your dad hit your mom? Remember that's why you don't live with him anymore? Well, guess what?"

"No!" he squirmed against his bonds.

"I don't care what you think of me," I said. "But I do care that you don't have a chance to lose your temper with your little girl the way you lost it with her mother. And since we're on the subject of what I do and do not care about, I do owe you for making me realize how much I care whether I go to jail. I was getting a little too passive, you know, trying to accept my karma and let my life run its course. I lost sight of the fact that I have a choice in the direction of that course, and I've decided I want to stick around."

"They'll get you on DNA," he said. "My blood is on that sword."

"Maybe, maybe not. I keep my things clean."

"I won't drop the charges," he said. "No matter what you do to me."

"The problem with playing chess with me is that I live by a completely different set of rules."

"Fuck you," he said, spitting. The saliva hit the oxygen mask and slid down the side of the plastic, ending up on his cheek.

"You'll be able to fuck all right," I said. "But you won't be able to have any more children. I can't have a killer running around having children, see? Not safe for the children; not safe for the world. So the Lopez-Famosa line ends here."

With that, I loosened his belt and yanked his trousers down. He went crazy, twisting and straining against the straps. The ambulance rocked. Preston turned to look, and I saw Kurt grab his head and turn it forward.

Lopez-Famosa's screams grew louder. "I can put you to sleep," I said. "But then you wouldn't feel the pain. I want you to feel the pain. Frankly, it's going to hurt more later—hopefully for the rest of your life. I'm a bit disappointed I can't use my sword; the nice police officers took that away. I can't use a scalpel, either, because my cutting technique might serve as evidence. Fortunately, I have this high intensity electric wrap."

I reached up to where the paramedic emergency supplies were neatly arranged on a shelf and pulled down the powerful electric blanket.

"Even in sunny south Florida, prolonged immersion in a swimming pool or canal or the ocean can lead to hypothermia, so some paramedics carry this handy rescue device," I said, plugging the blanket into the ambulance's outlet and then winding it around Lopez-Famosa's testicles.

His eyes went wide and he struggled against the straps again.

"Does that feel good?" I asked. "It won't in a minute. It heats up very, very quickly."

He screamed obscenities into the mask and I noticed tears on his cheeks.

"The testes are heat sensitive," I went on. "I won't burn your skin, so you'll have no evidence of this, but the heat will kill your germ cells. Do you know what they are? They're all the little Oswardos you've got inside—little Oswardas, too. They're made of proteins and I'm cooking them right now. Less than half an hour of sightseeing here and they'll all be dead. See how clever this is? No marks, no evidence, just utter and complete sterility. Don't worry, Ozzie. You'll be back home in no time, snug as a bug in a rug."

Lopez-Famosa arched his back and let out a yowl so loud it pierced the mask. Kurt Vanderkamp switched on the siren so we wouldn't have to hear it.

I turned up the heat.

41

Solomon opened his front door.

"I have to admit I am surprised to see you," he said.

"We have an appointment."

"Nevertheless."

I took a deep breath and let the moment build. It stretched and stretched. "About Tie Mei," I said at last. "You told me they sent you to keep an eye on her. I'm guessing they knew she wouldn't do what they wanted her to do over here any more than she had done it over there. After she quit, I mean. After she got herself caught."

"You live a fiction," he said.

"So you say. My answer is that you could say the same of anyone. We all have our stories."

"You want to change your story, Doctor. That is why you came to me, no?"

"I want to change some of it," I said.

So we went to work. The training room seemed smaller than it had before, perhaps because Darlene was there along with a broad-backed man. All three wore matching workout suits: black tops and black bottoms with white stripes.

"This is Marco," Solomon said. "He helps me at the shop and is training for his first unlimited fighting match."

Close up, Marco was young and big and strong, but his handshake was limp.

"Another snake fancier? I asked him.

"Turtles," he said.

"Ah, I like turtles, too."

"We have been discussing equilibrium," Solomon said.

"*Wuji*," I replied.

Solomon smiled slightly and nodded. "Please—explain."

"I know *wuji* means stillness, a state pregnant with infinite possibility. It's the void referred to in the book of Genesis—all there was before God created heaven and earth. It's also what the *Daodeqing* says preceded *taiji*, the state of binary forces harmoniously interacting."

"The *Daodeqing*," Marco repeated.

"It's a book about virtue," said Darlene.

Solomon looked at me inscrutably. "That is correct," he said. "Martially, *wuji* means you are ready for anything. In every fighting system other than the one I teach you there is a dialogue between you and your opponent. He gives you this; you give him that. I do not believe in that dialogue. Instead, I say forget what your opponent is doing and concentrate on your own state of perfect emptiness."

"Tie Mei taught me exactly the same thing," I interjected.

"Tie Mei, Tei Mei," Darlene clucked.

"Whatever your opponent tries to do to you, your only job is to respond in a way that maintains that *wuji*," Solomon continued. "If he flies through the air because of what you do, that is not your business. There is no bad intention, there is no good intention—there is only you keeping your equilibrium."

"But you gotta intend to drill the guy, right?" said Marco.

Solomon shook his head. "If your mind is cluttered with intentions, you are not free. You must not have any kind of plan."

The idea was so big it set us into motion. Marco began circling the room like a caged tiger. He bounced on his toes a few times and shadowboxed near the bag. I noticed that his heels came up when he punched and that his connection with the ground seemed weak.

"I just don't see how we can not have a plan," Darlene protested, dropping into a full split and leaning forward until her elbows touched the ground. "How about wanting to win?"

"We want to win. We want not to be hurt. But those are goals, not plans."

"I plan to win my UFC fight," said Marco.

"No," said Solomon. "That's your goal. And for practice, try defeating the doctor. Be careful of his fingers, please, and no elbow strikes to the back of the head or kidneys."

Marco and I each pulled on a set of open-finger mixed-martial-arts gloves and went at it. He dove for my legs and I stepped aside and twisted his arms, one high and one low. All of a sudden he was on the ground with a surprised expression.

"Finish him!" Solomon cried. "He is at your mercy."

"I don't need to do that to keep my *wuji*," I answered.

By way of proving me wrong, Marco sprang up and tackled me again, this time from the side. I tried a similar maneuver, but it was only partially successful. I ended up sliding across the floor until my heels reached the wall, then I pressed down on top of him. He suddenly swung his hips around on the floor like a circus performer and hooked his heels around my back. Once he had me there, he began to press his point, forcing me to the ground and locking my shoulder.

Darlene crouched next to us. "Marco studied jiujitsu in Brazil. It works, doesn't it?"

Marco increased the pressure on my shoulder. "Okay," I said. "That's enough."

The young baboon kept going. I felt the tendons at the top of my arm begin to separate. I tapped the floor as I had seen wrestlers do, but Marco seemed not to notice.

"Hey," I repeated. "I mean it. Back off."

Marco took it up another notch. Darlene smiled at me.

"Now you understand why you must finish an opponent when you have the chance," Solomon said.

"This isn't life or death," I gasped. "We're supposed to be helping each other here."

"You do what you train to do," Darlene opined.

My shoulder had about another inch to go. Darlene joined the game by jumping on my back and looping her leg around my other shoulder so I was pinned on both sides.

"No comment, Doctor?" I heard Solomon say. "You always have something to say."

I was in too much pain to answer his taunts. I arched my back to give my shoulders some room.

"You two better get off me," I said. "I'm not kidding."

Solomon moved close to me. My position on the ground allowed me to see his shoes but not his face. "Anger means you're out of *wuji*," he said.

"You set them up to this, didn't you?" I gasped against Marco's forearm.

"You are filled with thoughts of retribution: what you will do to them when you get free, what you will do to *me* for masterminding your pain. Out of balance this way, you cannot find a solution. This is the moment you've been training for, Doctor. You wish all kinds of bad things on these two right now. That is your urge, is it not?"

"I'd like to chop them in half," I panted.

"But that will not help you."

"I have to do something," I groaned as they tightened up even more.

"Transcend the white heat of your anger and pain. Think and feel your way to an alternative."

"Just tell them to let me go. They're going to break my back."

"And breaking your back makes you think of your girlfriend, Jordan, with the injured spinal cord. It brings up guilt and a rush of medical knowledge. Perhaps visions of being in a wheelchair yourself are making your judgment cloudy. You want to be a master. Let me tell you that the time to be a master is when things are tough, not when they are easy. You have lost your *wuji*, Doctor. If you *really* want to transcend who you are, you have to figure a way to get it back."

"This is too much, Solomon," I gasped, as Darlene planted her feet and yanked my shoulder up higher. "*You* are too much."

"If you can do this, perhaps Jordan will love you again," said Solomon. "Show yourself you are not controlled by anger and panic and perhaps you can convince her."

The pain drew a constellation in the space behind my eyes. I saw galaxies unfolding, swirling and spiraling. I saw arms of stars reaching out, each one replete with a solar system of planets. I saw infinite possibilities, but all of them glowed with my agony and therefore they could turn only one way, toward the heat, the hell, the burn of my torso. I was on fire and I could not think.

"Alignment," said Solomon, tapping a tasseled loafer on the floor.

Darlene had my humerus against the edge of the joint capsule. Another millimeter and my shoulder would dislocate. It made a loud, unhealthy noise.

"His shoulder's going," said Darlene. He can't get out of it. He's not as good as you think he is."

"The fisherman sits by the river," Solomon said with a resigned sigh. "The two boys sneak up on him. They put their hands on his shoulders and they shove."

At first I thought Solomon had gone completely crazy, but then I understood his craft and with it I understood the hint. My teacher was referring to a legendary movement Tie Mei had taught me many years before. The memory pierced the pain and I began to feel the places Marco was touching me in an analytical way. I felt the direction and quality of his force and suddenly the message of the galaxies came through. His movements were circular and therefore two-dimensional. To beat him, I needed to respond with a spiral.

I moved my shoulder blades down and tucked my pelvis, getting rid of the arch in my low back. I twisted my forearm and began to reverse Marco's lock.

"Fucker," he said, realizing what was coming but unable to stop it.

"I heard they don't like swearing in UFC," I gasped. "Doesn't sound to me like you're ready for prime time."

I worked the same reverse on Darlene and succeeded in slamming her face into the floor.

"I never liked you," she mumbled, her lips pressed against her teeth.

42

"Your shoulders are tight from riding your motorbike," Solomon said after the other two had left and we were alone in his kitchen and drinking tea.

"I'll work on it."

He showed me a movement to loosen them. It looked like he was swimming the breaststroke through the air, his fingers tucked high under his armpits as his hands came in. I tried it. It was painful but not as much as Marco's joint lock.

"Tell me about your research," I said.

"*Ti kuan yin*," he said, taking a sip from his cup. "Iron Goddess of Mercy—a very popular leaf. A friend in China sent this particular tea to me. It comes from a high mountain plantation."

"I'm not asking to pry. I'm a doctor. I'm fascinated by these things."

"Did you know that immunology began on Shan Mountain in China?" Solomon asked.

"Where you trained, yes?"

"Buddhists and Daoists have been there for a thousand years—probably more. Internal alchemists knew how to attenuate viruses a thousand years ago. They actually cooked vaccines using much simpler methods than we use now. There was some risk of human-to-human transmission, but overall they were better than 80 percent effective, especially on smallpox."

I looked around Solomon's modern South Florida kitchen, with its black marble floor and countertops, its recessed halogen lights and shiny stainless cabinets. I knew I had been with Solomon in many lifetimes, and I still marveled at the way karma reincarnates cohorts. I wanted to comment on the magnificence of the cosmic plan and to savor with him the remarkable flavor of this particular go-round—the woman that bound us, the link through my Judaism, through my grandfather, through medicine—but when I tried I couldn't put the feeling into words.

"Have you been vaccinating yourself against snakebite?" I asked instead.

Solomon looked at me strangely. "What makes you ask that?"

"Seems logical you would want to attenuate your risk."

"Attenuate," he repeated. "You have a way with words."

"You're the one who does. I just threw that out for a giggle."

He gave a tiny smile. "You can be engaging company."

"Thank you. As can you."

"As a matter of fact, I *have* been vaccinating myself. I use an old Daoist method of soaking a cotton plug with a tiny amount of diluted venom and inserting the plug into my nose. The venom is absorbed through the nasal mucosa. The sting is excruciating, and often my nose goes numb for days."

"Does it work?"

"I have been bitten a few times and suffered no ill effects. Beyond that, I cannot say for certain."

"You talk about alchemy. Tie Mei never used that term."

"Alchemy in Western terms is the science of turning base metal into gold. Internal alchemy in our martial terms is the science of improving the stuff of us, of turning our body into the organic equivalent of gold. Our art is built on a tripod of Daoist philosophy, Chinese medicine, and local martial arts. All three legs together make the process. You become stronger, more flexible, more resistant to disease, more able to manage stress, more clear thinking, and, of course, you live longer."

"I would still like to hear about your research."

He gestured for me to follow him. We went upstairs and into his bathroom and through the secret door and down into his lab. When we got there he donned his white lab coat over his sweats.

"Snake venoms are weapons in an evolutionary arms race," he

said. "The venom evolves to meet the challenge of the prey."

"Jordan has a theory that the prey wants the predator."

"She is correct. Such desire is a dance. It manifests, through evolutionary change, as tiny changes in the immune system of the prey—mast cells, mostly. Those changes answer related changes in the exquisitely complex venom molecules, which draw on a whole panoply of available proteins to fit the bill."

He opened the taipan's tank and with shocking speed snatched up one of the snakes and pressed its head into a milking vial. Muscles bulged in the snake's head as clear drops appeared through the glass and the reptile flailed and whipped helplessly in Solomon's hands.

"When we are young it seems that love should be simpler," he said. "Our lives, after all, are less complex, and we are often less encumbered. Sad to say, sometimes what should be simple is not."

"You and Tie Mei," I said.

He made a face. "You were quite right to guess she would have none of her assignments."

"They came through you?"

He shrugged. "Through me, through other channels. She knew I was there to see that she did them."

"And the crime bosses let her ignore them?"

"She was brave, and her life with you and your father made her braver. She was entangled in her new life and drew strength and succor from it. She defended herself against their advances on more than one occasion. I helped by reporting she was sick or confused in her mind."

"And she rejected you," I said. "She threw the baby out with the bathwater."

"The system was in equilibrium. She drew from me, I drew from her."

"Codependence."

"I prefer to call it the harmonious interplay of opposing forces," Solomon answered, putting the taipan back in the cage.

"So your research is on snakebite immunity?"

Solomon smiled archly. "There is no great fortune to be made immunizing snake fanciers, Doctor."

"No great validation of your theories in the halls of academe either, am I right?"

"*Wuji*," he shrugged. "In life, in career, in love, in combat, always keep your balance no matter what others say about you or do."

"Do you think bettering my *wuji* will free me from my urges?"

"What do *you* think?"

"I think that if it doesn't, there isn't much point to the training."

He dispatched a rat into the king cobra's cage. The animal reared up to an alarming height and caught the rodent in midair.

"There are anti-inflammatory and anti-tumor medications derived from vipers," he said. "Contortrostatin for slowing tumors—a product derived from a Palestinian species that slows tumor growth—and others. Viper venom is designed to breakdown the structural integrity of blood, yet its venom—in tiny and diluted quantities—seems to have the opposite effect."

"A vaccine for affairs of the blood."

"Your way with words again. Personally, I am working with venom from the cobra family—*Elapidae*, in Latin. These venoms attack the nervous system."

"You're saying you can repair nerve damage with the very thing that causes it?"

He shrugged. I looked about, seeing the equipment around me in a whole new light. I was no bench researcher and I hadn't been in a biochemistry or molecular biology lab in years, but I suddenly understood that there was far more expensive equipment here than was needed for merely extracting and storing venoms or, for that matter, analyzing or fractionating them.

"Yes or no? Have you synthesized an agent or is this just a theory?"

"I've had some modest success," he said. "Early trials of my own devising."

"Mammalian though, right? Rats?"

He nodded.

"Success how?"

"You can buy mice with diseases, did you know that? Genetically engineered to show Alzheimer's or Parkinson's or epilepsy. And, of course, you can cause injury and repair it."

"Regeneration?"

"The Holy Grail," he said. "The English language is so evocative sometimes."

I put my hand on his arm. "You're saying you can repair a compromised spinal cord?"

"Nerve repair is my field of interest."

"If you have something that works. . . . "

"I import exotic animals. Not a large sample, of course, as they are expensive. But I have tried it in rats and rabbits and monkeys."

"You injured them?"

"Peripheral nerves first," he said. "Fingers, toes, finally a large nerve in the leg."

"And?"

"It was amazingly quick. I had to go back in surgically because I do not have a scanner of any kind, but to the naked eye the repair was nearly invisible."

"How soon?"

"That is an interesting dimension of the treatment. The compounds in the venom are very powerful. If the toxins themselves do not function quickly, the prey animal will escape."

"So the repair was rapid?"

"Surprisingly so. A few days for small nerves; perhaps a week for large ones."

"That's not possible. What about function?"

"Function was restored. The animal had to relearn use of the limb, but animals are singleminded that way, undistracted as they are by imagination or conscience."

I gasped. It was an enormous medical breakthrough. If what he said was true, Solomon Yu was going to help countless people and in so doing become a fantastically rich man.

"What about spinal cords?" I pursued. "Where did you inject?"

"Through the dura and directly into the cord," Solomon said calmly. "Regeneration is a very complex process. It is driven by gene expression, and for it to happen properly the environment has to be perfect. The compound has to be in direct contact with nervous tissue."

"Difficult without a scanner," I said.

"I am certain I lack your surgical skills, Doctor, but I muddle through."

"How long after injury did you administer the treatment?"

"Experimentally it seemed to work better on old injuries than fresh ones, which of course is the opposite of what one would expect. I hypothesize that there may be substances at the site of a fresh wound that interfere with the integrity of a molecule as large as the regenerative compound."

"Excitatory neurotransmitters, probably. What was the longest you waited between the time of injury and the time of repair?"

Solomon walked to a row of rat cages and pulled out a black-and-white male. He turned the rat over and showed me a long, fully healed incision on its leg.

"I injected the compound into this one after a week," he said. "The sciatic nerve was bisected."

"What kind of dosage did you use?"

He put the rat down and it scampered away, showing no ill effects whatsoever.

"It turns out not to matter much because it is not carried in the blood. Absorption is topical and direct. I dose according to the size of the lesion."

"And you tested sensory function?"

"With needles, flame, and ice."

"And in monkeys?"

"I waited a month after the injury. Same results."

My heart started to beat quickly. "What did you do with them afterward?" I asked, filled with a vision of revivified gibbons swinging from trees at the local zoo.

"The monkeys?"

"That's right. I'd like to see them."

"I didn't have the luxury of keeping them as mascots, Doctor. After all, I am a businessman."

"You *sold* them?"

He inclined his head.

"So you think it will work on humans?"

"I believe so, but I have not yet tried."

"I could get you a subject," I said, my mouth so dry it was hard to peel my tongue off my teeth.

"Do you know how many people are desperate to get out of their wheelchair? I could have volunteers in a moment. I don't need a single subject; I need a clinical trial—several of them, actually. That requires time, effort, adequate funding, and the right pharmaceutical company. Seven years, maybe ten. Patent lawyers. Filings. Politicians. Surely you are not so naive as to think that we can simply invent a cure and immediately start helping people? That would be like young love, would it not, Doctor? Simple and unencumbered but full of curves in the road, consequences no person could predict?"

"My girlfriend, Jordan, has spinal cord damage," I said, growing agitated. "You know all about her. If there's even a slim chance . . . "

"Well," he said, briskly, disengaging himself and shrugging out of his white coat. "That is quite enough training for one evening."

"Oh, no," I said. "You can't let it go like that. Jordan Jones . . . "

"I have no hope to offer your friend and no pipe dream to offer you."

"But you said it works."

Solomon held up his hand. "This is not China. There are obstacles."

I grabbed him by the collar. "I love her. I'm desperate. I'll do anything to help her."

I saw rage flare up, and I watched him beat it down. He disengaged himself gently.

"Good night, Doctor."

The smile in his eyes was worse than hate.

43

The next morning, Wanda intercepted Detective Avery Billings at the last minute, her big SUV nosing out his Crown Victoria in a game of driveway chicken. They emerged from their cars as I came through my front door, and it was head-to-head at once. I knew Avery's power first hand, but I didn't give him odds against Wanda, who looked exactly like what she was—a big, strong policewoman protecting her family.

He pulled his shield and she pulled hers and I stood under the arbor with the firebush tickling my head and watched as they glared at each other, nearly touching noses, Avery in his ill-fitting sports coat, Wanda in a suit of her own, jacket over her shoulder, white blouse, flat shoes, modest taupe skirt.

"He's going down," Avery said.

"Not today," she replied.

"Tomorrow, then." He turned to me because he had seen me there all along. "You do know you're going down for this, right? A technical glitch, Japanese sword not Chinese—all that does is piss off the state prosecutor. He doesn't like vigilantes and I don't like vigilantes and we're not going to stand for it—not now, not ever."

"My sword," I said. "I want it back."

Gritting his teeth and avoiding Wanda's glance he stalked back to his car, yanked Quiet Teacher out of the back seat, and tossed it at me through the arbor. I caught it but only just, and the scabbard came apart in my hands because they had cut it open. The wood clattered to the ground.

"Destruction of private property," said Wanda.

Avery threw up his hands. "Evidence. And I didn't do it."

"What about the DNA?" Wanda asked.

"Damn lucky and a smart attorney and that's all. There was blood inside the scabbard, all right."

"But you couldn't use it," Wanda pressed.

"He cleaned the sword with bleach and oil and traces of both soaked in and denatured the proteins," Avery growled.

I smiled. I know I shouldn't have, but I did—mostly because I was thinking of Lopez-Famosa's damaged balls.

"You think this is funny?" Avery stepped toward me.

I stopped smiling but stood my ground.

"Jesus, Zee," said Wanda. "Maybe you should go inside."

"It's the doctor thing," Avery said, so close I could smell his breath. "They're all so arrogant."

Wanda picked up the broken scabbard. "You've made your point, Detective. Now stand down."

"Brain surgeon or not, you're just an overpaid mechanic," Avery growled.

"Until you need his hands inside your head," said Wanda.

"I ain't never having this guy in my head."

"You ask me, he's there already."

Avery colored at that and the thick muscles under his jacket, hardened from all that throwing and falling, visibly rippled.

"Axe," I said. "Can't we be friends?"

"That'll be the day."

"I'm not the bad guy you think I am."

"You sure as hell are."

"Think so if you must, but the rain you mentioned the other day seems like it's a long way off."

"It's early in the season," he said. "The way things look from here, it may be half a year before the hurricane hits, but when it does, it's gonna be a doozy."

Wanda stepped between us. "Tuck it back in your pants. Both of you."

I took a step back and Avery slowly sauntered away. He stopped to pick a Blue Daze blossom from beside the footpath and stuck it in his lapel. Then he got in his cruiser and drove off.

*　　*　　*

"I'm here for my mother, not for you," Wanda told me when we got inside. "Are we clear about that? I don't want her hurt, I don't want strife in her marriage. She cares about your father more than anything and what breaks his heart will break hers, too. I can't let that happen. Not on my watch."

"Nothing's going to happen," I said. "But thank you for showing up. As always, you have impeccable timing."

She handed me the scabbard. "It was pure luck. Anyway, all I did was stop you from making it worse."

"Stopped him, you mean."

"You were the one goading him and grinning like an idiot."

"But you defended me. Don't say you didn't."

She pushed a bit of stray soil off the path with her toe. "I didn't do a thing. The charges didn't stick."

I filled the teakettle and turned on the gas. While we waited for the water to boil, I used superglue to fit the pieces of Quiet Teacher's scabbard back together.

"Jordan made it for you?"

"That's right."

She nodded. "I'm not so sure you realize how close to the line you cut this time." She prowled around the room touching artwork, furniture, even walls, finally stopping in front of a print of a woman with an upturned face and her hair in twin knots.

"Is this old?" she asked.

"It's original, if that's what you mean—a Chinese woodblock print done by the Tashuawu printshop in Suzhou. Tie Mei said they are one of the best modern woodblock printers."

"Why didn't your father keep them?"

I shrugged. "I think he knew how much they meant to me."

"And this one? With the sword raised and the fierce expression?"

"One of my favorites. It's from Foshan. That's in Guangdong Province."

She pointed at the far wall. "And the man in the green hat with the purple top and the green mountains behind him?"

"That's from Chengdu, in Sichuan. Before the Communists, the Chinese made woodblocks just like the Japanese did. During the tough days under Mao they became a medium for creative political resistances."

"Sometimes I wonder what it must be like to be you, living in another time and place."

"I'm here, I said. "I just have tugs in different directions."

She shook her head. "You're a puzzle, that's for sure. One day I'll figure you out."

The kettle started to sing. I went to the tea cabinet and thought for a moment about what Wanda might prefer. I decided on some lychee-scented black. It was slightly sweet and wouldn't challenge her coffee-chugging palate.

"I think you'll like this blend," I said, putting some leaves in a strainer.

"I'm sure I will. Hey, remember Erkulwater, the trucker?"

"Of course."

"You thought his death was hinky."

I shrugged. "The guy popped pills."

"But you didn't buy the OD."

"His drug screen was negative the night of the crash," I said. "Some of that stuff is short-acting, some stays in the system a while. Kind of surprising it showed nothing if he was a user. And he was planning on suing Boniface and moving to Hawaii with his wife on the money. Already had a place there. What guy plans his future and then speeds over the edge?"

"The wife wonders the same thing," Wanda said. "She came in and made a statement. Said he didn't use, showed us an article in some trade magazine he'd written about the dangers of stimulants and the way truckers are pushed too hard. She thinks someone killed him."

I poured the hot water over the leaves to rinse them. Then I put the strainer in the brewing pot, poured the water again, counted to twenty, and pulled the strainer out.

"That's the clay tea set, right?" Wanda asked.

"Right," I smiled. "Yixing clay. Makes the smoothest tea. I've had the set for years."

"You see? I pay attention."

"Of course, you do. You're a detective. Don't sip it right away. It's hot. Give it a minute."

She took the cup in her hands and set it down on the counter. She pulled up a barstool. "So you think someone did the trucker?"

"The way he went bothers me, that's all I can say."

"And then there was the little girl's mother."

"Trust me, Lopez-Famosa did her."

"But he didn't do Erkulwater."

I shrugged. "Why would he?"

"Exactly. And why would he electrocute Charles Czarnecki?"

I dropped my teacup. It shattered on the floor, the shards surrounding the puddle of tea like tiny ships moored at the edges of a lake.

"We found him last night," she said. "A neighbor heard noises and called it in."

I crouched down to clean the mess with a sponge. My pulse pounded in my ears. Wanda came around the counter. The muscles in her legs looked huge. I decided she must be bodybuilding.

"What kind of noises?" I asked.

"She called it violent thumping."

As I dumped the shards into the trash, I felt a pit grow in my stomach. I'd liked the daredevil rider, despite his self-centered obliviousness. I'd felt a kindred spirit in his love of riding and even in his love of risk. He was an innocent, and my heart went out to him.

"Where was he?"

"At his computer."

"He was a software tester," I said. "He probably lived in front of the thing."

"He was playing a motorcycle race game," she said. "He had a contraption with handlebars, throttle, brakes, the whole deal. There was a headset for the display. You wouldn't think he'd put something on his head, the way his skull was, but he did. There were exposed wires, so the minute he booted up, he got juiced. I heard one paramedic lost his dinner when they took the helmet off."

"That makes no sense," I said. "Czarnecki was a professional. He'd know about the wires. And those things run on tiny current."

"This one was wired to the power outlet at the back of the machine."

"So you're thinking murder."

She nodded. "The officer in charge dusted the place. He found nothing. When I say nothing, I mean the place had been wiped down. Everything. The keyboard, the door handles, everything."

"Thorough," I said.

"But not clever enough to make it look like an accident."

"The truck driver looked like one," I said.

"We might have two killers, or the driver may have done himself."

"What's your best guess?"

"I'm not on the team. It only got around to me because I was a witness to the crash."

"That doesn't stop you from having an opinion."

Wanda looked me hard in the eye. "I'm wondering who had a motive."

"Of the people we saw hurt on the road that night, only a little girl is left alive. I suppose there's going to be an investigation?"

"Obviously."

"Tierra Jenkins has relatives in New Jersey. Please make sure she gets to them right away."

"I don't like Lopez-Famosa for this," Wanda said.

"Just to be safe," I answered. "Just so we all aren't sorry."

44

Tie Mei often counseled me to follow my instincts. It was her opinion that the rational brain so necessary to contend with the pace and intensity of modern life is wont to run roughshod over the faint but critical voice of intuition. Intuition communicates through emotion, she told me. It is infinitely subtler and more complex than logical thought and wiser than we can consciously know. After Wanda left, my intuition hinted that the killer was leaving a clear pattern, but somehow I wasn't seeing it.

I collected the mail and found another letter from Neptune. I puttered idly around, resisted opening it, but ripped it out of the envelope at last.

> Dear Vigilante Man,
>
> I can see your dreams, yes? I was with you when you were a general fighting the Mongols and when you stayed up all night watching flaming imperial arrows destroy your fleet. I can see into your soul. Darkness links us in the most wonderful way. Don't fight it!
>
> Reject those who try to change you—yes, yes, even the girl—just the way you would reject those who try to trap you and imprison your hands. Oh, those hands! You are the agent of God; you are the agent of karma. You know this. Of course you do. Yet you don't realize that it is not only your karma at work but that of others as well. The dead and the wronged work through you, too; their fingers are in the glove right alongside God's. The cutting and the bleeding have karma, too, and you are their necessary agent even though they cower, beg, and plead. You come to them because their karma draws you. You have no choice.

Do what you must to be at peace with the Dao. What other path is there? Where else does your river flow?

You know I'm right. I know you do because you haven't answered my letters, and you haven't made them make me stop writing them either. I know you've got connections to the cops. You could stop me if you wanted, just like you could choose not to cut if deep down you really wanted the sweet and squeaky life, the clean way, the easy way. You don't because you sense you are doing what you must, yes? Speaking of the cops—they're closing in. Can you feel it? I can—even the one who wants to protect you. They know about the man you are, darkness and light and gentle fingers and avenging grip. Be careful, please. The dark work must go on.

Watchfully,
Neptune

Imperial arrows? How could he possibly know that? The letter left me convinced that Neptune was part of my reincarnation crew, even if I could not as yet sense it. It also left me wanting to take my pills again just so I could manage a coherent argument against his. I warred with myself. There was, after all, the promise to Solomon, and I was nothing if not willing to put myself fully in the hands of a teacher. But there was the deep distress I was feeling, too, pulled one way and the other, feeling the seductiveness of Neptune's argument. It was easier to fend him off when I had the pills in me. I toyed with the bottle, popping the cap off and then putting it back on, popping it off and then putting it back on. After awhile I elected to stay clean and tortured just a little while longer in the hopes that by doing Solomon's bidding, by growing in my skill and believing in that growth and in my newfound capabilities, I would dispense with the need to prove aught to myself or anyone else.

I went to bed and lay down and closed my eyes. Hoping for a revelation of Neptune Cohen, I tried for a life regression. I'd had one the night I received news of what the Russians had done to Jordan. The memories came to me that horrible night as I huddled inside the stand-up safe in my bedroom closet—the safest, strongest, quietest, and most secure spot in my world. Flooding through me, they tore me from this world as painfully as if I were being dragged from a dream. I saw many lives that night, hundreds in fact, and I saw the coterie of souls that accompanied me in my transmigrations—Jordan chief among them, but also Tie Mei, my father, Wanda, and others I saw not as clearly.

An hour passed but nothing came to me except the ticking of my clock and the distant sound of the surf and through my closed eyelids the faint, regular wash of the beam from the lighthouse. As I drifted to sleep I hoped I might find an answer in my dreams. None came, but sleep did, and for that I was grateful.

*   *   *

At first light I slung Quiet Teacher on my back and rode to see Solomon. There was a low morning fog, and I navigated carefully, unable to see obstructions in the road. If I kept my helmet tipped up slightly, I could easily imagine the fog to be the top of the clouds. Suddenly, a wisp of conscious regression swept in, right there on the road, maybe because I was no longer trying. It wasn't a full memory—there was no story to it, no connection, no internal narrative—it was just a vision of the Manchurian steppe. I rode a horse and the fog was beneath me just as it was below the motorcycle, there on the road. I held a lance and the lance quivered as my horse exhaled to add to the murk. I could smell birch wood burning and human flesh, too. Momentarily consumed by the past, I ran a red light and was nearly t-boned by a newspaper truck, which let loose a horn blast that returned me to the here and now.

My heart pounded for minutes. I rode the rest of the way afraid that another disorienting flashback might come. None did, and I pulled to the curb by Solomon's house just as his garage door came up. The reptile king, wearing a bright red tracksuit, stood in the doorway to the house, his fingers on the alarm keypad. I brought my bike straight into the garage.

"I want your nerve formula for Jordan," I said.

He shot me an atrabilious look. His eyes flicked to the sword slung across my back. "I told you, subjects must come with grants and protocols and money."

"She can't walk. She has her whole life ahead of her. If she's willing to take the gamble—and I am sure she will be—I'll pay anything you ask."

Solomon shook his head. "I have spent my career developing this product, and I will not risk everything by assuming liability for a renegade human trial at this premature stage."

"Why premature? You've worked it on rats and monkeys. It's the logical next step."

"There are risks."

"What are they, exactly?"

"The toxin could interact with human tissue in a way I cannot foresee."

"You didn't mention problems when we talked about it last."

"Sometimes there is swelling at the injection site. And, of course, there is the issue of dose."

"You said you figured the dose by the size of the lesion."

"The manufacture is extremely time-consuming and difficult. Much processing and distillation are required. I have only a single small sample."

"It's worth chancing it to save a paraplegic."

"It's not worth the chance for me. It takes a great deal of time and money to make more, not to mention the liability if there is a toxicity reaction."

"I'll take full responsibility."

"Then you are even more reckless and impulsive than I thought," Solomon said. "I know you did not learn *that* from Tie Mei."

"Maybe I did," I said. "Wasn't she reckless to quit the triads? Wasn't she impulsive to embrace the American life and turn her back on China, on what she knew, on *you*?"

"Get in the car," he said. "I shall join you in a moment. We will have a lesson right now."

He was gone for several minutes, during which time I looked over the interior of the Aston Martin. It was opulent in the way Solomon's home was but modern rather than traditional, with a tastefully laid out dashboard and a console and seats exuding balance and style. I turned on the ignition and the radio and listened to morning news until Solomon returned with a long, narrow bag, which he loaded through the hatchback door.

"Beautiful coupe," I said. "The reptile business must pay well."

"It is the marque's entry-level model, but I enjoy it."

"It was James Bond's choice in the movies," I said.

"I know."

He shifted the transmission manually and made short work of a series of blocks punctuated by stop signs. We crossed Broward Boulevard and turned into Holiday Park, one of Fort Lauderdale's largest and busiest. Solomon drove to the far reaches of the property, away from dog walkers and joggers and the picnickers at the pavilion. He got out and withdrew the bag he'd brought along. It contained a pair of folded steel broadswords. They were far more finely wrought than my stainless-steel pair and bore sharp striking points on the pommels.

"It's not natural to withhold your cure from the needy," I said.

"*Zi-ran* is Chinese for nature," he said, laying the swords carefully on a towel. "It means self-thus. We do not think of it as something outside us. Nature includes us."

"Then do the natural thing and help my girlfriend."

He dropped into a Chinese split, his groin on the ground, his legs straight out to either side. Any teenage gymnast would have been happy to have his flexibility. He looked up at me.

"You say you can see your past lives?"

"Sometimes in meditation, sometimes in dreams, sometimes in a state of mind I can't explain," I answered.

"Yet you are trapped by your karma. Over and over, you go forth with your sword."

My mouth went dry. "I told you I had violent urges and hurt people," I said. "I never said anything to you about a sword."

He shrugged. "We're past all this, Doctor."

"You've been following me."

"Certainly I have not."

"So you've got your army of *gongfu* kids on the job. Darlene, Marco, and how many others?"

"Over and over, you make the same mistakes."

"No, I don't."

"Of course you do. You would not travel to Miami alleyways with your sword if you didn't."

The thought that came to me was more terrible than anything— it was a thought of subterfuge and gaming, a realization of betrayal of the worst kind, a violation of a student's trust.

"You followed me," I mumbled and then it hit me. "You did Erkulwater. You force-fed him the pills."

He frowned. "Pills?"

"You sabotaged poor Charlie's game."

"Talking gibberish will not work, Doctor. You came to me to work on a problem, and I need to know if my teaching is having any effect. I seek feedback, nothing more."

"You could ask me," I said.

"You could lie."

I wanted to rage at him for having the nerve to have me tailed, but I did not want to say anything that might cost Jordan a possible cure.

"Give me the formula for Jordan," I implored. "Do it in the name of Tie Mei. Do it because you know what it is to love someone and lose them."

Those were the last words I ever spoke as Solomon Yu's student. He picked up his sabers and regarded me with a snake's cool eyes. "Raise your sword."

*　　*　　*

Retrospection is a luxury only an armchair martial artist can afford, certainly not one facing a superior opponent, trying to juggle two lives while the police sniff around and the prize of prizes is tantalizingly within reach. All the same I had a flicker of realization that I'd seen this coming. There had been hints all along, maybe not so much of a coherent and well-conceived sham—that he was actually trying to help me or cared what I did—as a gathering storm, lightning bolts flashing across the firmament of Solomon's emotions: the way he saw himself, the raw register of his past as seen through the bitter lens of a man alone and bereft of his one true love.

I pulled Quiet Teacher from its scabbard.

"You want to hurt me because you think I cost you Tie Mei," I said.

He moved the swords to a ready position. "Who can fight a woman's bond with a child?" he said.

"If she had really loved you, someone else's child wouldn't have taken her away."

His eyes went wide and he raised his swords and his mouth opened in a scream. "She did love me!"

I had my *wuji* and he did not have his. I was determined to keep it that way. "I was four," I said calmly. "I didn't even know you existed. You were sent to make her do things she did not want to do. It's far easier to blame me than face the facts."

Enraged, he slashed the air in front of me with both swords. "I never forced her to do anything."

"I doubt you could," I said.

That made him even angrier. "I stood against them in the end. I was on her side. I helped her. She knew that and she loved me and you stole her, both of you! Everything I wanted, everything I yearned for, you took!"

His speed and skill were terrifying, yet there was a certain satisfaction in what was happening—almost as if I were scratching an itch. It was samsara—the wheel of life. With the breath of his blades on my face, I understood that he and I had been together many times, variously supporting each other and killing each other. That long-term, wide-angle view stood behind the surge of fear and the squeeze of adrenaline I felt as his blades closed in on my flesh.

"If I beat you, I get the serum," I said.

"If I beat *you*, I get your father."

I thought of Asher and his delicatessen soup. I thought of the life he had finally achieved for himself. I thought of the way he loved Rachel and of the way she baked for him and convinced him to exercise. Little details of his new life—his headband, his tennis shirts—all that was going to be destroyed because once again a specter from the past had risen to threaten our lives.

"No," I said.

My refusal of his terms set Solomon into furious motion. His right sword sliced at where my waist had been a moment before. It would have gutted me had it touched. A half second later the left sword came down diagonally from top to bottom. If I hadn't twisted out of the way it would have opened my carotid artery. I thrust my sword straight behind me as I turned and stepped away. The tip grazed the fabric of his sweat suit, piercing the jacket. I looked for the red-on-red blossom of blood as I turned around and brought Quiet Teacher up to guard, but I saw none.

Solomon advanced on me with repeating diagonal strikes. The straight sword is not as good at slicing as the broadswords are, as there is no radius to the blade. On top of that I had only one sword in hand to his two. The windmill of steel made entry impossible, and all I could think of was to work the angles, to find an opening beyond the spirals of his blade, a place where I could step in and thrust and be done.

"Different than slicing defenseless men, isn't it?" he breathed, keeping the blades flying, backing me up toward the live oak behind me.

"You're crazy," I said.

"On the contrary. I am defending myself against a known vigilante, a man who came to my house with a sword, leapt into my car, and forced me at blade point to drive until I managed to escape into the park."

His crafty reworking of reality startled me enough for his next move to catch me off-guard. He took a low cross step, scissored his blades, and caught me with the pommel. The sharp steel tip ripped across the line of my jaw on the left side and I felt a thin strip of flesh break loose. The pain seemed remote, like it belonged to someone else.

Do not become the sword. Let the sword become you. I could hear Tie Mei's admonition, but I could see Solomon was not following it. He had indeed become the swords. His rage and viciousness traveled the length of his blades like the glint of early morning sunshine just now beginning to burn off the fog. He thrust the other sword toward my belly with a turn of his waist. I figured the pommel strike had been a disorienting feint designed to set me up for a stab with the second sword. That deduction filled me with hope. Solomon had broken the very rule he had given me: he had made a plan.

I stepped aside just in time to miss the thrust and brought my empty hand down on his wrist. His weight was committed forward, so when I yanked him forward his blade sank deep into the heartwood of the oak tree. As he worked to free it I ran to his car and jumped in the driver's seat.

I started the car as he struggled to free his blade and managed to get it going as he finally worked it loose. I glanced in the mirror to see him running after me screaming, his remaining sword raised in the air. The mirror also showed me a ragged two-inch gash along my jawline, severing the external maxillary branch of the carotid artery. I knew a plastic surgeon or two who could help the look of the flesh, but I had to stop the bleeding. I drove one-handed while maintaining pressure on the vessel with my thumb.

When I got to Solomon's I drove into the garage, slung Quiet Teacher over my shoulder, burst through the door, and made straight for his secret laboratory. All I could think about was how badly I wanted Jordan to have her legs back. Regardless of whether she ever spoke to me again, I needed to set things straight and make up for what I had unwittingly done to her. Everything was as I had last seen it, and even though I tore the place apart I could find no trace of the experimental formula.

I paused in the search, stumped and weakened from the loss of blood. Dizzy, I lost my balance for a moment, the world went dark, and I slumped over. Trying to hold the artery closed with my thumb, I pitched forward into the rack of cages, knocking them against one another. They clattered to the ground. Groggily, I saw the thick, cream-colored bellies of the death adders turn upward as the cages tumbled to one side. The taipans pushed with their noses as if looking for a way out, the king cobra struck the glass like a prizefighter, the cascabel sounded an alarm with its tail, and the mamba and the bushmaster slithered back and forth madly along the length of their cages. Only the krait seemed placid about the upturn of his world, merely righting himself along the glass and coiling up in the corner.

As my head cleared, I saw that the rack had gone over because it was not fastened to the wall but set on casters. There was a small refrigerator behind them. As my head cleared, I bent and opened it.

Inside, the white wire shelves were packed with vials. I took them out and read their labels one after the other. They were venom samples Solomon had collected, and behind them was a single larger tinted glass bottle. The label on it read *Regeneration Batch 11 50ml Trial Six.* I remembered what Solomon said about being able to make only a small quantity of the trial formula at a time. This had to be it. I dropped the vial in my pocket and made my way back to the bedroom, down the front stairs, and through the front door.

Outside it was as if the fog had never been.

The day sparkled with promise until I thought of my father.

45

I steered the bike away from Solomon's house and toward the ocean, struggling to work the clutch and brake while keeping pressure on the wound. The big BMW has a terrific suspension, but the stretch of A1A between Las Olas Boulevard and the Hillsboro Inlet is marred by a merciless run of potholes and dips and the ride dragged the D rings of my helmet across my open flesh. I felt weak and nauseous as the pain grew familiar and the adrenaline left my bloodstream. By the time I got home I could barely focus. I nearly dropped the bike when putting it on the stand. I rushed inside, put on a butterfly bandage, and called Khalsa.

"I need a plastic surgeon," I said.

"We'll worry about prettying people later."

"It's for me," I said. "I hurt myself."

"Bad timing. I need you here. The suite is ready and Roan is waiting for you."

"The suite?" I said. "Roan?"

"Didn't you get my page?"

"Ah, no. I went out for some early exercise."

"Well exercise with your goddamn pager, Xenon. 24/7 when you're on call. Eugenia Wentworth is waiting for you in the OR."

"You talked her into the surgery?"

"I didn't talk her into anything. She tripped on the escalator at Neiman Marcus in Boca and fell right off her three-and-a-half-inch heels and onto her coccyx. She went numb and lost the use of her legs. She made the paramedics bring her all the way down here. Insisted, if you know what I mean. Caused quite a scene. She's got her legs back, but there's still transient numbness and the paralysis scared the hell out of her. Gus Wentworth has been exploring my anal cavity ever since she rolled in. She keeps repeating your name, and Gus keeps repeating your name, and goddamnit, you better get down here."

"I'm not feeling great," I said. "Better give it to Tremper."

"She's not the type who takes no for an answer, and neither is Gus. Substituting another surgeon will mean the end of your short, second career. This is a job for you and nobody else. Now get in here and do it."

"I'm on the way," I said.

As soon as I hung up I dialed Wanda. "I need you to get them out of town," I told her.

"What? Who?"

"Your mom and my dad. You need to get them out of town right away. Protective custody, whatever."

"What are you talking about?"

"Someone threatened them. Someone who knows me."

"Who is it? Tell me and I'll have him picked up."

I thought about it. Solomon would just say I had come at him with a sword. He would file charges. My fingerprints would be all over his house.

"Someone terribly dangerous and ferociously smart," I said.

"You're not talking about Lopez-Famosa are you?"

"Wanda, I need you to trust me."

"Ha."

"Just do it, okay? Put our parents in a nice hotel. Do it sneakily, as he may be watching. I'll cover the tab. Just get them hidden."

"You're going to explain this, right?"

"I'm going into an emergency surgery. I'll call you just as soon as I'm out."

I hung up and made some toast. I covered it with honey. I ate a banana. I took a quick shower, keeping the now burning wound on my face from the flow, and hopped on the bike.

*   *   *

315

Gus Wentworth was a florid-faced man with an alcoholic's nose. He owned a company that manufactured gyros for expensive yachts, and he was accustomed to micromanagement.

"What the fuck took you so long?" he said, bursting into the locker room just as I finished changing and scrubbing.

I didn't want him to see my wound but barely had time to raise my surgical mask before turning around to face him.

"I was jogging," I said.

"Jog with your pager. That's what we pay you for."

"Yes, sir."

"You're the best man for the job, is that right?"

"I don't represent myself as the best at anything, sir."

"Well you damn well *better* be the best."

I put my gloved hands up in the elbow-down fashion of the surgeon. It was a submissive gesture as well as a hygienic one. "I know you're worried about her, Mr. Wentworth. It's natural to be concerned. This is a major procedure and the stakes are high. All I can tell you is that your wife has lived with this problem all her life and she is strong and otherwise healthy. I am optimistic about the outcome."

"Medical mumbo jumbo," Wentworth muttered.

"I'd like to get to it now," I said. "She's waiting."

Before he could object I slid around him and out into the hallway and the OR. The quick breakfast grounded me a bit, and the sounds and smells of the operating suite created a comfortable cocoon. Khalsa was there and glared at me. Roan nodded. Vicky Sanchez—always my first-choice nurse—rolled her eyes at me as if to say Khalsa had been on the rampage and wasn't he just too much. I rolled my eyes back. Roan had Eugenia in a light, relaxed semisleep because she had insisted on seeing me before going under. I squeezed her hand and knelt to her and she opened her eyes and smiled.

"Tell me you're going to leave an invisible scar," she said.

"I'm sure going to try."

She beckoned me closer. I put my ear to her dry lips. The heat of her breath stung my wound. I worried my blood might seep through the paper.

"Lie to me before you cut me," she said.

I bent close. "It's not just going to be invisible work," I whispered. "It's going to be miraculous. You'll feel better than you ever have. A few weeks from now, you'll be pole dancing at the hottest club in town."

She smiled and I nodded to Roan and he turned up the gas and out she went. We turned her face down and wheeled up our recently acquired O-arm scanner, a mobile imaging device consisting of a large white circle protruding from a control platform. The circle opens to a "C," which we slid over and under Eugenia. She lay on a radiolucent table made of graphite and carbon fiber so when we closed the circle we were able to get three-dimensional pictures even more precise than the ones I had already seen. Looking at the images I identified a thin septum of bone at the level of the T9 vertebra. The spinal cord was literally impaled on the spike. Khalsa whistled.

"Can you believe she did yoga?" he said.

Roan stared at the image, tracing it with his finger on the screen.

"Something like this happens, you have to marvel that so many of us come out put together right," he said. "I mean, what are the odds that all our systems will be perfect?"

"Stacked against," I said.

Vertebrae have shark-fin-like protrusions called spinous processes. These are the knobs you can feel through your skin. While Roan hooked Eugenia up to a device that measured the electrical conduction of the spine in real time, I made a mark in the skin over the bone spike and marked off an incision from the spinous process of T7 to the one on T11. I was all set to cut when I realized something was missing and stopped.

"Zee?" said Khalsa.

"Music," I said.

Roan grinned. "Your pleasure?"

"Classical."

"Special request?"

"Smetana."

Vicky kept her eyes on Eugenia's back while Roan cued up *The Moldau*.

"What is this?" Khalsa sputtered.

"Czech composer named Bedřich Smetana," said Roan. "He wrote a cycle of symphonic poems celebrating the natural beauty of his country. This is the second one. It's about the running of a river."

"I know the piece," Khalsa interrupted. "I don't want music. I want progress reports."

I crossed my arms. "The music plays," I said.

Khalsa frowned but said nothing more. I made the incision and began to elevate the muscles off the bone. I favored specialized elevators for blunt dissection but needed to cut myriad small vessels, too, so I used monopolar cautery—essentially a knife that burned to coagulate the bleeders at the same time it cut. I exposed the laminae—the backs of the vertebral bodies—from T7 to T11 and confirmed their location using the image from the O-arm. I put a burr on the high-speed Midas Rex drill and was about to start grinding down the spinal processes and underlying laminae when I felt a sudden sharp pain in my cheek.

I reached up under my mask. My finger didn't come away bloody, but I suddenly felt as if my face was on fire.

"You all right?" asked Roan.

Before I could answer, a wave of dizziness hit me and I took a step back, holding the drill high in the air.

"Doctor?" said Khalsa.

In a flash I understood what was wrong and that I was in a race against time. I looked at Eugenia on the table and ran through the angles in my head.

"Zee?" said Roan.

How could I tell these people that Solomon Yu had done more than cut me? How could I explain that what I had taken for swords were actually fangs. I pieced it together from memory. He had gone back into the house to get his swords. That was when he did it.

That was when he coated the steel with venom.

"Sometimes I just have to take a moment to marvel," I said.

"What are talking about? Get back to work!" sputtered Khalsa.

"Working on something as incredible as the human nervous system fills me with awe, that's all. Can you imagine that the brain and spine are complex enough to cause consciousness to arise spontaneously? I'm not sure I believe that God is an old man with a beard and a staff sitting in a cloud looking down on us, but. . . . "

Khalsa turned red enough to pop a vessel. Vicky saw it and put a hand lightly on his gown. "I believe Dr. Pearl is saying he's glad to be back at work."

I took a deep breath and the music receded. I summoned all my focus and applied the whirling burr. I kept going until the laminae were paper thin then started looking for the septum in a head-to-toe pattern. I checked the O-arm image, all the while wondering what my prognosis might be and how I could get antivenin. Before I succumbed to the poison, I needed not only to finish Eugenia—I needed to treat Jordan with Solomon's potion. I knew it would work. Everything about Solomon—twisted as he was by a dream denied—bespoke consummate genius.

But what if it didn't?

Because the septum was probably attached to the underside of the bone, I could not just lift the laminae as in a routine procedure. So using small bone punches called Kerresons I removed the laminar bone piecemeal, working down from the top of T8 and up from the bottom of T10 until all that remained was the septum and the bifurcated dural tubes surrounding the cord.

Khalsa bent in for a look. "The spinal cord just treated that thing like a roadblock," he said. "Split into two, went around it, joined back up."

"That's just how I explained it to Eugenia," I said.

I opened the dura above the septum in the single tube, down the middle of both duplications and into the inferior single tube. I freed the cord's diaphanous arachnoid attachments—a delicate spider webbing that held it to the dura—and let it float freely in cerebrospinal fluid.

"Beautiful work," said Roan, looking over my shoulder.

I wanted to tell him that it damn well better be because it might be my last. Instead, I swung in the operating microscope, carefully dissected the dura off the bone spur, and then nibbled bone away with a rongeur, which basically looks like a tiny nail clipper. When I had bitten off all I could, I put a diamond burr to the last of the spur and then used the O-arm to be sure I'd gotten it all.

"That's it," said Vicky.

A wave of nausea hit me so hard I erupted into my surgical mask. Bile filled my mouth. I covered by making a loud belch. Just another few minutes, I told myself. Just hang on a little longer.

Sweat poured off my brow. Vicky patted it dry for me, giving me a quizzical look. I used the microscope to see the tiny needle and even tinier suture I needed to close the ventral and dorsal surfaces of the dura, making use of the gap between them. Vicky handed me the piece of artificial material required to give the cord room in its new home, and I shaped it to fit the opening between the previously opened halves. Then I switched back to my magnifying loupes and sutured in the patch.

"Any electrical changes?" I asked Roan, my voice sounding weak and pitched high.

"She's fine," he answered.

"Let's do a Valsalva," I said.

Roan's machinery was breathing for Eugenia, and he paused the breathing after a single inspiration. The pressure of the contained breath pushed on her cerebrospinal fluid and swelled the cord slightly. I surveyed my suture for leaks, saw none, but added a sticky mixture of cryoprecipitate and thrombin called fibrin glue to help seal the suture line.

"Yes," said Khalsa, whirling away from the table and clapping his hands over his head.

I became aware of the music again as I began to close up Eugenia. The stress of holding precise positions always wore on me, but in combination with Solomon's envenomation it was too much. I managed to line up the tissue layers through sheer force of will, barely daring to breathe while I finished the suturing. I wanted desperately to stay conscious so I could test the results by waking my patient for an evaluation, but the moment the last suture was in I collapsed.

"Zee!" Roan said, dropping to my side.

"Snake bite," I said in my last conscious moment. "Inland Taipan. Fierce snake. Australia. Antivenin or I die."

Khalsa roared something but I could not make it out.

46

My leather boots had thin, flat soles and I felt the stones beneath them. I smelled the strong incense, too, which was of pine and of sandalwood and of other exotic spices mixed in from the travels of our merchants but held only for the emperor and for these halls of the Forbidden City. I should have been proud and confident in my steps and because I was an imperial guardsman others should have feared me, but I was the one looking over my shoulder; I was the one afraid.

Change had become the rule. I tried to figure out my new place in the shifting sands that were the palace. Qianlong, the emperor, grew more and more senile and soft-minded while Heshen—whom I know now as the miniature Travis Bailey, major domo of my surgical office—gained power. Heshen was slight of stature even in that incarnation, but he commanded us with his unpredictable temper and his confidence and his eagle eyes and his habit of using his sharp dagger on those who got in his way. Two days ago I was an accidental witness to the murder of a staunch cavalryman who dared suggest Heshan was more politician than soldier. Heshan stabbed him next to a silk screen behind which I was sleeping and suffered no consequence for it.

After the murder Heshen grew bolder. He even went so far as to penetrate the quarters of the most favored imperial concubine and, yes, penetrate the concubine herself, not because she was the youngest or the most attractive but simply because the emperor preferred her.

Will this murdering schemer actually become the Son of Heaven? Can he who is so vile and conniving and low actually receive the mandate of the gods? Can a man who willingly kills someone just for speaking the truth be made a god? It won't be the emperor who stops him—that much is certain. Twice today I have been in the imperial presence. This Manchu emperor of the Qing Dynasty plays with toys like a child and drools into his soup. The empress and the cuckolding concubine wipe his chin and coo over him and wave their fans and bat their eyes while we soldiers stand impassively as if we hear and see and smell and taste nothing, as if we are statues, mute and dumb.

*   *   *

I felt a hand on my shoulder, shaking me. I was sure it was Heshen, and I brushed him off.

"You won't get away with it," I said. "People see through you."

"Zee. It's Roan. How does your face feel?"

I blinked and came out of the palace as if yanked from a dream. My friend came into view and behind him someone else I knew I should recognize but could not.

"Karen MacDougal is here for the neuro exam," Roan said.

"I took a toxicology internship at Duke," Karen said, putting her hand on mine.

It all came flooding back. I wanted to give them information they needed, but it was hard to breathe and hard to talk and the pain was everywhere.

"I can't move my hands," I whispered.

Roan nodded. "There's a neurotoxic component to the venom. We've got the antivenin in you. We think we can reverse it."

"Taipan," I said.

Karen nodded. "We're up to speed, Zee. It's a very bad snake— the worst in the world. The antivenin manufacture is limited. The antivenin bank in Miami gave us a few vials, which we put into you. We've got more coming from the Philadelphia Zoo. Do you want to tell us how this happened?"

"A friend has a collection," I said quietly. "I got careless."

"What a bizarre happening," said Karen.

"Bizarre, yes, but not unusual for our man here," said Roan, smoothing my cover story. "You'll find that out as you get to know him."

The act of speaking nauseated me, and I closed my eyes and concentrated on my breathing. I could feel the air going in and out of my lungs, but my diaphragm didn't seem to be moving. Roan addressed the subject as if he were psychic.

"Breathing feel strange?"

"Yes."

"Your phrenic nerve is affected. Your throat is sore because I had a tube in you until an hour ago."

"There are presynaptic and postsynaptic toxins in the venom," said Karen. "We've been dealing with paralysis and muscle weakness."

"How long have I been out?" I asked weakly.

"A day and a half," said Roan. "After you collapsed, it took me a while to get anyone to believe what you told me. The wound on your face doesn't look like a snakebite, and we couldn't find any other envenomation site."

"My kidneys hurt," I said.

"You're pissing brown from muscle lysis," said Roan. "It's not pretty, but we're beating it. I've been reading up on the snake. Online clinical studies, journals, the whole nine yards."

"The venom contains procoagulants and myotoxins," said Karen. "We've been watching you for internal bleeding. Your face will be okay, though. There are no necrotoxins to eat your skin."

"Basically, you got hit with the nastiest cocktail of organic poisons on planet Earth," said Roan.

"Yet it's a medicinal treasure trove," Karen added enthusiastically. "Some guy in Australia is using a derivative compound to treat congestive heart failure, and I wouldn't be surprised if another drug being developed from the stuff doesn't become popular for speeding clotting in trauma cases."

"Eugenia," I said. "How is she?"

Roan smiled. "You did good, buddy. The biggest problem we've got is keeping her out of your hospital room. She's only two doors down and keeps wanting to have us wheel her in to see you. She'll be walking before she loses much of that yoga muscle tone after all."

"Don't let her bend," I said. "She's going to push it and she mustn't. We have to let that dura heal."

"Don't worry," Roan said. "She's flat on her back and her husband is keeping her that way. John Khalsa gave him the talk. You don't want to hear what he has to say about you doing a surgery while some snake venom was eating you from the inside out."

"You're right, I don't want to hear. Is my brain bleeding?"

"No," said Karen. "And you're actually lucky. It seems you've been very lightly envenomated. Taipan fangs are long, but your wound is very shallow, like the snake couldn't quite get in."

"Oh, he got in," I said. "He was sneaky."

"Do you want us to call Jordan?" asked Roan.

I made a poor job of shaking my head. "I don't want her to see me like this," I said.

And then I was gone again.

*   *   *

The oxen pulling the ploughs stank and my donkey stank and I probably didn't smell any too fresh myself, but we were fragrant roses compared to the wafting odor of drying manure used to dress the Han Dynasty fields. I trudged along shouting out offers of sharpening service as the farmers hoed their alternating rows. For the most part the farmers ignored me because they were accustomed to honing their own scythes, though poorly.

I was in a valley somewhere in the center of the Middle Kingdom. The air was clear and the views to snow-capped peaks and thick forests and swooping eagles were salubrious. Now and then I heard the roar of bear, but no one else seemed to hear it, intent as they were on harvesting the crop and preparing the fields anew.

I dragged my little cart along a dirt path, a Chinese peasant with sun-browned skin and bare, widely spaced toes and pants that stopped above his ankles. A rock bumped the wheels of my wagon and my donkey passed wind and I stopped to watch the grain wave and saw a little girl approaching, dragging a spade behind her.

"My daddy says to make this right for him," she said, thrusting the worn wooden handle into my hand.

She was Jordan, this little girl, but with straight, thick, black hair and almond eyes. I searched her face for a sign that she knew it was me, Xenon Pearl, her future lover and the man for whom she would be maimed, but she offered me nothing save an impatient stomp of her foot.

"Well?"

"This handle is loose. The shovel needs repair more than sharpening.

"He said you would say that. Just fix it and sharpen it, too."

All in all I felt it might be too fine a day to engage so pedestrian a project and I knew there would be little money in it, but the little girl moved toward me again, coming so close she almost stood on my toes. She put her hands on her hips and stared at me until I went to the donkey for my tools.

It wasn't much to tighten the handle, just a nail that needed pulling and a new one to fit and some crimping of the metal edges down around the wood. I did all that while she watched and I saw her little shadow on the ground beside the round one of my wide straw hat. I tested my work by leaning into the blade and wiggling the handle; it held fast.

"Now make it sharp," she said, pounding one small fist into the other quickly.

I saw she had coins in the tight hand so I took my stone and crouched on the ground and raised the shovel blade high and began to work from near edge to tip, slicing and slicing and slicing away until the metal gave up the part of it that was not sharp and left the digging surface bright and gleaming.

"You missed a spot," she said, pointing to a region high up on the neck that would never see soil.

"That part is not important," I said.

"If you're going to do something, do it right. Especially with tools," she said.

And so I set to slicing that one lone spot, not for the few coins she held but because I loved her and had no other way to show it.

*   *   *

"It escapes me completely why you cannot simply live in a fashion befitting a surgeon of your caliber," John Khalsa said to himself, not knowing I was awake to hear him because I was holding on too tightly to the vision of Jordan to want to open my eyes.

"I'm not so bad once you get to know me," I whispered.

I heard the scrape of his chair legs on the floor.

"Ho," he said. "So you're awake."

"How are my bloods?"

"You've got some defibrination coagulopathy, but they're coming back in line. How does your breathing feel?"

"Easier," I said.

"Can you move your arms?"

I tried. They twitched. "Not much," I said.

"From what they told me that's better than before."

"Great news."

"It is indeed. I'm told that a rattlesnake bite does more tissue damage. One of the plastic surgeons did your cheek while you were asleep. Fifteen-minute job. You won't see the scar unless you're kissing close."

"Thank you."

The telephone rang. Khalsa answered it. "Yes, this is his room."

I watched his expression.

"Yes, he is expected to recover. May I tell him who's calling? Yes, fully. Apparently the venom dose was very light. Who is this? Hello? Hello?"

"Who?" I managed.

"Some guy," Khalsa said. "Didn't give his name. Said he was a friend. Look, you'll regain full function. We got the serum into you before there was any permanent damage. I ran the O-arm over you. Roan was with me, and Karen. I had two neuro-radiological consults while you were unconscious just because we knew you'd want to know for sure. The fangs didn't get far enough into you to do the kind of damage that was possible. Very light dose, that's what the panels show."

"How is Eugenia?"

"She sat up today."

"How long has it been?"

"Three days."

I tried to jerk upright and instantly felt needles in my abdomen.

"Whoa," said Khalsa. "Save your strength. There's a woman outside waiting to see you."

He got up then and I held my breath. The door opened and the door closed.

It was Wanda. "Look up drama queen in the dictionary and there's your picture," she said. "If it's not a deadly snakebite it's something else."

"Tell me dad's okay."

"He's fine. I've got them both at the Delano on South Beach."

"You're kidding."

"You said you'd pick up the tab, and I couldn't think of a better way to punish you for all this then a seven-hundred-buck-a-night suite. That was until I saw you. Then I figured you punished yourself."

"I got mixed up with a bad guy," I said.

"Ya think? Our parents are holed up in a hotel because you called me, panicked, and then went missing. Do you know I had to call hospitals to find you? As a patient, if you follow."

"I follow."

She reached around to adjust her shoulder holster and I saw she was perspiring under her arms. It dawned on me she was nervous. I'd never seen her that way. She was always a rock.

"Wanda," I said.

"Look. They tell me you're paralyzed. Are you going to be able to walk again or not?"

So that was it. First there was Jordan and now me and it all fell to Wanda to see—Wanda, whose job entailed more pain and more horror than any person should bear. She was right. I was the drama queen and she was the foot soldier who had to carry her dead and feel the spit and the ire and the hatred. I went righting wrongs in my own clear, cold way with no one to answer to but a teacher long dead, but it was policewoman Wanda who had to clean up everyone's mess.

"It's a toxic paralysis," I said. "I got a light dose. I can move already. Watch."

And there, for her more than for myself, I made the most gigantic, focused effort to lift one foot slightly off the bed and then the other.

The effort exhausted me, but the sheets moved and Wanda made a noise. I felt myself slipping away, but not before I saw her turn away from me to clear her tears.

"Lopez-Famosa's little girl," I said.

"She's up north with her family."

"I have the murderer," I whispered. "I know who killed the patients."

But I think my voice was too weak, for she seemed not to hear me.

*   *   *

I was so intent on sculpting my candle that I barely noticed the summer sun scorching my neck.

"Find shade," scolded the abbot. "The heat will melt the beeswax."

The abbot was Solomon—I would know those precise footsteps anywhere. Here, again, he was my teacher, but in this early life he wasn't out to kill me. I bowed my shaven head and picked up my candle and moved to a patch of shade by the monastery near a lookout space in the brick that allowed a view of Jinghang, the Grand Canal, the low sprawl of Tang Dynasty Yangzhou, and, beyond it, the Yangtze River. It was the fifteenth day of the seventh month, and the city was in a riot of music and colors and shouting because the ghost festival was upon us, and the baking of cakes was the thing and for us monks, the shaping of candles.

The festival was all about honoring the dead and celebrating their return as ghosts—a kind of Chinese Halloween. Monks had the additional charge of absolving our ancestors of sin and thereby releasing them from suffering. To this end, the candle I had in mind to be in the shape of the face of the Buddha, for it was he who taught us the paths and truths that saved us from woe. I willed myself with every fiber of my being to see the Enlightened One in my mind's eye and reproduce his heavenly physiognomy on the wax. I used a small chisel as a tool, sometimes cutting with the edge of it, sometimes shaving gently. The wax was a solid chunk, irregular in shape, neither exactly a sphere nor a block, but there was enough material there for the fashioning of an entire head.

I had never met an Indian prince, but I imagined his neck would be elegant and straight, and it came out that way—and easily. The eyes were more difficult. They needed to convey so much: penetration, surrender, acceptance, understanding, selflessness, and stillness. Most of all they needed to mirror impermanence, as impermanence is the defining rule for all life, especially in a city by the water so given to floods.

The aroma of a thousand dishes, savory and sweet, wafted up

from Jinghang on currents of air as I crafted those eyes, working from the inside out, starting with the pupils. I fashioned their circles with the backside of my little chisel, and once I had them, toiling there beside the wall, on the dirt, in my robes, I began to clear the space for the irises. These came to me powerfully, urging me to work faster. I carved the outline of the orbits and then the eyebrows, which I made fine and arched to lend the Enlightened One just the right ironic edge.

I did the bridge of the nose to ensure that the eyes were set evenly, for everyone understands that deviations in the shape of a face are nothing more than deviations in the shape of character; the face of the Buddha held no variance from the straight and the true. I made the nose aquiline as befitted an Indian prince. Once I had the tip done, I molded the nares, the very nostrils through which air was drawn in and processed and exhaled cleaner than before because the Enlightened One was nothing if not an engine of divine purification.

The lips came next, and I remembered that they had kissed a woman—indeed, played the overture to fathering a son—but they had performed far greater deeds later in speaking the truth to the disciples. To accommodate both, I gave them a hint of sensuality spiced with compassion and finished off their edges with sternness.

I resisted the temptation to make the ears pendulous as they were in the laughing Buddhas tradesmen put in their shops. Rather, I carved fine earlobes, smaller than the vogue but with intricate auricles that bespoke an ability to listen to the deepest possible message of sounds, the rhythms of nature that underpin our days but so often pass undetected. Whorls, I created, and whorls within whorls.

The cheekbones seemed to form themselves as naturally as mountains arise between valleys, and I could say the same for the line of the jaw. When the face was complete, I gazed upon it and felt the presence of the abbot behind me. With the two of us staring at it, the face seemed to come alive. The abbot murmured something about the crime of burning such a creation even though we both knew that was entirely the point, and as we grappled with our attachment to the beauty and power of the image a ghost rose up from the shade of the ramparts, in the dim place where the earth met the stone. It was the ghost of Tie Mei, impossible as she had not yet been born, and I reached out to her, calling her name even as I wrestled to reconcile this old life with my newest one. As I did, I heard a voice pulling me back to the hospital room, and this particular voice of all voices was the one I could not resist.

47

"You were crying," said Jordan. "And you had your arms out. It was so sad to watch. I just had to wake you."

I swallowed and rubbed my eyes and in doing so discovered I was in control of my limbs. The paralysis was gone.

"Thanks for coming," I said.

"I'm sorry it wasn't sooner. Roan only just called to tell me what happened."

She looked softer than she had the last time I had seen her, as if she'd been drinking lots of water and the fluid had filled in all the tiny lines life had added to her in the last year and smoothed out any sharp edges.

"You look beautiful."

"In the eye of the beholder," she said, as if she could read my mind. "And I don't want you to mistake my being here for more than it is. I'm visiting a friend in the hospital, Zee. That's all."

"Of course," I said, trying not to show how much that hurt. "Nice outfit."

"It's a Brazilian workout suit. Girls use them for yoga, I guess. I like the low cut and this shade of orange."

"I could almost juice you," I said.

She waved her hand. "If you start your business I'm just going to leave."

"Okay. I'm sorry."

"So how did this happen to you, Zee? How could such a terrible snake bite you? Roan said it's Australian. What does all this mean?"

"I've been working on my problem," I said, struggling to get up and finding my abdominal muscles too weak to lift me.

"You mean . . . "

I nodded. It was painful.

"You were trying not to be violent and you got bitten by a snake?"

"Not a snake," I said.

She blinked. "I don't understand. Roan said the venom was really bad. He said you almost died."

"It's a long story," I said.

She paused as if she were going to chastise me, caught herself, and produced a bunch of violet flowers. "I brought you these. Sorry I couldn't manage a vase."

I pointed at the plastic pitcher of water by my bed and she took the top off it and put the flowers in.

"They're nice," I said. "I'll take them home when I leave. Now, would you see if my clothes are there in the closet?"

She wheeled over and opened the door. "Nothing here. But there's a paper gown over on the windowsill."

She brought it to me and I slipped it on, moving carefully, thinking about every little piece of tension and relaxation, all the complex steps required of a routine task that had suddenly become hell. Jordan watched me through it and I saw a flicker of recognition at my struggle. I swung my legs off the bed and tested them, first hoping my sensory nerves were working because I felt little in my legs and then hoping the same for my motor works. I could stand, but when I tried to walk I stumbled. I tried to roll but the coordination escaped me and I would have fallen on my face if Jordan hadn't caught me.

"Your arms are strong," I said.

"It's the hand bike."

"Look, I need to borrow your chair."

"What?"

"Just for a few minutes. I need to get to the OR locker room."

"People who can't get around get attached to their chairs," she said.

"I promise I'll bring it back," I said.

She sighed. "You're not that great at keeping promises, Zee."

"Just five minutes. Not a minute more."

I helped Jordan onto my bed. Then I slipped into her chair and made for the door like a Formula One driver. There were no nurses in the hall, and I reached the locker room without anyone interrupting. Trying to get through the door was tricky but I managed. Inside, I opened my locker and slowly, painfully, got dressed. Solomon's vial burned against my skin through the fabric of my pants. I hoped and prayed that being removed from the refrigerator for so long had not degraded it; I had no way of knowing how temperature sensitive it was.

I wheeled to the nearest OR suite and pried the door open a crack. Scott Tremper and a host of nurses were busy at work and didn't see me. The moveable O-arm was not there and I needed it for what I wanted to do. I went to the next room and caught a glimpse of Vicky Sanchez through the window. She was alone and she happened to look up and see me. Her eyebrows went up but I shook my head and put a finger to my lips. She gave a tiny nod and went back to work arranging sponges on a tray.

I wheeled myself down the hall. A couple of nurses passed me and smiled. A gastroenterologist I knew slightly pointed at my chair. "Nice ride," he said.

I located the O-arm in the last suite. It was empty. I went back to my hospital room and found Jordan watching television with her toes peeked out from beneath the sheet.

"They have crap channels here," she said.

"It's not a value-added joint."

"Stop looking at my toes."

"I like the nail polish."

"I know what you like."

I stood up. "Come with me. We're going down the hall."

"You can walk?"

"The poison is out of me now. I'm just weak."

Using her arms, she swung her legs off the bed in practiced fashion and slid into the chair. "I've got to go," she said. "My mother is meeting me downstairs in five minutes."

"Call her and tell her you're staying longer. I'll have someone else bring you home."

"No."

"Yes," I said.

"Coming here was a mistake."

"No. It was perfect."

She stared at me. "Your lips are dry, Xenon."

I lifted the flower jug and drank from the water. The petals brushed my face. "Yum. Violet water."

"You're totally out of your mind," she said. "Plus, you need a shave."

"I'll get to it."

"When was your last meal?"

"I don't know. They've been feeding me through a needle."

"I'm going to get you some food," she said.

I looked at her and I knew she was lying. "No you're not. You're going to leave. That would be a big mistake because I'm going to give you your legs back."

She sighed. "We've been through this so many times."

"There's a new drug," I said. "It can repair your cord."

She narrowed her eyes. "Don't start."

"I'm serious."

"If that's true, why hasn't Dr. MacDougal mentioned it?"

"She doesn't know about it."

She took a moment to digest that. I saw her fingers play on the rims of her chair wheels. "So, it's experimental."

"Yes."

"How experimental?"

"It works on rats and it works on monkeys."

She wheeled herself to the door and reached to open it. "I'm not a monkey, Xenon, and I'm not a guinea pig either. I'm glad you're not dying from your snakebite or whatever it was. Now, my mother's waiting."

I reached into my pocket and pulled out the vial. "Things may not always come out the way I promise they will, but I know spines. Are you really going to turn away from walking because you think I'm unreliable? Forget about being angry. Forget about hating me. Just let me help you."

Her eyes filled up. "Hate you? I *wish* I could hate you. It would make everything so much easier. Why is it never easy around you? Not only is this an experimental treatment, it's not even a sanctioned experimental treatment. This chaos—this is why you're not the man for me. This is why I want you out of my life."

"If you'd rather spend the time in that chair than take a calculated risk, then you're not the woman for me either."

She started to interrupt, then stopped.

"Now we're going to the surgical suite," I said, taking hold of her chair and leaning on it for support. "I'm going to inject this stuff into your spine and let it regenerate your nerves. You never have to speak to me again if that's what you want."

She took the vial in her hand and examined the clear liquid. I could see the conflict in her eyes.

"Is it safe?" Jordan finally asked in a small, low voice.

"I think so."

"You think so?"

"There might be some swelling at the site of the injection."

"So the downside is some swelling and the upside is I might walk?"

"That's right."

"But it's only been tried on monkeys?"

"And rats. Look, the machine I need to look at your back is available. It's the middle of the afternoon. Somebody could need it any minute and we'd lose our chance."

"So this isn't a hospital thing."

"No."

"It sounds crazy and dangerous."

"Desperate times call for desperate measures."

"You're the one who's desperate. I'm dealing."

"Tell me you don't want to walk and I'll climb back into bed," I said.

She put her face in her hands and talked to me through her fingers. "The last time you helped me you lost your job. Now you have it back. Are you sure you want to do this? What if John Khalsa finds out? You would probably lose your license to practice."

"Use of experimental medications is a gray area," I said. "But however it plays out, you're worth it."

She raised the vial high above her head. "I should smash this right now," she said. "That's how I'm feeling. Pulled two ways like you always pull me. Disney should name a rollercoaster after you, Zee. I swear they should. The 'Black Pearl,' maybe, or 'Project Dangerous.'"

"Put it down," I said.

"No."

I could see my whole plan slipping away. "Tie Mei came to you," I said. "She said you'd walk. This is what she was talking about."

A hummingbird of doubt flew into the room. "She could have been talking about anything," Jordan said. "She could have meant years from now."

"No," I said. "She knew about this stuff."

Her arm came down slightly, but the vial was still in peril. "Xenon, that's ridiculous."

"It's not. Her old boyfriend is the scientist who made it."

She put the vial in her lap. "Her boyfriend?"

"We're running out of time," I said. "We've got a surgical window. I saw an empty suite."

"This is just like you," she said. "Impulsive. Crazy. Wild."

"Okay, okay! I'm the world's worst guy! But I'm not wrong about this stuff, Jordan. It's going to work. It *has* to work. Please let me try."

We endured a silence that seemed to last an hour.

"Please," I said again.

"It's not going to change what I've said about us, Zee. What I've said about you."

"I know."

She shook her head. "You say you know, but I know you're thinking that a miracle will change my mind, but I want you to know a miracle will only change my legs."

"I understand."

She fell silent again. Everything tottered and teetered and swayed. I closed my eyes. When I opened them she was still watching me.

"Okay."

48

We made it most of the way to the empty surgical suite before
Roan Cole ran into us as we came around a corner. His shock at
the sight of us was almost comical.

"What the hell is this?"

"There's something I have to do," I said.

He looked puzzled. "You really shouldn't be up. We've got to
run your bloods. Your kidneys took a beating and your liver hasn't
been so happy either.'"

"I'm ducking into OR 3," I said. "Do you have a minute to get
me a bagel from the cafeteria?"

He leaned his long frame against the wall and brought his hand
up to rub his chin. "A bagel?"

"Sesame. Toasted. Butter, no cream cheese. And a cup of their
horrible tea."

"He never drinks hospital tea," he said to Jordan.

"Never except today. Take the bag out of the water right away,
will you?"

"Ah ha," he said. "This is about a little OR nookie, is that it? A
passionate surgical rapprochement?"

"You're an idiot," said Jordan.

"A quarter of an hour is all I need," I said. "Run interference
for us, yes?"

"Roan Cole is not an idiot," I said when he was gone. "He's the
best friend I've ever had."

We pressed on to the OR. I got Jordan up onto the table, but
it wasn't easy. My leg muscles were still terribly weak and my back
muscles weren't much better. I gave her a paper gown and she put
it on by herself, bidding me turn around by order of her pointed

finger. Once she was prone I rolled the O-arm over her as I had with Eugenia Wentworth and lit it up. I wasn't an expert at the thing, but I knew the basics and within a few minutes the screen gave a clear view of what the Russians had broken seven months earlier and what I had managed to fix.

Jordan's bones were healing and the shards were cleared out. The cord still looked swollen, a good sign as it meant that despite her paralysis nerve death and atrophy had not yet occurred. I couldn't see the exact state of the cord, though, as it was beyond the capability of the scanner.

"Before you cut me again, I want to cut you," Jordan said, her voice slightly muffled against the table.

"I beg your pardon?"

"Give me a scissors, please."

"Jordan."

"A scissors. I know there has to be one on your instrument table."

"You can't touch it. Those pieces are sterile."

"Give me the scissors, Xenon."

There were several on the tray. I put one in her hand. She propped herself up on her elbows and motioned me closer.

"Kneel down," she said.

I knelt, taking her request for some sort of religious ritual.

"Turn your head."

I hesitated.

"You won't turn your back to me when I have a scissors in my hand but you expect me to trust you with my spine?"

I turned my head and felt her take my ponytail in her hand. I heard a snip.

"There," she said.

I stood up, speechless. Roan came in with a bagel and a cup of tea. He looked at Jordan inside the O-arm, a thicket of my hair in her hand.

"This is one kinky place to play barbershop," he said.

I reached for the hair, but Jordan wouldn't give it to me.

"I'm holding onto it for good luck," she said.

"Someone's going to have to clean that up," Roan said, inspecting the back of my head. "It's not exactly even."

Jordan beckoned with her empty hand. I bent to her again. "Last chance to not do this," she whispered.

I gazed at the expanse of her back and recalled the first time I had seen her unclothed, on the beach, in the moonlight.

"The wheel of life is already turning," I said. "Karma is strongly at work."

She sighed and closed her eyes. I took the vial from the tray and stabbed it with a syringe.

"Wanna tell me what's going on?" asked Roan.

I made a mark on Jordan's back. "Would you nerve block that area, please?"

"A spinal injection?"

"That's right," I said, drawing down what I figured would be enough to saturate the area.

"Something Chinese?"

That stopped me. I looked at the clear liquid and a sudden panic seized me. The dosage was a crapshoot. Hell, the whole thing was a crapshoot. What if I had I read Solomon wrong? Could the regeneration story be a hoax? What if he maneuvered me into dosing Jordan with something lethal? The idea started my hands shaking, and I paused with the syringe in the air, dripping thick, golden syrup.

"Zee?"

What if Solomon was playing me? What if I were about to poison my lover?

"What's in it?" Roan asked.

Tie Mei said intuition was king. She said it trumped rational thought. Well, intuition told me this cure was real. Every sign I'd received, every cue, every taste, and every smell told me that Solomon, tortured by lost love and driven by the need for redemption, was exactly the genius I read him to be.

"It fits," I said.

"I beg your pardon?" Roan said.

"It's outlandish and unlikely, but it fits."

"What's in the stuff, Zee?"

"A regeneration compound."

"What?"

"You heard me."

Roan wiped his face. "Her cord is toast, Zee. There's nothing . . . "

"It's experimental," I said. "Brand new."

"Really? How did you get it?"

I shook my head.

"All right," Roan said slowly. "Say there is such a thing. Say this is not a piece of pure derangement subsequent to snakebite. If something like that existed, don't you think I'd know about it? Wouldn't it be in journals or on the Web?"

"You should probably go, Roan," Jordan interrupted from the table.

"She's right," I added. "If you don't want to be involved, just make up a syringe and I'll do the block. That way you're free and clear."

"So you have informed consent," said Roan.

"Of course, he has consent," Jordan answered. "You think I'm lying here for a massage? Could we get on with this please?"

"All right then," Roan rubbed his hands together. "I brought the bagel, so I guess that means I'm in. You're going to feel a pinch, Jordan. It'll last only a second. Let me know when you're ready."

Jordan turned and looked at me with anger and hope and helplessness as Roan prepared his block. I bent down and kissed her.

"Do it," she said.

She gasped as Roan's needle went in, and a moment later the muscles of her back began to relax. I ate and drank, waiting for the anesthetic to take full effect. The bagel did me some good and the caffeine had an almost instant effect. I took a few breaths.

"You okay?" Roan mouthed.

I nodded. "When I'm done, will you take Jordan home?"

"I forgot to call my mother," Jordan said. "She'll be waiting downstairs."

"Do we need to keep her for observation?" asked Roan.

"She just needs to rest."

"You *both* need to rest."

I manipulated the image one last time to make sure I wasn't missing any lesions, then, satisfied, I slipped the needle through the dura and injected Solomon Yu's magic potion into Jordan's sweet cord.

49

The venom was neutralized, but the fierce snake lived within me. Riding home, I had the disconcerting experience not of entering another lifetime but of seeing this one afresh and with altered senses. I was extraordinarily sensitive to changes in temperature; I felt every tiny shift in humidity; I rode as a poikilotherm would ride if it had a steel horse and the power of internal combustion, which is to say I drafted the warm exhaust of vans and dodged the tiny turbulence that issued from the alleys between tall buildings, shivering at nothing, exalting in the blessings of an intermittent sun.

I made it home in record time. Once there I examined my face to see the plastic surgeon's work. It was excellent; the rip had been reduced to a tiny line, and in time it would pale as the skin around it tanned. I made a mental note to send the man a bottle of champagne.

I drew a bath, poured in healing oil, and turned the water hot and hotter. I floated with my eyes closed and could almost feel my scales. My lips were as a reptile's, blistering with heat-sensing pits. When I ducked my brow under, the cool and warm ends of the tub were as separate oceans to me. I added more heat, but even the scalding tap was not quite hot enough. I soaked and tried to will the last vestiges of toxins from my veins. In my mind's eye, I romanced a Jordan with strong legs and a healed back.

I thought about Solomon. I wondered whither we would go in this life. Had his enmity been extinguished by the act of nearly killing me? If it had, I would leave the matter be, such was the generosity of a spirit grateful to be alive, but I was woefully resigned to the knowledge I had not seen the last of him.

And then, with the sweet sandalwood steam tickling my face, I remembered that a murderer was at large—and unpunished. I bolted upright in the bath, and as I did I heard a faint noise at the front of the house. Dripping water from my bath towel I ran on still-unsteady legs and jerked the French doors of my bedroom open to the outside. The cool winter wind assailed the reptile in me, but I steeled myself and leaned over the balcony railing for a look.

I did not see a car outside, though certainly someone could have parked around the corner. I saw no interloper on foot. My Madagascan tree creaked in the wind. The Mexican Firebush rustled. Elephant Ear philodendrons rubbed my windows and crotons crackled, but I saw no evidence of intrusion or surveillance. I ran downstairs and walked the perimeter of the backyard like a diligent general inspecting his foxholes. I looked for signs the fences had been disturbed and checked for footprints in the grass. All I found was bamboo reaching for the sky and anoles nest-building in the cracks and crevices of my gazebo. I turned on my house alarm and activated all my external lighting.

In the house, I found a mushroom formula in a cupboard. A mixture of *Shizandra, Maitake, Ganoderma, Reishi, Cordyceps,* Lion's Mane, Turkey Tail, *Agaricus,* and more, it was Wu Tie Mei's secret recipe. When she first made it up for me, I had been tempted to use it as a tonic at the first sign of a cold or flu, but she had warned me off casual dispensing. Its effectiveness was diminished by casual use, she said, counseling me to save it for deep trouble. The last time I saw her, on vacation home from medical school, she had given me the formula printed clearly in her fine hand and told me I should always keep the recipe safe, even until I was an old man, and that any quality herb shop could fill it. When I asked her what deep trouble meant, she would not speak it, but I felt she meant a terrible diagnosis. It was the medicine of the forest, she said, found only by treasure hunters who knew which logs to upend to check the damp, dim places most eyes never see.

One night I took a quarter cup while in the grip of a terrible flu. I woke up the next day with nothing but fuzz on my tongue and the inside of my mouth. It was as if the mushrooms were vital beyond the ability of age and desiccation to extinguish them. I felt as if they had sporulated within me. The experience frightened me; I had not used the formula again until now.

The package was dusty with age. I brewed it with purified water and sipped it while watching the clouds scud by and listening to the last of my bath drain down the pipes. Then I stood quietly in meditation.

There was no caffeine-like rush from the medicine or even the twitching excitement of an adaptogen-like ginseng, but I felt the formula healing what the venom had rent. It worked on my blood, enhancing the ability of my erythrocytes to carry oxygen and my white cells to fight invaders. My tendons and ligaments seemed to chatter with enthusiasm for the special support the mushrooms gave them. I could almost feel the magic formula strengthening the lattice matrix of my bones.

When my meditation was over, I was not better than new, not even as good as new, but I was hungry and far stronger than I had been and that would have to be enough. I thawed a slab of corn-fed brisket and tenderized it with a mallet. I cooked it slowly, turning the meat, painting it with a marinade of balsamic vinegar and horseradish and olive oil. I ate it as the afternoon came down but only after I said my own form of grace, thanking the dead cow for its life-giving sustenance. I do this whenever I can, for I believe that to focus the mind on the sacrifice underpinning a meal serves to transmit life force and spirit.

Darkness fell. I took a nap. My exhaustion was total and absolute and no other noises got through to me. I awoke to the beeping of my alarm clock. The bright red numerals showed that it was 2:00 in the morning. I showered and dressed and nibbled a bit of the wasabi chocolate Darlene found too piquant. Then I slipped my high-quality digital voice recorder into my pocket. It was the same unit I used for patient notes and had good sound quality and a sensitive microphone.

Wired for sound, I retrieved Quiet Teacher from its lair.

This is the last time, I told myself. Really. Truly. No more after this.

Jordan, you have to believe me. There's not going to be any cutting.

I went to the garage and saddled the Teutonic beast.

* * *

Tiny traces of the snake remained within me and I felt a reptilian reaction to the weather, but I was heartened by Quiet Teacher and fortified deep in my carnivore belly. I was confident knowing I was merely out to do what I had been so often born to do. I rode west as I had before, along cool canals and through what had once been swamp. I had the uneasy feeling I was being followed, prompted perhaps by the noises in the night, but when I checked the mirrors I saw only anonymous headlights and none that seemed glued to me.

Weston came up quickly. I exited the freeway and made my way to the familiar subdivision, forgoing the printed directions I'd used the last time. I bumped up over the swale, gunned the bike past the lake from which I had yanked the alligator, and drove right into the front yard. I parked my bike in a dark corner of the driveway and rang the bell.

"Yes?" The voice came over the intercom, and it was Boniface's, soggy with sleep.

"How you doing, Jay?"

"Who's there?"

"Samaritan Hospital security. We need to have a word with you."

I heard a crashing sound and then a fumbling and then everything got quiet. Finally, he spoke. "It's the middle of the night."

348

"I'm aware of that, sir."

Two minutes later, Boniface was at the door. He yanked it open. The last time we met, I wore a helmet. This time, I let him see my face, but I kept Quiet Teacher tucked behind me.

"The hospital has you on tape," I said, flicking the voice recorder in my pocket to the on position.

"I don't know what you're talking about."

"There was a high-definition camera in Mr. Erkulwater's room. We recognized you from an interview about your films. Personally, I really liked *The Bitches of Eastwick* and *When Harry Ate Sally*. *The Rear Hunter*, too, though I guess that one's kind of dated by now."

"What do you want?"

"How come you killed that guy?"

He pulled his Dirty Harry gun out of the ample pocket of his robe. "Get in the house," he said, grabbing my arm.

And then he saw the sword.

His face went white as he tried desperately to put it all together. The first time round, he'd taken me for Charlie Czarnecki. Now he knew Czarnecki was dead. There were pieces missing for him and he needed them for the puzzle.

"You're not the biker," he said slowly.

"You mean the guy you electrocuted?"

"Who are you?"

"Clever, sabotaging that gaming headset the way you did."

"Drop the sword," he said.

I put Quiet Teacher down gently. "Let's talk about the murders," I said. "Erkulwater and his pills; Czarnecki and his computer games—you wanted the woman, too, didn't you? Lucky for you, she died. What about the little girl? I bet you'd like to do her, too."

Boniface nudged me forward with the barrel of his gun. We got to the kitchen. The air conditioner was howling even though it was the middle of winter, and I saw his bare feet were white with the cold. He pulled a barstool away from the granite counter and sat down, keeping the big Smith&Wesson pointed at me.

"You know where the kid is, don't you? Why don't you tell me so I don't shoot you in the face."

"You can't kill me," I said. "I don't come back, the tape goes to the police."

"You're bullshitting. There is no tape. If there's a tape, tell me what the fat bastard did when I put the pills in his mouth."

"He vomited," I said.

"He prayed, you lying fuck. He prayed with his cheeks full of pills like a chipmunk. Now, I don't know who you are, but you're no security guard. If you know where the little girl is, you'd better start talking or I blow you away and run you through the wood chipper and use you to fertilize my flowers."

"She'll be the last of them, right?" I said, leaning against the counter no more than three feet from the gun. "No more witnesses? Nobody to bring you down?"

"Shut up," he said, the glow from the microwave display clock emphasizing the bags under his eyes. "I worked my whole life for what I've got. No jury's gonna take it away because some whiners see an opportunity to milk a rich guy."

"It would be a crime to lose a genius like you."

"That's right. And they wanted to ruin me. They would have filed a class-action suit."

"Four people isn't exactly a class-action suit," I said, "but I can see how much you have to protect: *The Bourne Cunnilingus*, *A Rear and Pleasant Danger*, *Silence of My Ham*, *A Quiver Runs Through It*, *Forest Rump*. I like that last one, too, by the way. You really have a thing for Hollywood titles. I bet it's because you always wanted to make real movies but nobody would give you the dough."

He ducked and nodded like a waterbird. "In the beginning I had to do it all myself. Everything. Even the editing. Every last penny I made came from my own hard work."

I nodded enthusiastically. "So you went unrecognized and unappreciated. But I appreciate you. There's great dialogue in those films of yours. Real social conscience. Insights, too. They're spiritual, in a way, don't you think? The way you have the actors pray and look up toward Heaven?"

He was smiling now. "Most people don't even notice that."

"Well, I do," I said, barely able to keep myself from telling him I was spinning every word, that I'd never seen a single one of his films—though I'd looked them up—and never, ever would.

Suddenly he frowned. "Great," he said, slamming the butt of the gun down on the marble. "But I want that little girl."

"It all goes together," I said.

He peered at me. He moved the gun from one hand to the other and wiped his free palm on his robe. "What goes together?"

"The artist's vision and the grittiness of death," I said. "You're a man who really understands your place in the world. You're closer to nature than most people, a force of it yourself. Sex. Murder. You get right to the heart of things—no messing around for you."

As I said it, I realized I knew Boniface. I had always known him. During the White Lotus rebellion he had been my ruthless commanding officer. In the Ming Dynasty he had been a thieving foreign slave working at my shop at the provincial capital of Guiyan. He had been my cheating wife during my long trek across the Taklamikan Desert and my backstabbing brother in Souchun during the dynasty of the Northern Song. I stared at him with new eyes, suddenly recognizing the enduring evil in him and his pulsing need to work it through. Scarier still was the knowledge that I was just like him. I had murdered for my own sense of justice but murdered nonetheless.

Enraged, I made my move. The gunshot was so loud it left me deaf and dazzled, and I felt the vortex of hot air molecules pass my cheek. The tip of the barrel seared my palm. I twisted my wrist forward, which forced his wrist back. His index finger came off the trigger, and I used the revolver as a lever against his arm, closing the little bones of his wrist, one against the other, and moving the pressure of my spiral up against his elbow. He came forward off the barstool and went down to his knee, and then I had him. I pistol-whipped him across the cheek.

"It's not empty this time, is it?" I said, dropping the rounds from the cylinder and throwing the gun away.

A little trail of blood escaped his mouth. He spit a tooth and cleared his throat. "You're the same as me," he said. "You and your sword. The only difference between us is I do what I do so beautifully. You should have seen that motorcycle kid die. When the juice hit him his scalp stood straight up, just like in the cartoons. And your truck driver buddy? Before he started whimpering to Jesus he offered to suck me. He said he'd do anything. He kept babbling about his wife. I'm not kidding. It was a beautiful scene. Perfect, right down to the angles."

In that moment, I understood what the murders were to him.

"You filmed them," I said. "You filmed the killings."

He turned his head sideways and looked up at me from the floor. "I can find a stand-in for the little girl," he said. "I found out she plays the violin. I want the instrument in the frame, and I'll put one on the soundtrack. Jascha Heifetz playing something sweet from Beethoven or Brahms."

"Cello," I said. "She plays the cello."

He waved his hand. "Okay, so then I'll use Yo Yo Ma. Nobody's gonna know. I got cheated out of her, but either way the scene has to end with a kid. You're gonna help with that, right?"

"Where do you keep duct tape?" I said, opening one kitchen drawer after another.

His eyes answered the question, just a quick dart in the direction of a cabinet. I opened it and found a roll. I used it to strap him to a chair at his breakfast table. I did a harsh job, crossing his hands behind his back so the palms pointed away from each other and winding the tape ten times around his ankles before going to retrieve my blade.

"Forget wiggling out of this," I said when I returned. "Just tell me where the films are."

"I want a drink."

"You really had me fooled," I said. "Your righteous indignation. Peace and love. Reading the Dalai Lama's book on happiness."

"I wanna be happy," he said. "I got some great ideas from that book. Now how about that drink?"

"Sure," I said. "What'll you have?"

"Go to the left of the sink. Check the top cabinet. The bottle of red stuff there, that's Plymouth Sloe Gin—Alfred Hitchcock's favorite drink."

I poured some into a glass and held it in front of him.

"The movies," I said. "I really want to see what you've got so far."

"So let me go and I'll show you."

"Afterward," I said. "If they're as good as you say."

He considered the deal, chewing the inside of his cheek for a bit.

"You don't have a lot of choice," I said.

"They're in the study on the shelf above the TV. Now give me a sip."

I tilted the tumbler in the direction of his lips.

"You going to call the cops?"

"You bet," I said.

That was when Solomon Yu burst in.

50

My one-time teacher was dressed in a pair of blue jeans, leather driving gloves, and a loose-fitting car coat with a red plaid liner. He looked like he was on his way to a talk at the museum or maybe an afternoon coffee outdoors at South Beach.

"Who the fuck are you?" said Boniface.

Solomon ignored him. "You should be dead," he said to me, swiftly bending down to pick up the gun and pop a few rounds in the cylinder.

"So I *did* hear you outside the house," I said. "This time it was you, right? Not one of your kid soldiers?"

"You would never hear me. You heard a possum. I surprised it and it went onto your roof. You should trim back the trees around your house."

"I'll give you an A for patience. How did you know I was out of the hospital?"

He smiled a sick smile. "All the talk about patient rights these days and it is still so easy to get information."

"Somebody going to tell me what's going on here," Boniface interrupted.

"You are a thief," Solomon went on. "You broke and entered."

"Well, duh," said Boniface. "Take a look at me, why don't you? How about cutting me loose?"

Solomon didn't even look at him. "Just tell me how it is you are up and walking around."

"You didn't go deep enough with that poison pommel," I said.

"Return what you stole."

"Impossible. It's all used up."

"Give me the sword," he said, raising Boniface's revolver.

I got to thinking about guns and swords right then and about a conversation I'd once had with Wanda about how the blade is better at tight range, how cops are often cut before they even get their gun out.

"I know what you are thinking," Solomon said. "I know everything about you. The venom runs through us. The bite of the snake. Can you feel it? Do you notice the air-conditioning vents? Do you smell things you did not smell before? Can you sense chemicals in the air? Deodorizers and cleansers doing more harm than good."

"What a freak show," said Boniface. "Will one of you whack jobs untie me so I can get it on camera?

Solomon glanced at him as if for the first time.

"I wouldn't set him loose," I said. "He's killed two people that I know of and there may be more. I'm going to call the police."

"Give me the sword," Solomon repeated.

I suddenly felt the vibrations of a hundred lifetimes with Solomon. He was old when I was young; he was young when I was old; he was a woman when I was a man, he was a man when I was a woman. He enacted good when I ran amok; I tamed his excesses with justice. We forbore each other. We lived each other's karmic contracts, or perhaps we were just paying the same set of dues.

I laid Quiet Teacher down gently. He bent to retrieve it and for his eagerness received my foot in his face. The gun clattered away and he rushed me and took me to the ground. Solomon was strong and skillful and his training was evident and my nerves and muscles were still tremulous from the toxin. I simply wasn't up to the punishment. I rolled away and he came at me again. This time I used his momentum to bring him to my elbows and my knees. I tangled him up, but he was skillful enough to deflect my efforts. At an impasse we finally let go of each other, but not until we had tested each other's strength in every direction. The disengagement was like a bomb going off; it blew us apart and I hit a rack of copper pots, bringing them crashing down. He took out two barstools and bumped into the porn king himself, knocking him over in his chair.

We spilled out of the kitchen and into the killer's sunken living room. Tiny halogen spotlights lit up the porn posters, and breasts and buttocks cast crazy shadows on the carpeted floor of the pit. I threw a heavy wooden footstool and he responded by lobbing a crystal tongue. I brandished a fire poker and he backpedaled into the kitchen. I followed. He picked up my sword.

And that was when I smelled almonds.

*   *   *

Tie Mei wore a heavily brocaded golden gown bearing a background design of mountain cliffs and waterfalls, waves, clouds, and trees. The fabric materialized before there was any hint of her flesh, and I watched torrents cascade down cliffs and branches bend in the wind. Then my nanny's countenance slowly clarified and her pearly flesh gained substance and her eyes came clear and her high cheekbones gained edges.

"Why have you been gone so long?" I said.

She gave me that sad little smile of hers and it quickened my heart. I had a hundred other things to say and to ask, but she turned away from me and faced Solomon. I waited for a word that would heal our rift and calm him down. I waited for her to tell him she loved him, that she was sorry for the way things had turned out. None of that came, and oddly enough I felt badly for him.

Silently, she reached out for us both, one with each hand, and with her touch came the electric cool. The tiny static charge offered confirmation of her presence, but I don't know whether Solomon felt it. I saw only that he stared intently at the spot where I saw her face and that he lowered my weapon and his expression softened.

And then she was gone. That was it. That was her quiet lesson. We stood for a moment in her evanescence, and then I spoke. "You saw her, yes? We have to stop this—now."

"You tore her from me. She would have come to me if you two had only given her the chance. You should have seen us together, the places we went, the things we did."

I couldn't help but think of the difference between his look and Boniface's, between the gaze of a raving, homicidal maniac and the look of a wounded man, alone in a strange country, bleeding from old wounds no poultice would heal, crushed by love and twisting at the gallows of hate. I wanted desperately to hear some validation from him, to know that another human being had seen what I had seen, the ghost of my teacher. Instead of confirming the vision, Solomon turned away, and with no warning at all savagely brought my sword to bear on our host. The folded steel separated Boniface's right leg from his body, the long, straight blade slicing directly into the space between the head of the femur and the acetabulum of the hip. The hamstring muscles twitched a few times, dangling loosely. Boniface's mouth opened in a scream of horror, and his heart, working like a propeller out of water, sent a red stream across the kitchen.

"No!" I yelled, even though it was too late.

Solomon looked right at me and cut again, taking a diagonal line from the top of Boniface's right shoulder down toward the nipple. The blade got stuck in the bone, and Solomon had to drag it out, bringing bright white bits to air. Boniface started to twitch. The twitches grew more violent as dark, thick goo mixed with the spraying, spattering blood. The twitches became shakes and then terrible jerks that took what was left of him halfway across the tile floor.

It seemed the end would never come, but when it did, when the king lay still. Solomon thrust Quiet Teacher into my hand. "Good luck to you, Pearl. Good luck trying to tell them you didn't do it."

He backed away carefully so as not to get blood on his shoes and left the way he had come in. I heard the roar of the Aston Martin's engine outside as I sank to the ground, eyes closed to the butchery, and tried to calm down.

After a few minutes I shook myself back to the present and went to the library. I did my best to focus my attention on the collection of films. There was a long line of DVD cases on the shelf above the flat-screen television. I read each and every title. The porn king's crude attempts at humor were lost on me. I spoke the titles out loud. When I reached *Chipmunk Cheeks*—precisely the phrase he had used to describe Edson Erkulwater's look—I took it out and put it in the player.

I started to sweat the moment I saw the trucker's hospital room. All I could think about was the last time I had watched brutality on film and how that violation had changed Jordan's life forever. When I saw Edson's face and his hand raised in greeting, I pushed the stop button and removed the disc from the machine.

Charlie's End was more obvious. I watched enough to see the fake credits and the opening music with trepidation and bile. I saw the back of Czarnecki's head as he sat at the computer and felt my palms get cold when he donned his gaming equipment. I stopped the play just as the first wisp of smoke came out of his head and focused on my breathing to beat the reflex, using my thumb to work the nausea acupuncture point, *Nei Guan*—Inner Pass—on the inside of my wrist.

At last, I left the killing house. I saw with some satisfaction that the fat tires of Solomon's heavy Aston Martin had eliminated most of my motorcycle's tracks as he followed me across the swale, but I smoothed the single track through the grass with my boot. When I finally rode off, I used the driveway and the road and only detoured through some bushes when I got close to the guard gate so my departure would not be caught on camera.

51

Despite the trendy happy-hour crowd and the exotic fixtures and the infinity pool, the Delano Hotel is all about curtains. My father's suite had more than its share, billowing a bit because the windows were wide open.

"He won't shut out the sea breeze," Rachel complained to me, gathering a purple sweater tight around her shoulders. "Probably I shouldn't have pushed so hard for him to exercise. He says he doesn't feel cold now, says he doesn't feel pain either. Half a year of tennis and I'm married to a tough guy."

"We're here for fresh air, yes?" My father countered. "Who wants air conditioning when South Beach is right outside the window? Did you know Florida has some of the best air in the country? It's a peninsula, remember—a big thumb sticking into the ocean, wind blowing from this side, wind blowing from that side."

"Ach," clucked Rachel, waving her hand at him and embracing her sweater more tightly. "There's always a reason for his craziness."

I can't say I remember ever seeing my father bicker this way with Tie Mei. For some reason I found the sight heartwarming.

"Look at him," said my father. "Crying like a baby."

"I'm not crying," I said. "Where's Wanda? She asked me to come and told me it was urgent."

They looked at each other significantly. "You have something to tell us?" my father said. "You came to say good-bye, maybe?"

"I came to make sure you were all right."

"What's not all right about such a fancy joint?" said my father.

He said it casually, but he was clenching and unclenching his fists. He feels pain, all right, I thought to myself, but before I could say anything Wanda came through the bedroom door. She looked pale and haggard and drawn. Rachel turned away. My father went to the window, put his face out, and inhaled noisily.

"It's time to go," Wanda said, pulling handcuffs off her belt. "Every sheriff's deputy in Broward County is looking for you."

"I didn't kill Boniface," I answered.

Rachel made a small noise. Wanda nodded. "Of course not."

"I can prove it," I said. "And he's the man you want, not me. He killed Erkulwater and Czarnecki."

She gave a start. Apparently, she had not considered the angle. "What?"

"He filmed the murders," I said. "I watched the tapes."

She frowned. "He filmed them?"

"He told me. He bragged about it."

Wanda sighed. "This in a secret tête-à-tête?"

"But it's true Lopez-Famosa killed Kimberly Jenkins."

"So you say," she nodded, bending one of my arms behind my back as Rachel started to cry.

"There's proof. The tapes are at Boniface's house. I can show you."

"He was sliced to bits, Zee. Pieces of him are gone."

"They're not gone, they're just disconnected. If you've already been to his place, then you know about the tapes."

"I haven't been. Teams are still there. They say it's a bloodbath."

"It's a fantastic day out there," said my father, his back still to me. "Look at that beautiful ocean. Oy, what a color. Imagine weather like this in the deep of winter. In Russia even the sky would be frozen."

"Let's go," said Wanda, bringing my other hand around.

I resisted but gently. "Before you cuff me up, there's something you need to hear."

Slowly and carefully so nobody thought I was reaching for a weapon, I dug into my pocket and produced the recorder. I played the scene. It was all there, even the ambient sounds: the scrapes, the footsteps, the sound of duct tape ripping off the roll, the slam of a front door, the echoes of voices. Boniface's death screams sent Rachel running from the room.

"He's not a murderer!" my father cried. "This proves it."

"Give me the blow by blow," Wanda said, leaning forward keenly.

So we sat there, with traces of the islands coming in off the wind on the back of distant murmurs of the Latin pulse of South Beach waking from a siesta.

Wanda shook her head. "Two murderers on one tape."

"There's no tape," I said. "Digital. We'll have to copy the file. I haven't had a chance."

My father was fascinated by the sound of Solomon's voice. "You should have heard him grunt and stumble over consonants when he came off the boat. I can't believe the way he talks now. Not even a contraction! He sounds like a dictionary."

Wanda interrupted by asking for all the background information. My father explained how he and Solomon had once been rivals. Rachel came back in the room just in time to hear some gory details, and I could see she was thoughtful about it all, perhaps not having realized how deeply my father felt for Tie Mei. Wanda ended the reverie by announcing she would still have to take me to the police station.

"Just until we analyze the recording," she said. "You'll have to make a statement. They may lock you up for a bit."

My father put his hand on her arm. "No handcuffs, please."

Rachel went out and came back with a laptop.

"If that's a digital file, I say we make a copy right here and now. I don't trust that little recorder."

She took the device from Wanda and plugged it into her computer and downloaded the file. I saw her give it a title.

Xenon's Fate.

52

I waited for her outside on a little wooden bench by the front door.
I've got a staghorn fern above the bench, hanging from a nail. A
couple of Cuban tree frogs had used the suction cups on the end of
their toes to climb to the moist, leafy haven it offered. As darkness
grew I watched them emerge to hunt bugs, their dark eyes bulging.
When I got tired of waiting I went inside and had a drink of water
and then came back out again. I took in the front yard and realized
I'd let it go in the last few weeks. The Madagascar tree needed
pruning and the Mexican Firebush had run amok on the arching
arbor. I used a pair of pruning shears to trim it back a bit so that
visitors wouldn't need to duck to get to my front door. The wind
whipped my Royal palms around and I picked up a couple of husks
and put them in the trashcan; they stuck up like dry, brown golf
clubs.

A motorcycle came down the road, it's headlight gleaming. It
was a big, black sportbike and it rumbled more than most crotch
rockets do. It pulled into my driveway and Jordan swung a leg off,
using her hands to help it. She almost toppled over when her foot
touched the ground, but she got the kickstand down in time and
climbed off slowly and carefully. She took off her helmet and shook
out her hair. I found myself fighting for breath.

"Wow," I said.

"Makes you want to pinch yourself, no?"

"It does."

"Me too."

"So fast," I said.

"Eight days of relearning how to put one foot in front of the
other doesn't seem fast to me."

"So you're blonde now."

"I don't like it either. I'm going back to my natural color."

"And you learned how to ride," I said.

"I got a video. After all those times with you it wasn't that difficult. Day before yesterday the guy at the bike shop spent an afternoon with me in the parking lot. We started with a moped. He tried to teach me how to do a turn with the handlebars locked. You make it look easy. I would have fallen a hundred times if he hadn't been running alongside me."

"That's no moped you're riding."

She smiled. It was glorious to see. "I'm a quick study. I knew I wanted big and fast. You've always said a person should get what they want first time out or lose a fortune trading up."

"That's more than just big and fast."

The smile turned into a grin. "I know, right? It's the Hyabusa. Fastest bike in the world—named for a Japanese hawk that dives through the air at 250 miles per hour. It'll blow your Triumph into the weeds."

"Do you want to come inside?"

She got as far as the door and hung there, leaning against the jamb for support and trying to hide the fact that her legs were shaking.

"You look hot in leather," I said.

We made it into the living room. The shaking in her legs was worse. I reached over and put my hands on her waist, but she removed them firmly and moved toward the kitchen counter. She climbed onto one of my barstools. The shaking eased, but her leather riding pants hung off her lower half in folds.

"So you're out of jail," she said.

"Everyone seems surprised about that. I was just answering some questions."

"And?"

"And nothing. They needed some information and I gave it to them."

1

"I had a long talk with Wanda," she said. "She said what you told them checked out."

"I spoke with her after that. She said you looked great and she was right."

"You look pretty good yourself. Your face is healing well."

"The plastic surgeon did a nice job and I've been using one of Tie Mei's potions. What else did Wanda tell you?"

"She said there is some prosecutor in Miami who's gunning for you. She said he really hates you."

"So I hear. I don't even know the guy's name."

"He can't hate you more than I do."

I reached for the countertop to steady myself. "Please don't say that."

"You crippled me, you and your crazy past lives and your vigilante justice and your fantasy life and your madman ego. You crippled me and then you saved me."

"I'm sorry," I said. "But we turned it around. Everything is going to be fine."

"Fine, but never the same. Life's a giant tornado with you—some sort of cure for gravity. I get sucked up and twisted around and even when it starts to look like it might come out all right it gathers strength."

"I'll do better, I promise."

It was her turn to start crying. "I used to believe you when you said that, Zee. I really did. And even now I know you mean it. I know you want it. The trouble is there's nothing you can do. This is who you are."

"I've tried to change," I said, a terrible, bitter despair taking me. "I've tried so hard."

"Thank you for giving me my legs back, Xenon. Thank you for making me whole again so I can walk. God I love to walk. I love to walk. . . . "

Now she was really crying. I tried to hold her, but she shoved me away.

"You think you know me, but it's me who knows you," she went on. "I know everything about you. I've been talking to Rachel, to Wanda, to Roan. I talked to John Khalsa. I even talked to your dad. I know about the snakes. I know about the bite, the taipan. I know that Mr. Solomon Yu loved your Chinese nanny and blamed you when she wouldn't love him. She broke his heart and you broke mine and looking at you I see I'm breaking yours and there's so much breaking going on and that's what I can't take."

The words came out of her so fast that she was breathless.

"There's love, too," I said. "There's more than just breaking."

"I know," she said, the tears streaming down her face. "We're a kind of tragedy, I guess, or you are. I can't take it any more. I came by to thank you, Zee, and to say goodbye."

I couldn't stand up anymore. The weight of the last two weeks took me to the floor, where I found breathing an almost insuperable task. I felt the high senses of the snake in me. I saw Jordan's heat signature like an aura around her head. We stayed there, Jordan on the stool above me looking down, neither one of us able or willing to move, either together or apart.

"Does your back still hurt?" I asked, residing in that terrible place where every syllable has a moon's gravity and the silence between is a galaxy of needles.

"Yes, it hurts," she said, apparently grateful for a small respite from all the grief and the anger and the breaking and pulling. "A little swelling is what you said. I've got a sore spot the size of an orange back there, Zee; yesterday it was the size of a grapefruit."

"Let me see it."

"No. No more looking at my tender parts. You're not my doctor anymore."

I slumped.

"I vomited for hours from that stuff. I still have a terrible taste in my mouth and my tongue is still numb. He made it didn't he? That man, Solomon. The man who loved your nanny and who tried to kill you with his snakes. That man gave me back my legs."

You have to find him."

"The cops will find him."

"And if they don't you will, right?"

"Sure," I said. "Of course. We're not done with each other, Solomon and I."

She shook her head and her eyes lit up with anger. "Vintage Xenon. I'm talking about saving the handicapped and you're talking about some childish vendetta."

She started shaking again, but not from her legs. "I shouldn't have come here," she said. "I love you and I pity you. You can't know how that feels."

"I wish I had been there to see your first step," I said.

"My first step was when I was a baby. My life didn't start when I met you."

I put up my hands in surrender.

"I'm back to making swords, Zee. I have a bunch of new designs and techniques in mind, and I thought of a new way to make steel more flexible."

"The boron technique I told you about?"

"Not that, something else."

She stood up and went to the middle of the room. This time, her legs held firm. "I'm going now, Zee."

"Could we just give this time?" I asked from the floor. "You have too much on your plate to make big decisions now. Could we just take it slow?"

"I didn't make the decision," she said softly. "You did. You went out with the sword."

"I didn't cut anyone," I said.

"You didn't cut anyone, but the dead are everywhere. You said you had a solution. You said you had a process. You said the martial path would lead you to peace. It didn't, did it?"

I looked at the floor.

"There is no peace here," she said. "There is no peace anywhere near you. I've really got to go."

"You always came first," I said. "You will always come first."

"Take care of yourself, Zee."

I stayed on the floor as she went through the door. I heard her bike engine start and I willed myself to get up. I went outside and watched as she moved the kickstand up and juiced the engine. It roared. She clicked the transmission into gear and slowly let out the clutch, circling the bike around awkwardly.

I wanted to run to her, but I knew it would do no good. She turned her head. It might have been to check traffic, but I want to think it was to see me one more time.

Walking back to the house, the lighthouse beacon washed over me.

Traces of venom still in me, I felt like a snake raped by the moon.

53

I went to jail because I needed to, because there was something there that I could discover nowhere else. Waiting for clearance at the security desk I pretended not to mind that Wanda wasn't with me while I struggled to beat back irrational fears about being let in but not being let out. I had called the chaplain before leaving the house, so he wasn't surprised to see me, though his expression seemed a bit mystified.

"Thank you for coming back," he said.

"You look surprised to see me."

He laughed. "Well, you seemed agitated when you left the last time."

"I was a bit unnerved to be in a prison. I hope to make up for it."

He studied me. "We appreciate your dedication."

He led me to the same room where I had conducted the meditation session. The inmate named Irwin brought the group to order, putting them in lines to face me. The chaplain gave a wave and left.

"No Neptune?" I said to Irwin.

Irwin looked at me blankly. "Say what?"

"Neptune Cohen's not coming today?"

Irwin looked around at the men. "Anyone know that name?"

The men shook their heads.

"He was here last time," I said. "Muscular guy with small ears?"

The men exchanged glances. "No guy named Neptune at this facility," said the man at the back.

"Maybe he got transferred," I said. "That happens doesn't it?

Guys get moved?"

"There ain't *been* no guy named Neptune in the house," Irwin drawled. "You must've got the name wrong."

"I have the name just fine," I said. "He's been writing to me."

"Writing to you?" Irwin frowned. "You gave him your address?"

"No," I said.

"Nobody here knows where you live, Doc," Irwin said mildly.

I would not put it past Neptune to rope the whole gang into a collective torture-Dr. Pearl-game, so I searched the faces of the men for collusion—a twitching eyebrow, a drop of the eyes, a smirk, a smile. I detected nothing.

"Fine," I said. "His loss to miss the session."

We began our standing meditation. Some men had brought their sitting cushions and stood next to them, toes touching the fabric like a child might touch his blanket. I can tell a lot about a person by watching how they stand, and I was surprised at how serene the inmates appeared. I guess that's what happens when you wake up in a penitentiary every day. There's nowhere to go but inward to freedom.

Try as I might, I couldn't settle down. Neptune's absence bothered me too much. I heard four sneezes and three barks of intestinal gas, the last one going on as long as a movie trailer and eliciting more than a few snickers. One of the inmates suffered what sounded like a tubercular cough.

I said Neptune's name in a whisper. Where was the bastard? A couple of the men opened their eyes at the sound of my voice, saw my disquiet, and nudged each other. Within half a minute, the whole group was staring at me.

"I brought something to read to you," I said awkwardly. "But I really need to see Neptune Cohen."

Irwin squeezed his eyes together. "You all right, Doc? 'Cause you don't seem all right. We told you, there ain't no Neptune here and there ain't *been* no Neptune here."

I pulled a small paperback copy of Lao Tzu's *Daodeqing* from my pocket and cleared my throat to read:

"Weapons are tools of evil that are hated by many," I began. "Therefore followers of the Dao reject them."

The next line caught in my throat. Anxiety overcame me. I saw devils behind the faces of the men before me, and I felt a devil rising behind my own. I threw the book down. The men stared.

"Goddamnit, Neptune," I said.

A couple of the men winced. One looked like he would cry. Irwin's expression grew ever more boarish. A long moment passed, but Neptune did not appear. I could not stand there for one more instant. When I made for the door, no one tried to stop me. Outside the room, inmates passed by with barely a glance.

"Neptune!" I screamed.

I ran then. I took to that long hallway like a fighter jet on takeoff. I don't know if anyone ran after me, but I know they followed me with their eyes. Footfall after footfall, I had found my own quiet hell. In the deluge of my torment, the prison seemed impossibly quiet.

I pounded on the glass at the security booth, showing the little card the chaplain had given me. Frowning at my insistent behavior, the guards set me free. I dashed through the doors in the barbed-wire fences and to my bike, and I leapt aboard and set to eating the yellow horizon over the cane fields as if it were cake.

*   *   *

Wanda was waiting in my driveway with an impatient look on her face.

"You look like you've been here a while," I said.

"I asked the medical examiner to have a look at Kimberly Jenkin's remains," she said. "There's evidence of a strike to the face and we've taken a cast of your favorite Cuban fist for matching."

"Good news," I said.

"We went by Solomon Yu's house and found the animals in the basement. Brought in a trapper to take them to the Miami Metrozoo. Everything is neat and clean and orderly. A stop-mail order was put in but no return date given. His place of business is completely cleaned out. Not even a cockroach wing. It's like a careful hurricane went through there. Florida Fish and Wildlife is all over the place. Apparently they know Mr. Yu very well."

"Are they watching the airports?"

"They're on the lookout."

"Then he'll turn up," I said.

"Glad you're so sure."

I pushed the button on the opener. We watched the garage door come up as if witnessing a religious event—so quiet, the bricks beneath us full and heavy with everything we chose not to say.

"The prison chaplain called me," she said at last. "He said you came by for a visit and that it didn't go too well."

"A fair statement."

"He seemed genuinely worried about you."

"That's nice," I said, pushing the BMW inside.

"So you want to tell me what the hell you were doing at the prison without me?"

"I had to go."

"To see an inmate who doesn't exist and then run screaming out of the joint because you couldn't find him?"

"I don't want to talk about it."

"Would you rather chat about the special prosecutor out there with your name emblazoned on his forehead?"

"No."

"How about a certain Miami detective who has a pretty good idea who you really are?"

"Not about him either."

"He'll be sniffing your shorts for ten years if that's what it takes. He's a bulldog. I know his kind."

"You'll just have to keep your choke collar handy."

"Oh no I won't. Forget about help from me. I'm out of the game."

"I'm family," I said.

"Family? I wouldn't say so. You're the lunatic asshole who put my mother in jeopardy, made me look like a fool at the penitentiary, and abused my name at a cop dojo only to break the teacher's face. You've crossed into enemy territory way too often to be my brother."

"I didn't mean to do any of that," I said.

"You meant to, you didn't mean to—who cares? In the end it's all about you. There's a disease where the patient disconnects from the real people around him and sees characters who aren't really there. What do they call it?"

"Schizophrenia."

I went into the house. She followed. "Jordan tells me you're on some kind of medication," she said.

"I wish you wouldn't talk to Jordan about me anymore. It's not appropriate."

"I checked the prison records, Zee. There is nothing on a Neptune Cohen."

"He wrote me letters."

"Show me."

I riffled through the stack of mail on my counter, thinking a new one might have come in. I flipped through the envelopes until they flew. I reached into the trash, plunging my hand into the runny tops of a few tomatoes and some still-damp paper towels and piles of tea leaves. I dug through discarded coupons and advertisements and some twigs I'd picked out of the front yard on my way in the day Jordan brought her new bike to show me.

"Cupboards?" Wanda suggested, her arms crossed.

I opened a few, treating us to views of cleaning products, stemware, and dishes.

"This is nice," she said. "A tour of the house. What about your office, Zee? Could the imaginary letters from your made-up pen pal be hiding there?"

"Stop it," I said.

"No, you stop it. Stop imagining yourself some kung-fu warrior reincarnate. Stop endangering the lives of the people who love you. Stop dragging my name through the mud. Stop cutting people up. Stop ruining our parents' happiness. Stop breaking your girlfriend's heart."

"You should go," I said. "Really."

"Oh, I'm going," she said, her voice low and tight, her big frame humming with anger. "I'm going and I'm not coming back. Don't call me. Don't ask for my help. Don't cry my name when they drag you away—and they will drag you away, Xenon, maybe not today and maybe not next week, but you'll go out toes up in a bag or zipped in a jacket."

She stood there in my kitchen, breathing heavily, drops of perspiration coming down her face, looking at me as if she expected me to say something. When I didn't, she spun around and went to the door.

"What a pitiful, stupid, terrible waste," I heard her say.

54

Emptiness in meditation is a state of grace, but the emptiness in me was agony not insight and it burned like a torch that could only be quenched by steel. Quiet Teacher understood me and so I went to it after Wanda left and sat and let its carbon vibrate in sympathy with my bones. It brought me solace. I could not be lonely with it in my hand. I allowed it to move to me, trying to spiral beyond the searing pain of loss. When I bore a sheen of sweat I went to the chocolate closet and opened the door and reached up for a truffle to refuel me. I stopped, sensing something was wrong.

I did not see the king cobra right away. I know that sounds odd, but sometimes the sheer size and incongruity of a thing can confuse the senses. It was draped over several shelves, with a dark, gleaming body nearly as thick as my arm. Startled by the sudden inrush of light, it reared back and spread its hood. Its eyes stared at me unblinkingly.

"No," was all I could manage.

And then it was out. It glided toward me across the floor and I felt its mesmeric power, not merely the stuff of legend but the reptile blood we shared, the complex proteins, the serum, the filaments and strands and genetic building blocks, the transcriptions and codes built up over the hundreds of millions of years of ancestry we shared, and yes, the differences, too. Perhaps that's why I allowed it to get so close. We were kissing cousins, the snake and I, each in the grip of his passions.

The feathery vomeronasal taction of the touch of its tongue snapped me out of it, and I ran to Quiet Teacher and slid it from its freshly repaired sheath and returned to wield it, like a giant fang of my own, in the thick, hot air between us.

"You can change this," I told the king, even though I knew royalty was born to stay its course.

The eyes stayed with me as the body swayed, piercing me with a commanding look that might have riveted me to the spot had I not felt this empowering intimacy. I closed in, pointing the tip of my blade at its head, feeling as if I knew all there was to know about my foe. The king undulated sideways, accelerating all the while, and then struck at me, working the angle. Its shiny skin caught a sunbeam through the patio door and the sparkle distracted me, but at the very last moment I parried with my blade. It pulled back immediately then charged forward on a fresh route to my flesh. I heard the sound of its scales on the tile.

We circled and spiraled around each other, and the dance gained a musical score. I can't say what the instruments were, but the melody was haunting and Asian and it filled me with a sense that everything was happening just as it should. The king struck again. This time I actually caressed its head with my blade, twisting around it until it opened its mouth wide to show glistening pink and fangs.

I became aware of all my lifetimes at once, all the times I'd held swords and cudgels and halberds and spears. The intelligence of a thousand battles came into my feet and hands. The dance with the snake seduced me until I could barely sense the room around me. The energy circling in my body directed my blade—a hundred little muscles cooperating to create movement more intricate than ever before. One layer of my consciousness was entirely occupied by the deadly waltz, but another brought me a sweet realization that the depth I had been striving for had come to me at last. I was the martial artist I wanted to be. I smelled almonds then and I smiled.

"Thank you," I said, as I took its head.

I listened to my heartbeat in the silent house and thought about the finality of transection. One cut and the head was gone. No more problem. The snake would not bother me again. It was a simple, even mundane fact, but it meant the world to me.

I heard a bird chirp outside. I put the remains of the king outside by the French doors and cleaned the blood from the floor. I cleaned Quiet Teacher, too. I used paper towels to wipe every inch of it—first with bleach, then iodine, and then a film of light oil. A sterile sword had never been more important to me. When all traces of reptile proteins had been removed, I threw away the paper towels and pulled the white plastic trashcan over next to the bar. I hefted the sword in my left hand, marveling at how alien it felt, receiving new information about the balance of it and the grace. Jordan's masterpiece it was and ever more glorious when experienced anew.

I lay my cutting arm down on the bar's marble top and turned my palm upward. I took my time, inspecting each surgeon's finger as if my eyes had become magnifiers, seeing all the lines and whorls. I went inside the hand, layer by layer. I saw the gristle and tendons, the knuckles and phalanges, the ligaments and bones. I saw all the tiny scalpel-guiding muscles, all the nerves, and the blossoming, blooming, beautiful vessels of blood. I became aware of all the tough and breathtaking touches those fingers had managed, through the ages, life after life. I worked my way all the way to my wrist, where I saw the line I was after. It rose up out of my flesh like a bright red line separating the old life from the new. It was a piece of meat, that palm attached to fingers. It was no longer a part of me.

I turned my wrist so it lined up with the edge of countertop. My fingers hovered in space above the trashcan. I raised my elegant blade with my left hand. Mentally, I rehearsed the cut, putting all my power and technique into play, concentrating on the draw and the slice and the total and irrevocable severance.

I lifted my hand high.

"Tie Mei," I said just before I brought it down.

I knew the pain would set me free.

About the Author

Arthur Rosenfeld is a martial arts teacher, writer, speaker, and coach. His martial arts training spans more than twenty-seven years, and includes instruction in Tang Soo Do, Kenpo, Kung Fu, and Tai Chi Ch'uan. Rosenfeld is a critically-acclaimed, best-selling author of six novels (Avon Books, Bantam, Doubleday Dell, Forge Books), two non-fiction books (Simon and Schuster, Basic Books), several  screenplays, and numerous magazine articles (*Vogue, Vanity Fair, Parade,* and others). He consults for the pharmaceutical industry as a recognized expert on aspects of chronic pain. Arthur Rosenfeld resides in South Florida.

Photo by Vance Harris